COMMANDER WAYNE NEWELL: He wore his Navy uniform like a second skin and could get his men to do anything. All the while he was living the ultimate deception —as a KGB time bomb waiting to explode . . .

LIEUTENANT COMMANDER DICK MAKIN: The veteran XO believed his captain was the best in the fleet. But the sinking of two possibly friendly subs has pushed the crew over the brink—and Makin must choose between his captain and his conscience . . .

Praise for Charles D. Taylor's

Silent Hunter

(more)

CAPTAIN BUCK NELSON: He looked more like a college professor than a submarine captain. But his USS *Florida* is the only surviving ballistic missile submarine in the Pacific Chain—and he must take on a sleek and silent killer . . .

COMMANDER BEN STEEL: He'd served and socialized with Wayne Newell. Commanding the USS *Manchester*, he'd made a rendezvous with a lone Navy SEAL—who brought him top-secret information that would put him in a torpedo shoot-out with the man who had already destroyed two Boomers . . .

Praise for Charles D. Taylor's

War Ship

"RAZOR-SHARP, HIGH-STRESS SUSPENSE—AN EXPLOSIVE TALE OF AMERICA'S GREATEST DEFENSE SYSTEM HELD HOSTAGE."

—W.E.B. Griffin,
author of *Brotherhood of War*
and *The Corps*

ADMIRAL RAY LARSEN: The unconventional Deputy Commander for Submarine Warfare had to tell the President that the USS *Alaska* and the USS *Nevada* were missing—knowing that the wrong conclusions could push the world into nuclear war . . .

THE SOVIET GENERAL SECRETARY: The KGB had put the plan in motion. Intelligence agents were fighting to predict the next American move. He was the loneliest man in Russia—waiting for all hell to explode . . .

Praise for Charles D. Taylor's

Counterstrike

"A GRIPPING THRILLER . . . A CHILLING PEEK INTO THE CLANDESTINE WORLD OF SPECIAL WARFARE."
—Stephen Coonts

Books by Charles D. Taylor

Show of Force
The Sunset Patriots
First Salvo
Choke Point
Silent Hunter
Shadows of Vengeance (pen name—David Charles)
Counter Strike
Warship
Boomer
Deep Sting

BOOMER

CHARLES D. TAYLOR

POCKET BOOKS

New York   London   Toronto   Sydney   Tokyo   Singapore

An *Original* Publication of POCKET BOOKS

POCKET BOOKS, a division of Simon & Schuster Inc.
1230 Avenue of the Americas, New York, NY 10020

ISBN: 0-671-74330-9

First Pocket Books printing June 1990

10 9 8 7 6 5 4 3 2

POCKET and colophon are registered trademarks of Simon & Schuster Inc.

Printed in the U.S.A.

This book is dedicated to my mother,
Ruth H. Taylor,
whose support remains unending
and the memory of my father,
who said he was so proud that his son
was the first author in the family.

"A strategic balance acceptable to the United States must be consistent with our national security objectives and supportive of America's basic defense strategy—deterrence of aggression. Above all, it must provide a stable deterrent by ensuring there are no circumstances under which the Soviet leadership might believe it could execute a successful first strike against the United States . . . deterrence can only be assured by convincing the Soviet leadership that the probable costs of their aggression will exceed any possible gains."

> —from *Soviet Military Power: An Assessment of the Threat,* written and produced by the Department of Defense, 1988

"In the future, the U.S. SSN, designed for such long-range hunting, will find itself in a melee at close range, much like a knife fight in a dark alley."

> —from *Melee Warfare* by Lt. Daniel F. Nylen, USN, Proceedings of the U.S. Naval Institute, October 1987, pp. 57–64

"There is a great danger that you will solve political problems with military actions."

> —Robert S. McNamara, former Secretary of Defense—personal comment on the 1962 Cuban crisis on Public TV

Acknowledgments

In addition to discussing this book with a number of people, both military and civilian, I have read many books and military and professional journals. In attempting to translate numerous pages of my notes, I may inadvertently have used someone's words or phrases in dialogue or in simplifying technical sections. I would like to both thank the authors for the impression they made on me and apologize if I have altered their original intent.

For those interested in naval affairs, I can highly recommend the *Proceedings* of the United States Naval Institute, an organization I have been a proud member of for more than twenty years; their naval publishing program is without peer. The finest book available on the U.S. submarine force is *Silent Chase* published by Thomasson-Grant, Inc., with photos and text by Steve and Yogi Kaufman, the latter a retired vice admiral.

I would like to thank Dan Mundy and Bill Stritzler for their suggestions, Lieutenant Commander Jack Ward, USN, for coordinating one of my visits to New London, Bill McDonald for his never-ending interest in my books, Dominick Abel for managing the difficult role of agent and friend, Paul McCarthy for showing me how an editor's talents can make all the difference in the world, and my wife, Georgie, for her critical help as she survived yet another manuscript—and me. And special thanks to Nelson DeMille for allowing me to borrow a superb idea from his book, *The Charm School.* After I had completed the manuscript and turned Wayne Newell loose on the world, Nelson was kind enough to allow me even greater justification for such a heinous character, whom you will appreciate even more after reading Mr. DeMille's fascinating story.

PROLOGUE

Discovery

Impossible!

The odds of such . . . why, not even the Fates could be tempted in this manner!

Vice Admiral Mark Bennett stared blankly at the sheet of paper in his hand, no longer seeing the words. Instead, an image of *Nevada*—a blur at first, then a razor-sharp replica —swam before his eyes. He'd been aboard when she went on her initial sea trials. A fine submarine . . . a superb crew . . .

There was no reason to reread the message—he'd memorized those seven words instantly. Bennett was the single addressee—Deputy Chief of Naval Operations (DCNO), Undersea Warfare.

The originator, Rear Admiral Neil Arrow, was Commander Submarine Force, Pacific (COMSUBPAC). They were the closest of friends, classmates twenty-five years before at nuclear-power school, then six additional months at the same reactor. Arrow had sent the message under a security classification that he'd used only twice in his life, and both times to Bennett. For the second time that week Mark Bennett had been required to remove another one-time code from his safe, and once again he broke the

1

message himself: NEVADA NOW TWENTY-FOUR HOURS OVERDUE REPORTING.

These six words might not have been nearly so ominous if a similar report hadn't been received a little more than three days before, with equally frightening impact: ALASKA NOW TWENTY-FOUR HOURS OVERDUE REPORTING. And every four hours after that, following the rigid requirements defined for reporting such incidents, Arrow continued to confirm the fact that *Alaska,* a Trident ballistic-missile-firing submarine, was missing. Bennett had, of course, reported the situation to each individual in the chain of command with a critical need to know, ending with the President of the United States—eight men, no more. It was a relatively new procedure, secure, safe, and intended to reassure senior officers. But the loss of 192 strategic warheads, which each Trident carried, was hardly reassuring.

Two boomers, two nuclear-powered ballistic-missile submarines (SSBN's), vital links in the strategic triad defending the United States, had now failed to respond to a critical one-time safety report from their stations at the scheduled time—*Alaska* for almost sixty-five hours now. It had been an experiment, designed to evaluate the security of a new communications system. Under normal conditions there was no such thing as an SSBN violating security to send a message, not even a one-time-burst transmission. It simply wasn't necessary, not when stealth meant everything. Once an SSBN departed homeport and evaded her Soviet tails, she remained mute until returning home. She had to be in her assigned station *because she hadn't said she wasn't.* That's the way the system functioned. It was that simple.

Initially, *Alaska*'s failure was considered an equipment casualty. Communications gear had gone down at critical times in the past and it would again. This new system was untested under mission conditions, and the state of the world was deemed copacetic enough to run this single, critical test. So Arrow had instituted the standard procedures to reestablish contact with *Alaska* with a short, extra-low-frequency (ELF) query. *Nothing. No response.*

Both admirals concurred there could be any number of causes—that there was no reason to be concerned—but this second message . . .

Admiral Bennett's hand began to shake, but so slightly that he failed to notice the tremor even when the message slipped from his hand. He was shocked when he bent to pick up the paper and found it rattling between his fingers.

Bennett placed the message on his desk and smoothed it with his hands before depressing the button to the outer office. "Florence, would you please call Admiral Larsen's office for me. Tell him I'll be there in three minutes." He would need the first two minutes in the head to compose himself before walking into Larsen's office. Raymond Larsen may have been another close friend, but he was also Chief of Naval Operations and never overlooked a human weakness—especially from someone who might one day sit in his chair.

When he stepped from the private bathroom at the rear of his office, the red light was blinking on the interoffice communicator. "Yes, Florence."

"Admiral Larsen has Secretary Kerner and two senators in his office now. He asked that you come by about noon."

Bennett moved into the outer office and tapped his secretary on the shoulder. "Call back and tell him to throw out the senators. The Secretary can stay." The Secretary of the Navy was part of the chain. "Tell him it'll still be three minutes because I'm going to bring Admiral Newman with me." Robbie Newman was Director, Naval Nuclear Propulsion, one of seven full admirals in the Navy at the time. Bennett was out the door before Florence had gotten the CNO's office back on the line. Newman, who'd come from his Crystal City office, would be waiting outside Larsen's office.

The Chief of Naval Operations' office became deathly quiet after Mark Bennett explained as succinctly as possible that *Nevada* had now joined *Alaska* among the missing. Neither the Secretary of the Navy nor two of the Navy's most senior admirals could find the correct words. They stared at each other, eyes shifting from one individual back to another as if one of them would suddenly come up with an answer. It was a quirk of fate—if they hadn't agreed to this experiment, *just once . . .*

"One . . . possibly," the CNO finally murmured. "But two . . . highly unlikely."

"Two . . . almost impossible," the Navy Secretary concurred.

Silence once again dominated the room.

Then the Secretary spoke up again. "How many boomers do we have on patrol in the Pacific right now?"

"Including *Alaska* and *Nevada,* there are four," Bennett responded. "We have two in transit right now, four alongside the pier."

"I'd better inform Harry Carpenter now," the CNO decided. "He's going to fight me on this one." Carpenter was the President's Chief of Staff.

"The hell with him," the Secretary interrupted. He knew much more about the workings of the White House than he did about the Navy. "This is for the President directly. I don't want us wasting a second with Carpenter's bullshit . . . just in case . . ."

Long-range strategic bombers and intercontinental ballistic missiles, the other two elements of the country's triad, were more fragile. They could be shot down, destroyed in their silos, possibly sabotaged, but the SSBN's were supposed to be invincible, impregnable to Soviet intelligence efforts. They were the single element of the triad that kept the balance, and they carried almost half of the U.S. strategic weapons. One missing boomer was critical to United States security. But two of them gone left a gaping hole in American strategy—especially if they had been sunk—for the country was essentially on its hands and knees, at the mercy of its enemies.

How many more?

And how . . . ?

4

CHAPTER ONE

Looking Back:
How the Impossible Took Place

The American 688-class attack submarine (SSN) is slightly longer than a football field but only thirty-six feet wide, a sleek, silent hunter. Since she is nuclear powered and designed exclusively to deliver torpedos and surface-hugging missiles, creature comforts are respectable but secondary, unlike the immense SSBN's more than twice her size. The wardroom of this smaller submarine is the size of a dining room in a comfortable suburban home, perfect for a party of perhaps eight to ten people, a little tight for more. It is the place the captain meets with his officers.

With the exception of those on watch, all of the officers of USS *Pasadena* were now assembled in the wardroom at the captain's request. As a result, the most junior officers were unable to be seated, and leaned, arms folded politely, against the bulkhead.

Wayne Newell sat in his normal place at the head of the table as *Pasadena*'s commanding officer. This was his second tour on a boat of this class, and he exuded confidence in every aspect of his job as a result. Since he had already put in his necessary time on a ballistic-missile submarine, he

assumed squadron command might come with his immi-
nent promotion to captain.

Newell looked *Navy*. Even in the working khaki uniform
worn at sea, he was immaculate. His shirt was starched and
pressed knife sharp, like a Marine's, his commander's silver
leaves and submariner's dolphins reflected the overhead
light brilliantly, and three rows of service ribbons accounted
for his successful career. His brown hair, cut once a week,
was never ruffled. With his hands folded on the green-felt
table cover, his blue eyes fell on each of his officers as he
spoke. "Navy regs don't require a speech at a time like this."
A slight, comforting smile displaying even white teeth
appeared—a casting director's dream come true. "I'm sure
the rumor has already hit every compartment, and the
answer is—no, we're not involved in a nuclear war, at least
none that I'm aware of." More smile to put his officers at
ease. "But, yes, there appears to be a definite possibility."

This was one of a number of such wardroom gatherings
over the past week. Newell, aware that it was vital to keep
every member of *Pasadena's* crew well informed, had insisted that the contents of each critical message be known to
his men. From that initial warning—*this is not a drill,
repeat, this is not a drill*—every man had known that
international problems were escalating. They had also
learned that *Pasadena* might serve a critical role in the
coming days. Pride, instilled by their captain, had a great
deal to do with their performance since that first moment.
They were ready . . . committed . . . completely under his
control. . . .

"We are approaching our assigned station, which is a
point approximately fifteen hundred miles south of Adak
and three thousand miles east of the main Japanese island."
It was something they already knew, but Newell was repeating exactly where they had been ordered so no man could
possibly doubt anything during this patrol, literally a voyage
into the unknown. "We will shortly stream our antenna for
one hour in anticipation of our next set of orders. From
what little we have been able to gather, diplomacy is still in

effect—Washington and Moscow are apparently talking . . . common sense, I hope." The captain smiled again and glanced around a table of comfortable officers. He sensed that they knew they were well led.

"Captain?" The engineer officer raised his hand.

"Don't tell me we're running out of gas, Kirk." Newell chuckled. It was a joke that had continued between the captain and Kirk Wolters for the better part of a year.

"Not yet, sir . . . filled up at the last pit stop." Wolters had learned to enjoy the banter. His sense of humor had been almost nonexistent until Wayne Newell learned that his engineer needed to be drawn out. Kirk was the most serious of the officers, and his lack of imagination would eventually hurt his career pattern. But now Wolters, thanks to his captain, was even willing to have a few beers ashore with the other officers, something he'd been hesitant about previously. "It's just . . . well, how do we know this isn't an elaborate scheme to test our readiness?" He was as loyal as an officer could be, dedicated totally now to serving Wayne Newell.

"At this point, it would be one hell of a dirty trick, something I'd take right to CNO if it turned out that way. That's why I've had the XO right at my side since about thirty seconds after that first message was broken." He nodded at Dick Makin, his executive officer. "He agrees with me that they might have yanked our chains for forty-eight, maybe even seventy-two hours, but no longer than that."

"And there's no pattern to it," the XO added. "I've been through these things before on other boats. After a while you get to anticipate what comes next. Not this time," he concluded grimly. "Plus the first message, the one before they shifted us to another broadcast, was directed to every military addressee in the Pacific Fleet. It wasn't something designed to test just *Pasadena.*"

Each American attack submarine on patrol rose close enough to the surface at least twice every twenty-four hours to stream a floating wire just below the surface or raise an antenna in order to copy any messages directed to them and take a satellite fix. Soon after that first directive establishing an increased readiness condition for all American military units, *Pasadena* was requested to shift to another broadcast for operational purposes. From that moment on she appeared chosen to become a vital cog in an American plan to avoid a nuclear confrontation. On the fourth day, in the presence of his executive officer and department heads, Wayne Newell sliced open a packet he'd carried aboard just moments before *Pasadena* departed Pearl Harbor. They were informed that *Pasadena*'s operating area was in the vicinity of known Soviet SSBN patrol boxes. Her mission would be to intercept and destroy them if the order was given.

Wayne Newell and his officers were familiar with the objective. It had been established years before with the Navy's Maritime Strategy. *Seize the initiative:* wage war aggressively against the enemy's undersea capability—sink their ballistic-missile submarines to limit their desire to escalate to a nuclear exchange. And it was all based on the theory that Moscow would not employ nuclear weapons if there was a distinct possibility that the Soviet Union might trigger the nuclear devastation of their own homeland as a consequence.

"In any situation where the future of mankind is at stake, there are inevitably a chosen few. They essentially save the world." Newell had used this same message over the ship's P.A. a couple of times before to explain why he expected each member of the crew to do his duty, even if that meant sacrificing themselves and their ship. *"Pasadena* has been selected, I'm sure, because we have brought a new meaning to the term *excellence"*—and he seemed to give an almost religious symbolism to the word—"in every phase of our operations." *Pasadena* had won the E for excellence in each segment of competition for the coveted award. She was the top attack submarine in the Pacific Fleet.

"What the captain and I are assuming is that *Pasadena* deserves this mission." Dick Makin was as fond of his commanding officer as any man in the fleet. It was a privilege to serve under a man like Newell. If Makin never received another billet, if the Navy chose to overlook his potential for command, he was secure in the fact that he had served with the best. The XO still looked like the football player he'd been fifteen years earlier, broad-shouldered and thick-necked. But his face remained youthful even with a premature lack of hair. He was popular with the junior officers who kidded him about leather helmets and single-wing football. His dark eyes generally twinkled good-naturedly, and there was always an even smile, as long as things were going his way.

"It's possible one or more additional boats were switched to another broadcast also," Makin continued. "We could go back and copy one of the other circuits again, but the captain and I decided not to because of the danger that the enemy could compromise that frequency and broadcast conflicting orders." It was true. Newell was able to explain the critical nature of communications so that a child would appreciate the situation. Makin's eyes settled on the engineer. "You can imagine what a disaster that could be, Kirk. Believe me, the captain has involved me in every single decision. We've considered every possibility. This isn't a drill." He glanced at Newell for confirmation. "We are an integral part of Washington's strategy."

"Which brings me to the purpose of this little cocktail party." Newell grinned. "This is the toughest pill of all to swallow, and I'm going to give it to Wally to read." He removed a sheet of paper from his breast pocket and handed it to the communications officer. "You broke the message, Wally, so you win the dubious honor of reading it to the boys around the bar."

Lieutenant Junior Grade Snyder was one of those standing. He had to reach over the XO's shoulder for the piece of paper. The color drained from his face as he glanced down at the words he'd typed out so neatly after breaking the coded message for the captain. "All the messages on this broadcast are designated for *Pasadena*," he began haltingly. "It's our very own . . . ah, broadcast, as a matter

9

of fact. It's from COMSUBPAC." Snyder looked over to Newell for support.

"Go ahead, Wally. Your boys copied it. You broke it. You checked it twice to make sure there were no mistakes. You have the honors."

"Intelligence reports confirm existence of Soviet submarine masking device. Equipment imitates exactly American SSBN signature. Repeat, American SSBN signature. No means exist to break through device. Coordinates of *Pasadena* targets will therefore be designated by this command only. Regardless of apparent target identity, coordinates issued to *Pasadena* will be Soviet SSBN only. You are ordered to open envelope Bravo Delta Two Zero. Orders to follow Zero Nine Zero Zero Zulu."

Lieutenant Snyder's face mirrored the inherent doubt that existed in his mind. He would follow Wayne Newell to the gates of Hell, but he maintained a healthy suspicion for any wisdom emanating from Washington.

"Gentlemen, if you're ready for another round, you may serve yourselves." The captain waved in the direction of the coffeepot. "I'll wait until you're comfortable, since the rules of the game have just been altered drastically."

No one moved. The import of COMSUBPAC's message was simple enough. It was quite possible they would actually be ordered to sink one or more targets. War—so swift and sudden in its impact—was evidently at hand. *It was possible that their entire attack could be conducted against one or more targets that gave every indication of being sister ships— right up until the moment they were sunk!* But what if . . .

Their silence was ominous. No matter how long a man made a profession out of preparing himself for the possibility of war, the reality of the situation was still a shock. "Your message is received, gentlemen, and understood. The XO and I have been doing a bit of soul searching ourselves on this one." There was no effort at humor. Newell understood how each of them were reacting. You learned pretty quickly on a submarine how your people responded. That was an essential of command.

The executive officer was the first to react. "The captain has expressed his reservations to me already. That was shortly after he asked me to read that Bravo Delta Two Zero. I agreed with him that each of you should have your say because we could be ordered at any moment to sink a boat that sounds just like one of our own Tridents. I, for one . . . I might have a hard time giving the order. So I know how the captain feels at this point." Dick Makin was as assertive as an XO could be, and he'd been the one to insist Newell open the discussion to his officers.

The navigator was the first to speak. "Captain, if you have no objections, I'd like to ask for confirmation the next time we go to periscope depth. I know it's remote, but don't you think there's a chance that our crypto could have been compromised? Or maybe it was just a freak of nature, a weird something in the atmosphere that allowed them to interfere with that broadcast for just a short time." He shrugged. "I don't know, sir, maybe I'm shooting in the dark. But . . . but if we ever made a mistake, none of us could live with ourselves." He was the first since *Pasadena* got under way to exhibit signs of a new mustache, and he was habitually smoothing it with his fingers.

"That was my first idea, Andy. But we all know we're not supposed to be transmitting at all. If we're already involved in even a limited war on top, someone could intercept that signal of ours and have our position in no time."

Andy McKown was persistent. "We don't have to send a long one, sir, just a burst transmission, an interrogative referencing COMSUBPAC's message. You're talking seconds then. What are the odds of someone getting our position in that time? A million to one? A thousand to one? Even with a hundred to one, I'd much rather take that chance than sink one of our own."

"You're right, you know." Newell nodded in agreement. "We could never go back to Pearl again if we'd done something like that." He looked around the wardroom. "It's almost impossible that anyone'd ever pinpoint us. But I want to make sure there're no other arguments." By the expression on his face, they knew Newell had already made up his mind, but each of them also knew he enjoyed opening the discussion to them.

"Okay, Wally, go ahead and draft that message now. Put 'C.O. PASADENA REQUESTS CONFIRM YOUR' . . . whatever the date/time/group was. I want them to know it comes directly from me."

Wayne Newell was more than willing to acquiesce to that request, for he already knew what the response would be. He'd also anticipated each of the messages *Pasadena* had received since the crisis began. Newell was familiar with their contents beforehand because he knew they had not originated from COMSUBPAC. It had taken years to devise this plan, and its basis was exquisite. Code-named *Boomer* —since American SSBN's were the objective—patience became a way of life for those involved. The key to its eventual success was based on two critical points: Wayne Newell's promotion to command of a nuclear-attack submarine, and that vessel being assigned to the correct patrol area at the correct time.

The message from *Pasadena,* the one Andy McKown had pressed for, had gone out as an emergency and it came back at the same speed. It confirmed COMSUBPAC's warning. It also added a not-so-subtle admonition to her skipper: CRITICAL YOU CEASE TRANSMISSION PER GUIDELINES CONDITION ONE. It meant, in so many words, that *Pasadena* was to follow orders and await target assignment without further questioning.

Twenty-four hours later, what each man feared came as the ultimate message: PROCEED ZONE LIMA ECHO TWO SIX TO PROSECUTE CONFIRMED TARGET PER MY . . . and COMSUBPAC proceeded to list earlier messages, including the confirmation that the target was imitating an American boomer. But the most ominous part of the message was that the world situation had escalated to a conventional shooting war, with employment of nuclear arms anticipated.

Wayne Newell was in the control room when the sonar officer's initial report concerning their first contact echoed through the speaker. It was Steve Thompson's voice: "We've got machinery noises filtering through all that crap out there."

The change in the atmosphere was immediate, electric. Each man in control knew that sonar had been analyzing sounds radiating from the assigned sector, but until that moment there had been nothing manmade in the curious natural roar of the Pacific. If a war was indeed in progress on the surface, *Pasadena* remained blessed with ignorance—neither a hunter nor the hunted.

Quite suddenly that had all changed. According to their captain's op order, there were no other American submarines in that area. It was their sector to hunt and theirs alone. Any manmade contact would most certainly be the enemy.

"Very well. How soon can you give me a bearing?" Newell's slightly bored expression while the hours of search progressed had changed to sudden animation. The waiting was over.

"Still mushy, Captain. Port bow to port beam . . . need to close the contact to confirm."

Newell turned to his executive officer. "Station the section-tracking party, Dick. Slow to ten knots. We'll ease our way in. I'm going to put in some sonar time."

Pasadena had been on a northerly course. "Left ten degrees rudder, steady course three two five." Andy McKown was the OOD. "Ahead two thirds." He glanced over his shoulder at the XO. "Any special reason we're making a slow approach, sir? If we're so far away we don't even know what the contact is yet, the Russians don't have any sonar that can pick us out."

"Caution, I suppose, Andy. We can't assume any SSBN out in the middle of the Pacific is by itself any more than the ones they've got up under the ice. Those have guard dogs

around them because that's where they figure we'll attack."
He shrugged. "Only Washington knows. Maybe the logical
solution was to stick some of their big boys out here away
from the hassle."

"I guess that makes sense, XO. And I suppose he could
have some attack boats protecting him out here in the
middle of nowhere."

"That's why the captain's closing in this manner. Their
ears get better every day. He said he planned to maneuver
once we had a confirmation on the contact. Let him cross
our bow and make a pretty target."

Ten knots was generally a limit for 688s. That was close to
their *ambient limited speed,* which occurred when their own
ship's noise was approximately the same as that of the
ocean. The submarine didn't become any quieter by going
slower at that point, and it became more difficult to maneuver at lower speeds.

Pasadena continued to close slowly, silence being close to
godliness.

The watch changed. Those who were relieved carried the
latest details back to their compartments: machinery noises
first . . . then classified possible submarine . . . captain
maneuvered in an attempt to enhance the sound . . .
contact was still too weak for accurate target-motion
analysis . . . still too much background noise . . .

Newell ordered course changes, searching cautiously with
the towed array—listening for any sound that might indicate their contact was accompanied.

Nothing.

If a watch dog was near the boomer, it should make a
noise sooner or later. Dick Makin suggested that if there
really were an attack boat protecting this boomer, the logical
idea in that vast empty ocean would be to circle the boomer
you were guarding. She could, after all, be attacked from
three hundred sixty separate directions.

"That would require some speed," Newell agreed, "and
that would mean noise. We'd pick up one of their quietest
boats, even an Akula or a Sierra, after a while . . ." His voice

drifted off as he considered his approach. "Our contact could even be masking a watch dog now, on the other side, just like an eclipse, but sooner or later it'd have to show up."

They waited. Ten knots meant they were closing the contact at ten nautical miles an hour—that's if it were standing still. If it were on the same course and speed, there would be no approach, just the same distant unconfirmed sound depending on the condition of the water. On the other hand, if it came toward them, the sound intensity should increase. Sonar would analyze the target . . .

"Contact is improving . . . we have cavitation . . ." This time it was the voice of the chief.

"Any identification?"

"Classified probable submarine, Captain. I'm sure that's no surface contact."

"Thanks, Chief." Tommy Lott, the chief sonarman, had been an instructor before he came aboard *Pasadena.* He'd taught the fine points of analyzing contacts to hundreds of younger men in the fleet. "Now can you tell me where he's headed?"

"Give us a little more time, sir."

Twenty minutes later the head of the section tracking party announced, "Got a generally northwest heading, Captain. Recommend we come back on a northerly course to close—maybe a little east—and I think it would help if we could add a couple of knots."

"Go ahead, Dick, but not a sound aft. Tell engineering to ease that throttle," Newell said to his XO. "And let's man battle stations. If we're able to classify a probable already, along with a course for that sound, eventually we're going to be close enough to be heard."

The process was a quiet one for *Pasadena.* Her crew was efficient. They'd anticipated being called away to battle stations and looked forward to the order when it came. Until that moment, Newell had sensed a feeling of emptiness among the men. But it wasn't so much from their understanding that the world was on the edge of a nuclear precipice. Strangely enough, that had been accepted more easily than he anticipated. The past few days had demanded long hours of work from the crew as they prepared for what appeared to be a unique mission, and that was almost welcome.

What bothered them most, Newell learned, was their inability to share two of the most basic human reactions with their families—the fear of devastation and the hope for survival. For all they knew, the fear generated by a clash of the superpowers had become a reality on the surface. All the well-meaning efforts by so many leaders on both sides to diminish cold-war temperaments appeared to have collapsed. Conventional war on any number of battlefields could already be escalating toward a nuclear exchange. Until those orders arrived, they had been able to do nothing tangible, nothing that would justify *Pasadena*'s existence, nothing that would protect loved ones. Life beneath the surface of the ocean in a tiny tube called *Pasadena* had left them empty in crisis.

Now, according to their captain, they had an opportunity to become part of Washington's grand strategy.

The fire-control coordinator, Dick Makin, had been unable to generate an accurate set of cross bearings on the contact. "Captain, request we alter course. I'd like to try to get a better feel for his motion." Target-motion analysis was the process of obtaining a series of bearings on a sound, then changing course in order to obtain new bearings. The points where these second bearings crossed the first set would display the general direction the target was moving. Once they drew closer, these individual fixes could provide a fairly accurate course and speed for their target.

Ten minutes later, "Captain, I think our friend may have altered course. My old solution isn't tracking."

"Right. We'll hold this course and generate some additional bearings. Then see what you can do, Dick." Newell remembered the endless days of "the box" on a ballistic-missile submarine. SSBN's were assigned an operating area, exactly like this Lima Echo Two Six, and that was where they stayed. It was their station and theirs alone. In time of war the Pentagon knew that a particular submarine could be directed to fire if an action message was relayed to it via VLF from land or a TACAMO communications aircraft. The SSBN in that sector would fire its Trident missiles at preassigned targets from that specific point beneath the ocean's surface. There was a purpose, if one understood missiles and computers and the necessity to saturate an enemy, especially if that enemy was in the process of blanketing U.S. cities with the same nuclear devastation.

"The box" was home for a boomer until they were relieved by a sister ship on a predetermined date. They didn't move from that box. They might steam around the boundaries just as a fish swam interminably around the glass sides of an aquarium. They also maneuvered in relation to unknown contacts, because invisibility was the price of their mission. Other times, it could be caprice that determined their position within their sector.

Wayne Newell would have loved to bet that the contact would already be on a westerly—or easterly—heading, if it had appeared to be northerly before. Otherwise it would have to leave its assigned box. Perhaps they'd already heard him. But he knew he couldn't open his mouth. American boomers were the quietest submarines of all. Somehow, someone might begin to wonder why he knew a supposed Soviet boat was acting just like an American one. *Did anyone know how a Soviet SSBN patrolled its assigned sector?*

"Seems to be heading west, sir. Signal's no stronger."

"Dick, what do you think their boomers do? Do they steam around in circles, or boxes? Or do they just do whatever comes to mind?" Better someone else comes upon the answer.

"The Russians are precise," Makin answered. "If we've got one of their boomers here, the odds are that he'll head to the west for a while and then turn south."

"Good enough for me." The XO had answered Newell's question in front of everyone in the control room. "Since we seem to be astern of him, let's head in the same direction and kick up our speed again. He'll have a hard time hearing us if that's the picture." Newell was sure that was exactly what that boomer was doing. It was more difficult, almost impossible depending on acoustic conditions, to hear a quiet contact approaching from astern.

The contact *did* take a westerly heading. The signal *did* improve in sonar. "Captain . . . that's one of ours . . ." Even on the speaker suspended just above their heads in the control room, the attack team could sense horror in the voice that called out from sonar.

Newell looked over at his XO. "Dick, why don't you step in there and calm them down. It's a natural reaction. I can understand. I think they just used someone else to reinforce the situation. I know how tough it's going to be." His voice was sympathetic.

"Chief." Makin beckoned to Tommy Lott as he slid the sonar door shut behind him. *"That's not one of ours.* It would help a lot in the control room if your men could—"

"Listen to this," a young, still unnaturally high voice, unaware of Makin's presence, interrupted. "I fed the sound into the computer. That's a Trident out there. No difference at all. Whatever makes *Alaska* a bit different from the others, that's her signature. This computer doesn't screw up." The concern that had been evident in his voice in the control room increased in intensity. "Chief, you have to listen to this."

Lott's headphones were around his neck as he spoke. "I'll take care of it, XO. This is his first boat. He doesn't understand what it's like in the control room." The chief slid the headphones back over his ears without another word, and the executive officer returned to his station near the captain. Discipline on an attack boat was often silent, understood by all. A submarine was too small for conflict.

"We're going to take him on the southerly leg . . . if he turns to the south," Newell added. *If we've gotten this close without being detected, leave well enough alone.* "Come left to two two zero," he said to the OOD. Then he turned to

Makin. "I'm going to get into position and then wait for him, assuming we're right about the box. I can't imagine he has a guard dog or we would have heard something from it by now."

"Sonar would have had to pick up something," Makin agreed. "How many torpedos?"

"Two. I don't care if we're surprising him. I don't care if the first one's a direct hit. I don't believe everything I'm told about the Mark 48." It was designed to explode directly beneath the hull, creating a huge air pocket that would theoretically break the target's back. "Their double hull's more than likely made out of titanium, and it's a tough son of a bitch. I want to make sure it sinks the first time." He turned to Bob Holloway, his weapons-control coordinator. "I intend to fire two torpedos ten seconds apart. Get all your noise out of the way now. I don't want him to hear anything beforehand. The first sound's going to be the water slug sending that fish into his arms. We want everything ready—absolutely perfect—before we shoot."

Newell considered *Pasadena's* current position in relation to the contact. He intended to hit his target on its southerly leg. *Why not assume it was going to continue its apparent straight-line maneuvering?* He estimated his firing position very carefully. Once he was ready and was completely silent, it would be no different than hiding behind a tree. He'd be invisible. Satisfied, he asked the quartermaster to give the OOD a course to that spot.

When sonar eventually reported the target had turned down the predicted southerly leg, Newell checked his initial firing point again. "I want to be at a point exactly four thousand yards east of his estimated position . . . right about here." He jabbed at the chart with a finger. "We'll maneuver to remain absolutely silent until we shoot."

Pasadena was circling near her position, almost an hour before firing time. "I want to hold us at four hundred feet, stay below him," Newell said to the diving officer. "He could be running deeper than I'm estimating, but we'll fire from there." He had to be dragging an antenna—the boomers were in constant contact with the National Military Command System. Newell struggled to conceal his knowledge that this was a Trident with a communication buoy probably operating at no more than three hundred feet.

The weapons-control coordinator reported ready. The torpedos had been warmed, the tubes flooded and pressure equalized, muzzle doors opened—anything that would send a warning to their target had been completed beyond the estimated range of the target's hearing . . . assuming Newell was correct about their sound gear, he said. The XO claimed it still didn't have the sophistication of their own; Newell said he could take no chances. What he couldn't say was that he knew American listening devices were still superior to anything the Soviets made.

The weapons-control coordinator reported that all the presets—target's course, speed, range, aspect, optimum depth—were good enough to launch an attack . . . assuming the target made no further maneuvers. Nothing was absolute in the ocean depths, where sound could be twisted in strange ways.

"Range?" Newell's face remained calm as he asked the same question once again for the third time in ten minutes. Dick Makin knew exactly what was running through the captain's mind—emergency procedures, in case they'd been detected.

"About eight thousand yards."

"Any change in the sound?"

"Negative, sir. If they're preparing to shoot anything at us, they did it a long time ago. They're just cruising down the highway . . . not a care in the world. You know how these boomers are." But they weren't always like that. Quite often their maneuvers were pure whim, to put off any silent marauders.

"You'd think they might be a little more concerned . . . what with everything that's happening on the surface," the OOD said. This all seemed so easy to him, more like an exercise shot. Combat was supposed to be so much more complex. "You'd think they'd have as much information about the war as we've gotten. They have to remain close to the surface for messages."

"Hell, we're in the middle of nowhere," Newell answered. "It's just like being out in the desert. If there's a hawk around, you'll see him almost as soon as he sees you." He saw by the man's eyes that he wasn't completely satisfied. "You worried about the masking technique they're using?" Newell had heard others talking—whispering, really, because they didn't want their captain to think they were nervous about this new tactic.

"I guess so, Captain. Sonar's never reported anything but *Alaska's* signature since we confirmed the contact." He folded his arms awkwardly. "It's eerie." His eyes remained fixed on the control-panel dials before the helmsman as he spoke. "Besides, he's driving a straight line."

"You're damn right it's eerie," Newell answered. "I feel the same way. Hell, if we hadn't been warned about that masking device of theirs, we'd probably be asking them to exchange movies by now." He moved over beside the OOD and placed a hand on his shoulder. "And if we hadn't received that message, it's quite possible that by right this minute one of their torpedos would have split us open like an egg and you and I would be floating toward the bottom . . . and we'd already be compressed into a tiny piece of goo that even the sharks wouldn't touch."

The OOD's eyes moved from the dials to settle on Newell, but he said nothing.

"Myself, I'd prefer the Russians got their jocks blown off, Steve."

"Me, too, Captain," the OOD answered, his gaze moving back to the dials. "Me, too."

The silence in the control room seemed overpowering until Newell called out, "Range?"

"Coming up to six thousand . . ."

"Okay," Newell interrupted, "one more time. Firing-point procedures, tubes one and two."

The weapons-control coordinator went through the same reports. The torpedos were ready.

The fire-control coordinator, Dick Makin, repeated that the solution was ready. Although the target would be crossing *Pasadena*'s bow, they would fire before it reached that point. There was no reason to start it out as a stern chase for the torpedos. The target would turn away instinctively anyway.

They waited—silently—as their target closed.

Newell looked over to the diving officer.

"Slight up bubble, sir," he answered, anticipating the question.

His glance shifted to the OOD.

"The ship is ready, sir."

"The weapon is ready, sir."

"Solution ready, sir."

Newell's voice boomed out, echoing through the control room. "Shoot on generated bearings."

A water slug propelled the first torpedo out of the tube.

Ten seconds later, "Tube number two, shoot on generated bearings."

Every man in the ship was involved in his own thoughts as he felt the shudder of the slugs, yet each also shared a similar thought—this was the first time *Pasadena* had ever fired in anger, and they desperately hoped everything they had been taught would now save their lives.

"Both units running properly, sir."

"That woke him up!" the chief sonarman exclaimed a moment later.

"Evading?" Newell called out. So much time seemed to have passed—yet it was no more than twenty seconds since the second torpedo left the tube. There had to be some reaction from their target. There was no doubting your sonar when a torpedo was fired at you. It sounded like a train! Newell wanted to move, too, to evade whatever might be fired back at him. That's what they taught you. Yet he didn't want to break the wires that controlled the torpedos, that directed them right into an evading target.

Another pause. Then, "He's cranking it all the way up . . . probably going deep . . . probably turning . . ." The voice from sonar was tentative, breaking occasionally to listen, as it also attempted to report on what was occurring at the instant.

The torpedos shifted from a high-speed pre-enabling run to a slower snake search for their target. The wires had broken. *Pasadena* could maneuver whenever he wanted to.

"No noisemakers yet . . . wait one . . . yeah, there's one in the water, I think . . . if I didn't know different, I'd say it sounds just like one of ours . . . there's a couple more of them." Another hesitation. "First torpedo's out of search . . . homing . . . range gating . . ." The torpedo's sonar had locked on its target. Now it would close relentlessly, its speed increasing as it closed for the kill. "Christ, it's all so close I can't tell if it's locked on the target or the noisemaker . . . same for number two . . ." The voice was increasing in pitch. The entire process wouldn't consume much more than two minutes, just one hundred twenty seconds, hardly enough time for an unsuspecting submarine to evade a surprise attack.

"Steve." Newell's call to his sonar officer rose over the voice from sonar. "No counterattack . . . no snapshot?"

"Nothing like that, Captain. I don't think he'd have had a prayer evading if he tried to shoot. He's just playing rabbit for us."

A sharp blast whipped through *Pasadena* like a lash as the first torpedo exploded.

"Was that a . . ." Newell's voice was drowned out by a second, equally vicious explosion, an echo to the first.

"I couldn't tell, Captain. Too soon after he fired noisemakers. If I had to guess, I'd say that first was a direct hit."

"What about . . . ?"

"There's just a mess out there, sir." The chief had anticipated Newell's next question. "We're so damn close . . ."

Newell had already begun to speak to the OOD. "Let's move—just in case he's got one last gasp left." He called over to Bob Holloway, "Stand by tubes three and four." And to the control room as a whole, he added, "We'll prepare to fire again. Maybe we just blew up some noise-makers. Those titanium hulls can be pretty damn tough, but he's got to be hurting. Eight hundred feet," he ordered the diving officer.

The control room had remained silent, almost trancelike, from the moment the torpedos were fired. There had been no struggle, no frantic scramble, as they prepared for their enemy. They'd approached quietly while their target presented itself—almost an assassination. It had been little different than putting a gun to someone's head . . . akin to an execution.

They'd fired.

They'd waited for the body to drop.

But in this case they could not see it drop, not even through the miracle of sound. The turmoil caused by two torpedos detonating within seconds of each other had left a sound void in the water, and it was absolutely foolish to wait for it to clear. They could become the sitting duck without ever knowing it.

Pasadena returned to normal operation. The OOD and the diving officer brought her to life. Torpedo tubes were readied for another shot. The attack team began the process of preparing another solution—if a target still remained.

"There was at least one hit, Captain," Tommy Lott bellowed from sonar.

"What have you got, Chief?"

"Got to be going down . . . propellor's going crazy . . . sounds like he's trying to back out of trouble . . . blowing main ballast . . . want me to put it on the speaker?"

Newell was in sonar before the chief had completed his last words. And what he heard left no doubt in anyone's mind that there was a submarine struggling for life. That was just seconds before another sound came clearly through the water—crumbling, snapping metal.

Bulkheads were shattering.

Pasadena had been unable to hear that initial leak, if indeed that first indication of water had seeped into their target that slowly. But once through the hull, once that first trickle had grown to a flow—then a roaring, smashing cascade—the increasing pressure had burst interior bulkheads like eggshells.

The sound of tortured metal screamed across the depths as the engineering spaces imploded, tearing the frantically spinning shaft from its bearings. Each man in *Pasadena*'s sonar would retain a mental picture of exactly how their target was experiencing its final seconds, men and equipment alike bursting apart from the intense pressure. It must have been mercifully quick for most of that crew, even for those in the most distant spaces of the submarine who would have seconds more to imagine their fate before every compartment imploded from the pressure.

Newell turned slowly and walked back into the control room. As he reached behind to slide the sonar door closed, he said softly, "You can go back to business as usual, gentlemen. *Pasadena* has destroyed the enemy."

The men in the control room glanced briefly at each other, unable to hold anyone's gaze for long as they silently thanked their lucky stars that the other guy had been sunk. Their captain had brought them through.

Across the water the remains of their target plummeted to the bottom of the Pacific. USS *Alaska*'s pieces spread like windblown seed as they plummeted toward the ocean floor. Her Trident missiles would no longer threaten the Soviet Union.

When *Pasadena* went to periscope depth and raised her antenna for her normal messages that night, she received new orders. She was sent to a new sector, almost three days from her current location. Her target there would be another Soviet ballistic-missile submarine—and it, too, possessed the same devilish masking device that would imitate an American Trident submarine.

There were a great many similarities in the destruction of *Nevada*. The messages received by *Pasadena* communicated even greater peril, warned that her mission was even more critical to the safety of the nation, and described how the next Russian SSBN also carried a masking device that would allow her to imitate another American boomer, *Nevada*, perfectly. They were not to be deceived. They were not to question their orders. It was imperative that this Soviet missile submarine be sunk at the earliest moment, before she received orders to launch her missiles on America. Any hesitation by *Pasadena* could mean her own loss, and that could herald the end of the United States.

Wayne Newell reinforced this in his own way until his crew hungered for their new target. Only after *Pasadena* had successfully destroyed her second target, only after the explosion of her torpedos and the haunting sounds of the target's death throes, did they ponder the horror of what they had accomplished—another submarine, one that gave every indication of being one of their own, had gone to the bottom with all hands.

CHAPTER TWO

Looking Ahead

The dark brown, four-door sedan that pulled up in front of COMSUBPAC headquarters at Pearl Harbor was intentionally nondescript, as were the three men who climbed out. They were dressed in civilian clothes—short-sleeve shirts and slacks—as were most of the non-Navy types who worked on the base. They could as easily have been three of the myriad engineers who regularly visited the naval base to troubleshoot the sophisticated electronic equipment carried by the fleet. Anonymity had been their intention since departing Washington. If the Chief of Naval Operations, his DCNO for Undersea Warfare, and the Director of Naval Nuclear Propulsion had ever appeared there together unannounced and in uniform, circumspect articles would have commanded the front pages. Concerned dependents would instinctively have been clamoring for news. And, without a doubt, the word would have found its way to the Kremlin before the first report ever appeared.

Mark Bennett had flown directly from Dulles into Pearl to meet with CINCPACFLEET (Commander in Chief, Pacific Fleet), for indirectly the problem was as much his as anyone's, considering the chain of command. Then Bennett had been returned to the airport in civilian clothes. *No one ever noticed an admiral out of uniform.* There he rented the four-door sedan, and was waiting when Ray Larsen and Robbie Newman arrived on separate flights, one from San Francisco, the other from Seattle. It had been planned that way after the meeting in the CNO's office. Larsen needed to talk with the SSBN squadron commodore at their Bangor, Washington, base beforehand. Bart Bockman had been the last one to talk with the commanding officers of *Alaska* and *Nevada*.

As the car eased into visitors' parking there was no one to hold doors or make a fuss over three of the most senior admirals in the U.S. Navy. That was the way it would have to be—not the slightest hint that there was a crisis, no indication that the White House was on the verge of a military clash with . . . with the Kremlin, each of them assumed. After all, who else would be involved with something of this magnitude?

Once inside the swinging glass doors, a single officer, COMSUBPAC's flag lieutenant, escorted them to the large office where the admiral commanding all submarines in the Pacific waited for them. Neil Arrow appeared younger than one would have anticipated of the man who commanded the Pacific Submarine Force, but he'd been C.O. of both attack subs and SSBN's. He had been the next one in his class promoted to flag rank, after Mark Bennett.

Arrow was short and compact, like his submarines, with neatly combed, short, brown hair and inquisitive blue eyes. His voice was sharp and authoritative, even in simple conversation. "I was thinking accident when *Alaska* didn't report," he said after shaking hands with the others, "but there's something I haven't quite been able to put my finger on, even when *Nevada* remained silent." It was a way of opening a troubling discussion, words that he'd been considering since he'd come back to the building a few hours before. The only time he'd been out of his office in the past six days was to have breakfast with his wife and to see the kids off to school each day. "You see neither of them reported any troubles, not even a hint, before they got under way. Equipment casualties happen. I know that." He shrugged. "Yet both of them were as clean as Mother Hubbard's proverbial cupboard, according to Bart Bockman."

"I noted that," the CNO commented dryly. Larsen was a man who spoke only when he had something specific to say. He often made a statement out of a question, but left no doubt he was looking for an answer. "What's bothered me more since then is the late report about *Pasadena.*"

"We'll give the attack boats the benefit of the doubt, Admiral," Arrow responded. *"Pasadena* was ordered to shift patrol areas in transit. I assume they've been copying their broadcast. There was no need for her to acknowledge unless they had a problem. They weren't a part of that communications experiment. On the other hand, the boomers don't exactly ask permission to use the head, even when we really have something critical for them." He shrugged again. "If it hadn't been a special situation . . ." But there was no point in finishing the sentence, and his voice trailed off.

"And do you think the same thing that silenced *Pasadena* silenced the other two?"

Arrow shook his head. "Doubtful. They were in three different locations . . . three different situations. The operating sector for *Alaska* was well north of *Pasadena*'s last position, and *Nevada* was much farther than that. *Pasadena* had been asked to confirm at a later time—using a simple burst transmission that would be almost impossible to isolate. Acknowledging that message would be more courtesy than anything else, and the last thing we need in this Navy is courtesy. Otherwise we'd be encouraging a bunch of magpies out there. We may still hear from her. For all we know, Wayne Newell's busting ass trying to repair radio problems."

"No backup equipment?" Larsen inquired.

"Yes, there is," Arrow responded evenly. "But once again, considering security requirements, I'd give them the benefit of the doubt."

All the responses were exactly as Larsen anticipated.

Neither questions nor answers brought a solution. Submarines were like cats, or they were supposed to be—absolutely silent until they pounced.

There was an aspect still bothering Mark Bennett. "There's one thing I'm not sure of, and I'd like to see if your people can set it up for us. I'm a suspicious son of a bitch, and I want the location of every Soviet ship in the northern Pacific, and I'd like to see what they've been doing for the past four days . . . where they've been. Can you do that?" His eyes had never left Arrow's.

"Give me half an hour, maybe an hour if we're going to back them up a few days." Arrow stuck his head into the outer office and explained what had to be done to his flag lieutenant. Then he glanced over his shoulder. "Any of you as hungry as I am? Great way to kill time."

As they followed Arrow out of the room, a name that had been hovering on the fringes of Mark Bennett's mind flashed repeatedly, a gaudy neon sign in a sea of confusion. Since that initial message, he'd been asking himself if any single individual might be capable of meeting this unknown threat in the limited time span available. His answer was suddenly very clear—Ben Steel, captain of *Manchester,* the man he was sure would one day fill his own shoes. But was it possible . . . could he be close enough? Frankly, Mark didn't have the vaguest idea what *Manchester* would be close enough to.

The SSV-516 was barely making headway through choppy Pacific waters a few hundred miles south of the Aleutians. She was the largest intelligence collector in the Soviet fleet, a low, wide-beamed surface ship displacing almost five thousand tons. Much of her weight was electronic equipment, and she presented a strange sight with two spherical radomes for satellite communications perched on the forward deck housing. There were also three huge masts mounting a variety of intelligence-collecting equipment. The ship was squat and odd-looking, more than fifty feet from beam to beam to accommodate excessive storage space for long at-sea periods. She also possessed missiles and guns for her own defense, an unusual feature for a vessel never designated as a warship.

She'd been at sea for more than a month now, most of her time spent cruising the northern Pacific. A certain element among those people who sailed her were convinced that their ship would eventually be the most famous in Soviet naval lore. SSV-516 was already responsible for the loss of more enemy firepower than any other vessel in history. And she had yet to fire a shot in anger.

The reason for these unique victories was deep within the main deckhouse. There, nestled in the center of a restricted high-security area, was a compartment that few members of her crew could possibly comprehend. The single door was guarded twenty-four hours a day by burly, heavily armed individuals who were said to belong to the GRU, the military-intelligence branch of the armed forces. Those who were allowed inside the space had come aboard by helicopter two weeks after the ship had left her homeport. SSV-516 had steamed within two hundred miles of Petropavlovsk, a naval base at the tip of the Kamchatka peninsula, to receive the specialists.

The electronics within this room were highly sophisticated, so much so that few within the Soviet Union were aware of their existence. Using coded radio signals that could not be interpreted by any other instrument, these black boxes allowed the operators to activate a transceiver in a high-altitude, elliptical-orbit satellite. They could even reorient the satellite to direct its blue-green laser beam to a designated sector on the surface of the Pacific. The beam could penetrate several hundred feet of seawater. An aircraft or ship would have to be near the direct path of the beam in order to intercept—and the odds of that occurring were infinitely small.

The men who designed and operated this equipment had a single mission—to control the movements of an American 688-class attack submarine. They were able to accomplish that mission with relative ease for a single, simple reason—

the operators aboard the submarine had no idea that they were being so effectively manipulated. Their communications equipment had been specially adapted for that purpose by the replacement of a couple of harmless-appearing circuit boards during their last repair period alongside a submarine tender. Not only were incoming transmissions controlled, regularly received frequencies appeared dead. While seemingly impossible at first glance, it had not been overly difficult to achieve this modification, not when the years of patient, long-range planning were considered.

There are times when the outrageous becomes pathetically simple. Soviet electronics technicians, trained for years to operate under the guise of American technical specialists, had completed the alteration during the installation of updated equipment.

The radiomen and technicians aboard that submarine—USS *Pasadena*—had no reason to suspect the extent their communications system had been compromised. They maintained absolute, even blind, confidence that they remained in direct contact with their own secure system via satellite transceiver. In a way, that sense of security amazed the Russians. Even though these same men had arranged the alterations to *Pasadena*'s equipment, they remained astounded at the ease with which they sent the American submarine off on a third mission, following *Alaska* and *Nevada*. Boomer really was working exactly as it had been planned—after all these years of waiting!

Wally Snyder was *Pasadena*'s communications officer. When he appeared in the control room and glanced quickly at the faces on watch, he found himself almost pleased that the haggard expression gradually overspreading his own features was matched by those who happened to notice him. Wally was normally jovial, an easygoing individual, comfortable in any situation. But the pinched skin around his eyes mirrored the increasing tension of the entire crew. They were exhausted.

There was a war taking place on the surface, and they had

no idea which direction the scales were tipping, no clue whether or not loved ones were still alive. It might already have escalated into a nuclear exchange. Certainly, every single one of them had considered that.

But wasn't that why they had been sent on this mission— to take out Soviet ballistic-missile submarines that could wipe out every major city in the western United States, perhaps their own homes? It was entirely possible *Pasadena* was changing the face of the war. Perhaps they were actually saving their loved ones by the successful completion of each mission.

But why was there no news? Was America still untouched by the enemy—or was *Pasadena* now receiving orders from some underground command post that had been planted deep enough to survive annihilation?

So many questions remained unanswered. So many more surfaced as each hour passed. Ignorance became anything but bliss.

Snyder's eyes traveled from man to man in the control room until they fell on the executive officer. "Should I disturb the captain now, XO, or do you want to take care of this?" He waved his message board to show what he had.

"What've you got this time, Wally?"

"Another one of those commanding officer's eyes only, sir."

"One of those?" Makin didn't really mind that he wasn't the first one to see the message. A few words with Wally Snyder could always elicit the gist of whatever it was. The comm officer enjoyed the probing.

"They do seem to have a consistency to their approach, don't they?"

"Go ahead, Wally. He's been in the rack for a couple of hours. He'll get punchy if he ever catches up on his sleep." Makin, too, was tired—no, exhausted was more like it. But so was everyone else. If there were ever an unwritten rule for executive officers, it was that a captain was vital to the survival of the ship and the XO was responsible for seeing that he was as ready as possible to take his vessel into combat—in other words, sacrifice. Makin would grab some rack time once Newell was rested.

The captain's stateroom was just forward of the control room. Lieutenant Junior Grade Snyder was convinced the man was telepathic as he hesitated outside to marshal his thoughts. "Come on in, Wally," Newell called out in a firm voice at the first touch of the young officer's knuckles on the outer bulkhead.

The bunk light snapped on as Snyder stepped into the room. Wayne Newell was stretched out fully clothed. Though his eyes blinked briefly against the sudden brightness, he appeared fully awake. He stuck his hand out for the message board as he rose into a sitting position.

After a moment's hesitation, while his captain studied the message thoughtfully, the communications officer decided to express his concern. "Captain, doesn't it seem odd to you that they're sending us off after all these boomers? After all, you'd think some of the others could do what we're doing."

Newell studied him curiously. "What makes you think we're the only ones sinking enemy subs? Wouldn't you think Pearl was sending the closest boat to the nearest target?" He knew intuitively that Snyder was his sharpest junior officer, bright enough to question any unusual set of circumstances —*such as sinking submarines that sounded like your own.* Submarine captains, unlike many of their counterparts on the larger surface ships, had to know each member of their crew individually. There was no aloofness, no ivory tower to separate the men from their leader. Each man on a submarine depended on the next—and that meant the captain as well as the most junior man aboard.

Snyder considered for a moment before answering, "I don't know where this one is, sir, but we had to go like hell for three days to nail the one that sounded like *Nevada*. It just sort of made . . . made a lot of us curious. . . ." *There, it's out on the carpet.* He'd said what so many had been wondering, what his own men hoped he might gain an answer to. Sonarmen claimed they could detect the subtle differences in each submarine's sound signature even though the experts disclaimed that talent. It was eerie, so . . .

"Chalk it up to the best attack boat in the fleet, then," Newell said gruffly before forcing a just-between-us grin and a wink. "That's what they must think we are. If you don't bother about what goes on in your superiors' minds, then you won't have anything to worry about. There's a reason for everything in the Navy," he concluded, handing the board back. "Take this into the XO and tell him I want this plotted on the chart. I'll join him after I wash up."

That's it, Snyder thought as he turned back into the passageway, another sector designated, another submarine to be sunk. *Sooner or later, one of them's going to hear us coming . . . has to hear us!* An involuntary shiver coursed down his back, tightening in his crotch. He squeezed his thighs together. His entire body seemed to tingle.

There was an unusual taste in Wayne Newell's mouth as he leaned his hands on the tiny metal sink and stared into the mirror. It wasn't an especially bad taste, just one that hadn't been there before his communications officer delivered the message. He decided to brush his teeth while he was washing up, though he knew that wouldn't chase away that slightly metallic flavor that rose from deep inside.

While he toweled off after splashing some cold water on his face, he couldn't help noticing a flash of light out of the corner of his eye when he held his head at a certain angle. He stopped long enough to experiment, moving his head from side to side until he had the source. The bunk light was reflecting off the photograph of his family. Myra, his wife, stared back at him with a posed half smile. *Too put on, sweetheart . . . too cold.* On one side of her stood his son, Charlie, a sixteen-year-old. He was taller than his mother, just an inch or so shorter than his father. Fourteen-year-old Kathy stood on the other side and grinned back at him like a Cheshire cat. A handsome golden retriever, its tongue lolling out one side of its mouth, looked as if it was about to break Charlie's grip on his collar and charge right out of the photo. *Good old Jack Tar . . . not a complaint on his furry face.* They were all posed in front of a spread of palms with the warm Hawaiian waters barely visible behind them.

It was an all-American picture, Newell acknowledged. That's the way a picture in a naval officer's stateroom should look—all-American. One wife, two kids (one of each flavor), and the family dog, Jack Tar in this case. Right out of Norman Rockwell. He'd seen those paintings during his training at the "Charm School," even on covers of old *Saturday Evening Posts. That's the way I was designed,* he mused, *all-American, old-fashioned, apple pie . . .*

His eyes fell back on the kids. *At least I'm not an android. They may have programmed me and packaged me, but that family is one thing they couldn't manufacture . . . and I picked the dog!*

Wayne Newell loved his kids. He took secret pleasure in bringing up an adolescent son, even through all the challenges Charlie could throw at him. And Kathy . . . well, she was becoming a handful, what with all those pimply-assed orangutans she brought home, every one probably trying to screw her. You just had to show girls your love in a different way—by denying the sins that could spoil them for later.

But his children were something none of those bastards, the KGB types who ran the "Charm School" outside of Moscow, could have planned for him. *They wanted a pure American—they got a pure American.*

The wife he wasn't so attached to. She was more American, more suburban than he could imagine, more than most men could take no matter where they came from. *But that's the way so many of them turn out. It could be one hell of a lot worse.* Myra Newell wasn't so bad when he compared her to some of the other wardroom wives, especially some of those who'd been military brats or some of the husband-hunting debs who'd hung around the eastern shore waiting to grab unsuspecting middies when they graduated.

And that golden was all right. When Newell was ashore, he used to take long walks with the dog and discuss his situation in detail with the animal. Old Jack Tar never argued, never talked back, never suggested that maybe all this introspection might mean that he was gradually giving in to this American lifestyle. Hell, he'd thrown himself into it forever—that's what they wanted. Instead, Jack Tar would run ahead and sniff all the good smells, but not so far that he wouldn't come racing back to jump up for a pat and lick Newell's face. *Dogs don't care who you are, or what you are, as long as you give them a little affection. And, in turn, their love is unquestioning.* That had saved him much soul-searching.

It wasn't just Newell's dog ready to give him the benefit of the doubt. Myra had never really suspected anything about him, and she probably wouldn't believe it if she were told the truth. She was loyal. What more could a man ask for? From that first moment when he caught her watching him out of the corner of her eye when he was drilling the NROTC midshipmen at Berkeley, she'd accepted him for what he claimed. *How could you knock that?*

And there were so, so many others. Ever since he had been eased into the United States and assumed the name of the orphaned and now-dead Wayne Newell, there had been so many other trusting people. The administrators at Berkeley believed it, his professors believed it, the bureaucrats who got him into NROTC believed it, the girls he dated believed it . . . *hell, they all did! And Myra had swallowed it hook, line, and sinker.*

Most of all, Wayne Newell finally came to believe it. He couldn't remember the exact moment when he came to that conclusion, but at that point in time his transformation had become complete. He had been created by masters of the art of new identities, patient men who were willing to sacrifice so very many years to see their creation actually pay them back. But he was no android! *I am a father! I am a living, breathing human being, and there are a number of people who have grown to love me as Wayne Newell.*

The interviewer, the one whom he had no idea was a KGB agent at the time, the one who had used the android terminology, was also the one who remarked on his ability with languages—"not the technical aspects so much, but your ability to grasp the nuances of the accent." That's what had attracted them to him. And he had to admit they also understood his ego, even before he did. That was how they recruited him!

It was hard to believe that an actual school—no, not a school, almost a seminary, because its teachers were solely oriented to one goal—existed so close to Moscow. It might as well have been on Mars as far as foreign intelligence agencies—and the Kremlin power structure itself—were concerned. The less anyone, even in Moscow, knew, the better. The KGB had actually succeeded in developing a school that produced Americans; not a Soviet version but good, old-fashioned, all-American "Americans."

And no one could tell them from the "real McCoy," as they'd learned early in their schooling. That was because much of the faculty were the "real McCoy," *Americans,* pilots exchanged by Hanoi for missiles. There were some other native-born Americans who'd had the misfortune to disappear and end up at the Charm School, but Newell never learned whether they'd been purchased, too. It was a faculty that had been tortured and brainwashed until they weren't sure who they might have been, or become if they'd survived. But they never forgot the background that is forever imbued in each human being. It was amazing what could be accomplished with chemicals and new methods of mind control, for these Americans had once been the most loyal and patriotic of their generation. They now existed in a village exactly like one might find in the United States, except that it was just outside Moscow, and they trained Russians to become Americans—perfect Americans—so perfect that not one of the graduates sent off to the United States to assume their new identities had yet been found out!

When they graduated, they weren't replicas or mimics. They were real. They knew the music and the dances of their eras, they played baseball and they knew how to toss a bat to choose up sides, they memorized bubble-gum cards and batting averages, they knew Z-type cars, how to buy beer with a phony ID, local politics in the towns they would settle in . . . the KGB could go on forever describing how perfect they were, but they never said a word.

Wayne Newell was a perfect example of the Charm School, an ideal graduate who had achieved exactly what his KGB managers had in mind when they designed him. And Berkeley was a perfect place to be inserted. It was the type of school where no one questioned you, and that gave him time to assume a role that convinced even the Navy, who gave him an NROTC scholarship.

Conversations with a fraud—that was the terminology he often invoked when he considered the photograph of his family. They were real. They were flesh and blood—his flesh and blood. Love. Trust. Those were undefined gifts that he could never really return. And the only one who really understood and offered no argument was old Jack Tar, who just wagged his tail and offered an occasional slobber of affection.

Newell put on a freshly starched shirt and perfectly creased pants before he headed for the control room.

"Feeling rested, Captain?" His executive officer turned and smiled.

Even Dick Makin trusts me implicitly! "Just like I'd put in eight hours in the rack, XO." He rubbed his hands together enthusiastically. "Looks to me like they intend to keep the best sub in the fleet busy."

"Did you ever think it was going to be this way, Captain?" There was an odd inflection in Makin's voice, not challenging, not questioning authority, just identifying a concern that had not been evident earlier.

Newell looked at him curiously. "What do you mean, Dick?" he asked, using the XO's first name awkwardly.

"What's happening . . ." Makin hunched his shoulders as he searched for the proper words. "It's just so different. None of us ever expected it would end up like this—the war, I mean. It just seemed in the past that we'd see it coming . . . that we'd know we were going to war, that we were going out to do the job we were trained for, and kiss our families good-bye before we got under way."

"Like the movies, Captain." The quartermaster who was leaning over the chart balancing on his elbows looked up over his half glasses. "If this was a good story, we'd know why we were going and what the enemy had done, and we'd be real mad at him." His eyes went back to the chart.

"I see," Newell grinned. "We lack drama."

Makin shook his head. "More than that, Captain. No one knows why, or what's happened so far. We've got no idea if our families are even alive. We've been sent off on two missions and we succeeded in sinking two enemy boomers. That's great." He rubbed his bald head as he searched for the words. "But we don't have any idea if we're helping to win the war . . . or if we're just getting even . . ." His voice dropped off for a moment before he jabbed a finger at a point on the chart. "Right there, sir. That's where they want us. Only about forty-eight hours away this time at max speed."

"Fine. Give the OOD a course," Newell said. "And then why don't you come to my cabin. Maybe we can figure out a way to put everyone's mind at ease." He clapped Makin on the shoulder. "Then you need to get yourself a good sleep. I'm no good without an XO to make me that way."

That was exactly the way Newell saw Dick Makin, as a perfect executive officer. If there were distant, faceless people who had created a perfect Wayne Newell, he had created a perfect XO. There was a photo of a wife and children that Makin kept, but Newell couldn't remember how many youngsters there were. He'd met the family once, perfunctorily out of naval courtesy, after Dick reported aboard. And that was that. From then on he'd concentrated on turning the man into a perfect, faceless XO—so that the crew's loyalty would be wholly directed toward Wayne Newell.

These visual displays! Giant ones, and so damn clear. Mark Bennett never ceased to be amazed by these electronic wonders. It all used to be done by hand, by men writing backward behind huge status boards. Now computers made it all so much easier. The entire Pacific basin covered much of one wall in the darkened room of SUBPAC operations. The flag lieutenant had done a fine job on short notice. While the room was always manned for emergencies, the only time it would ever be activated to this extent was that fateful moment when war began—and he sincerely hoped that someday this room would be part of a past marked by generations of peace, a museum piece remembering those tenuous, dangerous years of the past—like Churchill's subterranean command post in London.

The locations of U.S. ballistic-missile submarines were marked by blue boxes indicating their sector assignments. Two of them were in high-speed transit from Bangor, Washington, to replace *Alaska* and *Nevada*. No one had ever imagined that such a gap could be opened in America's strategic defenses! There were a lot more SSBN's in the Atlantic because there were so many more Soviet targets close to Europe.

Attack submarines were blue X's, as opposed to the red X's for the projected tracks of their Soviet counterparts. The latter could be tracked for a while after they got under way, but it became impossible to stay on all of them forever if they didn't want to be followed. Sometimes they seemed to wave a red flag—*follow me*—when they needed to draw the Americans away from something else. Bennett accepted those posits with a grain of salt.

There were symbols for various types of vessels, surface warships of other nations, merchant shipping, and a special flashing red one for the Soviet intelligence collectors. The Russians always had a few trailing the aircraft carriers, others checking progress of fleet exercises, and certain ones whose mission was impossible to ascertain. At this very moment there were numerous intelligence ships in various sections of the Pacific, ranging from tiny trawlers to the imposing SSV-516. American intelligence always knew where that one was. Mark Bennett also knew they didn't have the vaguest idea about its mission at any given time.

The operating sectors for *Alaska* and *Nevada* jumped out

at him in blue slashes, one north and slightly east of the other. Bennett rose from his chair and sauntered over to the display until he stood directly under the last known positions of the two boomers. When he stared up, his eyes riveted on those slashes, he had hoped for some wonderful insight to suddenly overwhelm him. But nothing happened. There was no mystical prescience he could tap, nothing that would bring their fate to him in a burst of clarity. No Soviet boat's track gave even a hint of malice.

The intelligence collectors all seemed to be off on their own special missions, their tracks like that of a rabbit in the snow. Nothing solid there—except for that SSV-516.

She was that big one—the one the spooks were so excited about. They didn't know what she could do, but they were excited by what they thought she might have aboard. *Black boxes!* That was another method of explaining away intelligence weaknesses. Heady stuff. Cloak and dagger. And all of it bouncing around the ocean . . .

Mark Bennett's angular face, deep voice, and unruly hair were almost Lincolnesque. He was tall for a submariner, which was compounded when he bent slightly for doorways. On a submarine he seemed perpetually stooped, but the jokes about his size faded with the early talent he displayed.

Well, why not? Bennett decided. "Neil, I'm going to send some of our intelligence aircraft out to play with that Russian spook ship. I don't know what I'm looking for, but maybe something will happen. It's a start, at least."

"There doesn't seem to be any correlation," Neil Arrow mused. "I thought about it and decided it was too far away from those sectors."

Admiral Larsen listened to their conversation with interest but remained silent. He enjoyed watching others circle a problem. Even if his approach was unconventional, they sometimes provided him with the seeds for an idea.

"Black boxes, my friend. When you can't figure out what they're doing, you play craps." Bennett looked at Neil Arrow and then over at Ray Larsen. "It's a start. One thing we don't want to do is let the Russians know we're on to anything yet. If they're sinking our boomers, you can be damn sure they'll react if they think we're the least bit on to them."

That last comment struck a sensitive spot in Ray Larsen. The Chief of Naval Operations dictated Navy policy, but there were those rare times when it was also dictated to him. "I discussed that with the President not so many hours ago," he remarked sourly. "There's so goddamn many *ifs* involved here—*if Alaska* and *Nevada* are indeed gone for good, which is exactly what he said—*if* they were sunk by the Russians—*if* the Russians intend to take out more of our boomers, maybe here, maybe in the Atlantic, too—*if* their purpose is to unbalance our triad—*if* they intend to start shooting, or *if* they just plan to lay everything on the table and ask us to grab our ankles."

There was no absolute proof yet to lay at the President's feet. They knew, rather than sensed, that the two boomers were gone. But the man in the White House needed more than their inherent understanding of the situation before he used his tremendous power to threaten someone. He needed proof. All that the four admirals in all their wisdom could tell him was that the Russians seemed the only ones who could have accomplished what appeared to be an impossible feat.

Too often when the redheaded, crew-cut CNO spoke he had a disconcerting habit of pointing at his listeners with a large freckled hand. His index finger moved from one man to the next before falling back on Mark Bennett. "You can fly around that intelligence ship of theirs all you want, because we're always sticking our nose around it anyway. But you can't allow any overt moves that would make them think anything's out of the ordinary. The boys at the White House are jabbing their boss in the ribs every time he tries to think by himself. Don't do anything they can intercept electronically. Don't try to search the areas visually. Don't intimidate any Soviet units." Larsen's finger bobbed up and down as if he were scolding a child, and his blue eyes seemed to flash a warning. Ray Larsen had no idea he looked more menacing than his reputation, even among his peers. "Just don't try . . . just use your head," he concluded after realizing his old friend was already aware of everything he was saying.

Robbie Newman had been quiet until then. As Director of Naval Nuclear Propulsion, he'd become responsible for putting new nuclear submarines into the fleet. He'd gotten away from day-to-day operational responsibilities. He was in Pearl because there remained the distant possibility of fatal engineering casualties to *Alaska* and *Nevada* rather than a devious plot. But such an accident was so unlikely. Reactor accidents simply didn't occur. It could have been a valve or a vital piece of machinery, but the odds were too long to have two like this. "I'm not sure how many options we have open if we want to avoid broadcasting to Moscow, but am I correct in assuming we're not using ELF right now to communicate with our boomers?"

"Right," Larsen answered. "We'll use that frequency only once, if we have to, in the next few days—when we're up against the wall. The TACAMO aircraft are acting as communications relays because we may need to send more data. ELF's too slow for that."

"Then I think that leaves you with one choice," Newman said. "You've got to get some hired gunfighters to protect your boomers. And there's nothing sneakier than a nice quiet 688-class riding shotgun." He smiled. "That's my suggestion. You people know better than me how you want to work it out."

"I can read your mind, Mark," Ray Larsen said, turning to Bennett. "There's only one foolproof way we can get the proper message to them—at least without raising curiosity." He winked, pleased with his own idea.

Bennett waited because the CNO's finger was still pointing at him. Larsen wiggled the finger. "We send a simple message, a one-time code to the C.O. of each boat we want to use. That won't rattle Ivan's cage. Tell him to come to periscope depth at a certain time for a pickup, or however you want to word it. Whatever it is, even though the Russians know we're contacting some of our boats, which may be unusual, there's not enough there to point any fingers." The finger was pointed directly at Bennett's chest. "Then at the appropriate time, so they have a decent chance, we parachute a SEAL onto that point. Give the SEAL something to attract the boat's attention, anything that makes noise so sonar can localize it. They'll find him eventually—hopefully before he dies of exposure."

It did make sense. *Tennessee* and *Georgia* were in transit and should be safe. But *Michigan* and *Florida* were continuing patrol in their own sectors, unaware. They were in the most immediate danger, and *Florida* was about a two-day run from *Alaska*'s last known position . . . too close!

Bennett turned around to look back at the Pacific display. There were enough attack boats out there to more than cover the boomers. But they were beneath the surface, where they belonged. There were reasonably secure ways of maneuvering surface ships without spilling everything to your enemy, but too many unusual communications with a submarine presented some challenges. Using attack boats to ride shotgun made sense. Getting them there was something else. *But—yes, there she was*—Manchester *was there!* Bennett closed his eyes and said a silent thank you for his hired gun. *Ben Steel was there!*

USS *Manchester* was new, less than a year on patrol, and she was only eighteen hours from *Florida*'s sector. She was the second command for Ben Steel, who was considered by his peers to be the finest submarine captain in the fleet. It seemed pure luck to the others that he was the closest. Mark Bennett once again gave silent thanks.

Within an hour the message had gone out to the attack boats. It was very short and very simple—"package arriving surface"—and it included the time and position nearest their anticipated locations. There wasn't a commanding officer who would mistake its import. If the subs were near their assumed position, the SEALs would be found. Once aboard the submarines, they would deliver their message directly to the commanding officers. Then they would have no choice but to be submariners until the boats surfaced off their homeport, if they ever returned.

CHAPTER THREE

The quartermaster read *Manchester*'s position off the computer and checked it against his chart. "Five miles to the pickup point, Captain." He had three inertial navigation systems, the second serving as a backup, the third to monitor the other two for accuracy. "Give or take a couple of yards. Seems to match up with sonar's contact," he added.

"Very well. Sonar, what do you make of it now? Any change?" Ben Steel asked. It was habit. Sonar would have sounded off at any variance in the contact.

"Still directly off the bow, sir. No change in bearing. Intensity's just about the same as before. Looks like it's remaining in the same position."

"Classification?"

"Still manmade, sir." That was what they'd determined previously. "I don't know what the hell it is, but it's broadband, so it's obviously designed to attract our attention. No tonals. No cavitation. And the way the signal varies, I'd have to say someone's operating it."

Steel folded his arms and stared at his executive officer thoughtfully. "What do you make of it, XO?" It was the third time he'd asked the same question in the past half hour.

Simonds grinned and shook his head wisely. "You're not going to get me on that one, Captain. I'm sure no one's compromised that one-time codebook you have, so the message had to be authentic. My ideas haven't changed. Pearl's sending a present of some kind for us."

"Even if sonar thinks there's someone bobbing around on the surface?"

"COMSUBPAC's job description requires that Admiral Arrow knows what he's doing."

"Take her to periscope depth," Steel ordered. "We'll ease in closer, keep her at about five knots. But stand by to pull the plug." His last comment was more for himself. The emergency dive was second nature. Each watch stander was trained constantly for any emergency, but it made them more comfortable when Steel put the obvious into words.

With the voices of the OOD and the diving officer quietly conning the ship in the background, *Manchester* gained a slight up angle. Steel finally said to Simonds, "Why don't you step into sonar and see what you can make of it? Maybe there'll be a change as we close." Ben Steel had never been a patient man; he was doubly irritable when he failed to understand something. "That message didn't say there was any rush, and I'm not about to show my ass until I know who's looking for it." Ben Steel could have been Hollywood's idea of a captain—black hair, dark eyes, white teeth to set off an olive complexion. He was quiet when he was thinking, yet his voice boomed when he gave orders, a smaller version of John Wayne.

Simonds, as both men silently understood, was unable to come up with anything that sonar hadn't already indicated. Yet he accepted intuitively the processes his captain's mind employed automatically.

Steel was at the larger of the two periscopes, the one with a camera that would display whatever he saw on the remote units around the room, before the diving officer had achieved a zero bubble. "Put it all on the screen," he called out as he slowly circled with the periscope, scanning both the surface and the sky. His 360-degree rotation was an automatic—"dancing with the one-eyed lady" was the term. "I want backup." But there was nothing more than waves and whitecaps and a gray cloud cover obscuring anything that might be flying above it.

"ESM report?" Was there a hidden inaudible electronic something waiting for them?

"Not a thing, Captain. Nothing anywhere." There was absolutely nothing radiating any type of electronic signal that might be searching for *Manchester*.

Steel brought the periscope back to the bow, straining his eyes toward the horizon. "Nothing . . . not a goddamn thing," he grumbled, waving an arm at Simonds. "XO, you take a look. Maybe you can see something I can't."

Simonds put his eyes to the periscope, swinging it to either side of the bow. "I doubt it, Captain. I was looking at the TV screen, and that didn't show any more than you could see here." The television-type screens located in various sections of the control room had relayed the exact image appearing on the periscope, but Simonds didn't see the need to remind Steel of that.

The XO was a large, somewhat portly man for his age, who loved to eat and drink when he was ashore. His hoarse voice grabbed a man's attention because he often sounded like he was barking. The glasses that so often slipped down his nose when he was looking directly at a man could be a source of amusement *until* his small, dark eyes met those of the man he was talking to. They helped to emphasize that he was serious almost all the time.

"Range to contact?"

"A little more than three miles."

Steel turned to the OOD. "At two miles, I want you to turn to port and start circling clockwise. Let's see if we can get a rise out of whatever it is."

For the next hour *Manchester* held its distance, waiting for a change in the signal sonar had first picked up, searching the frequency spectrum with the ESM gear for any kind of electronic radiation that might indicate a trap, and staring through four-foot seas for any sign of their quarry.

Nothing.

"Prepare to surface," Steel said as he returned to the control room from his fourth visit to sonar. He, too, had to agree that the signals seemed to be manmade. If there were anything out there waiting patiently to trap him, there had to be a man there also—and who was crazy enough to bob around out here in the middle of nowhere with the specific intent of attacking *Manchester?* He had to agree with Simonds that it made sense to first find out exactly what this mysterious "present" really was as he gave the order to surface.

Scampering up the ladder toward the top of the sail, Steel called back, "Stand by to dive until I say otherwise. And catch me before I hit the deck." Ben Steel prided himself in clearing the ladder faster than any other C.O. in the fleet. The man came down from the top of the sail like a rock.

Manchester's captain, OOD, and a lookout emerged into a cool, gray day. Dark water surged against the black hull, washing across the deck with a brilliant contrast of white foam. The submarine rolled easily in the swell.

They were greeted by a vast, vacant nothingness as the three sets of binoculars swung across the horizon. There were no birds in the middle of the Pacific to greet an object that had not been there a moment before.

"Change course toward the contact," Steel ordered, his binoculars fixed just a little ahead of the port beam. He tapped the lookout on the shoulder. "Keep your glasses right where mine are and—"

"I've got a light, Captain!" the lookout interrupted.

"Right." Steel had seen the flash an instant before. "I've got the same thing. Don't bother trying to read it. Scan either side now to see if there's anything else out there." He pushed the button for control. "I need someone on that light off the bow."

"We've already got it, sir. Wait one."

While the signal light continued to blink back at them, the three men on the bridge, inherently suspicious of everything, scanned the horizon for any indication of life other than the blinking light.

"Come on," Steel shouted into the speaker. "I need a reading."

"Must be one of ours, sir," Simonds's voice answered.

"What do you mean?" The captain was impatient.

"Message is a bit rough. Basically it says—'what's keeping you?'"

"Exactly?"

"Negative, sir. That's what makes us think it's ours. Actual light says—'what the fuck's keeping you?' He's repeated it twice. The Russians don't have a sense of humor like that."

"I can see someone in a wetsuit, Captain."

"Right, I've got him now. Christ, no raft, no nothing. Just a life vest . . . I think. Let's get a rubber boat and crew on deck on the double," Steel called down. "No telling how long he's been out there."

The OOD maneuvered *Manchester* within a hundred yards before two sailors cast off in the boat. When they came back alongside, three more men were there to haul the half-numb figure aboard and assist him down into the control room.

Twenty minutes later, even before the diving officer had leveled the boat at four hundred feet, Steel called his executive officer to his stateroom, where the Navy SEAL had delivered his message. "Plot this on the big chart, Peter, and bring us to a course to the center of that sector. Flank speed." His face was grim as he studied the person who had delivered the message. The man had parachuted from a plane into the Pacific with not a sign of life for thousands of miles. He'd been in the water for more than eight hours.

There were other SEALs from his unit on the same lonely assignment, each hoping that a submarine would find them so they might deliver a message that could save the lives of

160 men aboard another boomer—and possibly maintain the thread that held the fragile American triad together.

It would have been next to impossible for the General Secretary to convene the entire Soviet Defense Council without the U.S. becoming aware of the matter even before the meeting was adjourned. There were too many individuals in Moscow willing to sell tidbits of apparently boring, useless information—such as the whereabouts of high-ranking officials on a given day. After all, what did it matter to the average person whether these men were in their offices or talking together in a large room? But it did make a difference to intelligence specialists. If too many of these powerful men were known to be attending a Kremlin meeting, then something vital had to be up. No one knew better than the General Secretary that it would be insanity to reveal anything like that to the United States at this stage.

Quite simply, the Russians were afraid that the Americans would assume any meeting of a number of members of the Defense Council would be an admission of culpability in the disappearance of the U.S. ballistic-missile submarines.

Truthfully, the few Russians involved had no idea at this stage whether Wayne Newell's mission had met with success. The patrol sectors for *Alaska* and *Nevada* had been furnished. After that the plan's success would be wholly dependent on Wayne Newell's abilities. It was quite possible they would not know until the Americans gave it away themselves, if they were foolish enough to do so. There had been no method of confirmation established to report the sinkings, if and when they occurred, because that would violate the security of the system. It was deemed too easy by Kremlin experts for someone on *Pasadena* to become curious if any odd message was sent, and doubly so if it were intercepted. It would have to be American reaction that would confirm Newell's success. There would be nothing if he failed.

So instead of the members of the STAVKA of the Soviet Supreme High Command gathering for a meeting that might be known about within hours in Washington, the General Secretary called upon only the Minister of Defense, the Chairman of the KGB, and the Chief of the Main Political Directorate. They often met during a given week, and there was nothing suspicious about their coming together on this day.

Much of their discussion was centered on "what ifs." What if, by some unexplainable fluke, the Americans learned too early of the loss of their SSBN's? What if the U.S. decided their SSBN's were being sunk by Soviet submarines, and what if they decided on a similar course of action by sinking Soviet SSBN's? What if the U.S. reaction was simply to unleash its remaining triad based on the assumption the USSR was about to do the same? What if the U.S. challenged the Soviet Union publicly—and for some reason could prove their allegations? There were so many "what ifs," and they had all been considered before. But now, with *Pasadena* hopefully fulfilling Wayne Newell's mission, they must anticipate and be ready to react instantly to any what if.

The General Secretary had experienced some anxious moments of introspection the previous evening. The "what if" that concerned him most was what his own reaction would have been if the Americans had perpetrated this action on his country. Though he tried to avoid the unpleasantness, he too often found that he was placing himself in the position of the American president; and, as a result, time and again he experienced a deep feeling of resentment toward the Soviet power structure after all the years of negotiating arms reduction and mutual pacts to avoid armed conflict.

The attempt to eliminate one arm of the U.S. triad had not been his idea. It evolved in the early eighties after it became obvious that the KGB had been immensely successful with their insertion of Wayne Newell. The next logical determination was how best to employ the man. The current plan had been proposed and the details worked out before he'd taken the leadership. Perestroika and glasnost were vital to the evolution of the "new" Soviet Union, but one-upmanship in throw weight never quite reached the back burner. Overwhelming power, currently considered retaliatory rather than aggressive in nature, continued as a military tradition.

As he considered his position the night before, the General Secretary compared himself to President Kennedy and the abortive Bay of Pigs invasion. *What an appalling experience that must have been—and to have inherited it from a previous administration!* History had already made that one of the most significant gaffes of the twentieth century, and he did not want this operation to match that Cuban abortion.

On the other hand, the world might someday look upon his country's removal of a threat to world survival as one of the premier contributions to world peace. *If by some quirk of fate the Americans could be brought once again to the table to discuss elimination of long-range missiles . . .* But that was a dream. He had erased the concept from his mind as quickly as possible.

His defense minister, who had been deeply involved in the project from the beginning, had much different ideas. He saw it as a method of conquest. If he'd been given his head, he might have planned on inserting more Wayne Newells, until the entire submarine arm of the American triad was history. But wiser minds, those who were suspicious of the plan initially, prevailed. Many even wondered how it had gotten this far, because they honestly hadn't settled on what the next step would be. How could they if the Americans had yet to acknowledge anything was wrong? A series of responses had been considered, maybe half a dozen acceptable to all four of them, but not one an absolute until the U.S. reacted.

The other three members in the room that day appeared to be experiencing a heady bout of belligerence. The American eagle had been challenged on his own territory. The gauntlet had been thrown down. To listen to the talk among the three of them, the General Secretary would have thought the U.S. was pleading for its very life. But such was not the case. There hadn't been the slightest peep from the American eagle.

The Chief of the Main Political Directorate said, "I think we are at the point of asking them if they intend to sue for peace. If not . . ."

"There is no indication from Washington that they are even aware of the situation," the General Secretary interrupted, "and I have no reason to believe any of their submarines have been sunk. Each of you bears exactly the same responsibility as myself—preparing for whatever action the United States initiates."

Wally Snyder paused for an extra ten seconds before he knocked on the bulkhead outside Dick Makin's stateroom. Are you absolutely sure you want to do this? he asked himself. He knew the XO had only slept for two hours, but he also realized he might not have the opportunity to talk with him privately again. His idea was a shot in the dark, a lousy bet if Las Vegas was setting the odds, but he couldn't live with himself if his sixth sense eventually proved correct.

Makin perched on the edge of his bunk and yawned deeply. "I think that the next time you find a few moments to slip into your rack, I'm going to pour cold water down your neck, Wally." He ended with a halfhearted attempt at a grin, then tried to flatten the remaining fringe of hair around the back of his neck with his hands. He pointed wordlessly at the only chair in the tiny stateroom.

Snyder turned the armless chair around and squatted on it with his arms leaning on the back. Then he looked closely at Makin to make sure the exec was awake.

"I feel like I've been dragged through the meat grinder backward. How about slipping down to the wardroom for some coffee?" the XO offered as he stared blankly at the junior officer.

"If you don't mind, I'd prefer to talk right here. It'll just take a minute." Wally's chin fell on his arms as he stared back at the XO. "It's just an idea I have, and I figured it would be better to bounce it off you first before it's mentioned to the captain . . . if you think it should be . . ."

"Go ahead, Wally. Make it good, though." The XO stretched, surprised at how muscles could tighten up even when they hadn't been exercised. Then he surprised both of them by yelping when he absentmindedly kicked the chair with his big toe.

Snyder glanced down at the foot and grinned nervously. "Maybe it's a feeling, sir, nothing absolute. It's just the communications gear . . . and everything that's happened the last few days." He extended his hands, palms up. "It's hard to explain exactly, but I'd like to run some emergency tests just to be sure. You know, there are some tests set up with shore radio, even at times like this, so you can make sure everything's working right. . . ." His voice softened until it was just a whisper. They were involved in a war. Everything had turned upside down, and here he was about to talk about an experiment—and one that involved breaking radio silence.

"Go on, Wally. What makes you think there's a problem?"

"Well, we've got communications . . . but since this all started we're receiving some general message traffic but we're not hearing anything sent specifically for other boats. The only messages we pick up are directed to *Pasadena*. Now I know we were told traffic would be restricted on this special net they assigned us if conflict intensified, but it . . . it just seems odd. Either there's no other boats capable of copying our broadcast or we're the only one left out here . . . or some changes have been made in the emergency op orders that we don't know about."

"Say you do the test. How does that work? We're not supposed to be transmitting. No matter what frequency we copy, we don't squawk word one. You know, radio silence and all that."

"It's pretty simple. It's designed for an emergency. Just a simple series of letters and numbers that we send so quick no one could ever fix a position on the sending station, or no more than maybe one in a million." His arms were folded across the top of the chair again and he leaned forward. "Then they answer us with a preplanned series of letters and numbers. It's a burst transmission, so there's no problem with interception. If their answer is correct, then I'm wrong. If not, well, then I don't know what to do next. But it would mean that something's not kosher and the captain better pay attention to the problem double quick."

Makin studied the young officer closely. "You don't like what we're doing, Wally?" he inquired curiously.

"Hell, sir, I don't think anyone likes sinking another submarine when it appears to be one of your own. Imagine if those two we hit really were ours." He cocked his head and stared back at the XO as if he were daring the man to disagree. "I'm not scared, if that's what you were getting at." A self-righteous frown knit his brow and his voice grew more assertive. "I really do think we ought to test our gear at this stage. We have no idea what's happening out there."

"Okay, Wally. I'll talk to the captain about it when I have an opportunity. But I don't want you bothering him about it now. He's got enough on his mind without worrying about communications tests." A good XO protected his captain from unnecessary items, especially when things were tight, and Makin considered himself a superb executive officer. "It may be a while, but I'll take a shot at it. Okay?" He had a habit of raising his eyebrows, which often coerced the other person into assenting.

Snyder stood up. "Thanks, XO. I appreciate it. I know it makes you look bad if I'm wrong." He hoped sincerely that the XO wouldn't put it off before they encountered another target that sounded exactly like an unsuspecting American boomer.

Dick Makin was more concerned than he'd let on to Wally. Perhaps it was a sixth sense with him too. Whatever, it was a nagging, bothersome something that had gotten to him even as he slept fitfully. But he wasn't about to burden Newell. The captain had said he would do everything in his power to get Makin a submarine of his own, and it wasn't so long ago that he'd shown Dick a copy of his letter of recommendation. Dick was loyal to his captain in the Navy tradition, more so to Wayne Newell for keeping his promises. He was a superb commanding officer.

USS *Manchester* was at battle stations. While this was a normal evolution at sea, each man knew this particular instance would be anything but normal. They waited with a heightened sense of anticipation for their captain to speak to them on the 1MC. It had begun when they were assigned to pick up the Navy SEAL who had parachuted into the Pacific. Now it was only too obvious that his specific mission was to deliver a message directly to their captain, one so sensitive that no communications system was secure enough. Since that initial moment when the SEAL was first spotted blinking at them, each rumor that spread through their tiny cylindrical home increased the level of tension.

"This is the captain speaking." From the instant they heard the familiar background drone of the 1MC, each man knew intuitively that Ben Steel would involve them completely. "I know you've been anxious to learn what's going on. I can assure you that, as usual, I will withhold nothing from you. It just seemed like a good idea to make sure that everyone was fed before we went to battle stations, since we'll start work right after this little speech." His tone remained soft and well-modulated, an example of the calm approach he expected from each of his men.

"As you all know, there are no secrets on a submarine, only rumors. And it is the captain's responsibility to come clean with his crew as quickly as possible before someone takes one of those rumors seriously.

"Our latest crew member, Lieutenant Commander Burch, the SEAL we fished out of the ocean more than an hour ago, is quite comfortable aboard submarines. As a matter of fact, he claims to have locked out of them more times than a lot of our younger sailors have ever crossed the quarterdeck." In an aside intended for everyone to overhear, Steel added, "Perhaps Commander Burch will learn to stand his own turn at watch in the next couple weeks, since he doesn't get home until we do."

Steel continued, "The commander is also willing to speak to any one of you to assure you that everything is still all right back home. If you have any doubts about who he is, you'll recognize him as the one in the XO's khakis . . . with a couple of extra notches taken in the belt.

"Lieutenant Burch obviously risked his life to bring us new orders of vital importance, and that's what I want to explain in detail so you will understand why I'm asking for 110 percent from each of you as long as this mission lasts.

"There are two boomers missing—*Alaska* and *Nevada*. One disappearing is possible; two, a long shot too impossible to consider. COMSUBPAC has to assume the worst unless some trace of either of them is located. He also has to assume they may have been sunk intentionally and that all our boomers are now at risk. The immediate solution is to provide protection until we learn exactly what has happened. We have been asked to assist *Florida*. In the old days, we would be called a hired gun. In this modern era of nuclear power, I'd like to think of us as"—Steel paused just long enough before concluding—"a hired gun.

"We don't know if there are any bad guys out there or, if there are, who they are. We can always figure that the Russians are behind this, but there are no certainties, no assurance of what we're looking for or how many are out there.

"We are proceeding to *Florida*'s sector at flank speed. We are at battle stations now because I want to conduct damage-control drills until I'm convinced we can save this boat from almost anything. After that, we will return to normal watches until we are three hours from the outer limits of *Florida*'s patrol area. So get as much sleep as you can beforehand.

"Once in the vicinity, we will attempt to contact *Florida* so she doesn't take a potshot at us. There is a way to do that, and Commander Burch has provided me with the appropriate signal. After that, we'll set up a screening plan of some kind, although covering 360 degrees around a boomer sounds as ambitious to me as it probably does to you.

"Now I guess you know as much as I do. The XO and I will be making the rounds of the boat in the next few hours, and we welcome any questions"—again Steel paused for effect—"and any ideas you care to offer, since none of us are experts in this type of mission."

With a metallic click, the background drone of the P.A. disappeared. An ominous silence settled through *Manchester*'s compartments, which left each man to his own thoughts. But there was one paramount in each mind: *Just how close could you get to war?*

As developments in electronics miniaturized both the hardware and the earth itself, the U.S. Navy acknowledged the increased pressure on its senior officers in this instant world. The result was a provision for added privacy when they were off duty. In places like Hawaii, they constructed decks and pools enclosed by fencing behind many of the grand old homes that once housed what was the social whirl in pre–World War II Pearl Harbor. Many of the old guard looked upon such luxuries with disdain. Others accepted such privileges with grace, especially when these became the only places they could escape prying eyes while conducting their business.

When the Chief of Naval Operations, his DCNO for Undersea Warfare, the Director of Naval Nuclear Propulsion, and the Commander of Submarines, Pacific, were together, they desperately needed as much privacy as possible. To be seen together unexpectedly in Pearl Harbor would have been no different than placing a sign in Red Square— *trouble*. There were few places these four officers could gather on the entire island without attracting attention, other than Neil Arrow's backyard. It was a retreat.

The afternoon sun was warm and a soft breeze rattled the palm fronds together with a lazy sandpaper sound. The pool was inviting, but not one of them would have considered putting on a bathing suit and going for a swim until after working hours. Disciplined work habits had been ingrained in them for too many years. But they did enjoy a lunch served on a shaded deck, and each man appreciated the change in scenery without mentioning it to any of the others.

Ray Larsen, always more silent by habit, was bothered when Robbie Newman maintained his customary long periods of silence. "You know you drive me crazy when you stare off into nothing like that."

Newman had a thick shock of unruly gray hair and often was quite happy to listen to others, even though he gave the appearance of being asleep with his eyes open. Newman's large, dark eyes slowly came around to the CNO. He said nothing.

"I used to think you were drunk years ago, Robbie. Now I know you're thinking." Larsen's blue eyes flashed and he grinned at the others. "A penny for your thoughts," he persisted.

"I'm imagining how ridiculously easy it might be to take out a boomer if you're willing to do a little constructive thinking." Newman's eyes were fixed on a palm tree beyond the pool as he spoke. "You see, we've covered every angle so well from our own point of view that we've overlooked how the other guy thinks. I've been trying to put myself in his place and sink a couple of submarines." He shrugged good-naturedly. "Is that worth a penny?"

"It's worth a hell of a lot more if you come up with anything," Larsen muttered. He rubbed a hand unconsciously through his crew cut, waiting expectantly to see what Newman had to say.

"Well, after considerable thought—which may have been all of twenty seconds—I decided that the only navy that really could take out our boomers would be Soviet. It doesn't really make sense for anyone else. But, we can't really track every single Russian submarine, can we?" Newman wasn't expecting an answer, and continued, "The diesel boats stay in their own op areas close to home, so I can discount those. That leaves the nuclear fleet, and there's no more than a hundred of those we have to worry about," he mused, "if we figure how many are up for repair at any given time. So we try to keep track of them and spend our next couple of days putting everything and everyone we've got into figuring out where they are and which ones may be the bad guys."

"You're making it difficult," Mark Bennett said. "That's not really your point, is it?"

"No," Newman answered. "But I'm not quite sure what my point is. I'm assuming since neither *Alaska* nor *Nevada* acknowledged that communications test, they're lost. My considerable experience says it's impossible for them to both be lost as a result of equipment casualties. My considerable experience also says that any Russian submarine that tried to come close enough for a shot at them would have blown his cover before he was anywhere within torpedo range. It's our old standby theory about equipment casualties, raised yet again—once, maybe yes, but definitely not twice. The Soviet boats are still easier to hear than one of our own. Remember, our boomers stream the towed array for the specific purpose of avoiding any such surprises." The towed array was a series of highly sophisticated listening devices implanted in a long rubber tube and towed well behind the Trident submarines to provide long-range warning of approaching danger. "I can't imagine either *Alaska* or *Nevada* possibly remaining unaware of any—and I mean any—type of Soviet submarine approaching within firing range."

Admiral Larsen stroked his chin thoughtfully with one hand. "That's worth a lot more than a penny." Newman had stated what they already agreed on—in his own terms. Glancing at Bennett, he asked, "How does that balance with your technical data?"

The Navy invested billions of dollars each year in an attempt to keep a reasonable accounting of Soviet submarine movements. Such intelligence would be invaluable in time of war. The initial step, and the least expensive method, involved spies who were supposed to report all ship movements. But that was only good until the ships were out of sight. Then there was an extensive underwater hydrophone network covering a large part of the ocean floor. It was linked to a computer system that attempted to follow each submarine's track as long as a contact remained within range. Beyond that, ships specifically designed to tow deep-running passive listening devices relayed every sound they detected via satellite to shore-based computers which analyzed and filtered out everything but the submarine. And there were air, surface, and subsurface antisubmarine groups that attempted to chase any unknown contacts until they were identified. The effort was magnificent, but the end result was sometimes disheartening to the educated observer. There were too many holes in the ocean. And the odds could not be overlooked. Submarines grew increasingly stealthy and dangerous. Submariners became increasingly skillful and cunning. But Newman was right. No Soviet boat should be able to sneak within torpedo range. They all knew that.

Bennett smiled wanly. "There are probably thirty of their submarines I couldn't even begin to locate. But we can tell you roughly how many may have been in or near those sectors in the past month, and I emphasize the 'may have been.' The tough part is that most of them are unlikely candidates to sneak up on any boomer."

"Could the same one hit both *Alaska* and *Nevada?*"

"You asked that before." Bennett was amazed how he and three other grown men could play word games like this, hoping that a new idea might suddenly be generated from the tired ones they kept repeating.

"You didn't have all the data you have now, Mark."

"It would have had to travel flank speed from *Alaska's* sector to nail *Nevada*. Russian boats are faster than ours. The ones that could have covered that distance make a lot of noise. I don't know of any in that region of the Pacific."

"How about SURTASS?" That was the towed listening device that relayed acoustic data to shore via satellite.

"We're rerunning all the tapes," Neil Arrow said. "The

first time through there was no Russian sub or subs that seemed to be in a position to take out one boomer, much less two. But how many times before have they surprised us?" he concluded. The answer—too many—was obvious.

Admiral Larsen turned back to Newman. "You know how to build them, Robbie. Could the Russians have something new out there . . . something quieter than the Sierra or Oscar or Victor Three . . . or even the Akula?" Were the latest classes of Soviet attack boats possibly as quiet as their American counterparts? Had some new, unknown feature been installed to mask their inherent sound?

"Negative." Newman knew more about the Soviet submarine research program than any non-Soviet alive. "Maybe their next generation of boats, but nothing in the water now."

Larsen drummed his fingers on the table. Then he looked at the other three men. A fresh breeze lifted the fronds on a palm that had been casting shade over them and the sun caught him directly in the face. Larsen looked back down at his fingers and flattened his freckled hand on the table irritably. "Do any of you feel that either *Alaska* or *Nevada* is coming back?"

He was met with silence. Bennett and Newman eventually shook their heads. Arrow murmured, "Never."

"I concur." Two of Larsen's fingers began to beat a tattoo again. He glanced at the offending hand as if that would control the motion. Then he folded his hands in his lap. "Perhaps it isn't the Russians . . . or at least not operating under Kremlin orders." Any wild idea was worth throwing on the table now.

The others glanced uneasily at him but said nothing. They knew Ray Larsen well enough to know he had more to say.

"Perhaps we've got a maverick submarine out there . . . anybody's . . . out of control . . . one with a crew that doesn't know what it's doing . . . or somehow the equipment's gone haywire. . . ." He was searching for something he couldn't put into words. "I don't know how to explain it . . . just something we can't understand."

Neil Arrow was the only one to respond. "With more than a hundred men aboard . . . it's impossible." He shuddered at what Ben Steel and *Manchester* might be facing if Larsen could even be close.

"You mean that a hundred men wouldn't be crazy enough to do something like this?" Larsen was leaning forward now, his arms folded on the table. Those menacing blue eyes shifted continually from one man to the next. "Maybe you're right," he added softly. "I hope I'm wrong. Maybe it could even be . . ." But he shook his head before uttering the word *sabotage*. Maybe that could happen on one boomer, though even that was pretty farfetched, considering how intricately the Personnel Reliability Program worked. No, never on two boomers. "But there doesn't seem to be anything else we can come up with here. Now you find out how it could happen."

CHAPTER FOUR

Working hours aboard a Trident ballistic-missile submarine on patrol are composed of regular maintenance, watch standing, studying for promotion, and performing exercises for missile or torpedo firing and damage control until most could be accomplished automatically. The remaining time is spent eating, sleeping, watching movies or reading, and looking for new ways to avoid the boredom that can be part of life aboard a boomer—thus the reason for two crews for each boat. Seventy days at sea spent navigating the restricted boundaries of an assigned sector in the middle of a vast ocean is considered the maximum a crew could take in peacetime without losing their fighting edge.

This particular day was one for exercising the crew of USS *Florida* in preparing to fire one of their immense Trident missiles. The encoded exercise message was broken by two people using independent sources from locked safes. Then Captain Buckley Nelson received the exercise message in his stateroom and forced himself through the painstaking details of once again opening his special safe to remove the launch instructions. At the same time, his executive officer then opened his own packet to confirm the coded authority in the orders. Only then could Nelson confirm his objective on the target-assignment list in his safe. Then *Florida*'s crew was called to battle stations missile. The countdown was initiated. Now they must function with metronomic efficiency.

Each step had been covered many times before, and Buck Nelson knew he would take his crew through the same process many more times before he received orders to his next duty station. He was anxious for transfer after eighteen months of this existence, and at this stage he wasn't as concerned about his next assignment as he should have been. There were days of such boredom that he had to convince himself that not every new billet would be better. The first two or three patrols had been well worthwhile, even exhilarating at times. Although there was no guarantee that he would make admiral, a good many men who commanded boomers had a hell of a fine chance if they didn't screw up. But the monotony gradually seeped into his bones, as it did with each of his peers, and there were times when a maximum effort was required to push himself after the first couple of weeks on station. It demanded more mental effort each day to convince himself to jog a mile or more. Perhaps it was the sameness of the track—nineteen laps around the missile compartment was equal to one mile; the scenery never changed.

If there was a primary, unspoken responsibility for Buck Nelson, it was to set an example. *Perfection* on a boomer was the key word, or as damn close to perfection as possible. Nothing else would do. This perfection, coupled with leadership, was supposed to flow downhill—from the captain to the XO to the engineer to the weapons officer and on down to the lowest man who was studying every waking minute to qualify for his dolphins. When his seniors on shore reviewed *Florida*'s promotions, her crew-retention rate, the number of newly qualified men, her exercises—their review and this information was passed on to a board in Washington that would decide whether Buckley Nelson would be selected for admiral, or whether they would send him a message by way of a dead-end billet.

Buck Nelson did not look like a submarine captain. His

appearance was undistinguished. In civilian attire, most people might have guessed him as a college professor with his rimless glasses, thin brownish hair, rather gaunt features, and almost colorless mustache. Yet he approached his job like a professional football coach, tough, demanding, and unsmiling. He also possessed a master's in nuclear engineering from MIT, which was followed by a doctorate in reactor design. It was no wonder that boredom overtook him so quickly on station, but his seniors in the Navy considered this a necessary step in preparing for greater things.

So this day was a good one to take his crew right through to the firing sequence. *Florida*'s missile-control officer reported the system cycled for launch. Each member of the crew reacted almost instinctively to his responsibilities as the minutes passed. The red firing key was removed from the safe and inserted. Continuous target information was keyed into the computer along with their current position from the inertial navigation system. The backup computer checked and rechecked every byte of data to ensure that information from each system was correct. When completed, the three-stage rocket would be ready to hurl its sixty-three tons as far as six thousand miles. Its eight warheads would be programmed to land within four hundred feet of their targets.

What was it that Nelson's father had once told him? *The United States pays fantastic sums of money to geniuses to design sophisticated weapons to be operated by underpaid idiots.* They weren't idiots; not the crew of *Florida*. They were all sharp, intelligent young men, more dedicated to their profession than most Americans. But to comprehend the power of *Florida*, to understand how each piece of equipment functioned in relation to the next—that was beyond him or anyone else on board. There were certain things one had to take for granted—and the first was that the system worked.

And it did work once again, right down to the final step when Buck Nelson watched the system abort the sequence as it always did, with the data that had been entered into the computers. It always worked that way. *Thank God it always worked that way!* The geniuses that designed even the exercises knew better than to trust human frailties.

"This is Captain Nelson," he spoke into the 1MC. "I thought it was a good idea on such a nice sunny day to continue what *Florida* does best—drill. Now that we've obliterated eight separate cities in the Soviet Union with a single Trident, we have to assume that the Russians don't want us to fire the other twenty-three missiles.

"So . . ." It was almost cruel to tease them that way. "The moment that missile broke the surface, it was detected by a satellite. We gave away our position. That data was relayed to an underground command center in the Soviet Union. There are no surface ships in our vicinity, but there are two submarines nearby, one only two hours away. The nearest is now closing on us at high speed. I think you now know how precarious our situation really is. You also see how our next exercise will evolve.

"Mr. Cross has already inserted tapes in the computer, and soon sonar will pick up the first target. The game takes about three hours to complete, and we will remain at battle stations until the end. If the computer reports us sunk, the XO will bypass and we will continue. Realism is a vital part of this particular game. While we will not waste real torpedos or decoys, we will fire actual noisemakers. Damage-control parties will react exactly as if we had taken a torpedo or experienced a close-in detonation. Casualties will be treated at aid stations, and none of them will be allowed to return to duty before the drill is complete."

There was silence as the 1MC clicked off, followed thirty seconds later by a report from sonar—the initial contact! The next three hours were the most rigorous *Florida*'s crew had experienced since they departed their Bangor, Washington, pier. Within ten minutes each man was willing to believe they were under attack. Realism was the key to a successful exercise, and the designers had programmed this one as a heart-stopper. There was no time for pondering the situation. As the first target fired two torpedos at long range, a second was isolated in sonar, too distant to classify. But rough cross fixes indicated it was also closing them.

Buck Nelson attempted to maneuver close to nineteen thousand tons of submarine like a cigar boat running from the feds. *Florida* dove and fired first noisemakers to mask his ship, then simulated decoys to attract homing torpedos away from her. Then he rose rapidly toward the surface to confuse the enemy weapons-control coordinator on the next spread. She went entirely through her own firing sequence a number of times in retaliation. She made radical turns that forced men to grab for handholds as the huge submarine heeled one way, then turned just as sharply in the opposite direction to evade. Nelson treated her as much like an attack boat as possible.

At the end of three hours she had been devastated by a number of near misses. Torpedos detonated close enough to spring seams, create shock damage to heavy machinery, devastate sophisticated electronic equipment, flood spaces, start fires, darken the ship, damage the steering gear, injure thirty men and kill another dozen.

She was also sunk three times.

When Mr. Cross's game was completed, the men who had stood six hours of watch before the exercises began fell into their bunks without food. It was realism at its most terrifying. It would be another couple of days before they would experience boredom again.

Master Chief Tommy Lott understood *Pasadena*'s crew as well as any man, probably better even than his captain. That would be expected by anyone who had earned his submariner's dolphins because Lott was chief of the boat. In that capacity, he served as the XO's right-hand man, the sub's master-at-arms for any disciplinary problems, and as the commanding officer's advisor among the enlisted men. Wayne Newell could call every man aboard *Pasadena* by name, and he often knew their wives' and children's names, too. But Tommy Lott made it his business to know everything about *every* man aboard. If a negative factor existed, it was that Master Chief Tommy Lott was overly sensitive to the men's innermost thoughts. The crew was as much his as the captain's. Technically, when he became chief of the boat, he was no longer a practicing sonarman—but he couldn't keep away from his first love and Newell had allowed the chief to spend some of the time in sonar.

Chief Lott was a sonar technician by trade, the man responsible for *Pasadena's* ears. Sonarmen could sometimes be dilettantes, imagining they should be coddled because their acoustic talents could stand between life and death if their submarine was among the hunted. Some of them even grew so absorbed with their unique abilities that they talked their way ashore intending to end their careers in comfortable sonar-school billets. But most men who wore the dolphins also found they wanted to get back to sea after a tour ashore. Tommy Lott was no different. Being chief of the boat meant much more to him after his last few years ashore.

Aboard *Pasadena* Lott won the respect of every man on the boat because there was no ego involved. He accepted his native abilities and was thankful that they had brought him to the top of his profession in his early thirties. Lott looked like a bulldog, short, built like a fireplug, an expanding beer belly hanging over his belt. Even though his entire career had been aboard submarines, he walked with the exaggerated swagger of a surface sailor. But that was also show. He understood the computers utilized in sonar as well as any man in the Navy, but that was second to his talent for analyzing sound. That particular skill had, in turn, contributed to some sleepless moments in the past few days.

Tim Sanford, the chief torpedoman and Lott's closest friend, stared at Lott across the naugahyde-covered table in chiefs' quarters and forced a weak laugh. "Tommy, you look like something I pumped out of the boat after breakfast."

No reaction. Lott seemed not to have heard him.

"Except this turd didn't have bags under its eyes like you do. What the hell's bugging you, Tommy? You're supposed to be setting an example for the crew of this famous boat."

"You mean we'll be famous if we ever get back home, and famous if there's still someone alive to give a shit?" Lott stared back at Sanford without expression. The war on the surface, the loneliness of not knowing, was draining the spirit from *his crew*.

"Oh, come on, Tommy. The world hasn't come to an end yet. They're still in contact with us." Sanford shared many of the concerns about the war on the surface with the rest of the crew. He had a family back in Pearl and he was as worried as any other man. But he also had spent enough years in the Navy to know there was nothing he could do for them and that his place was aboard his ship. Lott, too, had always shared the same feelings, until now.

"Who the hell's in contact? We get coded messages from someone . . . somewhere. It's not as if someone were actually talking with us." He looked down at his fingernails and squinted as if they needed attention. "All that comes through, Tim, is orders to sink another boomer. And someone, or something, warns us that it's going to sound exactly like one of our own . . . *but don't worry—sink it anyway!*" Lott shouted with a look of agony crossing his features. He dropped his hands to his sides and looked first at Sanford, then at the other two men at the table, who had been sipping coffee and listening. "And it always does sound that way . . . exactly like one of ours. You ought to hear it."

Chiefs' quarters in a submarine were separated from the rest of the enlisted spaces in deference to their special position, but it was still tight living. Awake and off duty, the chiefs either socialized with their own or slept. There was no place else to go. They learned each other's strengths and weaknesses rapidly, and it was always surprising, even shocking, when a trait appeared that none of them had seen before. Tommy Lott was chief of the boat, and the little bulldog had always been a symbol of strength and fairness since the day he reported aboard. But they had seen him change since *Pasadena* sank that first Soviet boomer. It started in his blue eyes, gradually spread across his plump face, and now expressed itself in his conversation.

"My friend," Sanford began softly, "I'll never have ears like those attached to either side of your head, but you'll never understand the beauty of a perfect torpedo like your Uncle Tim—" He halted his attempt at humor in mid-sentence. What he'd been hearing from Lott had just come through to him, a combativeness that had never before surfaced in his friend. Tim Sanford recognized an odd, distant glint in Tommy Lott's eyes that carried a simple message—*shut up!*

"I'm not shitting you, Tim." Lott's voice was sharp. "I've got it all recorded on tape. Why don't you come down to sonar with me now and listen? I'll tell you what to look for. If you're worth anything, you'll hear what I heard. They sound exactly like American boomers—right down to the beat of the props and the machine noises, they're American machines."

"Tommy, I'd never hear them," Sanford protested. "I'm sorry I said anything about—"

Lott was on his feet. "Come on. Right now. Let's go down there. I'll tell you what to look for. I don't know how anyone can reproduce sounds like that. You can imitate cavitation. You can imitate the standard sounds any boat makes. But each boat has its own personality." He leaned forward with his hands on the table and glared down at Sanford.

"Perhaps they've recorded our signatures—you know, got it down to a science . . ." the other began weakly.

"If the Russians can't quiet their own boats properly, how come they're suddenly so damn good at designing masking equipment which makes them sound just like our own boats that they can sail away after a friendly bubble or two in the water?" His last sentence seemed to run together in a single phrase. He continued to stare at Sanford, waiting, almost daring him, for a response.

"Now, Tommy, I understand what's bothering you." He knew Lott had been chief sonarman aboard *Nevada* in her first gold crew. As a plank owner, Lott still retained an emotional attachment to her and the men who'd served with him. It was disconcerting to see the father-confessor of the boat on edge like this. "Believe me, I do. But you've got to loosen up. We can't allow the best set of ears in the fleet to have a nervous breakdown. . . ."

"The best set of ears is still the best set of ears." Lott looked at the other two men for the first time and saw the same look of concern that Tim Sanford had. His eyes returned to his friend, and he saw that Sanford was patiently waiting for him to say whatever he felt was necessary. There was no tension in Tim's face, none of the anger that Lott knew was lurking just below his own surface. He sat back down. "I'm sorry."

"Nothing to worry about, Tommy . . ."

"But what would you say if you found out we'd been conned and those were real American boomers we'd sunk? Bud Perini and Charlie Javier were on *Alaska*. You knew Tony Aldo was still on *Nevada*. Christ, who else . . ." He silently began to tick off other individuals on his fingers who'd been aboard *Nevada* with him.

"They still are," Sanford said. "The captain was warned well ahead of time about this new device the Russians are using. Remember, he used the 1MC to announce it to the crew before we ever gained contact, so there'd be no surprises."

One of the other chiefs, a machinist, spoke up for the first time. "You know, Tim, one of my first class said that another sonarman was just as concerned the other day as Tommy. They were talking about it during chow. It really is eerie as hell—this masking device, or whatever the hell it's called. A lot of troops on the boat are talking about it. Everyone has a buddy aboard one of those boomers. Just imagine—" But he never had a chance to finish.

"Battle stations . . . all hands man your battle stations . . ." The 1MC echoed through every space on *Pasadena*.

It was a false alarm, set off by a sound that had traveled a tremendous distance across Pacific waters through some freak of nature and been picked up with the sensitive ears of *Pasadena*'s passive sonar system. It could have been a hundred miles away, or even three hundred. As *Pasadena* continued toward her next target, the sound faded forever and the crew returned to their work. But it was not the victorious crew that Wayne Newell wished for. It was a curious, introspective crew who worried about the fate of their families in a war they had been told was raging on the surface, and who were equally concerned about their friends sailing aboard American boomers.

The General Secretary of the Communist Party of the Union of Soviet Socialist Republics requests the pleasure of your company at the skyburst of America's initial multiple-reentry vehicle, courtesy of a Trident D-5 missile now less than forty minutes outside of Moscow. Smoked glasses will be issued to protect the eyes of those who might survive . . .

The General Secretary snickered silently to himself. The only sound in the room was the voice of the evening newscaster in the background. If anyone had seen his face, there would have been no alteration in his expression as he considered how hilarious that invitation might be to another generation, one not attuned to anticipating a devastating nuclear exchange with the Americans.

He looked over to his wife on the off chance she might have noticed this weird, silent little joke with himself. Married people got like that after a while. They could tell when the other was happy or sad, introspective or carefree, tired, hungry . . . every sensation a human being might experience. He reflected on their relationship over the years. That was one of the most pleasant aspects of their marriage, seemingly an extrasensory experience—not the ability to read the other's mind, but a sense of how the other felt. It was a benefit he had not expected, and one that he relished as he grew older.

It was wonderful to have her there, even when she quietly watched the television news and forgot that he was present. There was a feeling of warmth, of security perhaps, which he could not define, but understood without putting it into words. He poured another small glass of vodka from the bottle set in ice. The liquid was thick and reddish-colored and gave off a faint background aroma of the hot peppers that flavored the drink. Pertsovka was his favorite. The aroma, not an especially strong one when the vodka had been in the freezer for so long, tickled his nose.

Each gulp, if he helped himself to some of the smoked fish between drinks, provided a variety of sensory pleasures within a few seconds. First, there was the icy velvet liquid on the tongue—was it the sensation of fire or ice? Which was followed by the first spark of hot pepper on his tongue, then the definite heat on the back of his throat as the vodka warmed on the way down. The arrival in his stomach was the grand finale, like the single, powerful thud on a bass drum as the alcohol and pepper combined for a searing punch that rose back up his throat with hedonistic impact. Whatever man had decided to combine these two stimulants was indeed wise!

The General Secretary had enjoyed more than his normal allocation of pertsovka that evening. Normally wary of alcohol whenever there was tension in the Kremlin, he'd violated his principles that evening. If his dear wife noticed, she said nothing. That was another wonderful part of her makeup—she allowed him the rare privilege of being nothing other than her husband when he returned to their apartment on those rare evenings he could avoid the affairs of state.

When he plunked himself down in his favorite easy chair with that air of exhaustion that came with the job, she always gave him a kiss on the cheek, sometimes a pat on the shoulder, just to remind him that she still loved him. It was simple reinforcement, nothing more, oftentimes providing reassurance to the most powerful man in the Soviet Union. Then she would bring out the vodka and fish. It was a warm, wonderful ritual which only the two of them understood. There was no doubt in her mind that he would talk when he was ready to carry on a normal conversation. She could wait. And when he was ready for dinner, on those rare occasions he wasn't attending a state function, she would prepare something in the tiny kitchen. It would always be simple and easy to do, but it meant much to him. He loved anything that didn't taste of government chefs.

Although she did note that her husband was drinking more vodka than usual, she said nothing. The news had been full of the recent transgressions of the United States against third-world countries, leading her to assume that's what had been troubling him. But now there was a segment on the athletes training for the Winter Olympics. She loved anything on ice, the fragile beauty of the figure skaters, the grace of the ice dancers, the power of the speed skaters, the violence of the hockey rink. If her husband felt the need for an extra glass or two, she felt he deserved it. If he had one too many, she even looked forward to his habit of coming up behind her chair, kissing her on the cheek, and slipping one of his rough hands down the front of her dress. Though she counted the days until he would turn his responsibilities over to a younger man, she loved those moments when the man she had always loved escaped for a few moments— even if he sometimes needed a few vodkas to find himself.

On this evening he was having a great deal of trouble escaping from the shell of the man who ran the USSR. *The General Secretary of the* . . . No, that wasn't quite right. Too long to get to the punch line. They all might have been immolated before then.

Since this may be the only time in your life to witness the detonation of a series of American multiple reentry vehicles over the ancient capital city of the Soviet Union, the General Secretary . . . Yes, that was more like it. Get in the punch line before you lose your audience. Why had the absurd become so amusing this evening?

He poured one more glass of pertsovka. Then, being a man of some discipline, he took the bottle out to the kitchen himself and stuck it back in the freezer. Out of sight, out of mind.

Seated once again in the comfortable, threadbare easy chair that had followed him from one apartment to another, he raised the final glass to the light and swirled the liquid until it coated the inside of the frosty glass like the inside of a fragile, pale ball hung on a New Year's tree. It seemed almost too pretty to drink. But it wasn't really—it disappeared in a single gulp, followed by the internal explosives that appealed to him so much.

"My pet . . ." he began.

She jumped in surprise. Perhaps it had been the assumption in the back of her mind, as she delighted in the easy grace of the ice dancing on television, that his hand slipping over her shoulder would be the first sign. She turned and looked back at him with eyebrows raised in question.

"What would you think if . . ." He paused with a slight grin that she knew meant he had drunk more than he realized. ". . . if the Americans announced that we had pushed them to the edge and . . . no, that's not really what I mean. What I mean to say is that they had good reason to release their missiles—what would you think about the leaders of our country?"

"Do you think that it would be a good reason?" she asked calmly.

"If it were I in their White House, I think . . . yes," he concluded after a slight pause.

"And would there be something you could do to prevent it?"

"I'm not sure," he answered softly.

"Then I wouldn't be very happy with the man I trusted to lead the country. Most everything I see on television indicates that it's the Americans who are providing all these challenges to peace. Of course, I don't believe all that after what you've told me." Both of them knew that not a word of anything said between the two of them would be repeated outside the apartment. "Is that why you've had a couple of extra glasses?"

He snickered aloud. "You wouldn't believe me if I told you what had been running through my mind the past few minutes." He rose and walked over to her side, kissing her on the cheek and patting her hand. "An invitation to watch the fireworks," he sighed, "for all those who refuse to step back an inch." His hand began to slide down the front of her dress . . .

They were interrupted by the phone that sat on a desk in the back of the room. It was the Minister of Defense. "I have just received word that a number of American naval officials cannot be located in Washington." The minister's voice was high and excited.

"And they are important enough to call at this hour?"

"The Chief of Naval Operations, his deputy for Undersea Warfare, and Admiral Newman, the one who builds their submarines—is that important enough for you?"

"Where are they?"

"No one knows, but they could be—"

"I'll be in my office in twenty minutes. Make sure the others are there."

He pushed the button that would bring his bodyguard and alert his driver. Whatever surprise his wife had planned for dinner would have to wait. He wished he hadn't drunk so much of the pertsovka. But, on second thought, perhaps it would improve the situation.

Mark Bennett had few loves other than his wife, Judy. There just wasn't enough time, not when you were senior officer in charge of Undersea Warfare. But there remained a special place in his heart for Hawaiian sunsets. Whenever he was away from Washington, and there was a chance—and there'd been very few such opportunities in the past few years—he made sure that he reserved an evening for that specific purpose.

Promotion to flag rank was a wonderful, heady thing, but it also meant more time in the Pentagon, a place he could still get lost in, or at sub bases, buried behind a desk in an office with no windows. A man really had to hate sunsets, he often said to himself, to avoid them in Hawaii.

That same evening, troubled by the discussion at poolside, he'd taken the car by himself and driven out near Fort

Kamehameha. There was a point reaching out into the Pacific, rarely visited by others, that he and Judy had chosen as their own years before.

Such self-indulgence was rarely enjoyed in their earlier days together. But once their children had grown old enough to take care of themselves for a few hours, Judy Bennett might glance out the window late in an afternoon and marvel at the clear air. That was reason enough to call Mark at his office and let him know that he could work a bit later that evening.

Her timing would be superb. About the time he'd step out the office door, she'd pull up in front with the top down and a basket of fresh fruit and cheese in the backseat. A bottle of wine would be chilling in the cooler beside it. They'd drive off together like a couple of teenagers, the sunset a focal point for those rare times by themselves. Years later, Judy was quickly bored by the Washington social circle and often remarked how nice it would be to be junior and back in Hawaii again.

This time there was no wine, nor fruit or cheese for Mark Bennett. But there was a glorious display of color. Ewa Beach, across the water, and Barbers Point, a low headland in the distance, brought a flood of memories. One that had settled in the back of his mind today now returned to trouble him even more while the sun settled into the Pacific in a boiling, pastel blaze—Buck and Cindy Nelson loved this view as much as the Bennetts. Now, Buck was C.O. of *Florida*.

The Nelsons were probably the best friends the Bennetts had. With the constant change of duty stations in the Navy, it wasn't easy to stay close to other couples. And few of the old friendships remained as strong once a family went back to Washington with admiral's stars. But their wives had kept the men as close as they could possibly be. Judy Bennett corresponded with Cindy at least once a month, and it had been Judy who insisted they call and surprise Buck Nelson when he was given *Florida*. Now, as the southwestern sky modulated to a deep purple, Mark Bennett was sure *Florida* was the next target.

He selected a flat stone in the sand and skipped it across the smooth surface of the water, remembering how he and Judy would challenge each other with the number of skips into a particular sunset. The cheese and fruit would have tasted wonderful at that moment, the wine even better. It was time for a walk, time to dig into his subconscious for the answer that was escaping him.

A warm, gentle breeze ruffled Bennett's hair as he wandered down the beach digging his bare feet into the sand. The sea was calm, its quiet broken only by little wavelets that brushed against the sand like the steady breath of a sleeping child. The smell of the ocean was so much different than the waters in Pearl Harbor, no oil, no garbage, no sewage, none of the detritus that compounds man's waste. He scanned the horizon. As far as he could see, there was nothing out to that disappearing line to indicate what was taking place below the surface.

Mark Bennett struggled to blot out the sweet smell of the sea, trying to remember what the air was like in those nuclear boats silently hunting each other in the inky darkness hundreds of feet beneath the waves. It seemed so long since his last command, *Stonewall Jackson*, a James Madison–class SSBN that had prowled the depths of the Atlantic. He shivered when he remembered how cold even Charleston could be in the winter—no wonder he loved Pearl.

Old *Stonewall*'s air did have a different smell to it—it was coming back now—not so much a smell as a lack of one. It was constantly being scrubbed clean, monitored by a computer, sanitized to death so that it had no personality. That was the air's most distinguishing feature—no taste, no smell, no nothing. All the aromas of food from the galley, the smell of machinery, the leather shoes, soap, after-shave lotion, even the farts, were duly sucked into the scrubbers and cleansed. Only when they surfaced to enter port at the end of a long cruise did the contamination alarms go off—to warn they were about to breathe the unclean air that everyone ashore regularly enjoyed without a moment's hesitation.

There was another memory from his command of *Stonewall Jackson* that Mark Bennett was aware of every morning when he slipped on his uniform blouse—a medal that few peacetime officers displayed, the one that legitimately belonged to Ben Steel, who now had his own command—*Manchester*. But junior officers weren't awarded such honors for that type of action. They went to the commanding officer responsible for making submariners out of their young officers.

In that particular instant, old *Stonewall* had been on her way back to Holy Loch when she picked up a Russian submarine, a new nuclear boat that must have been on trials to prove how elusive her new design would be. Ben Steel was sonar officer, and one of his sonarmen had detected a strange sound when they were south of Greenland. There was nothing like it in the computer memory, but there was every indication this was a foreign submarine, one quite different than anything the Pentagon was aware of. Bennett maneuvered to get a track on it. Same course, about the same speed. A pure intelligence coup there for the picking. Could he . . . should he? An SSBN was on duty until she entered port. But this contact appeared to be on a heading for Holy Loch. His initial responsibility lay in the missile tubes aft, but if he could also track this one without losing that tenuous contact with NMCS . . .

Every sound during every minute of the following sixty hours had been recorded as they silently closed and then followed that submarine. Steel had been awake the entire time, directing his sonar team, analyzing the Soviet's abilities by her sound and tactics, and assisting Mark Bennett in one of the great naval-intelligence coups of the period.

Mark Bennett received a medal. Ben Steel received a letter of commendation for his service record. That's the way it had to be. But every senior officer in the Navy knew the story and agreed with *Stonewall Jackson*'s captain that someday Ben Steel would be the senior submariner in the Pentagon. It was just a matter of time.

Now he thought of Ben Steel on *Manchester* and where he had been ordered. He squeezed his eyes shut until they hurt. Somehow . . . somehow the best kept having to prove it. . . .

A hungry gull made one final, curious pass by the stranger wandering the beach in the gathering darkness. But there was nothing—no garbage to be carelessly discarded by this human. As it soared off, the bird broke the stillness with a scream of frustration, acknowledging there was no more chance of satisfying its hunger until morning.

Mark Bennett repressed the urge to scream back at the gull—or was it a desire to sustain that mournful cry because he, too, failed to understand why there were no answers to his questions? What was that elusive something lurking in the back of his mind? A controlling factor of some kind had been added to the puzzle of *Alaska* and *Nevada*, something that would clarify their disappearance. But a barrier existed to hide what he was so sure was the obvious.

Squeezing his hands into fists, he wished desperately that Judy were beside him. Her arm would be around his waist and she would match her stride to his and her presence would have comforted him until the answers came. And if, God forbid, *Florida* disappeared also, she would know how to explain it to Cindy Nelson, and she would rush to help all the families . . .

Bennett stopped abruptly and hung his head, his eyes closed against the phosphorescent sparkle in the sand. Then he felt lone tears squeeze out the corner of each eye and run down his cheek. The families of *Alaska* and *Nevada* . . . when would they be told? How long could Ray Larsen—no, it was all of them, not just Ray, *don't blame Ray*—how could they justify keeping it from those wives . . . parents?

He had no idea whether this hideous gamble of silence was saving any other lives. . . .

There was no physical sensation of movement aboard *Manchester*. It was much like riding a commercial airliner on a clear, calm day, although there was no takeoff or landing, no turbulence to experience. Even at flank speed, vibration seemed nonexistent once the human body became attuned to the submarine. Each functioning piece of machinery was designed to float on its mountings to avoid "sound shorts" which were caused by a piece of metal transmitting sound through her hull into the ocean.

As he sat at the desk in his tiny captain's stateroom, Ben Steel toyed with this oddity. He knew as well as the next man that complete lack of sound and motion were still humanly impossible. His body was moving with *Manchester* and he would be thrown forward into the bulkhead if she came to a sudden stop, no different than a car hitting a tree. He had also become inured to the everyday hum of her moving parts. Man had yet to achieve absolute silence with submarines, but he was damn close. Still, certain sounds did filter out into the water, and sophisticated listening gear did hear them over unimagined distances.

Man's knowledge of electronics was more advanced than his ability to silence tons of machinery. Steel had heard those telltale sounds so many times before in sonar. He remembered his tour on *Stonewall Jackson* when he'd put on the big, soft earphones each day and been patiently taught to discern manmade sounds from those of sea life. He'd even seen what those sounds looked like when displayed on a screen, *beautiful*—"the visual display of sound cascades down the screen like a waterfall." Where had he read that? It sounded like poetry. But he'd never gotten to the point where he could identify a sound visually. He understood sound, and he'd learned how adept he could be at using his natural abilities when they'd followed that Russian sub off Greenland. But the technical aspects, the fine points, those were beyond him. They were left to that rare breed called sonarmen.

But there really was no physical sensation of movement, no vibration in the seat of his pants to indicate that *Manchester* was moving through the ocean faster than most automobiles ever traveled through a city's streets. She was heading for a rendezvous with the unknown, a mysterious something none of them would ever see, and something Steel certainly hoped she would hear—before being heard.

Undersea battles were an everyday occurrence in the trainers ashore. And whenever you made the mistake of being sunk, the instructors started the game over again, working with the attack team to increase their proficiency. There was always a critique at the end of each day to evaluate why you had been sunk, or what you did to sink the enemy. Then you went out for a couple of beers. That element of schooling was called tactics. You lived or died by tactics in a dogfight—that's what the instructors hammered home again and again.

And, of course, the commanding officers and executive officers attended their own schools, where they were exposed to a great deal more than simple tactics. They learned how to build and nourish an attack team that might save everyone's lives in a melee hundreds of feet below the surface. Then, there was strategy, that grand study of the entire ocean battlefield where each submarine and surface ship was simply a number expected to contribute to the common good.

Steel considered everything he had learned over the years—*tactics and strategy,* all the special schooling, *strategy and tactics,* everything learned by intuition, *tactics and strategy*—and he came to the conclusion that there was very little he could apply to his current situation, for he had no idea what to expect. Only intuition could come to his aid on this mission. Some referred to it as imagination, others as luck. He maintained that it was intuition and hoped his own remained as expeditious as it had been in the trainers.

And was the selection of *Manchester* for this mission just luck?

"I believe it's a matter of being in the right place at the right time, Captain." The SEAL, Lieutenant Commander Burch, had been very matter of fact. Being dropped in the middle of the Pacific apparently hadn't fazed him any more than being asked to run down to the store for a six-pack.

After a few hours' sleep he seemed to be as good as new. "They did seem to have a great deal of confidence in you, but I think it was mostly because *Manchester* was closest."

"Who briefed you on this mission?" Steel inquired curiously.

"Admiral Bennett did most of the talking."

Steel had known Mark Bennett since they'd been together on *Stonewall Jackson* in Charleston—a solid officer still capable of using his imagination.

"Admiral Larsen mostly listened . . ."

Nice to know the Chief of Naval Operations knew who Ben Steel was.

". . . and Admiral Arrow and Admiral Newman had a couple of things to say . . ."

Ah, yes, the boss of all Pacific submariners—and "the man who would be Rickover," as they all jokingly referred to Robbie Newman behind his back.

". . . but essentially the orders were Admiral Bennett's."

Burch, Steel remembered with amusement, had sat back with a bored expression on his face and asked, "What could I do to help out here, sir? I really can't go back where I came from, and I'm not the type to stand still." The unique challenges of this mission didn't seem to affect him. SEALs seemed unconcerned with their environment.

Steel remembered that those had been the first words to amuse him that day—*I really can't go back where I came from*—and knew why he instinctively liked the SEALs. "Okay, Commander, I don't know if we'll have enough time to qualify you for a set of dolphins, but you can do a couple of things. I really was serious when I mentioned over the 1MC that the men could talk with you if there was something bothering them about this whole mess. Your first job is to circulate around the boat. Spend time with the enlisted men. Have a cup of coffee with them. Get down to chiefs' quarters. Talk with my officers, especially some of the younger ones, and tell them exactly who was present when you received our orders and what they expect of us. That makes you the morale officer," Steel concluded.

"Then," he continued with a grin, knowing there was so little time, "since you're a SEAL and a man of action, I want you to get hold of my weapons officer and learn everything you can about those torpedos we shoot and how we go about it. Don't take more than a few hours." Steel laughed. "After that, we ought to be at battle stations, maybe even using some of those torpedos."

"I guess you're right, Captain. There's not a hell of a lot of time. So it's a morale officer you've won for now . . ."

That had been five hours ago. Steel knew from talking to the XO since then that Burch had done a good job as morale officer because a lot of the men did talk to him. And the weapons officer mentioned in passing that the SEAL had already learned enough to shoot a torpedo if they were forced to go to local control during a firing sequence.

Ben Steel glanced at his watch and realized that his musings had taken less than half an hour, but every minute was critical. He had yet to determine a fixed approach pattern, or an attack plan, or whatever it might be called when you were sailing a submarine into harm's way and you had no idea what that harm might be. He settled once again on intuition as his most reliable guideline. If he found *Florida* first, he might be able to communicate their mutual problem. On the other hand, he was just as likely to come upon the enemy—if, in fact, there was an enemy submarine —and then it came down to whose ability—

There was a rap of knuckles on the bulkhead outside his stateroom. When it all comes down to the short and curlies, Steel thought as he settled back into reality, you have to depend on your intuition more than anything else. "What can I do for you?" he called to the individual outside.

"Four hours to the limits of *Florida*'s sector, sir." The navigator stuck his head through the curtain hanging across the door.

"Thanks. Tell the XO I'll be out in a few moments and we can all play games with the chart—figure out how we'll roll the dice," he added more loudly as the navigator headed back toward the control room.

Steel closed his eyes and imagined he was back at Pearl. It was an exercise—more a mind game, if he allowed his imagination to run—that relaxed his mind whenever sleep wasn't in the cards. He pictured a trip up to Makaha with his family to watch the surfing championships.

There was Connie handing the picnic lunch to the two girls, who were already in the back of their station wagon. It was a hot, sunny, late-January day, and they would take H1 out past Makakilo City, then head north on the coast highway. The Steel family always started early on those hot days so they could stop for a swim at some of the beaches they hadn't enjoyed in the past, or browse in out-of-the-way shops that always appealed to Connie and two teenage girls.

He never went in the stores. It was more fun to lounge outside and watch the people, especially the girls in bikinis when they were near a beach. Sometimes he would stop at a fruit stand. Steel had a passion for fresh fruit, and that was always an important part of his trip. If his three females could wander the stores, then the only male in the family was allowed to indulge himself when the opportunity arose.

When they arrived at Makaha, the girls would go off by themselves since they intended to stroll the beach in their bikinis like all the others their age and they were sure their stern father wouldn't approve. What they failed to understand was that their father only disapproved of *their* trolling for boys like that. Ben Steel's favorite pastime at Makaha was no different than his daughters', except that he was doing the looking. If ever he happened to see his girls out of the corner of his eye, he always pretended to be looking the other way. Connie would hold onto his arm as they meandered across the hot sand repeating every so often what a dirty old man she married.

Makaha was a wonderful way to spend a day. International surfers were the reason everyone gathered there, and it was all good-natured fun. The police made sure that the beer drinkers stayed under control, and the girls consistently went home with new phone numbers. It was always a superb day.

Steel opened his eyes and stared at the neutral-green bulkhead of the confining stateroom that surrounded him. It had been a lovely daydream for a few moments—he looked at his watch and noticed that this particular trip to Makaha had taken less than ten minutes. But now he was relaxed. There were times he often wondered if he really slept. Was it possible to order up a dream like that? Could it be so vivid if he were asleep?

Ben Steel stood up and stretched, then went over to the metal sink and splashed some cool water in his face. The figure that stared back from the mirror needed a fresh shirt. *Why not indulge yourself, Steel? You may never need another.*

CHAPTER FIVE

A cold wind, spawned in the bleak, frigid Laptev Sea, swept over the western Siberian mountain ranges, crossed the Kamchatka peninsula, then whipped down the Bering Sea across the Aleutians into the open ocean. There was nothing in the northern Pacific to stall its mounting fury. Wave heights increased dramatically. Gusting winds flattened the peaks of waves and blew the foam from the whitecaps horizontally until vision was five hundred yards at best. The ceiling was less than a thousand feet.

SSV-516 plowed through the heaving ocean on a course thirty degrees off the oncoming wind. Any number of ships longer and heavier could handle such a day with reasonable comfort, but hardly any could churn through such seas with the relative ease of SSV-516. She was a scientific research vessel, which was a charitable appellation for an intelligence collector. Her broad beam coupled with a full-load displacement of five thousand tons countered the tumbling seas effectively.

Her commanding officer, Captain Markov, remained in the pilothouse almost constantly in such weather. He had little concern for hull damage but worried constantly over the tremendous value of her electronic equipment. Just one slip by an inattentive watch stander and a series of heavy rolls would result in damage that could be both costly to repair and hazardous to her mission. Most of her sophisticated equipment was unavailable anywhere on the east coast of the USSR, and replacement parts would have to be flown in from the research centers west of the Urals. SSV-516's captain had been selected over a host of talented naval officers for his seamanship, common sense, and caution in such weather; he would not have been selected to command a man-of-war.

The ship was plodding along at seven knots, her bow occasionally plowing deep into the sea. Even in the pilot-house one could feel the shudder run throughout the ship when she struggled to shake the tons of green water spilling from her broad bow to either side of her main deckhouse.

Her nose was buried in dark water when the phone next to the captain's chair buzzed. "Yes."

"Captain, this is Lieutenant Peshkov. The American aircraft are at two hundred kilometers, still closing on a direct line."

"Have you learned if there are any of their aircraft carriers within range?"

"Negative. Definitely not carrier aircraft. We picked them up shortly after departure from their Air Force base in the Aleutians. I'd wager my next paycheck they're recon aircraft. What little electronics they're employing fit that ID."

"How are they armed?" SSV-516 shook violently as her bow lifted out of the swell, flinging green water to either side.

"They aren't. Purely intelligence gathering, the type that should normally stay about where they are now . . . just listen. That's what I was anticipating even though they're still closing the gap. It could be a standard intelligence mission . . . or they could be out here for a specific reason, maybe wondering if we have anything to do with those submarines of theirs." Word seemed to be spreading on SSV-516.

"Let me know if they close to a hundred kilometers." He cut off his radar officer and pushed the buzzer for his warrant-missile specialist. "I want your men on standby. A possible target is closing from the east."

Captain Markov felt much better after replacing the phone in its cradle. This world of electronics was a comfortable one, a world in which the human eye was no longer necessary. But somehow he had been intimidated, almost frightened, by the cloak of invisibility that the clouds and blowing spray surrounded him with. His missiles became a comforting shield—even though their range was no more than ten kilometers. He suppressed the knowledge that any self-respecting pilot would already be aware of SSV-516's defensive weaknesses and would find it easy to remain just beyond their reach.

It was an especially quiet watch in *Florida's* control room. The watch section was exhausted from Buck Nelson's intensive exercises, and the diving officer found it necessary to shift men at their positions more often than usual to keep them alert. It was also a boring watch, few contacts, smooth seas above. The OOD had little interest in maneuvering games. Their course was generally steady, speed and depth rarely changed, and sonar's only contacts were distant sounds that would have no effect on the submarine.

"Thirty minutes to the wall," the duty quartermaster announced in a bored monotone. He'd been replotting their position and reporting the time every five minutes to no one in particular—anyone who might listen—simply to keep himself alert. The internal navigational system's positions were determined by the computer and accurate within feet. A typewriter in the control room printed out their longitude and latitude every six minutes. But he had chosen to plot their location by hand, just as quartermasters had done before the Omega system became more accurate than the individual who operated it. The old methods were those he'd learned first, and now they were a welcome crutch to stay awake.

Captain Nelson's standing orders didn't require notice of a base course change, only reason not to have done so, but no one in the darkened control room minded if the quarter-master had decided to keep them informed. Each instance after the time to maneuver was called out, one by one the others ambled over to the chart table to study their new location—a couple of additional miles covered on an imaginary line superimposed over a chart of a single sector in the Pacific Ocean. The background was entirely blue, no indication of anything they might identify with. Only the neat, black numbers indicating ocean depths revealed any type of relief, and that was the bottom, miles below.

The quartermaster's line of advance and each position marked with a tiny X on the invisible sheet of plastic covering the chart were straight and efficient. His efforts were normal. All quartermasters tested themselves against the computers. The computers were always correct. The exact position of an SSBN was absolutely critical from one moment to the next since they might be ordered to fire a missile at any time. An incorrect position fed into that missile would mean a complete miss after traveling up to six thousand miles—and for all they knew, the single mistake could mean the end of their country. It was sensible to indulge the quartermasters, not to mention the technicians who maintained the navigational equipment.

So every five minutes the time to course change continued to be summarily announced, and in time visually noted by each member of the watch able to pass by the chart table. At precisely five minutes beforehand the OOD, without realizing why he did it, called the captain in his cabin to inform him of the maneuver.

Buck Nelson was stretched out in his narrow bunk, his pillow carefully folded in half under his head. His original intention had been commendable—to read until he was called to the control room. The light still burned over his head. Some of the handful of papers he'd been reading had slipped off his chest onto the deck when he fell asleep. For a moment the harsh buzzing of the phone became an integral part of a fitful, already forgotten dream, before it gradually dragged him from the oblivion of an exhausted sleep.

Nelson mumbled into the mouthpiece, "Captain here." The remaining sheets of paper slid off his chest as he rose on one elbow out of habit. "Very well," he responded, "come to your new course on schedule," without wondering why he was called.

He hung up the phone and allowed his head to slump back on the pillow for a moment. Waking like that reminded him of the few times he'd been drunk. Buck Nelson accepted the reality of command—never sleeping more than two hours at a time at sea. It was a fact of life. But he would never come to terms with the disconcerting effect of that buzzing phone jarring him awake. That was another fact of life that had no doubt raised his blood pressure every time it jolted him like that. It was something you put up with. A standard course-change report could just as easily be an emergency call—*a torpedo in the water!* Silly to think about. Yes. But that buzzer sure as hell got your attention, no matter what the reason.

There wasn't the slightest reason to get out of his bunk for a course change. The OOD had completed the same maneuver a thousand times, and this one would be no different. The point Nelson was making to himself at the same time he felt for his pulse was that commanding officers who reacted to every single evolution aboard their vessels probably weren't going to continue in that position for long.

Yes, his pulse rate was faster than it should have been. It couldn't have been that "all ships" message that implied in as few words as possible that an increased alert had been set—no reason why. *Relax. That's it . . . relax.* He'd seen those messages too often. Like all captains, he was certain they were sent by shore-based officers who had nothing better to do. The one he'd worry about would be the launch message. The soul of the engineer took over, relaying the messages to the body, explaining that tension was a state of mind. Only type-A personalities, highly nervous individuals, allowed the tension to rise like that. That was why they weren't fit to command a boomer. *But Buck Nelson is.*

If the pressures that were integral to commanding a war

machine as lethal as *Florida* got to any of the C.O.'s for more than a couple of patrols, it would turn up in their physicals. It didn't matter whether it was found out by one of the meticulous physicians responsible for the health of the men who commanded the boomers, or one of the shrinks who would ask something stupid just before delivering an incisive, demanding question out of left field that dug into your very soul. They had their ways—they learned pretty quick if that tremendous responsibility was getting to the man.

He took a deep breath, exhaled slowly. Then another. And another. *That's it, Nelson, relax. You have earned this fantastic ship and you don't want to screw things up with something as dumb as tension . . . nerves.*

This was the ultimate job in the Navy, as far as he was concerned. He was willing to argue that with anyone who claimed it was carriers. When you were promoted out of a boomer, there were big things ahead . . . as far as status was concerned. Your first star was most likely on the horizon. That was making it. But that star was nothing like command at sea; nothing was quite like command of a Trident ballistic-missile submarine, command of the most powerful weapon yet devised by man.

If an SSBN functioned as it was designed, it would never launch a missile in anger. It would deter. It would simply run around a box in a designated sector and its awesome capabilities would deter the other guy from challenging the effect of more D-5 ballistic missiles than would ever be necessary to wipe mankind from the face of the earth.

That was why it was the ultimate job—because as a single individual you served your country as well as any man ever had if you remained hidden from the other guy and the threat of your missiles kept him in line . . . *just as his kept your nation's leaders in line.* You were accomplishing more than all those people on Capitol Hill simply by the fact that you and your crew and your submarine existed and deterred the other guy. And if you were able to perform that job of deterrence, you were eventually promoted up and out of the best job in the Navy!

Nelson felt for his pulse again. Good. It was slowing down. *Relax.* That goddamn buzzer could give a man gray hair.

It would be nice to receive a star, Nelson admitted, even nicer to have some Pentagon job where he could get home for dinner with Cindy most nights.

But if that weren't going to happen, what would he do? The Navy didn't keep passed-over captains around forever. He'd always wanted to teach, and to get the type of position he'd dreamed of was only worthwhile if you had a doctorate. That's what Nelson had really been after years earlier—that one final year to complete his doctorate. It didn't hurt his career either. With that, along with command of an SSBN, there was a certainty of career movement in the right direction. He could be teaching now. But the Navy needed commanding officers, and Buck Nelson had received superior grades on his fitness reports in each command he'd had. So he'd wait.

Cindy did love that academic atmosphere. Oh, how she'd loved MIT and the Boston area. Because they were both older than the average graduate students when the Navy sent him off to Cambridge, it was almost like being part of the faculty. And he did teach some undergraduate classes. As a matter of fact, the two of them used to laugh together after those faculty parties when they were treated like a member of the department—even though Buck was technically a candidate for his doctorate. Yet he was making more money as a student than his professors!

He'd even thought once about resigning in order to teach. But a few weeks in an academic community changed his mind at his age. He learned how they treated each other at department meetings, when tenure was being considered, when applications for graduate admission were being considered. That had settled it. *He was Navy.* There was no comparison. The men you worked with in submarines were his kind of people, even if a lot of them were no longer interested in advanced degrees. On the other hand, a lot of the professors he met were okay . . . but sure as hell not out of the same mold. *Don't give up the idea, old boy,* a voice murmured from the recesses of his mind. *If Bill Crowe could make Chairman of the Joint Chiefs, there's room for one more egghead at the top.*

He stretched his toes toward the bulkhead and pointed his fingers at them. Then he relaxed his whole body. Point . . . relax . . . point . . . relax. That was it. He felt for his pulse once more. Good. Much better. *Relax.*

Nelson could feel himself drifting off. It was a good feeling. He imagined the family back home . . . Cindy . . . his two daughters, Jenny and Beth . . . their new house.

That house! That was the best thing that had happened to the Nelson family. When they moved to the state of Washington, it was the first house they could really call their own. In the past they'd gone to the older bases—New London, Charleston, San Diego, Pearl Harbor—and the places they'd lived were either apartments or rented houses, and they were always moving into something that someone had just vacated.

Bangor, Washington, was a base especially for the boomers, and Buck Nelson presented his family with a brand-new house that had been built on a freshly cleared lot in a lovely grove of Douglas fir. The scent of fir bark and needles was a constant, always fresh, but there was nothing like a clear day after a heavy rain when that heady aroma permeated the air.

It had been a little late for swing sets—the girls were already teenagers—but Buck Nelson's next major purchase had been one of those aboveground swimming pools, large enough to float in on one of those blow-up air mattresses. Pool days were rare in the northwest, and the giant firs blocked out enough sunlight to keep the air cool, but the Nelsons made the most of their "first real house."

His photo of Cindy and the girls was partially hidden behind a jumble of papers, and he sat up in his bunk to reach across the open desk and clear a path to that picture. He smiled at it for a moment, then sorted the papers on the other side and dusted off the glass with his handkerchief.

You're a lucky man, Nelson. Cindy was a lovely woman. Triple lucky, he decided after looking at the girls. It was hard to imagine how a man with his looks—thin hair, skinny, kind of nondescript—could be surrounded by females like that.

Jenny and Beth were growing up too fast. Just before *Florida* had gotten under way—the night before, to be exact—they'd given him a picture of themselves by the pool. The sun had been directly overhead and they were in their bathing suits . . . and Beth, the fourteen-year-old, looked just like her older sister. *Knockouts. That's what you've produced, Nelson—knockouts!* Too many of the younger men—both officer and enlisted—were in his stateroom every day, and he'd stuck the girls' picture in his drawer. It had seemed embarrassing at the time for the C.O. of a boomer to have to explain that those two luscious females were none other than his daughters.

Now, after also polishing it with his handkerchief, he placed it next to the other. Why not show off? Hell, maybe one of those youngsters would see it and ask who those girls were.

There was a sharp knock on the bulkhead outside.

"Come," Nelson called out huskily.

The curtain was pulled back and Delaney, the chief sonarman, a young man still under thirty, stepped inside. "Good morning, Captain, I—" He stopped in midsentence. "Wow, sir." His eyes were on the photo of the girls. "Who are those lovely young ladies?"

"My daughters, Chief," Nelson answered. He couldn't remember ever feeling so proud before. Not only did he command a boomer, but he was surrounded by three of the most beautiful women in the world.

Pasadena cut through the ocean depths at flank speed but there was little sense of mobility. One grew accustomed to the sounds of a submarine under way—the comfortable noises from the engineering plant aft, the creaking of the hull, the everyday hum of auxiliary equipment, even the muffled buzz of the men at their stations. Only hours after getting under way it all became an accepted part of each individual's integration with this huge machine; the only way that sound would ever be noticed was if something suddenly stopped. Then, that sudden silence, that unorthodox change in the submarine's rhythm, would be noticed by each man. If they were asleep, they would awaken quickly. That alteration in the ship's sound, her rhythmic heartbeat, would be no different than a rapid change in one's own bodily functions. It demanded instant attention to this great body that encased your own.

Wayne Newell's crew was tired; he could sense it. They were an integral part of him, and their weariness was akin to a numbness in his fingers or an itch between his shoulder blades that he couldn't reach. The men were scared and . . . no, they weren't scared. They were too well-trained. It was their families they feared for. No man who qualified as a submariner could be too frightened for his own life when he knew he was doing his duty—*as long as they continued to work together, they figured they'd get each other back home.*

It was *home* they were worried about. *Home, hearth, whatever you wanted to call it.* If there were a shooting war going on up on the surface, even if it was still limited to, say, a European land war between NATO and the Warsaw Pact, how long would it be before the first tactical nuclear weapon was used? Perhaps it would be an eastern front in Germany that collapsed, or Soviet forces pouring through the Fulda Gap so rapidly that only extreme measures would halt them. It might not even be that threatening, just something that the NATO commander acceded to when a hysterical field general saw his forces crumbling. Then the use of theater-sized nuclear weapons could lead to strategic threats followed by a decision to beat the other side to the draw.

It wouldn't take much to get to that same point of frustration about your home when you were six hundred feet below the surface of the ocean in an attack submarine. Not when you were racing at flank speed toward a newly designated sector to sink another Soviet ballistic-missile submarine . . . *another one that sounded exactly like an American boomer.* Not when you were increasingly terrified that your captain—or someone—could be making a terrible mistake and you were actually murdering your own people. And on the surface, perhaps that very moment . . . was someone murdering your wife and kids?

Wayne Newell understood the not-so-subtle element that was increasing the tension in his submarine. He also accepted the fact that it was solely up to him to make his crew as comfortable as possible with their terrifying responsibilities. They must be made to understand that there was absolutely no doubt in their captain's mind that they were doing the right thing.

Of course it was the right thing! In theory, the entire plan was working flawlessly. No . . . no . . . no—*not* theory . . . *those had not been American boomers they'd sunk.* It was *not* an elaborate masquerade to convince Wayne Newell or Dick Makin or *Pasadena's* crew that they were facing a cruel new device that was intended to deceive them into believing they were approaching one of their own boats. *Those really were Soviet boomers!* Wayne Newell now believed it in his heart . . . with all his heart . . . with his very being . . . and he closed his eyes and concentrated on that fact. *You must believe in your killing if you are to do a good job of it—and we are killing the enemy!*

He no longer acknowledged that their communications system was under the control of anything other than SUBPAC. He'd never heard of any SSV-516—it would have meant nothing to him anyway—any communications satellite, any blue-green laser. When the messages were brought to him, they were actually issued through the normal system, relayed by satellite transceiver to ensure secure communications between SUBPAC and *Pasadena.* Pearl Harbor had warned him beforehand, even issued the op order to cover this unique situation. It was in black and white, and his own executive officer, Dick Makin, had watched him open the secure envelope—sealed by COMSUBPAC in Pearl and handed directly to Newell as the commanding officer of *Pasadena. That's how it really happened* . . .

Those really were Soviet boomers! Those really were . . . *those really were* . . .

Newell's eyes clouded over as he considered each of their attacks—picture-perfect attacks! Cat and mouse! But the mouse never had a clue where that cat came from. Imagine the Russians trying to fool them like that. Perhaps they *might* have fooled another submarine, but not one with a superb crew like *Pasadena*. Wayne Newell had seen through their charade. With the help of an executive officer like Dick Makin, the best XO in the business for damn sure, he'd been able to warn his crew. He'd been able to convince them that they'd matured from America's first line of defense to a superb fighting machine able to breach perhaps the most sophisticated ruse the Soviets had ever attempted.

That was it! That was the way it was unfolding. It would be impossible to reinforce this . . . this undeniable truth for his men if their captain didn't believe it completely himself. *But he did.*

Those boomers at the bottom of the Pacific deserved their fate. They'd attempted to imitate American SSBN's in order to prepare to launch their deadly missiles at the United States. But Wayne Newell . . . SUBPAC . . . American intelligence had seen through it. His heart beat more quickly with the realization that he had acquired a new level of understanding in this complex game where nothing appeared as it really was.

It was critical to reinforce this understanding with his men. They—or at least some of them—were, he knew, faltering in their resolve. His executive officer had explained that some of them even wondered if *Pasadena* was the victim of a deadly hoax, or intelligence deception.

It wasn't that they mistrusted their captain. Nor was it the horrible responsibility of their mission. No, it wasn't that easy. It was a case of not knowing whether their families were alive or dead, of not knowing if there was a United States or simply a command post deep underground issuing orders—and the end result was gut-wrenching suspicion when the sonar told them they were about to fire on one of their own, *even when they had been warned beforehand.*

He picked up the phone and had almost touched Dick Makin's button before changing his mind. It had only been a few hours since their last discussion. As always, that implicit trust between them had been evident, but they had been unable to determine how to put the crew at ease. Maybe Dick had talked with some of the men by now. What the hell . . .

But why call Dick in here? He just might be in the next compartment. With that, he rose from his desk and stuck his head around the corner. There was a recessed light illuminating neat stacks of paperwork on Makin's desk. And there was the picture of his family. How long had it been since the XO left that out for everyone to see? Newell took another step so that he could look directly in. His executive officer was stretched out on his bunk with the light shining over his shoulder on a single sheet of paper—the one that explained the Soviet masking device that allowed their boomers to imitate the sound signature of American boomers.

"Ah, Dick, great minds and all that." He rarely used the XO's first name, but this was a time to do so. "You're thinking about exactly what I'm thinking." He stepped inside and reached for the single chair, turning it so he could straddle it with his arms across the back. "Mind if I make myself at home?"

"Sure thing . . ." Makin gestured as he began to swing his feet out.

"No . . . no, please, Dick. Stretch out. There's more room if you make yourself at home in your little castle." Newell waved him back down with a grin. "You're probably beat to shit like the rest of us." Newell's enthusiasm masked any weariness.

"I'm still pretty sharp." Makin forced a smile. Old quarterbacks never admitted to giving in to anything. "I've felt better before, but I can tough it out with the best of them. Hell, Captain, you haven't had much sleep yourself."

"The catnap was designed for me, Dick. Five or ten minutes here and there will do wonders, and whenever I can grab an hour undisturbed, it's just like a good night's sleep for most others." He nodded at the sheet of paper in Makin's hand. "Scared about that?"

The executive officer's forehead wrinkled in a frown and he shook his head. "No, not scared." He paused and looked hard at Newell for a moment. "No reason to be that I know of," he began tentatively, "unless there's something else I should be aware of."

"No, not that I know of either, Dick. I was just a little surprised that you were back into it again. I know some of the men have been concerned . . . and I sure as hell can sympathize if they don't have a full understanding of that explanation." He indicated the sheet of paper. "What do you hear?"

"I don't quite know how to put it into words . . . I've never been at war before, or . . ." He shrugged, searching for the right words. "I guess I don't know how men should react at a time like this. The shrinks covered a lot in prospective XO school in New London before I came out here, but I don't think anyone could imagine a situation like the one we're in." He glanced over at the photo on his desk and held his lower lip between his teeth for a second. "There's tension. Hell, we all feel that. And Wally's talked to me about—"

"Wally?" Newell interrupted. "What in the world could possibly be bothering him? I've already discussed everything with him," he added irritably.

"I know that, Captain. I know. But I promised I'd talk with you when there was an opportunity. He's kind of a sensitive kid, you know, and he worries when everything doesn't seem to be absolutely kosher—"

"I thought I'd explained everything as clearly as necessary," Newell interrupted again. "I don't give a shit who's sensitive—"

"My fault." Makin had developed a way of placing himself between the officers and the captain's rare streaks of irritability, just as he normally sheltered Newell from the everyday wardroom problems. "I didn't realize you'd already talked with him about that special communications check he brought up."

Newell raised an eyebrow. "Special communications check? I don't remember that I did. What's that all about?"

"Very simple, he claims. If a comm officer is worried about his equipment at all—and he seems to be bothered by the fact that most of the messages we're receiving are addressed to us, no other boats, no general addressees or information—you send a simple code on a burst transmission and the response comes back the same way. If there's no answer, then you know you've got a problem. Wally says it's designed for conditions like these, I guess to ensure security."

"No." The captain folded his arms across the top of the chair and rested his chin on them with a faraway look in his eyes. "No, I don't want to take any chances breaking communications security at a time like this. Maybe after we complete this next mission . . . yes. But not now, definitely not." His eyes focused on his XO's. "Want me to go over that with Wally directly?" It was almost a challenge, a rarity in their relationship.

"No. I'll handle him."

Newell glanced over at the photo. He'd already forgotten what Dick's wife looked like. She was an attractive woman, and he couldn't imagine why he'd forgotten that. Two kids, too. A boy and a girl. Perfect. Just like the Newells, except for . . .

"Fine," Newell said. "Now, what I really wanted to talk about was the tension problem. We talked about it a few hours back and decided we'd chew on it first and come up with a team approach. And that's what we need, Dick, a team approach, a united front to ease that tension." He leaned forward enthusiastically, balancing the chair on two legs. "If we don't go after it right now, Dick, there could be problems later. I don't want to be counseling crewmen at the same time we're coming up with a firing solution to take out a Russian boomer." He shook his head defiantly and the chair banged down on all four legs. "That's the way to get yourself sunk."

Makin rubbed his hands together thoughtfully. Wayne Newell's attitude was contagious. "I really have thought about it a lot, Captain, and there only seems to be one answer. I guess we've got to take the old-boy approach, sit down in each compartment and lay it all out again. Hell, we both have families. There's no better way than to tell them how we feel about our own—explain that we're all in the same fix . . ."

"You're right, you know, Dick. You always seem to have the right answer." Newell nodded sagely. "Just like politicians, we'll take our case to the people." His blue eyes brightened. "There's plenty of time, more than thirty hours, I'd say. What we need to do is get them mad, get them keyed up to get revenge for what's happening on the surface."

"They're tired, too, Captain."

"Understood. Work out a revised watch schedule for the next twenty-four hours so that everyone has a chance to rest. Better yet, have the chiefs take care of their own men and report back to you."

"That's the other thing I was going to talk with you about, Captain." The executive officer rubbed his hands together again until he eventually lowered his chin to rest on his thumbs. "I thought you might be resting when I stuck my head in a while back, and I didn't want to upset you then." He pursed his lips and chewed on his lower lip again before he looked up. "Tommy Lott . . . he really seems to be near the edge. Chief Sanford came to me about it. It seems our chief of the boat is very upset . . . trying to get other people to listen to the tapes of that last Soviet boomer we sunk . . . says you can't imitate a boat's personality and he knew *Nevada*'s signature like he knew his own heartbeat. He served aboard her before he came to us, you know. He's convinced we—somebody—made a mistake."

"Well . . . that's ridiculous!" Newell's enthusiasm vanished as rapidly as it had appeared. His tone turned suddenly ugly. "You know that as well as I do."

"I'm just passing it on for what it's worth, Captain. Next to you, Tommy Lott is the one the troops listen to the most. His shit doesn't stink, as far as they're concerned. They respect whatever he says, and he's right at the edge. . . ."

"Then I'll take the goddamn tape!" Newell snapped.

"Say again, Captain." Makin's hands were no longer occupied with themselves. The sonar tapes were a permanent part of the ship's record—like the log—and they were turned over to COMSUBPAC for analysis when a sub returned to port.

"That tape, or tapes, of whatever the hell Lott's yammering about—I want it." He recognized the surprise in his XO's eyes and tempered his next words. "I'll listen to it with him, but we're not going to do that with everyone hanging around us. He can point out whatever he wants directly to me, but I'll have none of his upsetting the rest of the crew—not at a time like this." Newell saw there was no change in Makin's expression. "If he can convince me, we'll break off this mission and attempt to establish communications of some sort with Pearl. But you see, Dick"—he was balancing the chair on two legs again, and leaning toward the other man—"we can't afford any morale problems like that . . . not when our mission means"—his eyes widening—"everything."

"I haven't talked with him yet. I felt this had to be your decision, Captain."

Newell wagged an index finger in Makin's direction. "I won't accept insubordination, Dick, not at a time like this. We may just have a new chief of the boat if Lott doesn't see things my way."

Dick Makin said nothing. His loyalty remained intact. But this was the first time he had experienced a twinge of concern about his captain.

CHAPTER SIX

Ray Larsen's fingers drummed, as before, on the worn tabletop. It was as if none of them had gone their separate ways after their last meeting. His piercing blue eyes skipped across each face before settling back on the fingers of his own large hand. They appeared capable of maintaining that steady beat without his cooperation. "I haven't talked with many others—mostly C.O.'s and one or two staff types who know how to keep quiet but they all looked at me like I had four eyes." The free hand passed over his crew-cut red hair a few times. "The consensus was—*impossible*. No one could conceive of either equipment casualties or sabotage, not with more than a hundred men aboard." The eyes once again circled the table until they settled on Mark Bennett. "Well?"

Bennett pursed his lips before he spoke, carefully choosing his words as he passed the question on. "Any new ideas from staring at that display of yours?" he asked Arrow.

The Pacific submarine commander shook his head. "Nothing yet. Something could come up any moment, I suppose—a new sound from a seafloor hydrophone, or maybe SURTASS might pick up something . . . who knows? My intelligence officer has a whole crew combing through every message from every station in the Pacific—ours and theirs, by the way—sniffing for something we might have overlooked. If he comes up with anything, we'll be the first to know, but he doesn't have the vaguest idea of what he's looking for . . . or why." He stared at the CNO's fingers drumming on the table. The habit was an irritating one, and he toyed with the idea of saying so. On the other hand, he knew Ray Larsen kept a mental scorecard titled: Lack of Patience.

Robbie Newman had nothing to say. He was shaking his head slowly before the other three looked in his direction.

"But they're goners," Larsen concluded softly, nodding in private agreement with his own foregone conclusion, knowing none of the others would respond. "And we haven't got the vaguest idea where or when or how. With all man's knowledge at our fingertips, we overlooked something that we can't understand." His final words came in a whisper, and not one of the men at the table had ever heard the Chief of Naval Operations speak in that manner.

It was all part of an endless litany, an effort to expunge the tragedy from their hearts so that their minds could pursue each angle unemotionally. It was also a way of saying—*let's get on with it, tears won't bring them back.*

Bennett responded just as softly. "Two boomers would never go down at the same time due to an accident or malfunction . . . not like this. There's no statistician alive who could find those odds no matter how long he banged away at a computer." His voice rose. "One . . . yes. Two . . . no. They were attacked and sunk. It's as simple as that. And there's only one nation that would even attempt something like that. . . ."

"The first thing the President will say is—'prove it.'" Newman was matter-of-fact in his conclusion. "And we can't. How do you go about telling someone to stop sinking your submarines, better yet threatening them, if you don't have a leg to stand on? No, Mark, we have to come up with something better than a simple conclusion. That's too easy.

Tell me how they sunk those boomers and I'll break down the door to that Oval Office to tell the man about it."

Peter Simonds's ample belly covered part of the vast ocean as he bent over the chart table. His elbows were planted in the South Pacific when Steel entered the control room. "Nothing but water out here," he muttered as *Manchester's* captain peered over his shoulder.

"Imagine how our SEAL friend felt when he looked out of that plane for the first time, XO. What if you'd been up there with him? Water, water everywhere . . ." Steel's voice drifted off as he winked at the chief quartermaster on the other side of the table.

The XO glanced from face to face. Simonds hated flying of any kind. Everyone on *Pasadena* knew it. "There's nothing quite like the comfort of a crash dive when I think about being up there." The idea of parachuting left a decidedly hollow ache in his belly. He placed a large index finger on the chart. "That's the middle of *Florida's* sector, according to the message. I didn't realize they covered so much territory."

Steel smiled to himself, remembering how surprised he was the first time he went out on *Stonewall Jackson*. It wasn't so much the size of the sector as much as the fact that he'd assumed without thinking that a boomer simply arrived on station and then maintained trim for weeks, close to the same position. But that wouldn't have made sense. That would provide an easier target if someone was gunning for them. A boomer remained within an assigned sector for very logical reasons, but it maneuvered around that sector much of the time like a mouse in a maze, never standing still, never satisfied . . . always nervous. Each watch was a series of course and speed changes and variations in depth, but nothing so radical that it might interfere with the antenna they were towing to receive messages. "She won't be under your finger," he said to Simonds.

Simonds looked over the rims of his glasses and grinned. "It would take the fun out of it if she was."

The chief quartermaster was holding a small sheet of paper which he kept smoothing on the side of the table. "I've got a new fix here, Captain, fresh out of the computer, no more than thirty seconds old."

"How close to the last one?" Simonds asked, glancing down at the neat X that had been marked on the chart to indicate *Manchester's* last position.

"About yea." The chief was holding up his free hand to show a minute space between his thumb and index finger. His grin seemed to stretch from ear to ear. The duty quartermaster snickered.

"He was waiting for you to ask," Steel said, winking at the chief, "and you stepped right into the middle of it."

"Is today the XO's day in the barrel?" Simonds asked good-naturedly.

"About thirty nautical miles, Commander," the chief responded, a large smile still on his face. The navigation system on a boomer was so precise, and the chief so meticulous in his care of it, that his original answer was one of his few attempts at humor. The effort was made with each individual who asked the question. He was especially appreciative whenever the captain acknowledged his little joke.

Simonds shook his head, looking sadly over the tops of his glasses. "I promise never to lead with my chin again, Chief, if you promise not to tell anyone ashore."

"Done, sir." The quartermaster was pleased with himself. "Where do we go from here?" They were approaching *Florida's* sector from the south, and Steel had set his course toward the southwest quadrant.

"For one thing," Steel answered, "we don't go charging into the middle of that sector sounding like the local garbage truck. What I want, Chief, is to hang right on the perimeter for a starter. We're going to spend all our time listening." He pointed a finger at Simonds. "I'm going to concentrate most of my time in sonar, or at least I'm going to be listening to what they have to tell me. Until we have a solid contact of some kind, you can wander, but let control know where you are. I'm going to turn east on the bottom leg of *Florida's* sector and start my coverage counterclockwise. Then we're going to be more silent than we ever thought of being before. You get someone with a stethoscope to cover every inch of this ship. We're not going to make a sound."

It would have been nice to contact *Florida* to let them know the "good guys" had arrived. But submarines didn't communicate with each other. They also would most likely have blown their secrecy if an enemy were lurking. Steel was sure *Florida* had not received a detailed warning, because any interception of such information would hurt them. More than likely, there had been a general message increasing the alert status for all SSBN's.

Within two hours *Manchester* had settled on a leisurely course to the east on the lower leg of *Florida's* sector. Her maximum speed never passed ten knots and she varied her depth according to instructions from Peter Simonds until the process became second nature to the watch section. And once they were lulled by this constancy, Steel's orders were to change their habits. If an enemy submarine were monitoring the surrounding ocean as closely as they were—and that was entirely possible, as far as he was concerned—that submarine's computers might eventually isolate this distant sound that exhibited manmade habits. And that would change *Manchester* from the hunter to the hunted. Common sense demanded an uncommon strategy to confuse those computers.

In *Manchester's* sonar, each individual sound in that vast ocean became a possible target. The passage of a noise through the water to a submarine's listening devices can be affected by any number of peculiarities: the salinity of the water, temperature variations, depth of the source/position of the listening device, physical interference between the two, the chatter of a hull responding to a change in water pressure, marine life forms called biologicals, along with any number of unexplained influences that man had yet to understand. The ability of acoustic engineers to screen out unwanted noise meant that a given sound could be detected at an even greater range. These sounds reached the submarine across a wide frequency band over untold distances, sometimes from ranges so far that changing water conditions might attenuate them before the computers ever had the opportunity to identify the source.

To complicate the situation further, *Manchester* did not know what their prospective target might eventually be. It could turn up before they located *Florida*. Ben Steel was searching for an unknown quantity based on information from a SEAL who had parachuted into the Pacific Ocean after a briefing by four senior admirals who knew no more than Steel did.

There was no specific reason for a captain to spend so much time in sonar. Ben Steel just felt comfortable there. His sonar officer, David Hall, was a gem, the chief and his technicians outstanding, and they all understood why he enjoyed kibitzing in the background in that small space chock-full of the most sophisticated electronic gear available. One of the first tales told to new students in sonar school was the value of acoustic intelligence, followed by the "sixty hours of *Stonewall Jackson*" and her sonar officer, Ben Steel.

As he watched his men at work, occasionally easing a proffered headphone set over his head when a new sound was located, Steel's thoughts returned to old *Stonewall.* That had been a wonderful tour of duty, better than anything he might have expected aboard a boomer, and the other officers had been terrific to work with. Her captain, Mark Bennett, had been a mentor, the individual singularly responsible for bringing out the best in him.

He'd bunked with the navigator, Wayne Newell, an NROTC graduate from the West Coast whom he'd known vaguely at nuclear power school. Steel remembered how different the Academy graduates initially found the NROTC types. Ben had always been a good athlete at Annapolis, and he and many of his friends remained frustrated jocks the first few years out of school. It was an Academy disease. The college-trained officers joined in, but their spirit wasn't the same. The touch-football games weren't as competitive with the non-Academy officers, nor was the basketball. They hadn't been instilled with four years of intramurals and simply didn't take such things as seriously.

On the other hand, Newell had been a company commander at Berkeley and was one of those who became dead serious about that. He wore his uniforms like a second skin. His neat appearance seemed chiseled from granite. Ben Steel's rough-hewn John Wayne countenance had been a little too raw for that; in that regard, he was the antithesis of the Academy-groomed officer.

Newell had been forgotten after nuclear power school, except for the times Steel had noticed his orders in the *Navy Times*. Then their paths crossed on *Stonewall Jackson*. The bunk in Newell's stateroom had just been vacated, Steel moved in, and they'd gradually grown on each other. It had been a polite relationship during their first patrol, with casual conversations during those few cherished spare moments when they were crowded in the tiny space together. It began with reminiscences of their midshipmen days and comparisons of the differences—Annapolis versus radical California campus—and Steel could laugh now when he realized how stuffy he and his Academy friends had been about those "outsiders."

It was their wives who had established a closer relationship. Judy Bennett, as the captain's wife, hosted monthly teas for the wardroom wives, and the two junior women gravitated to each other naturally. Unlike so many of the others—Navy-oriented women who had met their husbands at Academy dances and married them as fresh-caught ensigns—neither Connie Steel nor Myra Newell were able to identify with the Navy at first. Since neither one had ever spoken that insider's language, they found pleasure in their own unfamiliarity with this new environment.

Myra Newell had met her husband-to-be at Berkeley. Answering the age-old question of how they'd met each other the first time grew funnier over the years. NROTC was not popular on that campus. The midshipmen drilled on the practice fields because the athletes found them more acceptable than the liberal element that controlled much of the rest of the campus.

Myra was a part-time secretary in the athletic department, working her way through the university. She was the brightest student who had graduated from her tiny northern California high school and the first to be accepted at Berkeley. But she had never had a social life in her hometown because she'd been helping to support her family since the age of fourteen. When the quiet girl with the conservative upbringing appeared in Berkeley, she realized immediately that there was no way she could survive in the free-swinging atmosphere of her more liberal peers. The decision to accept a job in the athletic department was a logical one for her. It was even more natural to be fascinated with the men in the handsome uniforms who were drilling nearby.

Wayne Newell had seen the girl before. She was cute, and she was one of the only females who bothered to watch his company drill, at least without carrying a sign demanding that the military get off campus. The maneuvers he ordered were simple—the company marched to the left, to the right, to the rear—and before she was quite aware of how it had happened, he had brought them to a halt and he was standing beside her.

"How would you like to be the color girl at our ball?" He gave orders for right face, at ease, and called out to his company, "How about it? Does she fit the description?"

They cheered.

She turned a deep shade of red.

"Then it's settled. You've been honored. What do you say?"

She looked up at him for the first time. "I've never been so embarrassed in my life."

But she went to the ball—and fell in love with Wayne Newell.

It was the kind of story that Connie Steel loved. It was out of the storybooks, a true romance, and so different from the others that followed a predictable path either after graduation or shortly after the intense concentration on winning the submariners' dolphins.

Ben Steel had met Connie the night the officers from his first boat were celebrating his new dolphins at the officers' club. She was with a shore-based officer who'd become hopelessly drunk, and she was calling a taxi when Ben overheard her on the phone. "Please." His hand covered the mouthpiece. "Cancel it. If I don't have a date to take home, there's no way I can leave this party early, and my friends are going to get me very drunk."

"What's the party for, Lieutenant?" She held the phone tightly, suspicious, lonely, and unsure of her answer.

"New dolphins . . . special honor, special party."

"Who's won the dolphins?" For some reason which she later realized was absolutely irrational, she trusted the submariners much more than the men ashore. Somehow they gave the impression of being a lot more serious. She later learned that ended with working hours.

Steel brightened. "Me." He pointed to the shiny gold dolphins on his chest. "And it would really mean everything to me if you accepted. I hate hangovers . . . and I really would like to meet you. Honestly, my intentions are honorable . . . at least they are now." He grinned, taking his hand off the mouthpiece.

"Cancel the taxi," she murmured into the phone. "All right," she said, placing it back on the hook and nodding in the direction of the private room where the party was going on, "but I insist on a formal introduction before I go into that madhouse with you." She held out her hand. "I'm Connie."

It wasn't quite as romantic as the Newells' introduction—maybe the movies had overdone that approach—but it was different. The two women became fast friends as soon as *Stonewall Jackson* left on the next patrol. Two months at sea was an eternity for a wife on shore.

The Newells and the Steels remained friends for their entire tour, the men more so because they worked together and it was convenient, the women because they too often shared a unique loneliness. It was a relationship that was pleasant while they were all together, but there was nothing to bind it permanently when they left for new commands. Connie wrote to Myra often that first year, and was disappointed when the responses grew more rare, until Ben assured her that it was more likely Wayne Newell's attitude. Both men instinctively understood that Newell had little interest in maintaining relationships. He was friendly enough, respected others for their capabilities, and returned favors, but his job was his life. He preferred to maintain a polite distance. Eventually Connie understood, just as she gradually accepted other oddities concerning the Navy and its people.

Over the years, the two women remained casual friends-by-mail, until their husbands ended up commanding attack submarines homeported at Pearl Harbor. They found the ten years hadn't hurt the enjoyment they found in each other's company when *Manchester* and *Pasadena* were at sea.

The relationship that was to last from the days on *Stonewall Jackson* was between Ben Steel and his commanding officer, Mark Bennett. It was nurtured by the women because their husbands' respect for each other sustained itself through the years. It grew until the younger man commanded *Manchester* and was chosen by his mentor, who had become the most senior submariner in the Navy, to battle an unknown enemy.

The sonar chief announced another distant contact. Steel squeezed his eyes tight and strained for that mostly inaudible sound. It was next to impossible to continue his musings about the old *Stonewall* days at the same time. The mental images of Connie and the girls faded rapidly, and he said a silent little prayer for their safety as *Manchester* plunged ahead through the black Pacific waters.

Was the Kremlin conference room excessively hot, or was it just his imagination? The General Secretary dabbed at the perspiration on his upper lip, then ran the handkerchief over his bald head. The cloth came away damp. Damn! He should have known better than to drink that much vodka earlier in the evening. Wasn't it all just a simple matter of age? He couldn't handle it like he used to, and sooner or later he was going to have to admit it. But at times like this . . .

". . . and our intelligence operatives in Honolulu," the KGB head continued, "still haven't located the American admirals. However, there has been an increase in message traffic between Washington and Pearl Harbor, peaking at approximately twenty-seven percent over the past twelve hours. Also, their Trident base in the state of Washington was included almost fifty percent more as an information addressee than in the preceding six months. The codes being used are unusual for even highly classified operational traffic, and we have reason to assume that one-time codes are being employed."

"Stop!" The General Secretary's voice cracked like a shot through the Kremlin room. "I have no interest in that garbage. Answers, all I want is answers. Keep the details to yourself." A mild headache had commenced earlier behind his eyes and was now pulsating toward the back of his skull. KGB percentages had a great deal to do with magnifying what should have been bothersome, like too much vodka, but it shouldn't have been so irritating. There was no need to snap like that. Vodka hadn't contributed to discomfort of this nature in the past, at least not to this extent. "My only interest is the content of those messages. There are others to worry about the extent of message traffic and explain its meaning. We all know why this is happening, so tell us what will result." The anger in his voice was controlled but still evident.

"As I explained, their coding has created some problems and—"

"I came here at your request," the General Secretary interrupted. "I left the comfort of my home after spending a long day here because there was a grave emergency, as far as

I could gather from your phone call. That home was very comfortable. I'm no less tired than I was then." The look in the General Secretary's eyes was an unusual combination of impatience and outright displeasure. "A plan designed by men who no longer appear at this table has finally been activated. Those originators are either dead or sitting in front of a fire with a blanket over their withered knees, waiting to die. So please don't tell me about percentages. Just tell me exactly what the Americans are doing now."

It was the question they'd all anticipated, and each man at that table appeared momentarily lost in his own thoughts as the KGB head stared wordlessly back at his senior. Their reaction was automatic. To head the KGB no longer meant automatic invincibility. They were remembering the words the General Secretary had uttered earlier that day, no more than an expansion of what he had been saying for the past couple of weeks—they were a government so steeped in the past that they could only complete that which had been designed by an earlier generation of bureaucrats. And to compound that, their own decisions were doomed to be carried out by a succeeding generation, unless the system was radically altered.

That morning he had made it understood that he intended to change that system or die trying. Now he was angry because he was once again trapped by plans that he'd been forced to act upon. This time, it was the military who had insisted it be done. They contended there was no alternative. If the operation was suspended at this stage, regardless of its outcome, there never again would be such an opportunity to neutralize U.S. strategic power. Wasn't that the reason the original plan had been devised? Neutralize the threat? At that time, the men who determined how Wayne Newell would be used also felt that the entire operation should be seen through to the end once it was enacted—no getting cold feet at a later date. It was their singular contribution to the future. Russian leaders, the

General Secretary silently acknowledged, instinctively (or was it stubbornly?) stuck to such plans once they'd been formulated.

Even before he assumed the leadership, the General Secretary had developed a hatred for the overcrowded meetings so common in the Kremlin. Once it became his decision, he'd established a maximum attendance based on subject matter. Today there were only six other men in the room, still too many as far as he was concerned. His regard for the three military officers present had been decreasing over the past few days in proportion to their enthusiasm for what was now taking place in the Pacific.

The admiral in charge of submarine warfare made the mistake of holding the General Secretary's glance for too long, and he knew there was no choice but to take the initiative. "None of us can be absolutely certain what the Americans are doing or even thinking. We'd already be aware if they could substantiate anything. But if those four American admirals are indeed in Pearl Harbor now, I'm ninety-nine percent sure they're still in the dark about what has taken place—at least they have no more knowledge about exactly what has happened than we do. None of us can. It doesn't matter where they are. After all, only our submarine captain really knows. We can only assume—"

"Men who assume are doomed to experience failure. This strategy originated among men who expected that our intelligence capabilities would be at least the equal of our technical abilities. So far, one half of that expectation appears to be assumption," the General Secretary concluded acidly. "The first question I want answered is *how* the Americans are aware of any problem with their missile submarines at this time, if that is in fact why their senior admirals have suddenly disappeared from under our noses."

"We should have that—" the KGB head began.

"No!" Again the General Secretary reacted angrily to his closest advisor. "You *will* have it if you have to expose every one of your people. Just how do you think I would react if I thought the Americans had conceived of a strategy to neutralize our seagoing ballistic-missile system? Should I immediately launch every missile at my fingertips? Should I declare war? Or perhaps I should get on my hands and knees and beg for peace at any cost?" He folded his handkerchief systematically before he again patted away the perspiration. "They absolutely must have some inkling of what has taken place, possibly more than we do, or their admirals wouldn't disappear like this. It just may be likely that they already know more about the success or failure of this mission than we do—*and that is ludicrous!*" His words dripped with sarcasm. "It is more than likely that the American president knows more about the success or failure of our efforts than I do, and if he does, then he has a distinct advantage." His eyes held those of the KGB head. *"Find out what they already know.* And how."

Captain Markov responded slowly to the buzz of the phone beside his chair in the pilothouse of SSV-516. He had been dozing, oblivious to the heavy seas, and the irritating sound had been incorporated into a dream already lost to him as he reached for the instrument. Time meant nothing in the northern Pacific as the dark, gray days changed to black nights then back to dark, gray days again. Sleep came when he closed his eyes, whether he was in his bunk, on the bridge, at the dining table, or sometimes even standing, if he happened to be leaning against something. Wakefulness became a state akin to sleep, but years aboard ship had trained him to function regardless of his exhaustion.

"Captain here," he murmured into the phone.

"Captain, it's almost time to send another message to the American submarine."

"Then do it."

"But . . . the American reconnaissance aircraft—they could intercept our signal."

That was correct. Those planes had completely disappeared from his mind. Maybe he wasn't functioning as well as he used to. "How much time?"

"Thirty minutes."

"And if they don't receive a message in thirty minutes?"

"They would dive and wait for another three hours before attempting to copy their message traffic again." The satellite laser transmission could reach well below the depths of normal methods, but the Russians couldn't chance transmitting when *Pasadena* was deep. That could definitely compromise their entire system. So they were forced to follow the old methods.

"How critical is this message?"

"They're all critical, Captain. If I may recall for you, our instructions indicate that other members of *Pasadena*'s crew are loyal to the United States, and at a time like this we could be making a grave mistake if they had reason to doubt any little thing that's taken place."

"You're correct . . . of course." Captain Markov paused as SSV-516 strained to lift her bow from underneath tons of green water streaming down the forward part of the ship. She shuddered, shaking like a wet dog. "Where are the American planes now?"

"Circling, about the same range, maybe a little closer, but still out around one hundred kilometers."

"And their chances to intercept the signal?"

"They could pick up something on their equipment, Captain. It's almost impossible not to. But there's no absolute reason they should know what it is or where it's directed. After all, it is relayed to a satellite before being redirected to *Pasadena*."

"But if the aircraft do receive it?"

"I don't think they'd be able to interpret it accurately, not with the equipment they have. But they would pass it on to shore base."

"How much should this storm affect their chances of interception?"

"Everything is affected, Captain. That's why I can't say."

"There's no reason to raise any doubt, then, with the other members of her crew. Send the message."

CHAPTER SEVEN

Dick Makin was a realist. He anticipated the pressure that would come as XO of *Pasadena* when he first read his orders. That came with a career in the Navy. But he never once expected it to feel like this, not tension that you could cut with a knife. Through all his years in submarines—the equipment casualties, the emergencies, the agonizing personnel decisions—never once had he imagined that he would be questioning his own values. In his dreams he had always accepted the fact that someday he would have a command of his own and that he would be inescapably responsible for the safety of that ship and its crew. That was how he'd been trained, and it seemed natural to assume that was why Dick Makin had been put on this earth. He possessed the natural ability to assume that awesome responsibility, never once questioning that any other man in the same position wouldn't be his equal.

As executive officer, he was the chief administrator and business manager of *Pasadena*, the man responsible for ensuring that the captain's orders were carried out and that the ship was run smoothly and efficiently. Tommy Lott, as chief of the boat, was Makin's alter ego among the crew. Together they were a team. Their respect for each other was mutual. The chief of the boat's relationship with his captain should have been the same also. Until the last few days that had been the case within a military structure established hundreds of years before.

Now that age-old system was in question. Wayne Newell had refused to allow Wally Snyder to check his communications equipment even when the young officer had offered solid reasons for testing it. Newell had used security as a final reason, even though he knew the odds of Wally's burst transmission being intercepted and their position marked were very long. Nor would he consider Tommy Lott's professional analysis of the sonar tapes, a request that was becoming increasingly presumptive. For the first time, Lott's emotions appeared to be overwhelming his reason.

Now Dick Makin was rereading the latest message from COMSUBPAC just handed to him by Wally. It was short and easily comprehended, yet his efficient, well-organized world was indeed coming apart:

IMPERATIVE PASADENA REPORT RESULTS OF ACTION TO DATE.
YOUR SUCCESS CRITICAL TO NATIONAL STRATEGY.

There was no way of knowing it had been sent by SSV-516, nor that any response of theirs would be received only by the soviet ship.

They were asking *Pasadena* to violate security at a critical juncture in her mission. This after Newell had refused a less dangerous equipment test. If she were located by electronic-countermeasures equipment because of this . . .

"XO, that's a no-no," Snyder said. "I can't buy it. I was told in comm school this would never happen. Not a chance in the world that they'd do something like that right now."

"What about that communications test you wanted—"

"Comm tests, yes. A half-second burst transmission at best. No addressee involved, no chance to triangulate sources for a fix of any kind. They were designed for what I honestly consider an emergency now. But a message like this really scares me. It conflicts with everything I ever learned about naval communications. What can I say, sir? I smell a rat."

The executive officer understood communications security as well as Wally Snyder, as well as any other man on *Pasadena*. Submarines were on their own. The limited communications they experienced were generated by shore command. During wartime it was understood that submarines reported their successes only when they returned— otherwise assumptions were made for lost boats after the fighting was over.

"The captain's adamant about your request. We don't make a peep. 'That's doctrine,' he says." *So what would Newell's reaction be to this message?*

Wally Snyder glanced briefly at the XO. There was no doubt the case was closed, but he couldn't walk out. He had to make one more try. If their equipment checked out, he'd have more faith in this message. He leaned forward with his elbows on his knees, his knuckles pressed tightly together until he formed a steeple with his index fingers and touched them to the tip of his nose. Then he looked at Makin again. "I know there's something wrong, XO. I don't know why. I don't know what it is. But I know deep inside that I'm right. When they trained me, they didn't leave out anything. They turned out a damn fine submariner, too." He slapped his thighs with his hands and stood up. "Request permission to take this to the captain myself, sir." This was the way he'd get his point across to Newell. "I'd like your support."

Makin's lips tightened into that rare expression they all knew when he was about to dig in his heels. "I discussed this with him once. I won't a second time. He's got too much on his mind. You know you can talk to him anytime you feel it's necessary, Wally—when he's in the control room, in the wardroom, or you can go to his stateroom and knock—"

"But I want your backing, XO. I—"

"I have never in my career placed my captain in an awkward position with a junior officer and I don't intend to now." His eyes narrowed until the black pupils glistened with anger. "I've initialed that message. You may deliver it to him now and express yourself if you want to take the chance, but I'll back my captain a hundred percent. His reaction will be the same as mine. We'll remain silent until our mission is accomplished. The source of that message is secondary until our orders have been executed."

The communications officer's head inclined briefly in acknowledgment. "Thank you, sir," he murmured softly. There was no purpose in challenging the authority of naval command. He turned slowly and stepped into the passageway. Makin heard Wally whisper to himself, "Thanks a lot," as he moved away.

The XO rubbed his tired eyes slowly, pressing against his eyelids until multicolored stars glistened against the blackness. The United States was at war, not a show of force, not a localized action, but a terrifying confrontation with the Soviet Union. There were no boundaries. Civilians were as susceptible as the military. Every man aboard *Pasadena* had someone back home he was thinking of during every waking moment. Makin knew that each time he thought about Pat and the children in their new house looking down on Honolulu, he had to remember all the other families, too. But that was easy enough to say. It was next to impossible to do. The image of the three of them, Pat and the kids, kept pushing to the forefront, forcing all the others backward to merge in an incomprehensible blur.

That house was the first the Makins ever lived in that had a personality of its own. The others had been what a junior officer could get on a junior officer's pay in a military community. Those had been shelters—neutral, bland, unenticing to anyone with a sense of taste. And Pat had taste that she was willing to keep in check until their time came.

It came when her husband received orders to *Pasadena*. She had gone out to Pearl herself to look for housing while he stayed back in New London to attend pre-XO school and mind the children. An old friend told her about a perfect house that had been purchased by her husband's company when one of their executives was transferred back to the mainland. Places like that usually remained within the corporation in a tight housing economy like Honolulu, but it was a case of a friend of a friend who looked the other way.

Surprisingly, Pat had found a house they could afford with a view of the city and the water, and it was distinctive enough to have a personality of its own. The end result was a new personality for the Makins, a sense of pride and place that united them as a family.

It was the beginning of their transition. Dick had gone from a junior officer with ambition to the next stage, XO on an attack boat, which would make or break his career. And at the same time, the Makin family had established a sense of self. It had been a great year.

Dick smiled to himself when he realized his eyes were squeezed tightly shut. He wanted so much to retain that precious picture of Pat and the kids in front of that house that looked down on Honolulu and out to sea. But he shouldn't—he couldn't.

There were a hundred thirty other men aboard *Pasadena* who one way or another were projecting similar mental images. There were parents back on the U.S. mainland, brothers and sisters, and a number of the crew had wives and kids back there, too. He had no more idea than any other man whether they were already under attack. All-out war meant every place was a target, not just the military. For all he knew, for all any man aboard *Pasadena* knew, America could already be dead.

You always understood that such a situation was possible. But there was no real way to comprehend such horror until it was upon you. Beneath the surface of the Pacific, a few short words from a burst transmission were the only indication that their loved ones might have experienced a horrible death. The unknown was more ominous than any of them could have imagined. Their helplessness became magnified by their isolation. It had been only a matter of days since the initial war message, yet hours seemed days and the days seemed weeks. Only the two attacks they'd made interrupted the mental agony of not knowing. Ignorance was anything but bliss. Yet there was no desire for revenge, since they had no idea what type of vengeance they might exact.

Tim Sanford's large body eased through the door to the executive officer's stateroom before Makin had a chance to respond to the quick knock. "Sorry to interrupt, XO, but we've got to do something, sir." The chief torpedoman tossed his rumpled *Pasadena* baseball cap on the cluttered desk and pulled the single chair back to sit down, all in one motion. He was as comfortable with officers as he was in chiefs' quarters.

Makin's face brightened into a wide smile. Something about the unruly red hair hanging over Sanford's forehead and the freckles covering his broad Irish face was a source of amusement at a time like this. The man was obviously concerned, yet his good nature was still reflected in his eyes. Wally would go off in a blue funk and think dark thoughts for a long time. Sanford was exactly the opposite. He'd get whatever was chewing on him off his chest and then it would be all over chiefs' quarters and back to the men in less than an hour. "Well, Chief, let's try to fix whatever's got you down. Talk to me."

"Tommy Lott again, sir. He's losing it fast. And you—or the captain, I meant to say—put him off. Captain Newell even said he wanted the tapes—and you just can't do that. No one can. They belong to SUBPAC. You can't do something like that with Tommy. He's chief of the boat. Every man aboard looks up to him more than any of us. Now he's about as blue as I've ever seen him, sir, and it's spreading just like an infection. Every man's talking about him, and those sonarmen aren't helping—"

"Time out, Chief, time out." Those goddamn tapes! "Are we going to spend the rest of this patrol worrying over those tapes he's got of those Soviet masking devices?"

"Yes, sir. That's it. Only Tommy says there's no masking device any human being can put together that would sound like that. He's playing it for anyone who'll listen. He stops it, runs it backward, then forward . . . backward and forward.

Says it's like listening to ghosts." Sanford's freckles appeared to lose their definition as he continued. "Says each submarine has a personality of its own, and no computer could build a specific personality like *Alaska* or *Nevada*. And he points it out when he plays those tapes. Hell, I can't tell. No one else can either, except some of the sonarmen say they do. It's eerie, XO. Tommy says it's like being in bed with a woman in a dark room—you could tell who she was after a while just by what she did without seeing or hearing her. Do you know what I mean?"

Makin nodded. He knew. The ultimate comparison. That came to every man within days after they got under way. The memories increased rather than disappeared as the days on patrol grew longer. Each time you got in your bunk, the imagination would take over, no matter you were by yourself, no matter you were dead tired. You remembered that woman—just like Tommy Lott was absolutely certain he could sense a submarine's personality.

"What else, Chief?" He could see Sanford wasn't finished.

"Mr. Makin, the Navy's my life. It's the only one I know." He paused, pushing red hair away from his forehead. It fell back, as it always did, when he leaned forward. "I understand why Navy regs are the way they are . . . and I respect that." He bit his lower lip. "Tommy's the best friend I ever had, and he's the finest chief of the boat in the Navy. But it's almost as if he's gone out of his head. He's saying things about the captain that could get him in trouble, sir." The words spilled out as if an invisible switch had been snapped on. "He'll hate himself later. He can't mean what he's saying—and he respects Captain Newell as much as any of us—but—" Sanford stopped, searching for the proper words.

"I won't say anything to anyone, Chief. You know that. Everything stays right here for now."

"He thinks Captain Newell's the one who's flipped. He says the captain's refusing to listen to him and then wanting custody of those tapes are because he knows that was *Alaska* and *Nevada* we sank." Sanford pushed his hair back again before looking sadly at Makin. "I don't know what else to say, sir. I don't know what to do."

"You just did it. It's the best you could do for both of them. See what you can do to keep Lott under wraps for the next couple of hours. Better yet, I don't want to hear about him until I've had a chance to sit down again with the captain. Now go on—get out of here," he said with a half smile.

A telltale click preceded the hum of *Pasadena's* 1MC system as Chief Sanford moved off down the passageway. "This is Captain Newell speaking. As you all know, we anticipate contact with the next Soviet boomer within twenty-four hours or less. We know the limits of her sector, but she could be anywhere within it. *Pasadena* is privileged, perhaps one of the most honored submarines in American naval history. While we don't have the necessary backup information to confirm this, it appears to me that we have been singled out for a vital mission that all of us hoped would never take place. To date, we have performed professionally and with highest honor. I want each of you to know that I am unable to put into words the pride I've experienced in serving with you."

Makin nodded to himself. The captain knew how to control an audience with simple words.

"My purpose now is to let you know that I understand exactly what each of you is going through. I am experiencing the same doubts as you . . . even the same fears for my family ashore. But there have also been some advantages. I don't think any single event brought us so closely together as that final *Pasadena* cookout before we got under way. You met my family and I was honored to meet each member of yours. I was just in my stateroom looking at the picture of my wife Myra and those two beautiful kids of ours, Charlie and Kathy—even my pooch, old Jack Tar—and I got to thinking about your families in the same instant."

Dick Makin found himself staring at the speaker in the corner as Wayne Newell's evenly modulated voice flowed calmly into his stateroom. The man sure as hell had a talent—a silver-tongued orator! And timing? His timing was superb. He understood how tension was building. Hell, the two of them had been talking about it just hours ago. But Newell must have sensed the sudden increase . . . must have known the men were looking for something . . .

"I'm not sure why we were singled out to perform this duty, but I like to think it's because we're the best boat in SUBPAC. And I don't mind telling you that I've told Admiral Arrow time and again that I had the finest crew in the entire Navy. Anyway, it seems that our mission is to protect the mainland United States during our nation's most crucial moments. We have responded twice, and both times we have been victorious. We faced one of the most devious inventions in modern warfare, a device that would convince us that we were firing on one of our own. Only through the brilliance of our intelligence branch were we forewarned.

"If we hadn't known of that insidious masking device that imitates our boomers so perfectly, I can promise you that *Pasadena* and each one of us would be at the bottom of the Pacific right this moment." Newell drew a deep breath, audible in each compartment, before he added, "And our cities right now might have been smoking rubble, our nation driven to its knees by the Russians. I like to think that our homes remain intact because of *Pasadena's* actions."

Makin was surprised to find himself hanging on each word, acknowledging each statement as if he'd said those very words himself. He understood Newell's motivation, even agreed how vital it was at this moment. And he knew that if he were captain of *Pasadena,* it would have been unlikely that he could have employed either the timing or the sense of drama to put across such a speech. After what he'd just experienced with Wally Snyder, and the conversation with Tim Sanford, there was no doubt that Newell's amazing sixth sense was operating perfectly.

"My reason for this overly long speech is not just to congratulate you or build your egos. You know now how I feel, and each one of you should consider himself a king among kings. My purpose is to warn you against complacency—to say that there's two down and one to go. But that may not be the case. There may be more than that. The next Soviet boomer that we encounter may be the one that hears us first. There is no room for mistakes in our world.

"I also must caution you against rumor. Too often we are willing to accept secondhand information as gospel. Let me assure you that the intelligence received from Admiral Arrow's office just before our departure indicated that we might encounter this Soviet masking device on this patrol. The XO will concur with that. The intelligence report given to us was very slim. There was nothing to explain how the device worked or even what it might sound like. Perhaps COMSUBPAC's intelligence people hoped it might be a poor imitation. All they knew was that it existed, and they had to warn us of its existence. Luckily, they were able to tell us when it would be used. When we get back to Pearl, I'll damn sure tell them it's a devilish instrument that could beckon the best of us to our death. Although it was intended only for the eyes of the captain and the executive officer, I will be happy to explain as much as I can to any member of this crew who feels the need to know more about it. As a matter of fact, I'll show you the exact report.

"It is important to understand that our worst enemy could be ourselves if we fall victim to doubts about the identity of solid sonar contacts. We have been assigned the ultimate mission any one of us might ever hope for, and we must perform as if the existence of our country depended on each man aboard *Pasadena*. I sincerely believe it does."

Dick Makin picked up the phone as soon as the hum of the 1MC clicked into ominous silence. He couldn't depend on Chief Sanford to keep Tommy Lott under wraps. It had just become the job of the executive officer.

"I hope everyone realizes that if we were a destroyer plodding along in a sector like this, we could have a cookout on the fantail." Buck Nelson's voice was loud, intentionally so. He was demanding the attention of everyone in the control room. Outside of the common courtesies when he entered, they had all responded like so many bumps on a log—the drudgeries of patrol, no different from the last, or the next, could quickly make sleepwalkers out of professionals! Every commanding officer was aware of the problem. Breaking this almost hypnotic sensation of boredom had never been complex.

The helmsman was the first to respond. "Any beer at your cookout, Captain?"

"Don't I wish." Nelson chuckled. "No, even the skimmers don't get it at sea, regardless of what they might tell you," he said, referring to the surface navy. "They're just like us. They can't break out the suds until they're on the beach."

The quartermaster of the watch grinned at Nelson. "Would this be just a hot dog and hamburg cookout, Captain, or something a little special?"

"Well, what do you guys think? There're some terrific steaks in the reefer waiting to be thawed, I'm told. I figure if *Florida* ever has a chance, this crew deserves nothing but the best. Hell, this would be a real barbecue—steaks, maybe ribs, if the cook could whip up some Texas-style sauce and find some good smoke." Nelson leaned on the chart table and looked back over his shoulder at the OOD, who was watching him with amusement. "What do you say, Jeff, you know good barbecue. Think it could be done?"

"No doubt about it, sir." His voice carried the soft accent of the southwest. "Just let me find a little wood and I'll teach those cooks things they never learned in Navy schools."

"Now you're talking," Nelson agreed. "I never figured you were limited just to missile systems, Jeff. Another trade'll mean a hell of a lot someday, when you're finished with the Navy."

"Just one problem, Captain," the OOD said, winking at the chief who was diving officer on his watch. "There's just no such thing as barbecue without beer." His accent grew heavier. "Back home, we used to say that was like going to a nuns' beach party."

"Well then, I guess we're just going to have to wait to the end of this patrol, because I don't believe in *Florida* doing anything half-assed." Nelson grinned at the quartermaster. He'd started out with a little blue-skying just to get their attention. Now it sounded like a great idea. "I hereby promise that when we get back to Bangor and the blue crew takes her out, we'll have one hell of an outing. No hot dogs or hamburgs. Just steaks and real barbecue, and Mr. Sones is going to teach our cooks what real Texas-style sauce is all about. He loves the hot stuff. And I bet I can have a couple of bags of hickory or mesquite or whatever you need sent over from Seattle. What do you think of that, Jeff?"

"I think y'all got yourself a deal, Captain." Jeff Sones's accent brought a snicker from the diving officer.

"We're all witnesses, sir," the chief agreed.

"How about the beer, sir?" the bow planesman reminded.

"Beer, too, Cody. As long as we're ashore, I think everything can be arranged." Nelson moved over behind the planesmen, his eyes darting from the bubble to the depth gauge. There wasn't much effort required of a good man to hold depth when you were moving so slowly. He bent closer to Cody's ear. "You are old enough to drink beer legally, aren't you?"

Just as Nelson anticipated, that drew a laugh from the watch. Although Cody was near the end of a six-year enlistment, he was baby-faced. "Aw, come on, Captain. Not you, too!"

"Cody, my friend, you offered me a target. I couldn't resist. As a way of apologizing for teasing you like that, I'll use my authority right now and appoint you head bartender for our barbecue. How's that?"

"All right," Cody exclaimed enthusiastically, taking care that his eyes never left the dials in front of him. "You just hired the best bartender on *Florida,* Captain."

"I've been watching that depth gauge since I wandered in

here, and I don't think it's varied a millimeter, Cody. I wouldn't be surprised if maybe you're one of the best planesmen, too."

The helmsman, who also controlled the stern planes, had remained silent until then. "Hey, Captain, Cody's got the easy job now. Those bow planes hardly do a thing at this speed." He never looked away from his dials either. "I'll give him a run for his money any day."

"I don't doubt that, Smitty. I guess it'd be unfair to pick out anyone in this watch section or any of the others." Nelson turned toward his OD, who was standing relaxed with his arms folded behind the diving officer's station. "I'll bet it feels good to have men like this standing watch with you, Jeff. I'm going back to try to get a little paperwork out of the way, so why don't you run them through some drills. A man can get stale as hell out here."

"Sure enough, Captain. I was planning on giving you a buzz to get your permission anyway."

The captain removed his rimless glasses carefully with his right hand at the same time he was pulling a handkerchief from his back pocket with the other. He held each lens to his mouth and breathed on it before systematically polishing each glass. Then he placed them neatly back in position on his head with both hands. "And I want everyone here to remember that barbecue. Mr. Sones has been appointed head chef and Cody's the bartender." With that, he left the control room.

Buck Nelson experienced a feeling of self-satisfaction when he settled in the single chair in his stateroom and turned the handle to pull down the desktop. There was no doubt about it. Life could be boring as hell aboard a boomer on patrol. Maybe he'd promote a couple more chefs and bartenders from the other watch sections in the next few days. *Florida* definitely needed something to look forward to.

"I suppose I have to talk to him . . ." The grin on Admiral Larsen's face at the start of that sentence was meant to express his lack of enthusiasm for the President, but it faded just as quickly. "Don't I?" he concluded, realizing that he, in fact, was overwhelmingly sympathetic to the man at that very moment. "Put him through on the secure line," the CNO requested.

There was no response from the others. They understood why Ray Larsen had begun that way and why he acknowledged his relationship with the President just as quickly. The man in Washington had not been kind to Larsen the past two years, not when it came to budgets. He said that the Navy was pretty well-heeled from previous administrations and it was his job to make sure the other services got a fair shake. While Larsen could admit privately that possibly his commander-in-chief might have a valid argument from the taxpayer's point of view, publicly the two men remained in opposition to each other. Unlike a politician, Ray Larsen also possessed an inherent respect for the office and its responsibilities, regardless of its inhabitant.

"This is Admiral Larsen, sir. This line is secure."

Bennett, Arrow, and Newman quietly studied the change of expressions on Ray Larsen's face as he talked with the President. There was no speaker phone; a secure line would automatically cut out the feedback. Listening to a one-way conversation is much like eavesdropping, though there is no guilt since only one individual is under direct observation.

"Our conclusion could as easily be based on our combined experience. But to reinforce that, it appears statistically almost impossible that two of our boomers could be lost as the result of an engineering casualty in this manner."

Eyebrows raised in frustration.

"I fully agree that anything's possible, sir. However, the number of reasons one would disappear without our having some prior knowledge of a problem, either through an analysis of earlier engineering casualty reports or an unanticipated emergency, is almost zero. It would almost have to be human error. But two of them like this—no chance, in our opinion."

A nod as his explanation was acknowledged.

"Yes, sir. Admiral Bennett, OP-02; Admiral Arrow, Pacific Submarine Force Commander, and Admiral Newman, Director of Naval Nuclear Propulsion."

A slight smile.

"I'd have to agree with you. If they can't figure it out, then no one can," he added for their benefit.

Knit eyebrows—a question he hadn't expected.

"Beyond the Russians, only the French and British have that sort of capability, and I can't imagine a scenario that would cause them to do it. They have nothing to gain, sir, nothing I could possibly imagine in my wildest dreams. On the other hand, the Soviet Union has a thousand and one ways to benefit."

Larsen shook his head.

"Well, sir, you are privy to much more intelligence, but my personal knowledge of their naval leaders would still negate even that. Sort of like cutting their own throats, you might say. And I think the fact that they have no SSN's anywhere in that vicinity or even close enough to have an impact should knock them off the list."

Ray Larsen was jabbing his finger at a point well to the left of Robbie Newman, as if the President were actually in the room. Bennett found Larsen's habit even more disconcerting when he was gesticulating into blank space.

"That's right, sir. To be absolutely honest, Admiral Arrow's people have been using their computers to project possibilities based on last known position and possible tracks . . . and they've come up with nothing yet. I wish I could offer some hard facts, anything other than my personal suspicions. It's just that I've been in this business for—"

The CNO wasn't used to being interrupted, and there was a surprised look on his face.

"Thank you, sir. I realize we've had our differences and I appreciate your confidence."

Larsen listened and stroked his chin thoughtfully, occasionally glancing across his desk at the others. Then he shook his head forcefully.

"Damn. I can't believe it. No indication whatsoever. That was going to be my next question, sir. I thought sure our intelligence people would come up with some hint."

He leaned forward, cocking his head slightly to one side. "Yes, sir, I'm sure of that. If there's anything at all, you can be certain I'll be in touch immediately."

When he replaced the receiver, Ray Larsen chewed on his upper lip before he spoke. "Can you believe there's no sign at all in Moscow that anything's up? Not a whisper." He exhaled slowly. "Our commander-in-chief expressed the desire that we come up with something plausible pretty quickly. He said that when there's no light at the end of the tunnel, then you go to the next tunnel. We'll set the Russian theory aside if we don't come up with something damn soon."

"Where else would we look?" Robbie Newman inquired calmly. "Every single engineering report since *Nevada* and *Alaska* began construction has been sifted through our computers. I couldn't put my finger on anything unless I found the wreckage."

"He doesn't understand that," Larsen responded irritably. "You see, he understands that there are hundreds of *Alaska* and *Nevada* survivors out there who have no idea their men are gone. Each hour we wait makes it all that much uglier . . . for him . . . for all of us . . ."

Mark Bennett tried to imagine how Judy would have reacted if old *Stonewall* had gone down, especially if the information had been withheld from her. In those days, the kids were still around home. The loss would have been blown out of proportion. But that was years ago. Now they were on their own and Judy—well . . . he wasn't sure how she'd handle it. He knew damn well how he'd feel if he were in her shoes and it was Judy who was lost at sea. . . . *That was it.* Now he knew.

"We've got to go to the families soon," Bennett said. "They deserve it. I think we've got to make plans to have someone knocking at each door, and I think we'll have to isolate Bangor for as long as possible. You know what I'm thinking about here—the-Navy-takes-care-of-its-own approach, so the media doesn't get wind of it right away. Maybe by the time they do, we'll have something to go on."

Neil Arrow didn't like the idea. On the other hand, he had to admit that eventually there'd be no other choice. "Okay."

Markov grasped the arms of his captain's chair as SSV-516 slid down the side of a huge swell and heeled heavily to port. A screaming wind tore the foam from the tips of waves as high as the bridge and swirled it in a gray mist that enveloped them. The ship hung for an instant, the inclinometer passing thirty-five degrees before beginning the long swing over in the other direction. This was a better course for the safety of the vessel, because they were keeping the sea on the starboard bow rather than burying the ship's nose deep into each immense wave. It was easier on SSV-516, harder on her crew. Sleep had become just about impossible. Eating was for a select few.

The phone on the bulkhead buzzed. Markov's grip on the chair tightened with one hand as he grabbed the instrument with the other. "Captain here," he growled.

"The American aircraft is closing, sir. Now on a direct course."

"When did it turn?"

"As soon as the last signal to the American submarine."

"Range?"

"About seventy kilometers."

"Call me if there is any change in the American's direction."

Captain Markov hesitated. There was no way that aircraft could get a visual on them in this dismal weather. But, he eventually reasoned, it was all a matter of electronics these days, so seeing your enemy no longer had meaning. He pushed the button for his warrant-missile specialist. "Our target is closing now. If he reaches forty kilometers, I want you prepared to launch on my direction. Is your kill range limited that much in this weather?"

"Negative, Captain. They're heat seeking."

"Then there's no warning signal to the aircraft once they're launched?"

"They have to know our radar's on them and they're being tracked, but they can't tell exactly when we launch. Of course, they could pick them up on radar. But that's highly unlikely in this mess."

"I want you to fire all four missiles in the launcher. I don't want them to have an opportunity to report any attack."

CHAPTER EIGHT

Peter Simonds, *Manchester*'s executive officer, had never in his life—not once, not even in his single days when he partied every night with the other bachelors—considered becoming a SEAL. As an ensign there had been early signs of the stomach that now hid his belt buckle. He was a fancier of fine women and food and drink and had grown accustomed to that belly to the point that it was a comfortable friend. While it created an annual problem at the time of his Navy physical, his talents outweighed the spirit of the regulations. Peter's good intentions expanded each year, enough to escape each doctor after a halfhearted warning. The result was that he continued to avoid anything vigorous that would take time from his favorite habits ashore.

There was a time when Peter considered settling down. It was the one memorable point of his single tour on a missile boat, *Lewis and Clark,* and at the same time the lowest point in his life before he'd grown to understand his good fortune. The incident occurred far enough in the past that he had finally been successful in moving it to the rear of his mental filing system.

He met her the first time they pulled into Holy Loch for a refit period with the tender *Simon Lake.* Any of the older officers in the wardroom could have warned him against falling in love with a girl he met in a bar, but it was something everyone had to learn. As unfortunate as it was to learn the hard way, Peter would no more have interfered today with one of his junior officers than his XO did with him at the time—"the school of hard knocks," his captain said later on in a consoling voice, and "better than knocked up."

Her name was Mary, simply Mary, none of those lilting Scottish names for her. She was pretty and talked with a pleasant, rich accent and she drank much too much of the local whiskey. But for a young, single officer in a foreign country for the first time, that was exciting. The fact that she didn't take him to her flat until the second night convinced Peter that she'd decided he was special. When she told him she loved him, he sincerely believed his dashing charm had simply bowled her over. Not once did it occur to him that he was a ticket out of the life she had succumbed to in the past years. Not an officer in Holy Loch, whether stationed there or just passing through, had the heart to tell him who and what she really was.

When *Lewis and Clark* got under way for the next patrol, Mary possessed his undying love and the ring that had been given to him by his grandmother.

When *Lewis and Clark* returned to Holy Loch, he went directly to her flat, racing up the stairs and through the door like the lovesick puppy that he was. The man in bed with Mary claimed that he'd paid for the entire night but had no interest in a fight. He had no objection if Peter wanted his ring back, so he calmly pulled on his skivvies and headed down the hall for a hot tub.

Each year that passed dimmed memories of pretty, sweet Mary and her lovely accent, until there were months that he never thought about her. Nor did he ever interfere with the painful love lives of his junior officers. His grandmother's ring remained buried deeply in his jewelry box. Peter remained a contented bachelor.

Yet there was also a contrariness surrounding the XO. At

sea he was considered an exceptional submariner, an action-oriented officer who would relish contact with an enemy boat. He especially enjoyed the SEALs who came aboard his submarines, although their stays were short. They were rarely aboard longer than it took to transport them to their lockout point near an unfriendly coast, but he found them more interesting to him personally. Their attitudes were the same as his.

Too many of the younger officers were inordinately intense, no matter whether they were qualifying for their dolphins or competing to become a department head before their peers. It was always a race for them—yet it shouldn't have been a race, not from Simonds's view. Regardless of their abilities on paper, too many of this new breed never seemed to become an integral, functioning unit of the submarine, no matter how hard they worked. Peter Simonds wore a submarine like a second skin. He was a natural. And he also took the time to learn from people beyond the submarine navy—like the SEALs.

Simonds found Lieutenant Commander Burch, the SEAL they plucked from the ocean, where he expected he would—in the torpedo room. It was the last space the XO was checking for extraneous noise. He already knew it was secure and there would be no noise until the time came to reload tubes. And at that point such sounds would no longer matter. The torpedo room was also where Simonds knew he'd run into Burch because SEALs found any unfamiliar weapon a challenge.

"I suppose if there was an easy entrance to that missile launcher tucked way up in the bow, I'd have to crawl up there to find you." There was almost always a happy lilt to Simonds's hoarse voice. "Can you imagine someone my size crawling through that access trunk just to shoot the shit with you?" He laughed.

There was a single, small hatch leading from the torpedo room into the missile space located all the way forward on the lower level. There were twelve vertical tubes, each one containing a Tomahawk cruise missile, set between the pressure hull and the sonar sphere separating the torpedo room from the bow.

Burch had recognized the other "natural," in addition to *Manchester*'s captain, within an hour after he'd come aboard. He understood intuitively why Ben Steel was so confident in leaving the control room to Simonds during the search phase. "I haven't been shown the missiles, but I'll take your word for it." The chief torpedoman was nearby, arms draped comfortably over one of his weapons. "The chief's been teaching me how to ride one of these devils."

The torpedo room was the entire width of the submarine, and the area up to the tubes and the instrument panel was mostly for torpedo storage. The torpedos, close to two feet in diameter and twenty feet long, were cradled on hydraulically operated racks that could be adjusted to shift the weapons from their original storage place to a position where they could be loaded into the tubes. The four tubes, two on each side, canted outward at an angle, surrounded by a mass of gauges, valves, and piping. Between the tubes were the torpedomen's control stations. The actual firing was done from the control room, although it could be done by hand from the torpedo room in an emergency.

"Are you getting aboard one of those fish before or after it leaves the tubes?" Simonds wandered over and leaned casually against the same torpedo as the SEAL.

Burch was a stocky individual, all shoulders and chest and muscles. "You flatter me. The chief explained what it was like inside one of those tubes. A bit of a tight fit. Looks like I'd have to catch it on the way by."

The XO pushed his glasses back on his nose. "It's comfortable in here, isn't it? Smells good, too. Other than preparing for a firing sequence, I'd prefer to be in here myself." He took a deep breath and inhaled the intoxicating aroma of grease and metal. "You ought to be here when they're reloading. Less than seven minutes from the time we fire until we're ready again. Not quite as fast as being in a gun mount but a hell of a lot more exciting."

"The chief tells me he can do it a hell of a lot faster."

"That's when we don't have any observers aboard with their goddamn checklists. Seven minutes is what we tell the paper pushers in the commodore's office. They like doctrine. When the chief's not running by the book, then it's really something. Oh, shit," he exclaimed happily, "you ought to see them when we're going through an attack sequence—setting up the target solution, firing, maneuvering to avoid counterfire. Christ, Ben Steel drives this thing like a race car, diving, high-speed turns, everything. Then he's calling down here for the next firing run, never figuring that all these guys have had a chance to do is hold on for dear life. And the chief almost always tells him he's got at least two tubes ready." He slapped the side of one of the torpedos and pushed his glasses back again. "You'd love it," he said hoarsely.

Burch asked the chief, "How about it? I'm an odd man out on this boat. Need an extra body if the shooting starts? Maybe we can break your record."

"Well, sir, I figure we're faster than any boat in SUBPAC now. When the XO reported aboard he promised me we'd be the fastest because he said there was no reason for a submarine if we couldn't sink everything that came anywhere near us." He winked at Burch. "He also said I'd end up on shore duty on some ice station counting polar bears if we weren't the best. What do you think, XO?"

"Not only are you now the best, Chief, you have just been given the opportunity of hiring a SEAL to improve on that. I've always had a love affair with these guys myself."

"You've got a deal, sir." The chief reached across the torpedo to shake Burch's hand. "Think we're going to be able to use these babies, XO?"

"That's a promise, Chief." Then the XO headed back toward the control room, knowing he would find Steel close by in sonar.

Ben Steel was peering over a sonarman's shoulder and he sensed his XO's presence rather than heard him. He removed the large set of sonar headphones and hunched his back to stretch tight muscles. "I was looking for you a minute ago, XO. In the torpedo room again?"

"The only place on this ship that smells better is the galley, and I sure as hell have been trying to avoid that place," Simonds answered. "What's up, Captain?"

"Nothing other than prying, even though I know the job's already been done. Maybe it's nerves in my old age." Steel cocked his head to one side. "Any new and interesting sounds we're sending through the hull to the curious?"

"Not a thing. This old boat's quiet as the proverbial church mouse. The way we're creeping along, we'd have to be clanging away on that church bell to attract any attention." He pushed his glasses back on his nose. "We covered every inch of the ship, Captain." As self noise was reduced, even those sounds normally unnoticed by humans, sensor detection range increased. Aboard SSBN's a computer identified every self noise other than those in the baseline survey.

"Like I said, nerves. My apologies. Honest, I'll try not to ping on you again, XO."

"Never say that, Captain. Not at a time like this. Just one time one of us overlooks something that's chewing on us, that might be the fatal mistake." Simonds noticed Moroney, the sonar chief, eavesdropping, and waved an index finger at him in the dark, blue-lighted room. "How many stories can the greatest sonarman in the world tell us about that one little mistake someone made that told you they were out there?"

"These ears have heard more than you'd ever care to know, Mr. Simonds. The hiss of a beer can at a hundred yards . . ."

"Don't remind me, Chief. You're bringing tears to my eyes." He nodded toward Steel. "The chief's got a good point there, Captain. Manmade sound. That's the only thing I can't guarantee. If we're going to give ourselves away, it has to be something like that. We're as tight as a tick otherwise."

"Okay. We'll take that opportunity away from the bad guys. Why don't you secure the galley for now, except for sandwiches, of course? Have the cooks get everything they need out of the reefer now. Then they haven't anything to play with but a few knives, that sort of thing. Pass the word through each compartment that regular meals have been secured, and keep the sandwiches rolling for anyone to grab when they're hungry. No maintenance—so no tools adrift. If anyone has a problem that needs fixing, they ask your permission first. We'll continue the current watches until sonar picks up something solid." Steel wrinkled his forehead and rubbed tired eyes as he settled the headphones back over his ears. "Maybe some of the crew'll catch up on their sleep."

The process of finding out how much the Americans already knew about the fate of their boomers was indeed complex, much more complex than the KGB director could explain to the General Secretary.

Assuming the three Washington admirals would eventually end up in Hawaii at SUBPAC headquarters, operatives in Honolulu were ordered to undertake a painstaking search. Eventually, once it was agreed that the Americans had thrown them off the trail by avoiding easily traceable military transportation, it was a process of elimination among civilian passenger agents. They learned that the Chief of Naval Operations had arrived from Seattle. The Director of Naval Nuclear Propulsion had been on a flight from San Francisco. The Assistant CNO for Undersea Warfare had come from Washington. He'd also rented a car. All traveled in civilian clothes, using the names of enlisted men who had arranged reservations for them. The trail ended at the gate to the sub base. But it was enough to substantiate their assumption that the elimination of U.S. ballistic-missile submarines was indeed a probability. So many senior admirals on the hoof in the same place was a rarity, indicating an emergency of some kind.

Analysis of the message traffic concerning the SSBN's once again was based on assumption. Considering the sheer volume of military communications over any twenty-four-hour period, it was akin to untying a Gordian knot—and there was no opportunity to slash away at it with a great sword. There is a statistical possibility of breaking any code, though the probability lessens proportionately to security requirements. It was known that one-time codes, which were in the possession of only the people utilizing them, were being employed. In essence, that meant that the actual use of the code for breaking a message also resulted in that code's destruction. Luck would have a great deal to do with finding even a single word in such a message.

The most talented individuals in the Soviet Union dropped whatever they were doing to take part in the process. Mathematicians, engineers, computer scientists, linguists, and those few mavericks who possessed a natural bent toward code breaking were called upon to prove what the Kremlin power structure wanted to confirm—that their orders had actually been carried through and that in all probability they had been successful.

Four admirals disappearing within the Hawaiian naval base seemed to indicate success. The amount of high-priority message traffic from and to specific commands seemed to acknowledge it. Even the use of so many unknown codes substantiated it. But it was a simple American voice communication to an Air Force intelligence aircraft closing SSV-516 that seemed to confirm their suspicions. That voice was intercepted not by SSV-516 but by a remote communications facility in Siberia. It ordered a KC-135 tanker aircraft to rendezvous with the Air Force plane regardless of the weather conditions. The pilot of the KC-135 was told in no uncertain terms that his mission would have grave impact on national security and must be completed regardless of hazard to personnel and equipment. It was that single voice message that convinced the KGB director and the General Secretary that Washington was indeed working very hard to disguise a critical situation, for refueling in that weather was certain suicide.

A third method of confirmation was also employed at the same time, one primarily designed to infuriate official

Washington. It required the efforts of a uniquely trained Soviet commando unit, called Spetznaz, that had been infiltrated into the Puget Sound area the previous year. Their duties ranged from military and industrial sabotage to infiltration, small-unit actions, assassination, and chemical/biological shock efforts in time of actual war.

Each individual in this particular unit spoke English as well as any student at the University of Washington. They'd arrived individually in the Seattle/Tacoma region with Social Security cards, drivers' licenses, passports, and a thorough knowledge of the northwest and its lifestyle. Even if their existence had been known, identification would have been almost impossible.

The officer in charge had assumed the name of David Lundgren, and his blond hair and blue eyes complemented his new identity. When he appeared at Chicquita Mc-Carthy's door, he carried credentials as a reporter for the *Seattle Post-Intelligencer*. "Good morning, Mrs. McCarthy. I'm Dave Lundgren." He presented his newspaper photo ID to her. "I hope you might allow me a few moments of your time."

Chicquita McCarthy had been taught to be wary of newsmen. Her husband Paul had explained when he took command of *Alaska* that too many considered the wife of the captain of an SSBN to be a shoot-first-ask-questions-later person. *Look out for traps,* Paul had said. "Just exactly what is it you want, Mr. Lundgren?" she inquired politely.

"Just a few questions for a story we're trying to get a handle on. It's nothing—" But the young man halted in midsentence and looked down at his shoes. Then he raised his head and looked into her eyes apologetically. "No, that's not it. My apologies. I wouldn't have been honest with you to say that. We've picked up some rumors from one of our stringers in Washington, D.C., and my editor wanted nothing to do with it until we could confirm more of it."

Chicquita could imagine another story critical of the Navy and the men who manned the strategic-missile submarines. "I'm really not at liberty to talk about the ships.

Besides, I'm afraid there's nothing I could tell you that you don't already know." She looked down the street nervously. "I really make an effort not to know . . . and I don't ask questions."

The young man was growing increasingly nervous. "No, no, that's not it, Mrs. McCarthy." He shook his head sadly. "I don't like this any more than you do, but it's my job. I already know how you feel about the media around here . . . and I guess I can't blame you . . ."

"I'm really sorry I can't help you." The reporter's nervousness was adding to her own uneasiness. "I'm sure the base public-information officer can take care of your questions."

"Mrs. McCarthy, the base PIO refuses to talk with us. His office won't return any calls. This isn't something that any of us at the paper like," he blurted, "but we've got to find out, in fairness to you and the other wives as much as anyone else. We understand one of the submarines—both *Alaska* and *Nevada* have been mentioned—is missing on patrol, and we have reason to believe the Navy is withholding information. Can you help me?" Lundgren's hands hung at his sides, his face a mask of sadness and apology at the same time he seemed to be pleading for help.

Chicquita McCarthy's mouth opened very slowly. There were no words. Her eyes never left the reporter's. Very calmly, she folded her hands and raised them until they were level with her chin. She made a steeple out of her index fingers and bent her head until her lower lip touched her fingertips. "No, Mr. Lundgren, I haven't heard a word." Her voice was very soft, without expression. "I'm sure if there was the slightest chance of an accident of some kind, I would have been informed immediately." She dropped her hands to her sides. "And I have nothing to say."

"I'm sorry, really I am. If I've caused any—I mean . . . Mrs. McCarthy, I really do hate my job in a situation like this. I sincerely hope the rumor is false. I . . . I'll leave you alone." Lundgren turned on his heel and walked down the front walk, turning to his left at the street and heading for a nondescript car that was too distant to read the license plates.

The wife of the commanding officer of *Alaska* wouldn't have noticed anyway. Before the blond, blue-eyed reporter had turned from her front walk, she ran into her house for the telephone. She punched out the number for the direct line to the desk of the commander of Submarine Squadron 17. "Bart, I need to know if Paul's all right . . ."

A tingle of fear traced down Captain Bartholomew Bockman's spine as he listened to Chicquita McCarthy's frantic words. The order from Neil Arrow that preliminary preparation should be made to inform survivors had come less than thirty minutes before. Once they were ready, it would take hours before they were prepared to send the right people to each home. No sooner had he given a lame excuse that he'd check with Pearl Harbor and call her back, then he fielded direct calls from the wife of the captain of *Nevada* and the wives of the chiefs of the boat in both submarines. It was both hideous and terrifying at the same time. *He had no answers!*

The nice young men who identified themselves as reporters that day left absolutely no trace of their identity. Those in the military establishment who realized what had taken place now understood the extent of Spetznaz infiltration into the Puget Sound social fabric. There seemed far more to be concerned with than two missing SSBN's. It seemed that the Russians, by the very fact that their curiosity had gotten the better of them, were giving good reason to the Americans to believe that Moscow was involved in the disappearance of the boomers. In fact, the Soviets were so curious about how effective they had been that they were willing to antagonize. But there was as yet no clue as to how they'd gotten to *Alaska* and *Nevada*—nor what their goal might be. Moscow remained silent.

"There's nothing more to say." Once Wayne Newell's mind was made up, his expression was as firm and obvious as his voice. "The country's at war. *Pasadena* is right in the middle of it, and I'd argue with anybody right now that we're the key to swinging the balance in America's favor. We're the pivot point. None of us have any idea whether the U.S. is under attack or if our families have survived." He spoke to his XO in a pronounced tone with an almost religious fervor. He wholeheartedly believed in what he was saying. "When each man on this boat is wondering whether his family is alive, I can't have someone like Chief Lott magnifying our problems."

Dick Makin wasn't happy with what he was hearing and he held the captain's eyes without responding. He could tell Newell wasn't finished. The man's solution to the problem had come as a shock, even though Makin was in agreement that a solution was necessary. It was just that the XO had never heard of any situation where the chief of the boat had been relieved like this. Tommy Lott, he knew, understood exactly what insubordination was—and there couldn't have been the slightest doubt in the man's mind that he was undermining his commanding officer's authority by speaking out about the sonar tapes.

"I want you to have Chief Crowell put Lott under sedation for the duration of our mission. I can't have him causing more trouble when we could be facing combat any minute. Once he's quiet, that'll shut up any others. Close off one of the staterooms in officers' country as a temporary brig. And I want an armed guard assigned on a twenty-four-hour basis with orders to use his weapon if necessary." He waved his hand as he changed his mind. "As a matter of fact, I'll pick out the men I want to guard the brig. I want to make sure they understand my instructions. Tim Sanford will be the new chief of the boat . . ." Newell paused and tapped his index finger on the tip of his nose as if he were trying to make sure he'd covered everything.

This didn't make sense—drug the chief of the boat? The men might just turn against Newell on this one. "Captain, he's Lott's best friend and I don't think—"

"Don't bother," Newell interrupted rudely. "I know exactly what I'm doing." He'd been staring into the light over his bunk as he outlined his plans to Makin. Now, sensing how curt he'd just been to his executive officer, he turned with a smile on his face. "You know I didn't mean to be sharp, Dick. I'm sorry. I guess the tension can get to any of us. It was stupid of me." He recognized the set of Makin's jaw. It signified an innate stubbornness, like waving a red flag. "I really do apologize. Accepted?" He raised his eyebrows as if he expected his XO to accede automatically. It was decided. There was no room for argument.

"Captain, I can see why you want to get Lott out of the way. I'm the first one to admit there's no room for what he's saying." The XO's jaw remained outthrust, his lips pursed. He was second in command of *Pasadena.* "But Chief Sanford isn't going to be happy about leaving his buddy comatose. I'm not so sure I like it either. Perhaps I could still sit down and talk with him."

Newell waved his hand again to show he'd made up his mind. "No time, Dick. We could pick up our next target any moment now. We're not out on exercises, remember. We're fighting a war. Can you imagine trying to coordinate an attack with a man who's decided he doesn't like the target we've been assigned . . . not to mention he's the chief of the boat who's been insubordinate and is attempting to turn the men against their captain?" Newell shook his head briefly. "Nope, not a chance. I really appreciate your concern and being a sounding board for me, but we don't have a moment to spare. You tell Chief Crowell what has to be done and send him to me after he's taken care of Lott." He folded his arms.

"Yes, sir." Makin stood up and turned away slowly. Then, looking over his shoulder, knowing he'd feel guilty if he didn't mention it, he said, "I guess I'd better ask about Wally Snyder. He's no help right now, talking about phony messages, and I guess he's even talked with Chief Lott about that. . . ." If that's the way the captain felt about the chief of the boat, then it was the XO's duty to cover all the bases. Less than an hour before, he'd been isolating his captain from Snyder's bitches. Now it was time to get everything out on the carpet. "I think the situation's pretty much the same with Wally."

"Send Wally in to me. I'll settle this with him directly." Newell's blue eyes were piercing, his lips a sharp, gray slash etched on his face when he added, "I'll complete my mission if I have to sedate every disrespectful son of a bitch on this boat."

The communications officer looked miserable when he knocked at the captain's stateroom and stuck his head inside. "The XO said you wanted to see me, Captain."

Newell glanced up at Wally Snyder with a look of contempt. "Step inside, Mr. Snyder."

The young officer reached tentatively for the back of the vacant chair.

"No need to sit down. This will be quick. You'll either have a change of attitude or find yourself wading in deep shit."

Snyder nodded. "Yes, sir."

"Do you think I'm stupid, Mr. Snyder?"

"Of course not, Captain."

"I was a comm officer once. Years ago. Things were different then, but I did a hell of a job. Do you for even a moment think I forgot everything I ever learned?"

"No, sir." Snyder rocked slightly on his heels as he realized how his captain was setting him up—*and how defenseless he was at that moment.*

"Is it possible that COMSUBPAC might have made *me* more aware of the strategic situation and his communications intentions than he did *you?* After all, I am commanding officer of this submarine."

"I'm sure he did, sir."

"Then why do you continue to question my judgment when *Pasadena* is in a state of war with a foreign nation?"

"It's not that, sir. I simply feel that—"

"You're not in a position to make decisions for me, or to question the orders that I give." Newell's eyes had narrowed once again, until the pupils were barely visible. "Is it fair to assume you are aware of that, Mr. Snyder?" He pronounced the young officer's name as if it were a foul taste he needed to clear from his mouth.

"I didn't intend to—"

"I have no interest in intentions. We are on a mission of grave importance to our nation, and you have not only questioned my decisions, I understand you have also been comparing notes with the chief of the boat. Are you aware that Chief Lott has been relieved of his duties and no longer has the run of the boat?"

"Why . . . no, sir. I had no idea . . ."

"Well, now you do. *Pasadena* has destroyed two Soviet boomers and we're on the track of a third. Luck had nothing to do with that. Superb intelligence, superb communications, and a superbly trained and closely knit crew accomplished that. I intend to maintain that peak efficiency until we either shoot our last torpedo or are ordered to return to Pearl Harbor. I realize the pressure on the crew of this submarine and I also know that the slightest hint of insubordination can harm our mission. Do you concur, Mr. Snyder?" Newell's voice dropped until the final words were a bare whisper.

"I do understand, Captain," the young man answered softly. No one had ever treated him in this manner since he'd earned his commission. His eyes centered on a spot in the middle of the captain's chest.

"Look at me." Still a whisper.

Wally Snyder looked up.

"I expect your verbal support among your peers in the coming hours. If you as much as hint at any dissatisfaction with the manner in which I operate this vessel, I promise you will find yourself facing a court-martial. And since I consider us in a state of war, the punishment I would insist on is death." The last half-dozen words became a hiss that punctuated his threat. "Can you think of anything you want to say, Mr. Snyder?"

"No, sir."

"Then get out of here and do your job . . . and I'll do mine." Newell waved him away with a flick of his wrist.

Once Snyder was gone, the captain's head sank slowly until his chin rested on his chest. His entire body shook with exhaustion.

Why . . . why the hell do I have to straighten everybody out? Just for once couldn't people get their own acts together? Christ, it was just like being back home with the family.

Newell actually shuddered when he thought about that confrontation the last time with Kathy and that young punk . . . whatever his name was. Boys were no different than they were when he was that age. All they wanted to do was get their hand down some girl's bra, then go tell all the other guys about it. That's exactly what he'd told Kathy, and she had no right to go off crying to her mother. *Myra had no more idea what went through a boy's mind than the man in the moon.*

And, goddamn it, that Snyder kid had no more idea what went on in the enemy's mind. They were just as devious, except the game out here wasn't to get a little bare tit. This was the big game. They were going all the way, cover all the bases, then slide into home a winner.

There is just no reason to put up with that kind of crap out here, not while I'm captain of Pasadena.

And there's no reason to lower standards at home either!

Oh, Christ, I'm tired, he thought as his eyes fell shut and his mind went mercifully blank.

The first missile from SSV-516 exploded in the fuselage of the American intelligence plane. The blast wasn't powerful enough to bring her down, but one of the electronics technicians was killed and the other badly wounded. The second missile, only seconds behind the first, struck the starboard wing, rupturing one of the fuel tanks. Burning avgas swept back along the fuselage and through the ragged hole made by the first explosion.

The aircraft was mortally wounded at that stage but still capable of ditching. The frantic pilot put his violently bucking plane into a turn toward the Alaskan islands at the same time his copilot instinctively shouted a Mayday over the radio. But neither the maneuver nor the emergency call were ever completed.

SSV-516's final two missiles exploded in the cockpit, ripping the nose from the aircraft and hurling both men into the stormy Pacific.

CHAPTER NINE

Through the course of naval history—triremes, papyrus reed boats, war canoes, sailing men-of-war, ironclads, PT boats, nuclear submarines—a few great captains have appeared whose names survived through the ages. Somehow, by the time a man is considered for command, there are few incompetents who have slipped through the cracks in the system. There have been some bad ones, many capable ones, and a vast majority who were a credit to their ship. What history has taught us is that it takes a truly unique individual to achieve *absolute* mastery of his ship—one who possesses that rare understanding of the complex process that blends a man and his ship into a single identity.

Buck Nelson's unique gift of mentally positioning himself in the geometric heart of *Florida* was a source of relaxation for him. It was a mental exercise hinting of almost mystic experience. The ability to accomplish this feat was a talent he never dared mention to another soul. At times it could be disturbing, for he found himself projecting even when he hadn't willed himself to do so.

If he found himself alone in a space close to the epicenter of the submarine, the simple act of closing his eyes coupled with intense concentration allowed him to project his mind throughout the moving cylinder that was *Florida*. He seemed to be floating in a weightless state much like an astronaut. Yet here there were no compartments or bulkheads or miles of piping, not even a reactor, just an immense empty cylinder slicing silently through the depths. It could happen in the missile control center, the computer room, sometimes even the engineering spaces, and once even in the wardroom when he was fortunate enough to be alone.

Nelson had often read about mind control. Eventually he decided his unusual talents were akin to yoga, that age-old method of relieving tension and stretching one's mental capacity. He said nothing about it to anyone because he knew Navy doctors, especially those who constantly evaluated the captains of boomers, might determine he was unstable.

He found time to read only when he was at sea. It was a method of confronting that final stage of physical exhaustion that prevents one from sleeping. It was also an opportunity to absorb the fantasies of an author's mind while relaxing his own. The concept of man's limitless mental capacity especially appealed to him. It drew him back to memories of his childhood, to those special times after he was tucked into bed and the lights were turned out. There were moments when he was consciously aware of that netherworld between wakefulness and sleep, when his mind was somnolent—yet alert. He could withdraw to an imaginary world where he was sure he was capable of far greater understanding of the universe around him. It was a game for a child with a brilliant mind like Buck Nelson's, one to be cherished and kept to himself.

As he grew older and immersed himself in the things that most normal boys do, this unique talent gradually receded into his subconscious. It was a lost ability until he found himself on those long, lonely patrols at sea. At first he experimented with once again projecting his mind, and learned that he couldn't force himself to achieve the same experience. But eventually, once he decided it was a matter of self-discipline, it returned to him. It was mind expanding and harmless and Buck Nelson found that he was gaining an improved understanding of himself in relation to the submarines he loved so much.

When he took command of *Florida,* the responsibility was mind boggling. The ship was so huge—at 560 feet, longer than the Washington Monument, four decks deep, close to nineteen thousand tons submerged—that he at first had trouble conceiving of himself as an integral, operating unit of that vessel along with one hundred sixty other men—*yet totally in command.* It became necessary to withdraw mentally in order to enlarge his understanding of his ship.

As he lay in his bunk one night, too tired to sleep, he remembered standing under the giant hoop constructed outside the Submarine Force Museum in Groton. Its purpose was to provide a graphic display of the circumference of the Ohio-class Trident submarine, yet it was also a symbol to Buck Nelson of the creative power of man's mind in relation to his physical size.

With that impression in his mind one exhausted night, Buck Nelson closed his eyes and projected himself into the epicenter of *Florida.* He was floating—or rather, his mind was—through his submarine. Now he was able to comprehend what it had taken so many hundreds of marine designers so many years to build. He saw how each of her thousands of complex components became a whole, a vast ship capable of providing a deterrent that likely was saving man from himself. *Florida* became an integral part of Buck Nelson.

While the Navy provided highly skilled individuals to operate this technical marvel, Buck Nelson understood *Florida* completely in a period of time he could not measure. If his brain had been capable of controlling the vital machines and electronic suites that made the submarine what she was, there would have been no further need for the other one hundred fifty-nine men. His mind was in each of the spaces throughout the ship at the same time. He could have handled her as easily as a pilot wheeling a jet fighter toward an enemy at supersonic speeds.

It was seemingly an out-of-body experience when he considered his enhanced understanding of *Florida*. He desperately wished he could somehow convey these powers, even transfer them to other commanding officers, for he was sure it might someday save their lives. But Buck Nelson was also a rational man, and he could imagine the field day the Navy shrinks would have if he so much as uttered a word about his oneness with his complex and powerful submarine.

He was stretched out on his bunk, the lights out in his stateroom, once again attempting to project himself within *Florida,* when the phone buzzed on the bulkhead. "Captain here."

"Captain, this is Mr. Sones." The OOD's voice was soft and calm in his ear. "No problems in control. Sonar has an intermittent contact they thought you should know about. Appears to be manmade, probably not a surface contact."

"Have they contacted Mr. Mundy yet?" The sonar officer loved these games.

"Yes, sir. He's on his way."

"Do we have a convergence zone that would allow us to hear something from another submarine op area?"

"The chief says anything's possible, Captain. But he doubts there's anything that could be one of ours unless it's time to rewrite the laws of physics."

That would be Chief Delaney's response. He could be expected to qualify every answer with a word game. "Very well. I'll be there in a few moments. Please inform the XO, too."

Nelson flipped on the light switch over his head and blinked at the sudden brightness. Then he made a fist and rubbed his eyes. There was still sleep in them, and he could sense his muscles lagging behind the messages the brain was sending as he swung his feet out of the bunk and stood up. Cold water was the answer. He ran a sinkful, tested it with a finger and found what he already knew—the water produced by a submarine was never ice cold—but it would still wake him up.

After rubbing his face with a rough towel, he pulled night goggles over his eyes to accustom them to the dimmer light in the control room and sonar. Peering in the mirror, he decided to run a comb through his thin hair, then smoothed his mustache with his fingers. A clean shirt and freshly pressed trousers helped to give him a more commanding appearance, but he knew it was the captain's eagles on his collar and not a rough and ready appearance that made the difference. *What the hell, Captain,* he said to himself, *looks don't make the man.* Then he smiled at his image—*but silver eagles sure do!*

There was a comforting sensation, almost one of self-satisfaction, as Nelson moved toward the control room. He knew innately that he was perceiving the entirety of *Florida* —they were a part of each other—as she continued her tedious mission.

It was equally important that he sense *Florida's* position in her sector, just as he understood his own within the giant vessel. The picture formed in his mind was similar to holographic imagery. Now he could withdraw to a position where he could see *Florida* in relation to her sector, yet he was also an integral part of that picture. A complete grasp of everything was critical to relating to this unidentified sound that sonar had isolated.

"Good morning, Jeffrey . . . or good evening, or whatever the hell it is," Nelson said to the OOD as he entered control. "I never looked at my watch," he added, glancing at his wrist. It was easy to lose the sensation of day and night after an extended period under the surface. When one's existence was based on six-hour watch sections separated in time by sleep or paperwork, light and dark had no bearing on the system.

"Morning, Captain. Still dark on the surface, but they tell me the sun's going to take another turn shortly," Lieutenant Sones answered pleasantly.

"Where are we this fine morning, Jeff?" Nelson moved around the periscopes to the chart table toward the rear of the control room. "Someplace new and exciting?"

"Well . . . we are going to change course soon. And we've varied our depth a few times this watch. That was exciting," he added without expression. Sones's calm, easy nature matched his captain's. Nelson would prefer him in control in any sort of emergency.

Nelson glanced casually at the X's on the chart identifying *Florida*'s track since he last was in control. They displayed precise geographical positions, but there was nothing on the chart noting the normal variations of course and speed and depth that were a standard part of each watch. Those subtle changes would be in the ship's log, to confirm that *Florida* was making every effort required to randomize her movements, if there were anything out there capable of detecting her. This class of SSBN's was by far the quietest afloat, and it would be a freak of nature for an unfriendly submarine to hear her before they had already been identified. The only ones that had ever gotten close were their own 688's.

"You'd prefer a roller-coaster ride if you had the chance, wouldn't you, Jeff?"

"It would be a nice change of scenery, Captain. If you decide on something like that, I hope you'll let me do the driving." A man with a dry sense of humor.

Nelson ambled over beside his OOD with a grin. Both of them paused in their conversation to pay silent homage to a habit that likely originated with the first modern submarine. They studied the gauges and dials on the panels above the planesmen and the diving officer. It was customary, a practice engaged in by everyone who passed through the control room. In addition to the diving officer there were always two men on watch who controlled the submarine's course and depth by means of simple-appearing steering wheels which could also be pushed forward or pulled back. One of these controlled the rudder and the fairwater planes mounted on the sail, and the other the stern planes. Although each man passing through the control room paused to study those gauges, none of them would have dared to say a word to the planesmen. That was up to the diving officer on watch.

Nelson watched those dials, too, but said nothing to the men. "Anything else from sonar?" he asked Sones.

"Not really. Still intermittent. Dan Mundy just wandered in there grumbling about being woken up in the middle of the night. He had the last watch, so he was probably figuring on catching an uninterrupted six. Chief Delaney can't figure it out, so he told me it's something from another world—par for the course, I guess."

"Okay. I suppose the last thing they need is another body in there, so I might as well add to the crowd just to keep Delaney on his toes. Don't run into anything," he grunted as he headed for sonar.

The normal watch in sonar, four men, was more than adequate for the size of the space. Along with Chief Delaney, the current watch section had been joined by the executive officer, Jimmy Cross, and the sonar officer, Dan Mundy. Buck Nelson now made it seven. The room was designed primarily to house complex sonar equipment and the associated gear to allow *Florida* an advantage over an approaching enemy. Any people other than the normal watch section created a traffic hazard.

"Morning, Captain," Jimmy Cross murmured. People in sonar always seemed to talk in hushed tones. The XO had just removed a set of spare headphones and handed them to Dan Mundy.

"What do you hear, XO?"

"Not a damn thing . . . at least nothing but a few horny fish somewhere out there crying for a little action."

"No one setting up an attack on us?"

"Hell, no." Cross was a southerner, and he drew out phrases like "hellnoooo" so that they ran together. "I haven't got the vaguest idea what these guys with fancy ears have picked up this time. Since I've been in here, they haven't heard a thing that sounds like what they woke us up for, Captain. Wouldn't surprise me if it was one of Delaney's stunts." He winked at the chief. "He's got spies, you see, who let him know whenever we fall asleep."

Nelson winked at Delaney, too. "You must have had a hell of a good reason to time it so well with me, Chief."

"You mean I let you sleep too long, Captain?" He had a hand extended so that one of the sonarmen would hand him a set of headphones.

"No, Chief, you timed it perfectly. I was just about in dreamland when that goddamn phone buzzed. Mr. Sones tells me you've found something from outer space."

Delaney smiled at his own humor. "Might as well be, Captain. The way it's playing with my watch section, you'd think so." A headset was placed in his hands and he hung it around his neck like a towel. "One of the men picked it up about half an hour ago. It's about as faint as it can get without being nothing. I suppose since there's nothing else out here, that's why he picked it up. Just something barely audible on broad band."

"You're sure it's manmade?"

"Listened to it myself." He shrugged. "Then fed the recording through the computer."

"Could be a surface ship."

"No . . . no, I don't think so. We probably would have picked up some screw noises or surface effect with it if it was." Delaney turned away and placed the headphones over his ears as one of the sonarmen waved a hand at him. "Just a second, Captain. I think we've got something again."

Nelson glanced over at Dan Mundy, who was staring vacantly at the deck while he concentrated on the sound coming through his own headphones. He began to nod to himself as if the space were empty. Then he flipped the recording switch on the panel behind him before beckoning to Nelson. "Here, Captain, try these," he said, lifting the headset off and offering it in his direction. "Something there again."

Nelson pulled the headphones over his ears and listened. He heard the rush of nothingness, the sound of the living Pacific Ocean, indistinct yet existing beyond their hull. But there was nothing else other than *Florida*'s own minimal noise signature as it slipped through the water, not even when Chief Delaney wagged an index finger at him and then pointed at one of his ears with his eyebrows raised. *There was something there*—Nelson was willing to acknowledge their abilities to discern what was nonexistent to the normal ear—*but, no, nothing he could identify.* He handed the headphones back to Mundy.

"See what I mean, Captain." The XO nodded. "They're all crazy."

"Look at Delaney. He acts like he's listening to the Boston Pops."

Cross nodded sagely. "Like the sound of one hand clapping. What would we do without them?" It was easy to joke about it, even easier to dismiss if each of them didn't realize that this indistinct, unidentifiable sound that had just traveled through untold miles of saltwater could be an enemy. There was no reason for it to exist in this section of the Pacific. And Delaney was sure it was another submarine!

The chief spoke to Nelson without looking in his direction. "Captain, we're going to clarify that and amplify it before feeding it into the computer and then . . . oh, shit!" He lifted the headset off and draped it around his neck again. "There it goes. But I think we got enough."

Nelson noted that his sonar officer was still listening, a troubled expression on his face. "Chief," Nelson said, "the XO and I are going to wake up with a cup of coffee in the wardroom. Why don't you and Mr. Mundy come on up there when you've decided why no one wants us to sleep." As they left the sonar room, he added over his shoulder, "If you come up with something we can have fun with, you might even get a doughnut out of the deal."

"Give us fifteen or twenty minutes, sir."

Less than fifteen minutes later Dan Mundy came into the wardroom with the chief. "Delaney was right the first time, Captain," he said as he poured two mugs of coffee. "Manmade . . . and subsurface."

Each man looked at the other silently, seemingly embarrassed that there was nothing definitive any of them could say.

"Whose?" Nelson inquired softly.

Delaney looked apologetic as he reached for a doughnut. "Can't tell yet. Too far away, I'd say. We've been experiencing some odd temperature gradients out there for one thing, and I don't think our contact is burning up the ocean either. That's why whatever we pick up keeps drifting in and out. We've got to have a steadier sound for a while before we can analyze it properly. Or we've got to find some spot out here where water temperatures are constant and he lights up for us like a neon sign."

"I suppose we're going to have to wait to get any target-motion analysis." Jimmy Cross spread his hands on the table, palms up.

"All we can be sure of is that it's off the port bow now," Mundy responded. "Could be doing anything."

Nelson ran the back of his hand across the stubble on his chin. "And we've got nothing of ours operating nearby?" he asked the XO again.

"Not unless there's been some drastic changes in op areas that they didn't give us before we got under way," Cross answered.

"Then it's Soviet." Buck Nelson shrugged and spread his hands. "No one else is running submarines out here."

There was no response from any of the others.

"So, my friend," Nelson said to Mundy. "No more sleep for you, I'm afraid." He grinned at Delaney. "You see, there are ways of getting even, Chief. Until we know better, your contact is assumed to be unfriendly. I want you to do everything you possibly can—and then some—to identify it and track it. We'll keep the rest of the crew on regular watch until we have something. We're going to turn to a southerly leg shortly, and that'll bring your contact to the starboard bow, maybe close it a bit."

"Suggestion," Cross said.

"Shoot."

"I'd like to have the OOD's exaggerate their base course

maneuvering, try some more radical depth and course changes. If sound conditions are as difficult as the chief claims, we might as well cover ourselves as much as possible . . . make it equally difficult if they're looking for us."

"Go ahead. Mr. Sones has been looking forward to something to kill the boredom. That ought to make him happy."

No more than a couple of weeks had been necessary for COMSUBPAC's flag lieutenant to become comfortable around admirals. His job required that he work closely with one daily, and he had lost track of the number he had met since he was ordered to Neil Arrow. At first, totaling up the number of stars he came in contact with had been a game—one for a fresh-caught flag officer, two for a rear admiral, three for a vice admiral, and four for a full admiral. But he lost track when he passed one hundred thirty, so he decided to break off his count at the end of each week. He was also getting tired of all those stars. Admirals had become a dime a dozen.

It was quite different, though, when the CNO and the three most senior submariners in the Navy gathered in one room. The stars totaled fourteen, although it came to eighteen whenever PACFLEET joined them. That was the very highest end of the scale, if his averages included stars in a single room at one time. And not only were they an imposing group, these men were also family—on a first-name basis and well aware of each other's strengths and weaknesses. One man's thoughts could easily be verbalized by another.

"Right there." Neil Arrow tapped the spot on the northern Pacific with a pointer. "Last-known position. They were closing on that Soviet intelligence vessel."

"I thought they were scheduled for refueling," said Admiral Larsen.

Arrow nodded. "They already had rendezvous instructions. The pilot rogered them—so he had to have received them properly—then he continued with something else that was garbled. Weather stinks up there. Must be three or four fronts trying to pass through all at the same time. Communications were limited at best."

"But they'd found something out, your flag lieutenant said?" Larsen inquired.

"I'm not sure what. That's the message, or whatever we could put together from it." He nodded at the flag lieutenant. "Give Admiral Larsen a copy of that, please. You see, Ray," he continued, "it just came to me about fifteen minutes ago, and it was so nebulous I couldn't see dragging you out of the head to read it, since you were going to be in here in a few minutes anyway. All we can figure is that the pilot was closing that Soviet intelligence ship because he apparently thought he had something. He probably figured the weather was screwing everything up and it was worth a shot to come in on top of them."

Mark Bennett's eyes had never left the spot where the pointer had been. Christ, what a godforsaken place! South of the Aleutians—where elephants went to die. There wouldn't be a trace of that plane by the time the weather cleared, and sometimes it was like that for weeks on end. "What a hell of a way to go. I hope they were dead before they hit the water." He was aware of some of the grisly sights rescue craft found after men had struggled to survive in those waters. "They deserved better than they got."

"We don't know for certain—" Newman began.

"No, we don't, Robbie. I guess that's the least of our concerns, isn't it? No backup for them?"

"Weather closed in worse than when we sent them out," Arrow answered. "We were advised to wait a couple of hours to see if it would lighten up. It's not going to."

Bennett stared at the aircraft's last position. "When they do send a new crew out, tell that pilot to stay away from that Russian ship."

"I figure that's what got 'em, too," Larsen agreed, "but we'll probably never know." He pointed a finger at Mark Bennett and waved it in a circle. "You were going to locate that attack sub of yours . . . *Pasadena*," he recalled.

"Nothing. No response during normal communications periods. We've had some aircraft in her operations area the past few hours searching, planting sonobuoys . . . everything. Not a sound. My boats don't operate that way—" Bennett stopped in midsentence and stared back at the CNO, then waggled a finger back at him. "Now, damn it, Ray, stop pointing that thing at me. You really piss me off sometimes. I've got enough to think about without having to convince myself not to take a swipe at the Chief of Naval Operations—and believe me, I've thought about it the past twenty-four hours. So . . ." He couldn't think of another thing to say.

Larsen's face expanded into a huge grin. His normally penetrating blue eyes twinkled. He turned the finger that was still pointing in Bennett's direction around and stared at it. "Looks like a regular, run-of-the-mill index finger to me." He raised his eyebrows. "Never shot anyone with it yet." Then he uttered a short, sharp sound that was intended to be a laugh. "So I was intimidating you with it." He looked at the finger. "I often wondered if it was working that well, but I never had the guts to ask anyone." He glanced over at Neil Arrow. "Does it piss you off, too?"

"You're damn right it does, Ray. We're not a bunch of telephone commanders trying to act important. It irritates the hell out of me." There, he'd made his own point.

"Well, all you've got to do is say something," Larsen said, pleased with himself. "It's just a bad habit, I guess." But just as quickly he wheeled around and pointed it at Arrow's flag lieutenant, whose mouth had dropped slightly at the shift in conversation. "If I ever hear a story about this conversation, I'll know exactly where it came from, young man."

"My lips are sealed, Admiral." Once again the young officer was the picture of perfect naval decorum.

"Back to *Pasadena*," Larsen said. "You think the same thing happened to her that got your boomers?"

"We haven't got the vaguest idea what happened to *Nevada* and *Alaska*, plus you're talking about two different classes of submarines. No one's reported any unidentified contacts that might be her. And the op areas were too far apart." He pointed out the last locations of the three submarines. "Look at that distance. No one's going to break their orders and go chasing all over the Pacific."

"Engineering casualties?" Larsen glanced over at Robbie Newman, aware that the question had already been dismissed with the boomers.

"Doubtful again. More likely human error, if she really is gone. *Pasadena* was in beautiful shape. I had my boys in Washington comb her files. Nothing."

Larsen's eyes fell on Mark Bennett. He held his right index finger in his left hand as if it might escape. "I've got it under control now. See?" He held the trapped finger up for all to see. "How about the crew?"

"Wayne Newell is one of the best. He was one of my officers when I had *Stonewall Jackson*. Dick Makin, his XO, is a superior officer, too. There could have been an accident, but . . ." He finished the sentence by shaking his head.

"There's no choice, then." Larsen's eyes were narrowed now into their familiar slits to display his unhappiness. "I haven't got any proof, but I've got to tell the President that it appears our problems are due to enemy action—and the only enemy that I can imagine out there is Soviet . . . even if we haven't located any of their submarines. He has to make a decision."

"Captain, really . . . believe me, if I so much as hear a peep that sounds the least bit odd, you'll be the first to know." Moroney had been chief sonarman aboard *Manchester* for eighteen months, even before Ben Steel had assumed command. Up until now the captain had been what the men considered "cool." Never flustered. Not a sign of anger unless it was obviously called for. He handled himself well in any situation. But now there were signs that he was anxious, an omnipresent figure lurking behind the sonarmen on watch, asking them questions every few minutes, borrowing headphones to make sure they were functioning properly. Moroney could see signs of irritation from his men.

"Am I that obvious, Chief?"

"Like your fly was wide open and the flag was flying, Captain. You know . . . when you're looking for a contact, it takes twice as long to find it than if you just wait for it to show up. I've been in this business all my life, and I guarantee that if you're not looking too hard, they just come to you."

Steel felt a smile beckoning at the corners of his mouth. Moroney was right. That old saying about the chiefs running the Navy was right, too. If you let them do their job, you were running your ship properly. "Okay, Chief, you win. I'll stay out of your hair. I can't will a contact no matter how bad I want it. I promise I'll stay out of your hair for the time being. But you got to understand it's not easy for an old sonar officer."

"Now, sir, you don't have to ask permission to visit. We wouldn't know what to do if you didn't stop around for a cup of coffee. It's just that I think you'll be more ready for an attack when the time comes if you take it easier . . ." He was fumbling for the right words.

"Say no more, Chief. I understand. As usual, you're right."

Moroney could feel his face warming. "I didn't mean—"

"You're just like my mother, Chief. She was always right, too. It just took me a little longer to admit it. I'm on my way to control to bother Mr. Simonds. Then maybe I'll grab a little sack time while you're all busting your asses. That's the soft life of a captain." Steel was tempted to clap Moroney on the shoulder, as he might do to encourage the younger officers, but it didn't seem the proper thing to do. The chief already had the headphones back on his ears and was leaning over one of the sonarmen's shoulders, pointing at something on his screen.

Steel took the few short steps that brought him into the control room and stopped, gently sliding the sonar door shut behind him. It was almost as quiet as sonar. Each man was immersed in his job. Only the diving officer was talking, softly explaining something to one of the planesmen from his position to their rear. From the raised platform behind them the OOD quietly noted the displays on the control panel, one hand gripping the brace hanging from the overhead. The duty quartermaster was at the rear of the control room punching buttons on the navigation computer which would provide him with an accurate ship's position. Two others were working on the fire-control equipment on the starboard side of the space.

No one noticed Steel until a radioman appeared from his tiny space situated back near the entrance to engineering. The radioman headed through control toward the forward passageway and glanced at his watch before saying, "Good morning, Captain."

"Good morning, Wirtz. Got anything for me?"

"Negative, sir. We don't go up to copy our broadcast for another couple of hours. If you're headed for the sack, sir, you'd better grab a few quick hours. I'll be the one waking you up then."

Steel nodded. "Fine. Maybe I will try a few hours' snoozing." He caught the OOD's eye. "Is Mr. Simonds taking a nap?"

"No, sir. He headed back to engineering about twenty minutes ago, after Chief Moroney told him there was some sound from aft passing through the hull."

"That's right. I remember." And he should have remembered. He'd been standing beside Moroney when the chief had picked up a sound he thought was a wrench coming from the aft section of the submarine. The call had gone to Peter Simonds, just as the captain's orders had indicated, and the OOD had reported immediately that the XO was on his way aft. Maybe he should try to sleep.

"Want me to call him for you, Captain?" the OOD asked. "Or maybe you want to take a nap."

Steel shook his head. "Don't bother. I think I'll chase him down myself."

As he climbed through the hatch back by the navigational computers, Steel once again appreciated the different world in the rear half of *Manchester*. The well-lighted engineering spaces were a world totally separate from the darkened, red-lit forward control area. They housed the power plant that made the true submersible possible—the nuclear reactor. It was here that the controlled atomic reaction produced the heat that not only moved *Manchester* through the water at tremendous speed, but allowed her to remain below the surface as long as sustenance for the human body lasted.

It was clean and neat back here. The power plant literally ran itself. The engineers seemed merely there to monitor, to ensure that every piece of machinery operated as it had been designed to do. In addition to the watch officer, there was a reactor operator who controlled the rods, main cooling pumps, and the reactor's instrumentation; the throttleman who turned the large wheel that released steam to the turbines to turn the shaft; and an electrician who regulated the distribution of electrical power. They watched dials intently, recorded data constantly, performed routine maintenance, kept their space clean enough to eat off the tile-covered decks, and responded to the maneuvering orders from control. The place even smelled different, more like a hospital, sanitary and neat, everything in its proper place—a world apart from the weapons systems and control room forward!

He found Peter Simonds in the maneuvering room in conversation with the chief engineer and the main propulsion assistant. "Well, setting up a subsidiary wardroom back here?" Steel said.

"Hey, Captain," Simonds answered jovially. "We've got enough for bridge if you brought a deck with you. But I want the engineer for my partner."

"No cards, thanks, XO. Just heard you were back here and thought I'd stop in myself. I haven't been back recently," he said lamely.

"That's right, Captain," the engineer agreed. "I'll bet that TLD hanging on your shirt doesn't know how to react to radiation. We ought to have bells and whistles any moment now."

"Bullshit," Steel snorted. "I've been around here more than that." It was pleasant to be somewhere on *Manchester* where they didn't ask him when he was leaving. "What's going on back here that needs such important people?"

"I just came back to search out a little noise Chief Moroney picked up a while ago, and found the men that make this boat go were playing some games of their own," the XO answered. "Actually, Captain, they're fine-tuning her like a race car. We're going to be the fastest boat in the fleet, except I told them they're going to have to make the last adjustments like they were mice."

"I'm told that silence is golden, sir," the MPA said. "This really wasn't routine maintenance. I know we're running silent. We just had a valve that needed a little adjusting, and the XO comes in here like we were playing with a jackhammer."

Simonds inserted his thumbs in the top of his pants and lifted them higher on his belly. "I had to give a sonar lesson to these pups, Captain. Told them they'd be swimming home otherwise." His hoarse laugh filled the space. "Really, it was nothing much. Just something they wanted to check before you called for all the horses—if you have to." He looked more closely at Steel. "Say, Captain, everything is so damn quiet now, you look like you could use a few hours in the sack. Believe me, we've got everything nailed down. She's as ready for action as she ever will be."

"All right, all right. Everyone seems to think I'm on my last legs. I'll head for my bunk," Steel answered with exasperation. He wheeled about and headed for the forward hatch.

"Captain," Simonds called as he stepped through, "I didn't mean to upset you. I . . ." But his words were lost as the captain closed the hatch behind him.

After Steel had closed the curtain in his stateroom, he snapped on the light over the mirror and peered closely at his face. What the hell were they all talking about? There was nothing he could see that should worry them. His eyes looked fine to him. What the hell. He'd try to grab an hour or two. Sleep never hurt anyone.

Ben Steel closed his eyes and was asleep instantly. He never shifted position nor heard a thing until the radioman, Wirtz, woke him almost three hours later. "Good morning, Captain. Everyone's sure glad you had a chance to grab a few hours. Bet it did you a world of good."

The young man was right. Lack of sleep could hypnotize you after a while. He did feel like a new man. He also was sure this would be *Manchester's* day.

CHAPTER TEN

A soft breeze drifted across the shaded, open patio, muffling the conversation of nearby diners. It was barely enough to cool the sheen of perspiration on Myra Newell's neck, but it did waft the smoke from her cigarette across the glass-topped table. She noticed her luncheon partner's nose contract at the sharp aroma. "I'm sorry. No one likes secondhand smoke. I'll put it out."

"Don't be silly. I'm one of those reformed smokers who needs a whiff every so often to remind me just how much I enjoyed past sins." Connie Steel leaned her head forward and sniffed in an exaggerated manner, as if another trace of smoke might drift her way. Myra had been more than polite in asking if the cigarette were all right, then making every effort to keep her smoke away from their table. "Now if Ben were here," Connie continued, "he wouldn't say anything, but he'd look at you as if you'd just done something very gross."

"Wayne's no different. Mr. Pure—nothing stronger than a beer on a hot day. That's why I don't smoke when he's ashore anymore. I can hear it now—'It may not kill you, but you can be damn sure it's never going to do you any good.' Before *Pasadena* left, his latest suggestion was to take everything I spend on cigarettes and put it in a coffee tin

177

until I had enough to buy an exercise bike. He believes that would double my money because I'd be giving up impure habits and buying good health."

"But I'm sure he means well. He probably picked that cute line up from Ben."

Myra smiled, a knowing, long-suffering expression on her face, and ground the butt out in the ashtray. "He does mean well, and he's sure the world would be a better place if we were all just as perfect as Wayne Newell."

"Come on. You're being rough on him. I'll bet you miss him as much as he misses you right now."

"No, I miss him even more. He tends to forget everything when he gets back aboard that submarine. But for us, life really is so much better when he's around, or at least he tells us that it is," she concluded softly. Then, more resolutely, "For all my bitching about little things, my world changes for the better whenever he comes through the door." She reached absentmindedly for a cigarette until she noticed Connie watching with interest. "Not on your life—I'm not the one who's going to get you started again." The pack went back in her purse. "What you need is a teenage boy whose world revolves around his gonads, and you'd know what I'm talking about now. Wayne understands Charlie—and I don't. Even old Jack Tar! That mutt mopes around the house like he's lost his best friend until my husband takes up residence again." She smiled a sad little smile. "I guess I do miss him. I'd even give up smoking." Her eyes brightened. "Maybe I will when he settles down for some shore duty."

"Is that what he wants to do?"

Myra Newell pouted. "What Wayne really wants next is to be the most junior commanding officer of a submarine squadron." Her voice deepened in an effort to imitate her husband. " 'That is the path to an early star.' "

Connie nodded and fluffed her blond hair as another breeze danced across the patio. The restaurant where they were having lunch was new to her. It was a small place Myra had discovered when she was showing her brother and his family around the island. It was up the coast from Makaha near Kaena Point and sat on the top of a bluff looking westward. Myra had said the food was as pleasant as the isolation, and she was correct. The tables on the patio were well spaced, so that your conversation didn't become a part of someone else's; none of the other customers looked familiar; and the tropical drinks were twice as good because they were served in large glass bowls rather than the touristy pineapples and coconuts. And the charbroiled fish wasn't covered with fruit or nuts—it was grilled as it was supposed to be.

"Ben would love this place. Of course, he'd insist on a martini because anything with fruit juice in it is intended to hide the taste of good booze. Have you ever brought Wayne?"

"Once. And he enjoyed the food. He still doesn't understand why people have to drink liquor first when they know it's going to ruin the taste of their food."

"I remember when he used to take a drink or two. That wasn't so long ago."

"Try three or more," Myra said, laughing for the first time. "But you're giving away your age if you think it was recently. Wayne was always a serious guy, even when we were at Berkeley, although I admit he could be susceptible at times. His problem was that once he started, he never stopped. I think the last time he ever drank was just after he reported aboard *Stonewall Jackson*. That's when you and I met. Remember the night he was ready to defend the honor of the Navy against half a dozen Marines, and Mark Bennett saved his neck? Wayne still can remember Mark's exact words—'Any man who decides to mix it up with our Marines probably doesn't have the judgment to make decisions on a boomer.' And that was the end of a less-than-honorable drinking career."

"Ambition reigned over small pleasures?"

"That and a latent inability to sip. Wayne Newell remains a man fully committed to whatever he undertakes. One hundred percent full steam ahead in everything. No deviation once he has a goal. And moderate drinking was just asking too much of him—so he quit. 'It's all a simple matter of discipline,' he says in a grand manner to anyone who'll listen. Now, since he's cleansed of one more sin, he doesn't understand those who enjoy it. My good husband has so little imagination that he just assumes everyone must have the same problem with alcohol that he had."

"And I suppose the same goes for smoking," Connie said with a grin.

"He'd be a chain-smoker." Myra took out the pack of cigarettes again and looked at them longingly before returning them to her purse. "Too soon after the last. How about something for dessert?"

"Not a chance. I put on weight every time Ben goes to sea."

"That's funny. A lot of us lose."

"Some women stop eating when they're alone—I make a pig of myself. It seems that I don't cook any less for three than I do for four, and teenage girls eat like birds so they can fit into their bikinis. Who eats the rest?" She spread her hands in front of her before turning them around and pointing both index fingers at herself. "Mother! I haven't been able to waste food since my parents used to tell me about the starving Korean kids."

"Every generation has their own method of shaming a kid into eating." Myra winked across the table. "And you've become a real, live victim. But no one would ever know, kid. You don't look an ounce different than the days we used to force-feed our little monsters while old *Stonewall* was at sea."

"You're kinder than Ben. He claims that he sees so many overweight sailors who only stand watch, eat, and sleep that he doesn't want to come home to a wife with the same problem."

Myra nodded. "It doesn't matter that they're on different submarines or that they've both gone their own way, does it? You know . . ." she began, before pausing to search for the right words.

Connie Steel blotted her lips on her napkin and waited

patiently. Her friend across the table had something she really wanted to say, and there was nothing to be gained from interrupting her. Myra was still nodding, staring out at the Pacific Ocean, silently agreeing with what she'd just said and what she was about to say.

"There's something about little boys growing into big boys but still loving the same toys they grew up with. That's why our husbands pick up right where they left off after they've been away from each other for years. It's not that they love each other so much or that they're such great friends. We're—you and me—much, much closer. It's those submarines they play with."

"Their toys," Connie agreed.

"Wayne's probably into it more than Ben. Your man has room for you and the girls when he's ashore. I've seen him—believe me. He gets his heart and his mind away from that boat for a while when he's in port. Wayne never does." She sighed. "He'll throw a football with Charlie. He'll take Kathy shopping, unless he's bitching about her boyfriends. And of course he takes me out to dinner and then comes home for a romp in bed." She turned away from the ocean and rested sad, brown eyes on Connie. "But after each of those pet habits—those naked urges to preserve the images of father and husband," she concluded bitterly, "he's back on *Pasadena.* Sometimes, I'm sure his mind is with *Pasadena* when we're making love—just a different ride." She blinked away what might have become a tear. "Does that make sense?"

"Can I tell you how many times I've heard that?" She thought about the cigarette pack in Myra's pocketbook. God, how beautiful one of them would taste right now. "Do you remember the time Judy Bennett said something like that—about the different ride, I mean—at one of her wives' luncheons when Mark was C.O. of old *Stonewall?*" She waved her hand. "Don't bother to answer. It just proves we're all in the same position at one time or another, if you keep in mind the Bennetts are considered the perfect Navy couple. It was an extra glass of wine or so that brought that

out—and from the wife of the commanding officer, no less."
Connie giggled and wagged a finger in Myra's direction.
"You were the one who whispered to me that it was never
going to happen to us, that it was more likely a problem for
horny old Navy wives with teenage kids. And I think I said
we'd be different because we'd seen it firsthand. So . . ."

"So here we are . . . having lunch by ourselves because
their toys keep getting bigger and faster and quieter and
more lethal—the perfect piece of ass, I guess—while we get
a little older each day." Myra Newell gazed back across the
Pacific. "I'm still not complaining . . . that much . . ."

"Neither am I."

"But there is a difference. Your man makes an effort to
come back to you for as long as he can. Wayne tries—or he
used to. Now he's thrown himself so completely into
Pasadena that I don't think he has room for us anymore. It's
not just that submarine. There's more, but I don't know
what it is." She took two cigarettes from her pocketbook and
placed one in Connie's outstretched hand.

An aroma had settled in *Pasadena*'s sonar room that was
decidedly human. It wasn't necessarily considered a foul
smell at that stage, more one that develops when normally
clean people are too tired to shower and fall into their bunks
with their clothes on. Then there's no time between watches
to catch up. Once it becomes universal, it also becomes
acceptable—a hazard of the workplace.

Tension was also part of it, something undefined, an
essence that contributed to the aroma and reflected itself in
the unease of the men. They weren't snapping at each other.
No fights had broken out. It was more their silence, a desire
to be isolated from the world around them. Too often they
found themselves looking away from their friends rather
than beginning a conversation. Responses to questions were
shortened to one word or however many were necessary to
convey an answer. Men no longer greeted each other by their
nicknames. Officers were acknowledged more out of habit
than basic discipline.

Pasadena's crew was exhausted, physically and emotionally. They were at war. They had sunk two enemy submarines threatening their homeland. They had been ordered after a third. Yet there wasn't a soul on board who had any idea whether his loved ones were alive or dead. Was there a reason to mourn? Or would they return to Pearl Harbor as heroes, saviors of their country?

They also knew they were again ordered to find and sink another enemy that could be much like the previous two—this new target would give every indication of being an American missile submarine! Their captain had once again indicated the target was approaching under the guise of an American boomer which they must sink before it sank them. *It was the only way they could save America*—and the doubters among them had been silenced by their captain. Not a man could remember as bizarre a situation in the history of the sub force.

Dick Makin slipped into sonar and closed the door behind him. "Christ, how can you guys hear anything when you smell so bad?" It was intended to be funny. There was no response.

"Thanks for coming in, XO. I guess you might as well be the first to know about this contact."

Makin couldn't make out Steve Thompson's face in the dim blue light and he was sorry the sonar officer couldn't see his. "Oh." It wasn't the response he'd planned, but he hadn't expected that approach from Steve either. This wasn't the normal method for prosecuting a contact. The OOD had located him in the ship's office and said that Lieutenant Thompson in sonar had something on tape for him as soon as he had the time. "Where's the captain?"

"Haven't bothered him yet, sir," Thompson responded. "Too indistinct. It's really not worth his time yet."

"What do you have on tape, Steve?"

"Nothing special . . . the contact, or actually just a sound we picked up . . ." He was uneasy.

"Well, is it a contact or not?" The executive officer was as tired as any other man on *Pasadena*. A man could get along without sleep for longer than he would have imagined, but his temperament quickly became a major part of the sacrifice, even more so in a submarine at war. It was impossible when you had a sonar officer who had suddenly become incapable of expressing himself.

"I guess it's a contact . . ."

"Shit, Steve, no one in New London ever taught you to guess. Do you think you're pregnant, too?"

"Sorry, XO," Thompson snapped back. "I meant it was intermittent, nothing positive yet, no reason to get our asses in an uproar."

Makin folded his arms across his chest. Even in the semidarkness there was no mistaking the way his jaw jutted. "Talk to me, Steve. Tell me when a contact is not a contact. I seem to need a briefing on new ASW procedure. Or maybe I just need to have you tell me why you haven't called the captain yet. We both know his orders."

"The sound is weak enough so that it must be a good distance from us. No way to track it yet that I know of. I couldn't see the sense in disturbing him when I had nothing specific."

"That's never bothered you before. You just about dragged him out of his bunk by yourself and carried him in here when you picked up a trace of that initial target. You getting jaded in your old age?" Then, his anger close to the surface, he added slowly, "Did you also forget the captain's standing orders?"

Steve Thompson was taller than the executive officer by half a foot. The difference in their heights usually was less noticeable since they remained at a reasonable distance when they talked. But Makin was as close as as he could stand now, both because of his anger and a desire to keep as much of the conversation as possible just between the two of them. Even in the dim light the younger man could see the creases around the XO's eyes and the tautness of his lips. This was an entirely different man than he'd anticipated. "I really wasn't trying to contradict anything, XO. It's just that a lot of us are as exhausted as you and the captain, and we don't want to make any mistakes or bother you before you need to be bothered. I wanted to be sure what we had before I put the captain to any trouble."

"Okay, Steve." Makin took one step back. "What do you think you have out there? Do you want me to listen to it?"

"There's really nothing out there you could call solid, sir. I don't think we have anything right now." He tapped one of the sonarmen on the shoulder. "Do you have anything on that new contact now?"

The man shook his head.

"You can listen to the tape if you want, sir. I doubt it'll tell you anything I haven't already said."

"Computer come up with anything?"

"Not really. It's not biological."

"How about one of their boomers?"

"Well, I don't know . . ."

"Steve, what you don't know is one hell of a lot, like how far away that contact might be. It could be something completely different from what we're looking for and a hundred miles away. Or you could have one of their boomers moving along at maneuvering speed, hardly making a sound and only five miles away. Perhaps they could be lining us up for a shot right now. Or, God forbid, we're about to hear their missile doors open for a full-scale launch." He covered the single step, which once again brought them almost together, and looked up into a young face that was now deeply lined by lack of sleep. "I'm going to find out from the OOD where the captain is right now, and then I'm going to have him man battle stations until you have a better idea of what's out there. For all you know, it could be sitting close by with its muzzle doors open, waiting for us to drop our drawers. As soon as I know exactly what our situation is, I may have time to sit down and have a serious talk with you." He took a couple of steps backward. "I sincerely hope we're both alive to have that talk."

Makin stepped out into the control room. "Where is the captain right now?" he asked the OOD.

"Torpedo room, sir." The OOD grasped the support bar

above his head with both hands. He appeared to be swinging from it as he leaned slightly forward to peer at the XO. A broad smile seemed to punctuate the dark circles under his eyes. "Probably recounting the number of Mark 48s we have left," he said with a mix of humor and sarcasm.

"Save it," Makin snapped. "I'm on my way to the torpedo room. When we get back here I expect you to have the battle stations party ready to function." He halted as he was about to step into the forward passageway and looked back over his shoulder. "You should be ready for a snapshot any time. That funny little noise no one seems to be too upset about could be completing an attack solution right now. Or you just might have to evade without firing. That means a wall of noisemakers."

"Yes, XO." A concerned expression quickly erased the smile on the OOD's face.

Dick Makin had little time to consider the varying attitudes he'd encountered the past few hours as he trotted down the ladders to the torpedo room two decks below. Each of the crewmen who'd talked with him during that time was superb. He'd written or reviewed the officers' fitness reports and the enlisted evaluations. Together, he and Wayne Newell had managed to transfer any individual they doubted. *Pasadena*'s crew was as close to 4.0 as any he'd encountered. They had been trained ashore and at sea until they acted as one, and that had been evident in the sinking of those two enemy boomers. The preparation and attacks had been perfect.

Yet a couple of these supposedly superior men had already broken, or appeared close to it, even after their captain had explained in detail the sinister masking device employed by the Soviets. If Captain Newell had not been warned about this new device before their departure, perhaps there might have been room for doubt. But it had been explained in black and white. Makin had read it himself—a hideously ingenious device could be employed in a head-to-head confrontation to deceive sonar teams on American submarines. And *Pasadena* had luckily been ready for it. Intelligence had been on top of the Russians once again!

Then . . . then what motivated these superb men to question their leaders? As fearsome as it was to destroy another submarine, especially one that sounded like one of your own, the only alternative was your own death. And in your last moments you would have prior knowledge that your enemy now had free reign to saturate the United States with nuclear warheads. Each individual in the submarine force knew that in the event of an actual war certain of them would be chosen as a first line of defense. It was the roll of the dice. But it hadn't sunk in completely until it became a reality.

Why, then . . . why were these men questioning authority at this stage? Was it a form of mass hysteria?

He found Wayne Newell perched slightly back on the warhead of a Mark 48 torpedo, joking pleasantly with the first class torpedoman and the new chief of the boat, Tim Sanford. As chief of the boat, Sanford was technically no longer a torpedoman; his appointment had given him a new trade. But at a time like this, Newell still wanted him close to the torpedomen, close enough to keep the weapons functioning as perfectly as they had when they were managed by Sanford. Newell knew he'd have to stay close to Chief Sanford after placing the chief's best friend under arrest. Everything in this space was orderly. The balance of the torpedos had been repositioned to racks that would facilitate reloading. A combination of polished and painted metal heightened the special smell that Makin associated with the torpedo room.

There was no need for darkened lights here. If there was a space on the ship where actual physical action was involved with killing an enemy, it was this one. This was where the torpedos were loaded in the tubes, the tubes flooded with water and their pressure equalized with that outside, the muzzle doors opened, and the critical dials and gauges read and reread to insure a successful firing. And if an electrical casualty occurred in the miles of cable between the control room and the torpedo room, the tubes could be fired locally.

As soon as that tube was empty, the muzzle door was shut, the water drained from the tube, and the torpedo reload party would position the next torpedo with the hydraulic racks. It was a sensitive process to slip almost two tons of torpedo into one of those tubes without damage to the weapon or the tube itself. There were also myriad critical mechanisms within that tube involved with inserting target information into the weapon and preparing the tube once again for firing. The process was even more precarious when a submarine was maneuvering like an aircraft to avoid a homing enemy torpedo. If the control room was the brains of the submarine, then the torpedo room was the brawn. Makin loved the space as much as Newell.

"Looks like no one in this space has any problems," the executive officer began.

Newell cocked his head to one side. "Does that mean there're problems somewhere else?"

Makin had expected a smile of some kind, some friendly expression that came with their special relationship. There was none. "Nothing out of the ordinary, Captain. Everyone's beat to hell, of course. But I think they're as ready as ever." He brushed an imaginary speck off the torpedo next to the one Newell was sitting on. "Looks like we might be able to use some of these soon. Sonar's working on a contact . . ."

"Contact? Why wasn't I informed?" Newell had been relaxing astride the torpedo as if he were allowing it to graze. He straightened his back and placed both hands on the warhead, ready to dismount. "I expected to be notified right away."

"Nothing to be concerned with yet, Captain. Just picked up something out there, probably at a distance . . . intermittent . . . too mushy to classify at all. Computer can't do anything with it yet."

"What direction, Dick? Port or starboard bow?" *Pasa-*

dena had been approaching the boomer's sector from the southwest.

"It really is intermittent, Captain," the XO assured him. "Much too early to tell. Somewhere ahead of us. The OOD is manning battle stations."

"Well, certainly!" Newell jumped off the torpedo. "Just because you have an intermittent contact doesn't mean they can't blow you out of the water at any time." Newell turned to Tim Sanford, who had remained silent. "Hell, Chief, sometimes we can hear an enemy captain fart before his boat makes a sound."

The space was quickly filling with torpedomen who had been awakened when battle stations were called. They did not arrive on the run. They appeared stretching and yawning. "Come on, gents, get the lead out," the chief bellowed. "Hopkins, make another pot of coffee and inject some of that into these sorry creatures."

Newell waved a friendly hand back at the chief as he followed his executive officer up the narrow central pathway between the torpedo racks. "Wish I was going to be down here with you men. Good luck!" The special pleasure Newell now experienced in offering a few words of encouragement to his enlisted men was doubly pleasing. He saw himself as beneficent. These were the men who always supported him no matter what the situation. He appreciated that. In his exalted vision of Wayne Newell as the soul of *Pusadena*, he almost saw himself blessing these loyal men. He was exemplifying the balance between good and evil. *This is what it means to lead!* He was at peace with himself.

Newell fairly pushed his XO up the ladders to the middle level, then to the upper level toward the control room. He nodded a brief greeting to the OOD as they entered control but turned immediately left to the entrance to sonar.

There were three receiving units in sonar that could be switched from one mode to another, passive or active. The sonar officer was leaning over the shoulder of one of his sonarmen staring at the visual display when they entered.

Newell placed a firm hand on the sonar officer's upper arm. "Well, Steve, are we ready to blow away our next boomer?" His voice was as hearty as if he'd just slept ten hours.

Thompson squeezed his eyes tightly shut and gritted his teeth before saying, "Dixon, I missed that completely. How about you?"

"Yes, sir, I picked it out."

"That could have been what you're talking about, Captain," the sonar officer said, his eyes still shut. "I hope we got it on tape."

"Got it," Dixon said. "Want me to replay?"

"Do you still have it?"

"There's *something* out there, sir," the sonarman answered tentatively.

"Classification?" Newell snapped.

"No idea yet, Captain."

"Bearing?" Newell asked quickly.

The sonarman leaned over to the man beside him. "Look like port bow to you?"

"That's as good as any," came the muttered answer.

"Port bow is close as we can say, Captain," Dixon answered.

Newell plugged in a headset. "I want to hear that tape."

"Dixon," the sonar officer asked patiently, "will you help the captain out?"

The sonarman turned in his chair and set the necessary switches. "It's pretty hard to sort out, Captain. Kind of mushy, but there is something out there."

Makin studied the intensity on the captain's face. He pressed the headset to his ears as if willing the sound to come to him. There was no change in his expression. Finally, he lifted the earpieces away from his head and asked, "Did you play it?"

"Yes, sir."

Newell tore the headset off irritably. "Couldn't hear a goddamn thing. I guess that's what we pay you experts for. What do you think it is, Dixon?"

"If my neck isn't on the line, I'd say that's probably manmade."

"Submarine?"

"Probably. A surface contact would be giving us a bit more ID by now. But I don't want you to bank on me, Captain."

"Port bow," Newell murmured anxiously. His lips were pulled back from his teeth as he thought. "Okay. Battle stations manned. We could fire a snapshot in an instant if we were surprised." He glanced over at Makin. "If we can hear him, and if that's a boomer creeping along as quiet as a mouse, then he ought to be able to hear us at about the same time. Dick, tell the OOD to bring us down to ten knots, maybe a little less to be really sharp. We're going to creep in until we get a positive ID on this one." As if he were sure each man in sonar was about to ask him the same question, he announced in a clear voice, "I can assure you all that if this contact is a definite submarine, it will sound just like one of our own boomers when we're able to classify it. Don't let that fool you—and don't let that classification go beyond this space. Anyone who is fooled by a masking device like that is sure to be a dead man."

CHAPTER ELEVEN

The General Secretary of the Communist Party of the Soviet Union, sitting alone in his Kremlin office, understood the true meaning of loneliness for perhaps the first time since he was a teenager. But those solitary periods of his youth had been during the early 1940s. It was a time when many of his friends had lost at least one parent, and all of them knew of relatives who had been killed in the Great Patriotic War. Yet it had still been a shock to learn that both his mother and father had died together when their village had literally disappeared during the great Battle of Kursk.

In retrospect he knew it had been much easier to accept then. No Russian family escaped that immense human tragedy. Millions of them died to preserve their homeland from the invaders. That ultimate sacrifice was certainly preferable to being enslaved by the Germans. For him there were no decisions to be made, no village to return to, no friends to search for. Everything was gone. The state took care of orphans like him, and there was never a moment to stop and think about personal loss when the war was over. No one possessed the luxury of spare time. Like everyone else, he took part in rebuilding his devastated nation.

And there were advantages to being an orphan. Since there was no village, no family, no mouths to help feed, he was able to exhibit his natural abilities at an early age. This opportunity gave him the chance to be selected for advanced education which, in turn, allowed him to display military talents he might have remained unaware of. With the loss of a generation of young men, there were few people to block his progress. He recognized the advantages in the KGB, and used that organization as a stepping-stone in the Communist Party itself.

The ease of accession to each level of leadership within the party infrastructure constantly amazed him. The power he attained allowed him luxuries that were limited to just a few thousand individuals in the USSR. With each new position, he achieved new respect, which brought introductions to great men and relationships with beautiful women. That was how he'd had the good fortune to meet his wife. Being an intelligent man, and one who'd shaken the wildness of youth at an early age, he understood his luck at meeting her and treasured her undemanding, unending affection for him. He loved this woman who aspired to most of the same pleasures of life that he did.

Yet at the pinnacle of his power, when the citizens of the world anxiously anticipated each word he uttered, when he might have had anything he wished, right at this moment he was the loneliest man in the world.

The head of the KGB had presented each of the reports that had been required of him in less time than anticipated. Most of the events that had taken place in the Pacific were exactly as planned so many years before. Those were the days—and thankfully they were gone forever—when *first strike* seemed the only option for the future. No . . . it wasn't necessarily a first strike they were planning. It would be unfair to saddle them with that. They weren't positive of exactly what they were planning, because the world had changed so much in a very short time. What they were doing, or trying to do, was take away their enemy's firststrike capability. But that was so ambitious. They were only partway. Did they know what they really wanted?

Today the situation was different, radically different. No

longer did old men spend their waking moments planning how to gain the strategic advantage so they might end the waiting. Those veterans of the Great Patriotic War were mostly dead. Yet now, those angry old men, many of them ghosts, had returned to haunt the General Secretary. Their final plan, or at least its early stages, had succeeded—no further proof of the loss of *Alaska* and *Nevada* was necessary. Both submarines had apparently been exactly where intelligence said they would be, and the most brilliant ruse of the century was undoubtedly successful.

Those angry old men were pounding on the lids of their coffins. It was their turn to dance. The U.S. intelligence aircraft that seemed the only opportunity for Washington to learn how their ballistic-missile submarines were being located and sunk had been shot down. It appeared from electronic analysis there had been no chance for the plane to even send out a Mayday.

How could those old men, most of them now dead, have been so fiendishly accurate concerning an action that would take place years later? The General Secretary had grown to detest them for their prejudices and belligerence, their twisting of the future. About the only element they couldn't have foreseen was the intelligence plane the Americans had sent out to investigate SSV-516. And that had been a minor inconvenience easily remedied.

There was one historical aspect they had not anticipated however. Not a single one of them had expected that their mighty, aggressive Soviet Union would experience the economic problems created by them and their predecessors. Nor could they possibly have understood that cooperation with their natural enemies might be preferable. If only the Americans hadn't continued to expand their nuclear stockpile and improve their delivery vehicles, the General Secretary might have been in a position to . . .

If there had been more time, would the other members of the Defense Council have gone along with his opposition to activating this strategy? Doubtful. The USSR was led by a single individual in a figurehead position—the General

Secretary of the Communist Party—but it was governed by that party, and neither he nor any other man was capable of mandating what the senior party members had not agreed upon. And they had decided, without his concurrence, to activate this man who had been so successfully planted within the U.S. military framework so many years before. The plan had been originated when the General Secretary was still outside the KGB, and now he bore the burden of responsibility. Why did their government function this way? Why was the system incapable of halting something like this? A few of those old men who originated that plan were still alive—and, though not a one of them had a word to say, they would be ecstatic with its success if they'd known.

The loneliest man in Russia rose from his desk and strolled slowly to the window. One-way glass prevented anyone from looking up at him, but it also produced an odd glare that altered his perception of the people on the walkways below. He couldn't see whether any of them were familiar to him—but he was sure none of them wanted to die that day or the next, nor would they appreciate the sacrifice of their families in a nuclear exchange with the U.S. The people no longer harbored the hatred for Americans that he and his friends remembered and that the old men retained with a vengeance. Most of them—those under forty, anyway—actually believed that the two nations could live with each other; separately, because they were so different, but many no longer saw the necessity for the ascendancy of only one system of government.

Less than an hour before, the KGB head had explained that the President of the United States remained behind closed doors with his closest advisors. There had been no response, no statement. Even his most highly placed intelligence operatives in Washington reported they had no access to any rumor of what might be taking place. Therefore, the assumption among his own advisors was that the White House was plotting revenge on the Soviet Union. *Wouldn't that be Washington's natural reaction?*

Now, before the discussion had even opened, it seemed a

majority of the Defense Council was for carrying out the original intent of those past leaders—continue to destroy the SSBN element of the American triad. The USSR could neutralize the balance of U.S. striking power. *A successful first strike by the USSR would eventually be a definite possibility.* That's exactly what one of them said, and others had enthusiastically agreed with him.

The General Secretary had questioned how the loss of just two SSBN's could justify that position. After all, there were a number of others, not to mention missiles and bombers. The answer had been that another American SSBN was about to be destroyed in the Pacific. One more after that would definitely alter the strategy in that part of the world. In the Atlantic, sufficient plans had been activated to neutralize enough of the *Lafayette* and *Ben Franklin* class of SSBN's to keep U.S. retaliation within acceptable bounds. *Acceptable bounds!* That's what he was facing now.

His expressions of repugnance at the entire plan had fallen on too many deaf ears. More members of the small group than he anticipated—too many—now wondered if a first strike might not be their only solution now that they had gotten this far. He found more disagreement with his position than he would ever have imagined, enough so that he had been given time to reconsider that position. That meant that a silent revolt against his leadership was a distinct possibility. And he had few close associates he could depend on.

That's what happened when a man distanced himself from the loyal party members. It was almost like being a prisoner in his own—no, not almost—he was technically a prisoner within the Kremlin if he did not accede.

Who should he turn to? Was there a single individual whose support would force the others to rethink their positions? He doubted that.

In the end the loneliest man in the Soviet Union called his wife and asked her to join him for dinner at his suite within the Kremlin. She was neither a lover of Americans nor a supporter of the party leadership, but perhaps she might offer a solution. At the least, she wouldn't complain about the amount of vodka he anticipated drinking.

She'd understand.

If he could convey the gravity of his personal situation, she would understand and perhaps, just perhaps, bridge the widening chasm. . . .

"Hell nooo . . ." Jimmy Cross answered. His standard response, the affectation he assumed everyone enjoyed, was for Buck Nelson. They were the only ones in the wardroom. The question *Florida*'s captain had just asked concerned whether or not the sonar contact had been identified. "If I had to guess, I'd say it was a Russian submarine out to find out a little more about an American boomer."

"That's pretty definitive, I'd say." Nelson was carefully polishing his rimless glasses with a wrinkled handkerchief. "What makes you so sure?"

"Well, all things considered, I can't come up with anything else. Although we've been maneuvering to get a track on it, it still seems to be on the same general bearing, so that means it's probably coming toward us if its sound remains as solid. It also means it probably could pick us up by pure dumb-ass luck. There's no possible way it could know about our sector." The executive officer was explaining his reasoning in his normal, slow drawl. Nothing was ever hurried with Jimmy Cross, and Nelson had yet to see anything that would ever excite his XO. Corn-patch hair fell over his forehead like a Grand Ole Opry star's, and he looked as if he'd be just as comfortable in overalls and bare feet. Yet the man was more effective in an emergency than anyone Nelson had ever worked with. He fooled most people.

"Why couldn't it be one of our own?"

"It could be, Captain. But they shouldn't be in our sector without some warning to make sure we didn't blow their ass out of the water. Perhaps if sonar conditions were better, we'd have an ID by now. When in doubt . . ." He shrugged without finishing the sentence when the phone buzzed.

"Captain here." Nelson listened patiently. "Thank you.

I'll stop up if you need me. Otherwise . . ." He hung up the phone, then replaced his glasses very carefully, balancing them precisely on his nose with the thumbs and index fingers of both hands. "There. Perhaps you have a point, Jimmy. That was Dan Mundy and he says there's a definite change in the sound clarity of that contact. Maybe he slowed down."

"Which means that he figured if he hears us, then we may be able to hear him. And if he's as smart as we are, he's going to reduce his noise signature as much as possible to see how close he can get." Cross rubbed his chin with the back of his hand to see if he needed a shave. He always claimed it was tough to see the blond stubble, which was preferable to admitting he could forget simple, personal hygiene during those periods when he never slept. His inability to note the passing of days was a direct result of catnapping at sea instead of sleeping for any regular period of time. "You know those Russians like to sneak in from behind and just listen."

"Dan said the chief just couldn't classify a type or anything like that, so we have to assume he's probably still at a distance." Buck Nelson was peering over his glasses now in a manner that said he was looking for a suggestion.

"Don't let him sniff our butt, Captain. That's what I say."

"Me, too." Nelson picked up the phone and pressed the button for the control room. "Jeffrey, we're going to let you take the ride of your life—so strap yourself down. Wind her all the way up to fifteen knots and change course to the southeast corner of the sector. And continue the roller-coaster ride, too." He listened to the response from his OOD, winked at Cross and said, "That's right, you could be the next galloping ghost."

"He needs an attack boat his next tour," the XO said, "something he can use to go charging after the bad guys."

"Sometimes I think he should have gone to Pensacola and got himself some wings. He's good enough to do anything he wants. So tell me, Jimmy," he continued in the next breath, "what would you do if you were a Russian sub who just happened on to an unfriendly boomer and then found you were losing contact?"

"Speed up."

"Make more noise?"

"It's all relative if I thought my contact had turned away. Hell, if you're aggressive, you go after the other guy. You'd be chickenshit if you didn't."

"That ought to give us a better idea of what we've got. We'll just have that towed array hanging out back and listen until he speeds up enough to tell us who he is and what he wants." Nelson smiled. "I'm like Jeffrey. I was getting kind of bored myself. Why don't you go on back up there and explain to everyone what we want, and maybe I'll get myself a nap until something happens."

Back in his stateroom Buck Nelson removed only his shoes, placing them neatly on the deck where his feet would land if he were called in an emergency. Then he stretched out on his bunk. Better to grab an hour or so now. If they were really being followed by a Soviet attack boat, he knew he probably wouldn't get any sleep for who knew how long.

He closed his eyes. They snapped open by themselves. What was it that Mark Bennett taught him once when sleep wouldn't come? There really was a method of relaxing. If you were willing to work at sleep . . . work at sleep? When you're this tired?

He began with the same old method out of habit— inhaling deeply, exhaling slowly, tightening and loosening the muscles in his arms and legs one at a time. But when he closed his eyes, his brain immediately took over and started to design something—*what the hell will it be this time?* Why couldn't he just turn it off? Why did he have to design things when he wanted to sleep?

Their house in Bangor had been completely laid out in his mind before the land had ever been bought. Once the property was theirs, he sat down at a table with Cindy one day and put it down on paper, the location on the lot, the outside from foundation to peak, each room, even the amenities that made it more livable than any of the places they'd ever rented. It was a compilation of everything he and Cindy ever talked about, and it flowed from his mind like water from a pitcher.

He'd done the same thing with submarines. If he'd been a naval designer, the submarines would have been a hell of a lot different. More livable certainly, especially the attack boats. But they also would have cost more, and that's why Buck Nelson drove them and others designed them.

This time his mind was playing games. Damn if he wasn't designing a miniature submarine just for Jeff Sones. The kid wanted to drive boats like he was a fighter pilot. Okay, Nelson's mind was in synch and putting together one that would blow Sones's mind. What a power plant. And steering surfaces that would put Sones and his crew in harnesses like those pilots. Before his brain let him go, Buck had created the most beautifully maneuverable submarine in the world. No torpedos—but one hell of a ride!

Then he fell asleep.

Neil Arrow, arms swinging with his step, was in the lead, walking at a steady pace down the wide dirt road in the Waianae foothills. It was his turf, his idea, and he'd guaranteed they could do it without being seen. So all four of them, still in civilian clothes, had piled into the rented car and Arrow had driven them to the hills west of Pearl Harbor, where they could stretch their legs and get a little exercise.

"Why not?" Larsen had agreed when Neil suggested they get away from the base. "Spruance and Nimitz used to do it all the time. Spruance was a health nut. He'd get out beyond Makalapa with his commander-in-chief and walk Nimitz's ass off. Let's see if you gents can keep up with me."

They'd gone at least a mile at full tilt with Ray Larsen in the lead before he abruptly slowed down and said, "Okay, now that you've all met your maker, Neil can take the lead. The horse knows the way." The CNO was sweating profusely and droplets rolled from under his red crew cut down his neck to stain his shirt.

"Ray Spruance was a generation too early. He would have

loved to know you," Robbie Newman muttered. He was the least athletic of the group and was puffing visibly. "I was damned if you were going to get the best of me, but you came close to having another casualty on your hands if you kept up that pace."

Larsen held up two fingers and grinned. "Two casualties, Robbie. Look at OP-02 over there," he said, pointing at Mark Bennett. "He can hardly catch his breath. What do you say there, Admiral? Going to issue a directive on physical fitness to the sub force?"

"I'm going to call your wife when I get back and tell her she was almost a widow." Mark Bennett glanced over to Arrow. "You were thinking about it, too, weren't you?"

They were strolling easily now up a gentle path with heavy undergrowth on either side. The air was thick. It seemed to Bennett that the birds chattering in the canopy of trees over the path were making an effort to compete with the conversation.

Neil Arrow let out a sigh of relief. "You're lucky you gave in, Ray. None of us would have ever blown the whistle on the other guy."

"You were right, you know, Neil," Larsen answered. "This really is relaxing. I needed it as much as anyone. I think we were definitely getting too close to the problem."

Arrow could sense the undercurrent of frustration and resentment that persisted among the four of them. It scared him. Decisions made in the heat of anger could come back to haunt you. In this case, there was no margin for error. They weren't in the driver's seat on this one, never had been. Every bit of information that came to them, as meager as it was, was new. Someone else was calling the shots this time. Their initial goal was to confirm just who the enemy was in this case. *It had to be the Soviet Union.*

But this was so unlike the General Secretary's recent efforts. Why was he pushing a nuclear confrontation? That was the only purpose they could envision. What mistakes had been made on the U.S. side so far? They had to neutralize the situation and then come back swinging. It was necessary to be rational, consistent, cautious, regardless of what was happening. Anger had no place in their decisions.

Each of them had been mulling over their own thoughts for a few moments when Arrow turned toward Ray Larsen. He opened his mouth to speak, then realized his thoughts hadn't fully jelled.

"Go," said Larsen, jabbing a finger in his direction, then dropping it to his side with a sheepish smile.

"You don't have to give up your bad habits completely, Ray. We wouldn't know how to react." Arrow tried to glare at the CNO but his expression became a satisfied smile. The man was set in his ways but he was trying. "I've got an idea we ought to be thinking more about *Pasadena,* other than her being lost."

"Why?"

"That's a point," Newman muttered to himself. "She was in absolutely superb shape." He saw submarines as machines that either functioned perfectly or sank. It was black and white. As far as he was concerned, there wasn't the least hint that *Pasadena* could perform any other way but perfectly. The so-called "deadwood" that Newell, her captain, transferred off his own boat were considered excellent performers on others. Therefore, why not consider other aspects? If human error was a possibility, why not human fallibility?

"What'd you say, Robbie?" Bennett asked.

"Pasadena. She was in terrific shape. That's Wayne Newell's boat. All of his have always been 4.0, engineering-wise, I mean."

"Whatever way you want to look at them," Bennett commented. "He's so goddamned squeaky, I'd hate to work for him."

Larsen looked in Bennett's direction briefly. "How well do you know him?"

"He was one of my officers when I had *Stonewall Jackson.*"

"Was he like that then?"

"I don't know when he wasn't like that."

"You don't like him, Mark?"

"I wouldn't pick him out to go drinking with . . . even if he did drink," he added as an afterthought.

"How about fighting a war?"

Bennett glanced at the CNO, who was staring straight ahead. "He's driven to perfection. He would either sink everything that came anywhere near him or go down trying. And before you start telling me that's the only way to do it, Ray, you were the one who told me there's no point in sacrificing a submarine for a single target unless you were sure it was the ultimate target."

"Did I say that?"

"You're damn right you did. Newport. Naval War College. Visiting lecturer. I was a student, and I'll regurgitate everything you said that day, even most of the percentages you quoted."

Newman moved up beside Larsen. "Sounds like he's got you." He could sense the tension had disappeared somewhere during the first mile. "Why are you so interested in Wayne Newell?"

"I don't know," Larsen answered uneasily. "I hadn't even thought about him until you brought up his name. I guess I get scared by perfect people. Maybe it's a sixth sense. I didn't even think of who *Pasadena*'s C.O. was until you mentioned it, Robbie."

"He's good, isn't he, Mark? I mean beyond your distaste for his drinking habits," Newman asked.

"Yeah, I recommended him for an XO's billet when he was ready to leave old *Stonewall*. He wouldn't make mistakes. Like we've all said, it would have had to be human error for her to disappear."

"Come on." Larsen turned abruptly to the rear. "I feel better now, Neil. Maybe Spruance had the idea first, but you hit it right on the head this time. We all needed this. Let's take another look at *Pasadena*'s position."

"What are you thinking?" Bennett asked.

"I'm not, not really. I'm just taking shots in the dark." He looked over his shoulder. "Come on. Let's pick up the pace again. I feel like a new man." Robbie Newman hadn't really said what he was thinking, but Ray Larsen was sure at that moment that he'd read Robbie's mind.

Manchester had been running east on the bottom leg of *Florida*'s sector at about ten knots, varying her depth to counter the temperature gradients that affected sonar conditions. She had yet to detect a sound that could be considered manmade. Frustration, compounded by hours of anticipation, had become an enemy.

Ben Steel was experiencing an increasingly uneasy feeling that it had been a mistake to undertake his search by starting out on the perimeter of *Florida*'s patrol area. He remembered that Mark Bennett's method of covering a sector was no method at all. A boomer on station was boring enough without sacrificing imagination completely. Bennett had a policy of offering a day's maneuvering to individual OOD's—they could choose their own courses, speeds, and depths within reason. Drills were also conducted by the same individual, and the captain always made sure that each of his OOD's covered the entire spectrum during a patrol. It was a method of training and a means of keeping his men sharp.

So now, tell me, why are you undertaking your search by the book? Steel asked himself after the radio messenger had awakened him to explain there were no messages. *When you've been taught by the best, why not follow his example? Only the standard functions of a submarine need to follow the book. The hunt is limited only by your imagination.*

The unusual lack of messages at this time—especially with their unique assignment—meant that Pearl Harbor was probably being jammed. Of course, it could also be that they simply had no interest in singling *Manchester* out as an addressee. Even if a secure code was employed, any traffic analyst would recognize that she was involved in something special. Whatever the reason, no submariner ever waited to be force-fed information.

Steel's first question when he entered the control room was, "Where's our favorite SEAL today?"

"Most likely the torpedo room, Captain. He seems happiest down there, according to Mr. Simonds."

"Well, call down and ask him to please join me in control. Tell him he's going to learn how this boat really operates," Steel added, heading to the navigation table at the rear of the control room. The quartermaster had superimposed *Florida*'s sector on the chart to provide *Manchester*'s location within that area.

There was nothing imaginative about that line—that straight, black line that indicated their track. They had reached the lower boundary after a full-power run from the south. Steel's reasoning had been based primarily on the hope that *Florida* was anywhere but the opposite end of the sector. She should be picked up by sonar, he'd decided, on a sweep covering first the lower limits and then moving in a circular counterclockwise manner.

But it wasn't just *Florida* he was looking for. Those boomers were exceedingly quiet and she would be tough to locate. There must be another boat somewhere out there, an enemy submarine. What other reason could there be for two missing Tridents? It would be even better if they could isolate that one first. Only . . . what flavor? Russian? On the assumption it had to be Soviet, that other boat would be louder than *Florida*. His mission was to protect the boomer, to place *Manchester* between them if possible. He had been given the designated sector that was *Florida*'s home for the duration of her patrol, but he had no idea which direction the other sub might approach from.

Lieutenant Commander Burch appeared comfortable in his borrowed uniform when he arrived in the control room. "I understand you're looking for an expert boat driver, Captain."

"Well, maybe *drive* isn't quite the word I'd begin with. I

wasn't about to replace any of my OOD's. But I need someone who's unfamiliar with our normal tactics to help us out. Take a look at this for a minute." He beckoned Burch to follow him over to the chart. "You see, we're right here now, approaching the lower right-hand corner of *Florida's* sector. She's got to be in here somewhere, and it would be nice if we found her before the other guy did." His hand covered most of the area. "The submarine we assume is after her can be coming from anywhere—big ocean." He swept his hand in a circle around the sector that now appeared tiny.

"Harder to locate," Burch remarked. "How far away can you pick up the bad guys?"

"If you were aboard a little longer, you might say it would be mostly luck to pick up either of them. Russian subs are noisier but still tough to detect. It'll be almost impossible to find *Florida*. Those boomers are about the quietest things afloat, and they don't do anything to make it any easier to hear them."

"What if they hear us?"

"If they identify our sound signature, they'll leave us alone and hope we don't hear them. No one, not even *Manchester,* is supposed to know about these patrol areas. If they don't figure out who we are, they'll do whatever is necessary to disappear without being heard—go completely quiet, turn away, whatever needs to be done. The idea is that only those who need to know have any idea where a boomer is hiding."

"I suppose they can get mad, too," Burch said.

"That's why there's a signal to identify a friendly. If they're in a corner, they're just like a dog—they bite."

"But in our case . . ."

"I have no idea what's happened with them. I know as much as you do. It's possible somehow they've gotten the word. That would make them very nervous."

Lieutenant Commander Burch was as curious as he was perplexed. There were rarely any ifs in his world. A SEAL on a mission normally only ran into bad guys, and they were quickly dispatched. "It's beyond me what you think I can possibly do, Captain."

"You can find either *Florida* or the other submarine just as well as any of us, maybe better. Or at least you can provide us with the means. I had a captain one time who spoke about the value of imagination in a situation like this. I know how I'd probably run my search, and that could be exactly the way I'd locate my targets. I might also miss them completely by being so damn precise and acting just like a submariner, particularly if one of them hears me first. It's easy to see what we have to do, and all I want you to try is to place us where it seems we have the best chance of finding our quarry."

Burch glanced curiously at Steel. He was uneasy with the idea. "I don't think I could offer any more than any of your own men. It seems pretty obvious . . ."

"I couldn't agree with you more. That's the only reason I called you up here. The obvious could be our biggest mistake. It's the luck I'm looking for, that extra something that we might overlook. Go ahead. The quartermaster will put an overlay on the chart so you can play with it without messing up his pretty picture. I already know what I'm going to do. I'm going to bring us around to head toward the middle of the sector right now. We're pretty sure we know where they aren't. That's where we've already been. So why don't you come up with a couple of ideas for me to find out where they are. When I'm sure you're pissing up a rope, you'll be the first to know. What could be more fun?"

After a short lesson on the capabilities of the various sonars on board, from the sphere in the bow to the hull-mounted hydrophones to the array towed aft, Lieutenant Commander Burch experimented with possibilities until the chart overlay looked like a madman's scratch pad. There were diagonals, star-shaped tracks, geometric designs, and spirals. The final determination was simply that if they had been following *Florida* without success and were now turning away from her, they would have to sweep back. The other OOD's each took a turn at analyzing the problem as soon as they realized Ben Steel was looking for the optimum possibilities for locating the needle in the proverbial haystack.

Burch learned as he watched. It was Steel who let him decide that it was better to search the area they had been moving away from and then sweep back in a long spiral to catch their prey if they had indeed been following it. After turning more to a west-northwest course, Steel was satisfied that they had incorporated not only the most logical approach, but also the one that allowed a bit of luck to ride with them.

"I want to be ready for a snapshot," he told Peter Simonds. "Our intruder could be just sitting by himself waiting for a target to show up. I can imagine that we might be on top of each other before we know it. I hope so." If the enemy submarine was able to remain as quiet as *Florida*, it could be just like an ambush. The first one to shoot would be the likely winner. The only difference was that the loser who went to the bottom after a single shot would take more than a hundred men with it.

CHAPTER TWELVE

Pasadena had come close to periscope depth momentarily to copy her broadcast before returning to depth to continue her search pattern. As she came to a zero bubble at three hundred feet, the ominous click of the 1MC system echoed through each compartment. There was a time aboard *Pasadena* when an announcement had been something for the crew to look forward to. But at this stage of their existence, that had become ancient history. It had been only a matter of days—was that all?—yet to most even this small pleasure had disappeared in the sands of time. The announcements had become tedious, overbearing lectures.

Tension was thick in the air. It was beyond the scope of even a genius to invent a scrubber capable of purifying that. Every man could smell it! Feel it! It was transferred from one watch section to the next. It came from the man next to you, oozing slowly across the deck, up the bulkheads, along the overhead, and it gradually covered each of them. They were at war . . . with the Russians? Or was it with themselves? With each other? With their captain? They didn't know, not really, and when the 1MC clicked on there was an increase in the tension, a silent electric discharge creating a human aroma of ozone.

"This is the captain." Who else could it be? Newell was

the only one who had used the system in the past two days. "Once again, *Pasadena* is approaching a moment in our mission that may influence American history beyond anything you can imagine. In the past few days, each one of you has faced tremendous odds and reacted in a manner that has brought honor to yourselves and your families. You have shown the world that one hundred thirty distinctly different individuals can be molded into a crew capable of preserving the ideals upon which our nation was founded."

That was what they had expected, what they feared most—another pep talk, a morale builder. It was the opposite of what they wanted. News was what they cared most about. But *Pasadena* seemed cut off from the world—except for orders from SUBPAC. What was happening at home, if there was still a home? Was this the end of the world? Was it . . . ? Anything but this.

Newell's voice sounded deeper than usual and seemed to catch when he uttered some of the pat phrases he'd selected. *Pasadena*'s captain was a true believer in motivation, and he was a student of human behavior. He'd observed the attitudes of his men the past few hours and the results were patently obvious. Every word he had ever read about men in war, battle fatigue, personality conflict in time of stress, was displayed on each face he'd encountered. The men had expressed their concerns—yet not one of them was afraid for himself. Their only fears were for the war on the surface and the danger to their families. That was something he couldn't help them with. Those who controlled *Pasadena*'s communications had chosen to isolate her. This type of problem had been overlooked. If he could have come up with something, anything, it might have helped—just this once—but he remembered nothing in his background that could fashion an answer to what they were looking for.

The information that had come to *Pasadena* was in the form of succinct naval messages. That was a format that contradicted the imagination. Of necessity, it was vague, businesslike. Their orders, their mission—that was all that the Navy was concerned with at this stage. That only encouraged each one of them to interpret for himself exactly what was happening on the surface.

Yet there was an ominous note to those few, short messages, a hint that the civilian population of the United States must be in peril, perhaps already under attack. That was what lurked in each man's mind.

Wayne Newell would be the first to acknowledge that sonar's initial identification of the two submarines they had sunk had magnified his problems. But what was certainly weighing on their minds even more, *the fate of their families,* should be of even greater concern. He would make it so. Was there a home they were still fighting for? Or would they find scorched cities if they ever returned? He wanted them to have something more to worry about than the masking device that made Soviet boomers sound American.

The recent communications received by *Pasadena* had been calculated to enhance the importance of her mission. The continued existence of a Soviet ballistic-missile threat at sea was vital to *Pasadena's* maintaining a high degree of readiness. Their morale, their sense of mission, their unselfish efforts, might just save their families. This he believed with all his heart.

"I want to share a message just received," Newell continued. "It says: 'Imperative *Pasadena* locate and destroy enemy SSBN in assigned sector. Mission critical to survival of land targets and strategic negotiations.' While that is open to interpretation, I believe that there is a definite probability that our families may still be safe. I was informed before our departure that Soviet targeting included many of our cities, so I can only assume our efforts may be vital to their survival. And if there are actually negotiations under way, that could mean that our success on this mission could strengthen U.S. terms." An audible sigh escaped over the speaker in each compartment. "I can only repeat that I believe *Pasadena* is in the right place at the right time. We have been chosen to defend our nation in a strange and unanticipated way . . . and I just wanted one more opportunity to express my deep pleasure in serving with each one of you. I'm not repeating a speech we've all heard in the movies. That comes from the bottom of my heart. The next few hours in our lives will mean so much to those we love."

That was what they wanted to hear—what he wanted them to hear.

When Newell replaced the microphone, Dick Makin saw droplets of sweat coursing down his cheeks. From the manner in which the captain had spoken, they could just as well have been tears. His final words had been spoken with his eyes tightly shut, as if he were in prayer. The executive officer of a ship was closer to the captain than any other man, and Makin understood Newell better than anyone aboard *Pasadena.* He had seen more emotion from the man in the past six hours than since they'd first met. Newell was as dedicated as any commanding officer in the fleet. Yet his personality also appeared to be changing radically as the pressure increased with this new target. Wayne Newell had never been an emotional individual before. He had been cold, calculating, efficient. Now there was a new, almost human, element. The change was rewarding in a way, yet also . . . frightening.

"Well, what do you think, Dick? Any doubt in your mind after that that we're all in this together?"

"None at all, Captain." He watched as the handkerchief came out of Newell's back pocket. It seemed to wipe away his emotions at the same time the perspiration that was now staining his collar disappeared. It was an eerie sensation to watch the cocky smile of confidence blink on like a light bulb. "I hadn't had a chance to see the messages yet. I'm surprised we're getting detail like that in this situation."

"Me, too." He gave Makin a friendly poke on the arm and added softly, "I must admit I found it necessary to add a little something extra—for the troops, you know." Then in a louder voice, "But I guess that shows SUBPAC's confidence in us. I'm only sorry we couldn't respond so they'd know for sure we already took out two of those bastards. This submarine deserves to be the pride of the fleet."

An unexpected warning chill surprised Makin. He was

watching Newell's eyes move about the control room. The man wanted to make sure he was being heard. His words were for everybody on *Pasadena,* not the executive officer he'd been speaking with. The captain seemed to be addressing his destiny. And that chill was more pronounced . . .

"Captain!" The voice that interrupted them was from the sonar officer. Only his head was visible from the entrance to sonar.

"A steady contact, Steve?" Newell was beaming as he covered the short distance to the other compartment.

"Yes, sir." He held up a cautioning hand. "But Dixon thinks he may have something different this time. It's nothing clear, but the computer seems to indicate it's not the same thing."

Newell saw that Steve Thompson was bent over the shoulder of one of his men. He tapped him on the shoulder. "Still out there on the port bow, Dixon?"

Dixon shook his head without looking up.

"Maybe we ought to be ready for a snapshot, Dick," Newell called excitedly toward the control room. "Inform the torpedo room." Then in an even louder voice than he'd expected himself, "Is it solid, Dixon, close enough to track?"

Again the sonarman shook his head.

"Well, for Christ sake, what the hell is it?"

Dixon glanced quickly over his shoulder at the sonar officer. There was a pleading look in his eyes.

Steve Thompson edged over beside the captain and whispered diplomatically, "Please, Captain, they're trying as hard as they can to classify it. And it's still too far away to be sure of anything. I think it's manmade." He remained conscious of the recent confrontation with Dick Makin. "When I called you from the control room, I just wanted you to know we had something."

Newell's brow furled in frustration. "But you said it was different."

"That's right, Captain. It doesn't appear to be the same one we picked up earlier. I didn't mean to—"

"Mr. Thompson, Dixon's got the original one again," another sonarman interrupted. "Still faint . . ."

"Get a comparison."

Even Newell remained quiet while they waited.

It was less than a minute before Dixon said softly, "Two definite . . . manmade. One off the port bow. One to starboard. No definite bearing yet, no target motion. I'm pretty sure they're both far enough off so there's no immediate danger, Captain. The one to port is still very faint, so he's either awfully damn quiet or a good distance away."

"Target motion," Newell barked. "I need target motion."

"Captain," Dixon began in the same soft voice, "I can't—" Not even maneuvering would help at this stage.

"Steve, you know what I want. There's no such thing as"—but he'd already turned away in anger, and it was Dick Makin who heard his final word—"can't." The captain's arms were folded across his chest. His teeth were clenched with determination. There was no room for disagreement when he knew there were sonar contacts ahead . . . and they had to be moving . . . somewhere.

"Captain," the executive officer said, "I think we could add another couple of knots' speed without giving ourselves' away to anyone. The Soviet sonar isn't as good as ours."

"Dick, this is wartime," Newell snapped, "not an exercise. I know goddamn—" He had been about to say that he was more worried about American sonars anyway. But Newell cut himself off without finishing and nodded curtly to Makin before striding purposefully into the control room. Makin could hear him say to the OOD, "Add two—no, make it three—more knots, same course until we have a better picture from sonar." Then he was back in the tiny room. "Good thinking. We have to take chances."

About ninety minutes after *Pasadena* increased her speed, Dixon said, "Captain, the best I can say at this time is that the bearings of those two contacts seem to have shifted enough so that perhaps they're headed toward each other."

"What's your basis?"

"Well, sir, the bearings are still pretty vague for me to be saying something like that but"—he was holding his hands apart in front of Newell—"if we're in the middle here, I'd say maybe—just maybe—they were narrowing like this." He moved his hands slightly closer, no more than half an inch toward the middle. "That's the best I can say."

"Which one's the boomer?"

"Oh, I'd be taking one hell of a gamble, sir, if I said which one at this—"

Newell's voice intruded sharply. "Which one?"

Dixon's head inclined and his eyes fell to the deck for a second. His hands were still raised toward the captain. He closed the fingers of his left hand. "This one, Captain . . . the one to port."

"Why?"

The sonarman's eyes raised, though his head remained down. "If we're getting closer, its sound is remaining steadier, and damn quiet, too. So it's probably closer to us than the other one. Boomers are quiet as hell when they're ambling along at maneuvering speed—at least ours are." His eyes returned to the deck. *There, he'd said it!*

"You're not going to give me any of that shit, are you, Dixon? I don't want to hear that kind of garbage now."

Dixon was silent.

"How about you?" Newell challenged one of the younger sonarmen. "You hear what Dixon just said?"

No one seemed to be breathing in sonar. "Captain," Makin said softly, in an effort to place himself between Newell and the men, "I'm sure he can't hear you with those headphones on."

Newell reached out and yanked the headphones off the sailor's head. "Did you hear Dixon? He was intimating that the contact to port could be one of *our* boomers. What do you say?"

The whites of the sailor's eyes stood out even in the dim, red glow of sonar. His mouth hung open in shock. No officer, never mind the commanding officer, had ever acted like that on any submarine he'd been aboard. He never blinked, nor did he respond. He simply stared back at Newell.

"Don't you understand what I'm asking?" Each of Newell's words were spoken softly and distinctly, with the definite hint of a threat in the background.

"I . . . I can't ID that contact yet, sir." The sailor's eyes were a captive to Newell's demanding gaze.

"Try an educated guess then. Could that contact to port be a *ballistic-missile submarine?*" The final three words were pronounced so slowly that there was no mistaking the answer desired.

"I guess so, sir. It's pretty faint . . . but the Russian boomers are noisier—"

"Could it be a Russian ballistic-missile submarine?" Again Newell left no doubt about the answer.

"It . . . it could be, Captain." The sonarman blinked once, then twice more.

"Could it be a Soviet with a masking device exactly like the others we have encountered?"

There had been no movement in sonar. Each individual witnessing this exchange appeared transfixed, frozen by the words being spoken. Even Makin was caught in the electric exchange between Newell, Dixon, and the younger sonarman, fully aware of the captain's influence on the youngster.

The sonarman blinked again and his eyes flickered briefly in Dixon's direction. But he could see that Newell was also watching the other. There was no escape. "It could be, Captain."

"Mr. Thompson," Newell continued in the same soft voice, "I suggest that Dixon and each one of them continue to evaluate both contacts, but I expect you to personally analyze the recordings and the computer results, because I think you will come up once again with that infernal masking device that has somehow confused some of our crew."

"Yes, sir," the sonar officer answered.

"Mr. Makin and I will leave you alone. We'll be in control where we belong, preparing for our next attack. I intend to open the doors on two tubes with the hope that it is early enough that our contacts don't hear us. We don't have the luxury of waiting for our target to come to us, so we lack the element of surprise this time. The attack team is going to be ready. I expect you will find that the contact to port is our next target."

In the control room Newell grasped his executive officer's arm and said in an expressionless voice, "I expect you to take care of any problems with the men if the Russians are employing that masking device again." His fingers tightened until Makin looked at him questioningly. "You may do whatever is necessary to silence any dissent."

Buck Nelson woke with a start. *What . . . ?* He turned and saw a form in the entrance of his stateroom outlined by the light in the passageway. He reached for the rimless glasses that he'd carefully placed on the chair beside his bunk.

"Just me, Captain," Jimmy Cross said, "your ever-faithful executive officer reporting. I did knock, by the way. Y'all were sure as hell sawing up a cord of wood there."

Nelson smelled after-shave lotion as Cross stepped inside. That meant the XO had probably grabbed one of his hour-long naps. And for once he'd also remembered to shave before he began his never-ending inspection of *Florida*'s spaces.

"You come in here to inspect the C.O.'s stateroom? Or is there something else that decided you on disturbing my sleep?" Nelson asked with a trace of humor in his voice.

"None of the above." Cross waited until he saw the glasses carefully perched on the captain's nose and then he swung the chair around and sat down. "Thought you might have some interest in that contact that we turned away from."

"Don't tell me, Jimmy," Nelson said, smiling. "I should have stayed awake. Right? Or has he disappeared?"

"None of the above, again. He must have picked up speed like I said he ought to, so we seem to have a stronger sonar contact—still intermittent sometimes, but stronger. He's off our starboard beam now on this new course of ours so I'd guess he may be intent on trying to close us."

"Why didn't you wake me earlier?"

"When the captain of a ship is incapacitated, the executive officer shall be in charge of—"

"Jimmy, you having fun at my expense?"

"But you feel better after a couple of hours in the sack, don't you?"

Nelson nodded and stretched, hunching his shoulders before he swung his legs over the side of the bunk. His feet landed on top of his shoes, just as he had intended.

"Danny says he wouldn't be surprised if this contact's one of our 688's bird-dogging us for some reason. That's why I didn't bother you, Captain. I figured you could use the sleep more than me waking you up to tell you that."

"That a definite ID?"

"Not for publication, I suppose." Cross shrugged. "But from our no-nonsense sonar officer, I have to think it's pretty good."

"What do you think we ought to do, since it seems to be one of our own?"

"Maybe give our sonar people some practice on it, maybe even play with a couple of attacks. Whoever it is would be awfully surprised to hear that they've been sunk a couple of times."

"What's to keep him from doing the same thing?"

"I don't know, Captain. But my idea . . . also," he added with a serious expression spreading over his face, "was to be ready just in case he wasn't one of ours. You see, I checked the fleet scheds we picked up before getting under way, and there just ain't supposed to be anyone even passing close to us." He sucked the side of his cheek in like a cow chewing its cud. "That's also why I woke you up." Cross grinned crookedly. "I figured you also would have been bullshit if we found out an hour or so from now that our contact not only has closed us, but that it was also a bad guy who'd been taping every little sound we made."

Nelson bent down to tie his shoes. "What would I do without you, Jimmy? They say executive officers are made, not born. But in your case, I think you're a natural. And you have so much fun yanking my chain."

"Only to decrease the boredom on patrol, Captain. Chief Delaney seems serious enough about this contact—the way it's acting, I mean—that I decided to keep my natural sense of humor in check long enough to listen to him and Dan Mundy. That contact also appears aware of us, and my recommendations would be either to turn away now or tiptoe and see what they do."

Nelson rose to his feet, yawned, and stretched again. "Why don't you have the OOD reverse course. If they turn toward our present course or toward where they think we're headed next, we may get an idea about whether or not they can track us. Then we'll just have to see what they do. I'm going to wash up a bit. My mouth tastes about as bad as it can get. I'm going to discourage our iron-bellied supply officer from putting curry on the menu for a while."

"Right, Captain. Sounds fine to me. Grits at least twice a day would be perfect." Jimmy Cross rose to his feet and pushed the chair into the corner. "If I'm wrong about this contact, I'll be the first one to admit it."

"In this business, every contact is an enemy until they show me otherwise, Jimmy."

Pertsovka!

The General Secretary had forgotten about that bottle. It had obviously been in his freezer for some time. When did he . . . ? Then he remembered. That was a happier time. It was a gift from two Congress of People's Deputies members who came from his hometown. It was a local brand they'd carried to Moscow with them, and they had taken great pains to make an appointment with him to present the bottle.

How proud they'd been. He remembered offering a glass to them. They insisted that it should be iced first and after all . . . yes, he remembered they had been shy about drinking with him because he was the General Secretary. So he had reached into that same freezer and taken out a frosted bottle of lime vodka and poured three glasses before they could decline.

Yes, more than they would ever know, he had enjoyed those few moments with men who could tell him what things were like back home. And then they were gone, proud that the General Secretary had been willing to have a drink with them. Oh, how he longed for the simple pleasures of camaraderie with one's own kind.

The bottle of pertsovka was instantly covered with a layer of frost, and he could tell the removal of the cap was going to be a slippery contest. He reached in his back pocket for a handkerchief and was struggling for a grip with that around the top when his wife brought him a towel from the wet bar.

"Here, hold the bottle with this. That will make it much easier, and you wouldn't want to drop it, would you?" Her sad smile mirrored her understanding. She was aware of the gravity of his problems. It wasn't a day for friendly teasing.

"This is a wonderful bottle of pertsovka from a little town where I once lived. I'm sorry you don't care for the pepper flavoring . . ." He had been clasping the top of the bottle tightly in his hand and the heat had melted the ice around the cap. It unscrewed easily then and the very faint aroma of the hot peppers escaped. "Ah, don't you wish you liked this?"

She had gone back to the pantry for glasses and found two cold ones in the refrigerator. "I think perhaps there has never been a better time to learn." She went up on her tiptoes and gently kissed his cheek. "I will enjoy whatever you're having."

He poured a couple of ounces of the rusty liquid into the glasses she held. It looked perfect, flowing thickly, like reddish oil. She handed one of them to him and they silently touched the glasses together. His was drained in one gulp. She sipped curiously at first, then drank half, holding it on her tongue for a moment before swallowing.

"Well?" he inquired as the liquid hit home and the heat bounced back from his stomach.

"It's better than I expected." She imitated him and tossed back the remainder without holding it in her mouth. Then she smiled and tilted her head to one side, pushing a wisp of gray hair off her forehead. "Come." She held out her hand and led him to the sofa at one end of the room. "Let's talk, before we drink too much of this. Tell me what you are thinking."

How he loved her at times like this. There was no one else—none at all—to listen. It was one of those rare moments he could say whatever came to his mind without being accountable for it later. He poured two more ounces in each glass. "I'm not sure what I'm thinking . . . or if I'm thinking . . ." And then the rush of diverse thoughts in his mind coalesced into a logical explanation of the entire situation. The reasons for his frustration became more clear as he related his concerns to his wife. She listened patiently without interruption.

"What you're telling me," she responded when he finally stopped long enough to pour them both another glass, "is that you are trapped by other men's philosophies. You don't believe—"

"I don't know what to believe," he interrupted vehemently. "I don't know whether a first strike is an inevitability . . . a culmination of our historics." He sipped at the liquid in the glass like a puppy, taking little tastes. "Or if I will become a traitor to our history. Or, for that matter, perhaps there will be no further need for history."

"Do you have any indication of what Washington is thinking?" His wife had never cared for the Americans. They were too unpredictable.

"They've done nothing yet. They know their submarines are lost. But I have no idea if they know why. My intelligence agencies seem to have more advice than hard facts."

She could feel the warmth of the vodka penetrating her soul, an indulgence she rarely allowed herself. Life was good, at least it was if they could occasionally find moments like this one. "How many of them are really loyal to you . . . and how many are loyal to that original plan?"

"It can almost be broken down by age."

"You can always give an order to fire the missiles, if you absolutely have to. But there is a time to follow your instincts, and yours are to wait . . . just a little longer. But I think you must arrange for the old ones to disappear now."

CHAPTER THIRTEEN

Peter Simonds folded his arms and stared blankly across at the chart table. The quartermaster had just wandered aft. *Manchester's* executive officer was seated at one of the four attack console positions on the starboard side of control and had swung around to gain a view of the entire control room. It was tempting, habitually so, to get up and take a look at the chart. But he knew that their last position, marked with a neat, black X on the overlay, would be no more than a quarter of an inch from the previous one. And when the quartermaster returned with Lieutenant Commander Burch at his side, the next position would advance no more than that same distance on the projected course line that the captain allowed the SEAL officer to lay out.

Simonds unconsciously pushed his glasses back up the bridge of his nose with his right index finger. He continued on to his right ear and scratched just behind it as each man in control knew he would. Then he shifted his ample weight and scratched one of his buttocks. That had also been anticipated by the entire watch.

The OOD was in his usual position behind the planesmen and diving officer, his hand wrapped around the overhead support. When he heard the diving officer snicker, he glanced over at the XO, nodded and smiled, and turned back to murmur something to one of his planesmen.

"Mr. Simonds." It was Chief Moroney standing in the entrance to sonar just a few feet away. "There's something off our port bow," he commented matter-of-factly.

"Talk to me, Chief." The XO was on his feet, tucking his shirt into the back of his pants. "I was beginning to think the only thing we were going to hear was constipated whales for the rest of this cruise."

"No whale, sir," Moroney answered calmly as the XO stepped into sonar. "It's another submarine. At least I'm pretty damn sure it is."

"How do you know that so soon?" His hoarse voice carried a tone of exasperation. "You just picked it up. What's happened to the old chief I remember who used to keep us hanging forever without a classification in the middle of all those exercises?"

"I don't have any instructors leaning over my shoulder grading everything I do, XO. There's only one thing we're looking for now, another submarine, so that makes it all a hell of a lot easier when you're evaluating a contact."

Simonds picked up a set of headphones and pulled them over his ears. "Can I hear it?" he asked, his voice an octave higher.

"How about it, Billy? You got anything on that contact for the XO?"

"A little faint, Chief," the sonarman responded, "but it's there." He looked over his shoulder. "Got it, sir?"

The XO pushed his glasses up again. "You're yanking my chain." He glared over the top of his glasses at the chief before looking back down at the sonarman named Billy. "Am I really supposed to be hearing something?"

"Actually, XO, that's pretty clear, considering how long we've been dry. I'd bet we had a sudden change in sonar conditions—maybe when we rose above three hundred feet—and that's what made it so unusual. It may not mean anything to you, but we've been in outer space for so long in here that this contact sounds like a bell to us."

"What's our depth now?" Simonds asked.

"Two hundred eighty feet. We've been level for about the last thirty minutes."

"Keep at it, Chief." The XO was already out into the control room. "Hold your depth," he said as he passed the OOD. "I'm getting the captain. And don't change a goddamn thing. Just thread the needle like you're doing as long as sonar's holding him."

Ben Steel had eventually decided it was unbecoming to display his growing anxiety in any other space on *Manchester*. His solution had been to hide in his stateroom, perhaps catch up on paperwork, or that had been his excuse to Peter Simonds. When the XO raised his hand to knock on the bulkhead, he heard, "Come on in. I've been sitting here with my thumb inserted, staring at all this paper and wondering when someone was going to tell me to switch."

"Looks like your idea to reverse the search pattern paid off. Contact off to port. Chief says sonar conditions appear exceptional right now." The excitement mirrored on his face was contagious.

Steel slapped the top of the desk with the flat of one hand, then lifted it up with both and slammed it shut. There was a clatter as the contents fell inside. "What is it, Peter? Our boomer, I hope."

"Could be, Captain. Sonar's positive it isn't biologicals. Moroney seems to think it's a submarine."

"Where's my cap?" Steel pushed the chair back and stood up, his eyes searching for his baseball hat.

Simonds pushed his glasses back and grinned. "Don't need one, Captain. Anyway, I think it fell in there." He pointed at the closed desk. "I wouldn't open that now if I were you."

"You got a deal." Steel rubbed his hands together excitedly. "Let's hit it." He placed a hand on Simonds's arm and smiled broadly. "They will let me into sonar now, won't they?"

"I'll give you the password if they do ask, Captain." He

stepped into the passageway ahead of Steel. "But Moroney's so excited now he'd probably invite the mess cooks in."

They entered the control room and made the sharp left to sonar without a word to the OOD or the watch standers. The sonar room was no different than before. The bluish glow revealed Chief Moroney and his duty sonarmen concentrating quietly on their equipment. Their passive listening devices swallowed a profusion of sounds from the ocean— *Manchester's*, the sea life around them, and that of the contact. The unpracticed ear would have heard nothing unusual. But that specific sound they had searched for was separated electronically, the background sounds filtered out. As it became isolated for their analysis and fed through computers for identification, it was also recorded. Skilled sonarmen with unique auditory and technical abilities were required for such exacting work. Their silence, their intense concentration in the midst of the sounds they were analyzing, was a measure of this special talent.

Chief Moroney remained unaware that anyone was behind him. The sonarmen communicated with their hands. Touch was a means of drawing attention. Pointing at a graphic display where the sound indeed appeared as a waterfall, or a switch, even tapping their own headset to indicate there was something coming through that required more than one set of ears, was a part of their silent language. The chief was the conductor, orchestrating the capture of these sounds neither the captain nor the executive officer could hear.

Steel resisted an overwhelming urge to ask questions.

Moroney reached behind to turn on a switch and instead found his hand resting on Simonds's belly. Even then he was preoccupied, reaching around the XO to flip the switch. Only then did he recognize Steel. "Oh, didn't know you were here, Captain."

Steel resisted the urge to ask for one of the headsets. He wasn't sure what to say. "We might take a shot at whatever you have, Chief, if it's one of the bad guys. Within range yet?" he added lamely.

"Limited target motion right now, sir. I think it's just good sonar conditions. It's not strong enough to be that close."

"You still think you've got a submarine there?"

"Has to be."

"Our boomer?"

Moroney looked up at Steel thoughtfully and shook his head. "I don't think so, Captain."

"There's only one other choice then," Simonds muttered. "The bad guy that's after him."

"Why don't you move into control, Peter, and set up for an attack—"

"Captain," Moroney interrupted, his voice strangely tense. "I can't identify a Russian sub here. It's far enough away so only the computer could possibly identify it, so I've been comparing this to the tapes we've got, and it's definitely not one of their latest—not an Akula, or Sierra, and I don't think it's an Alfa or Victor either. Billy's been running it against the best we have for an Akula signature, and I don't think so . . ." His voice drifted off as he replaced the headset. "I'll run them all again to be double sure. . . ."

Simonds hadn't yet gone into control. "It has to be one of them, Captain. No one else is operating out here, and there's no reason anyway for any of our friends to be near our boomers."

Steel put a finger to his lips. He could sense the strain on Moroney. "Where's David?" he asked the XO.

"Right outside by the console." David Hall was the sonar officer. "He stuck his head in when you were talking with the chief and said he'd stick out there until there was more space in here."

"Go on out there and get set up, and send David in. He's spent a lot of time on these tapes. Maybe he can come up with something that the others have missed."

Chief Moroney looked up as Hall slipped into the tiny room. "Here, Mr. Hall." He stood up and handed the headset to the officer. "You take a shot at this. I'll bet my left nut that's no Russian boat out there. Shit, I'll put 'em both on the line."

"What do you think you got, Chief?"

"Please, sir, just tell me I'm right about the Russian thing first." Moroney's forehead was knit in a frown.

The sonar officer operated exactly as his chief had, playing the recording of their contact again and again for his own benefit. Then he fed it into the computer for analysis against their tapes of comparable Soviet submarines.

Steel fidgeted, folding and unfolding his arms, then shifting his weight from one foot to the other. It was pure frustration to be a fifth wheel on your own ship. Most of this time, Hall's eyes were closed in concentration, opening only when he flipped switches. At one time Steel was sure he heard the other whisper to himself—"You're right, Chief"—but he knew it wasn't his place to ask any questions then. Moroney, who was standing right behind the sonar officer, seemed oblivious to the captain.

"Nope, none of them, Chief," Hall eventually said over his shoulder without looking up. He listened a little longer, his chin perched lightly on his fingertips, until he began to nod his head as though agreeing with something that none of the others had heard. Then he removed the headphones and offered them to Steel. "It's not making much noise, Captain, and it's still a fair distance from us. But he might be wondering about us, too. I'll go along with the computer and put down even money that's one of ours."

Steel held the headset at chest level. "A 688?"

"That's right, and certainly very quiet. If sonar conditions weren't so good right now, we might have passed through this area without knowing the other was around."

"My understanding was . . ." But he let that slide. There weren't supposed to be any other U.S. submarines in the vicinity. Burch, the SEAL, had made it quite clear that *Manchester* would be the only one involved. "Which one?"

Under normal conditions, there probably were no more than half a dozen of the 688s home ported in Pearl Harbor at sea. The rest would be tied up at the piers for required maintenance. Each class of submarine had a specific sound signature of its own, no different for identification than human fingerprints. It was a matter of comparing the current contact against tapes in their library to determine the class. Sonar experts claimed that within a reasonable distance the trained ear could even identify a familiar sound by name. For David Hall and Chief Moroney, it was a game, but their accuracy was sometimes phenomenal. Like a few of the others in their unique business, they claimed each submarine had its own personal quirks that appeared as an oddity in its sound signatures.

"It just might be *Pasadena,* Captain."

What in the world would Wayne Newell be doing out here? Newell possessed an ability to turn up at the strangest places . . . even to say the oddest things. Steel grew to understand over the years that it was his nature. The man's instincts were amazing. Much of the time that strange place was also the right one for Newell. He never seemed to make mistakes either. Rather, it was a talent he took advantage of, making the best out of a difficult situation, profiting on the negative, turning a loss into a gain!

Was it possible he might just have ended up out here by pure happenstance? Ridiculous! Steel wasn't about to convince himself that this was one more situation where Wayne Newell had fallen headfirst into the pile and was here to give *Manchester* an assist in a hairy situation. *Chance might play a big part in a lot of things that happened to Newell—but not something like this.*

Ben Steel understood even before he was ready to admit it that there was no possible way he would talk himself into adding one more gold star to the Newell myth. It was better to sit back and analyze the situation and let the other captain initiate something. *Be coy!*

And that was no sea transit *Pasadena* was making. She was evidently moving quietly—as if she were tracking someone. . . .

* * *

The weather in the north Pacific had deteriorated even more. It was beyond anything the captain of SSV-516 had ever seen. Captain Markov had experienced violent winter storms in such forbidding seas as the Barents and the Norwegian and even the North Atlantic off the coast of Labrador. He'd also come up against summer hurricanes and cyclones in southern waters. But the combination of storms that swept across Siberia and the Bering Sea down onto SSV-516 actually frightened him.

The wind force increased—steady winds crept over a hundred knots, with gusts well beyond that—until the anemometer was ripped away. Windblown spray that tore at exposed skin made it impossible to determine the types of precipitation that froze to the pilothouse windows. Immense waves, some of them towering above the bridge, seemed to attack from every direction. Captain Markov was attempting to hold his bow at an angle into the wind. He'd been forced to reduce speed for safety purposes until he was just making bare steerageway. Time and again the helmsman was unable to get the ship back on course and they were forced to steer with their engines.

Waves continued to crash down on the bow, pressing it beneath tons of water. Each time, the ship won the titanic struggle, shuddering against tremendous weight as she rose against the suffocating ocean. The combination of wind and sea on either beam would push SSV-516 over on her side and hold her there until crewmen wondered whether she would ever right herself. And when the ship was twisted down forward and over on her side, a wave might strike from astern, lifting her stern so high that the screws were exposed. This would drive her bow farther beneath the surface, leaving her momentarily without steering control or power.

Internally, anything that hadn't been lashed down was hurled about until it either smashed or was secured. Food had become a memory. The galley remained secured. The groan and screech of metal echoed through the entire ship as seams were stretched beyond their designed endurance.

Those crew members off watch huddled in silent groups. Sleep was impossible. There was a constant rattling against the outer bulkheads as small, external pieces of their ship were sacrificed to the storm.

It was during an especially deep roll to port, over fifty degrees, with the bow deeply buried beneath tons of water, that a huge wave swept over SSV-516 from starboard. She was forced deeper beneath the sea. The men in the pilothouse watched the inclinometer surge past sixty degrees, then hold at that angle for what seemed an eternity before she began to right herself.

Then a second wave swept over her from the same direction. The forward radome was wrenched away with a horrible grinding sound that roared through the entire ship. The surging water swept it back into the mast, then tumbled it against the second radome before it bounced off the stack and was carried away into the darkness.

A frantic voice came over the speaker in front of the captain. "Pilothouse . . . we've lost all communications . . ."

"Can we still send to the American submarine?"

"Negative. Nothing. No satellite contact . . . nothing . . ."

Captain Markov's fear for his ship disappeared for an instant as he realized that their mission—the control of *Pasadena*'s message traffic—had just been lost.

Wally Snyder emerged from the radio shack near the entrance to the engineering spaces and wandered aimlessly into *Pasadena*'s control room. The stricken expression on his face instantly ignited the aura of fear and suspicion that had overspread the submarine. His demeanor was totally at odds with the man that everyone had known until that moment. His *Pasadena* baseball cap had been misplaced. His hair was rumpled and his uniform shirt hung loosely outside wrinkled pants. His eyes, until that moment the mirror of an outgoing personality, appeared lifeless and vague.

His gaze fell without recognition on each of the men who watched his progress through the control room. Catching sight of the captain, he ambled up beside Wayne Newell. "Captain, I need to talk to you." His voice was a monotone.

"Not now, Wally." The captain never looked in his direction. "We're in the process of prosecuting a couple of contacts . . . gonna man battle stations shortly." Newell had been pacing, peering over the diving officer's shoulder on one side of control, studying the settings on the fire-control officer's console on the other, glancing at the chart on the navigation table. He'd been standing beside the OOD when Snyder appeared at his side, rocking on his heels nervously. "This is what we've been waiting for and—" His words were uttered in a tone that would have convinced any other individual that he obviously had nothing of value to contribute.

"Captain," the young officer interrupted, "I really do need to talk to you." His voice remained calm and unexpressive, in direct opposition to the harried expression on his face.

"Wally," Newell responded irritably, glancing quickly in his direction for the first time, "perhaps you don't understand. Let me try this in English," he explained acidly. "We have a mission. There is a Soviet boomer to port that needs to be sunk, and she may have a watch dog guarding her."

"Should I explain my problem right here?" They were standing alongside the periscope. Wally's voice was a monotone. "It concerns us all anyway." He wasn't about to be put off.

Newell, one ear cocked, took a few steps in the opposite direction, trying to hear Steve Thompson's voice from sonar. He couldn't quite make out what was going on in there, but it was something new and he was curious. Snyder was only serving as an irritant. "Yeah, go ahead," was the eventual response.

"We have no satellite communications, Captain." He waited for a response before continuing. "We raised the antenna about forty-five minutes ago during our regular comm period and there was nothing . . . absolutely nothing."

He had gained Wayne Newell's attention. The captain's eyes were riveted on his own.

"That's right, sir. Zip . . . zero . . . squat . . ." His voice remained totally devoid of expression. Only his eyes now revealed the stricken look of a man who has known absolute fear. He had just imagined the world totally devastated, barren, devoid of . . .

"And you raised at the right time?" It had never occurred to Newell that the concept of war he'd worked so hard to establish would actually convey a picture of Armageddon to someone like Wally.

Snyder paid no attention to the question. "Our gear seemed to be working just fine. I don't think it's that at all. Maybe there's no point in trying to blow anyone else out of the water, Captain. If there's nothing left out there . . . no one to communicate with . . . then there's no reason . . ." His gaze settled on the deck as his voice faded.

The control room was absolutely silent. The normal soft chatter that was a part of a functioning watch had ceased altogether. Each man easily understood, in his own way, what Wally Snyder had concluded—the possibility that the war had expanded to the point where there was no longer any contact with SUBPAC could mean that their families were . . .

"Mr. Snyder, that is absolute drivel." Newell's voice crackled with anger. "This is another one of your"—he glanced at the OOD and then around the control room. Every eye was fixed on the two of them—"tricks designed to create problems to disrupt our mission." Everyone knew that the captain felt Snyder was creating as many problems for him as Chief Lott. And they'd seen what happened to Lott.

"I played around with some other frequencies, but they all sounded like they were being jammed. So, I asked the electronics technicians to dismantle the gear," Snyder continued softly. "I thought there was something wrong before. You remember you wouldn't believe me when I said so. And now we're going to see. Otherwise . . . there's nothing out there. No one. So there'd be no reason to continue . . ."

Newell pivoted on his toes to face the comm officer. His arms hung loosely at his sides, his hands knotted tightly into fists. "You can't secure that gear without my permission," he shouted. His fists rapped against his thighs in an effort to maintain control. "You tell those technicians to get that gear back on the line immediately. Do you understand me?"

Snyder's eyes remained on the same spot on the deck. "I got to find out about that radio. I think . . ."

Silence, as deafening as it was inaudible, pervaded the control room. Not a soul was looking toward the two men, but they were the center of each man's world at that moment.

"Mr. Makin, please escort Mr. Snyder to his quarters." Newell's voice was as calm now as it had just been on the edge of losing control moments before. "I want it placed in the log now that Mr. Snyder has been relieved of his duties for cause and confined to quarters until *Pasadena* reaches port or until I review his case. I will instruct the ET's to place the equipment back on line in the most efficient way possible. Do I make myself—"

"Captain!" Steve Thompson's voice calling from the entrance to sonar overrode Newell's angry reaction. Even Wally Snyder turned in his direction. "Target motion on the port contact is northwest about eight to ten knots. The other may be doing approximately the same—"

"Is that a boomer we have to port?" A smile of satisfaction overspread Newell's face. His attitude had reversed itself completely. Even before he received the response, he was calling over his shoulder to the OOD, "Come left to an intercept course and increase your speed two knots to close him." Then he was looking back at the sonar officer, who was staring at him uncertainly.

"Yes, Captain, most likely a boomer . . ." Steve Thompson responded disconsolately. "Apparently employing a masking device—just like you said it would." He glanced at Wally Snyder contritely for a moment before his eyes fell to the deck.

Newell's eyes darted from Thompson to Snyder and back to the sonar officer again. Then he looked around the control room. Every eye was on him, waiting, wondering what his response would be. He could sense the sudden increase of stress, almost a latent hostility, as if the chief engineer had just reported a valve opened to the ocean.

The diving officer's high-pitched voice broke the silence. "Watch your bubble," he snapped to the bow planesman.

"XO," Newell growled. He indicated Snyder with a slight nod of his head and jerked his thumb over his shoulder. "Get his ass out of here. We're going to make history."

"Yes, Captain." The executive officer placed a tentative hand on Wally Snyder's elbow, but he found himself unable to look at the man he was about to remove from control.

The communications officer gently lifted Makin's hand and let it drop. His eyes never left the gray deck as he shuffled out of the control room in front of Dick Makin.

The battle-stations team—*his first team*—had appeared after a short break without being noticed. Newell nodded in satisfaction to himself. With Snyder gone, the pressure appeared to drop in control. Each man seemed to have returned to his job, the confrontation with the comm officer forgotten. It was a comfortable feeling. *Don't allow a bad apple to spoil the whole basket!* he muttered silently to himself. "Course to intercept?"

"Actually, just about due north, Captain," the OOD responded.

"Very well, I'll be in sonar with Steve for the time being." He took one step toward the little compartment just forward of the fire-control consoles, then stopped. Newell folded his arms across his chest and fell deep in thought, clenching his lower lip between his teeth. When he spoke, it seemed to be to himself, yet it was also for everyone to hear. "We're not fooling them this time, not a chance. Before, we were waiting quiet like a goddamn lion in a tree. Now we're chasing 'em down. And they'll have their towed array streamed aft. It'll pick us up eventually. Not a chance in the world to sneak up on them. We gotta be ready . . . decoys . . . the works. A dogfight, a real dogfight. Okay?" he ended in a loud voice. It sounded like a question.

There was an embarrassing silence before one of the planesmen responded without enthusiasm, "We'll be ready, Captain."

"Good . . . good," Newell murmured. *Amazing how you could turn things around with a few well-chosen words.* Then, "Damn, I forgot those ET's in radio . . . messing with that gear." He pointed at the OOD. "You get them to put everything back together right now, hear? We'll worry about communications after we paint one more Russian boomer on our sail. Stop 'em right now, okay?"

"Right away, Captain."

As Newell entered sonar, the words were already tumbling from his mouth, "Ready to blow away another boomer, Steve?"

The sonar officer's glasses had inched down his nose until he was looking over the tops. "Captain, that's one hell of a masking device they're using." He removed the glasses and rubbed his eyes. "Dixon was asking me how we know so much about it if we're the first ones to ever run into it."

"Intelligence, Steve. It's about time those spooky guys turned up something useful to the fleet like this. But they weren't about to broadcast it all over town. Let people without a need to know hear about that device and it'd get back to the Kremlin in no time flat. So SUBPAC kept it to himself . . . except for those of us who might need it right away, of course . . ." His voice drifted off again. "Enough of that. We've been through it before. I want to get us in there and take this one out as fast as possible." He rubbed his hands together. "Are we going to have any problems about that masking device or has everybody got it together for this attack?"

"I guess we're ready to go," Thompson agreed forlornly. "But what about that other contact?"

"Other contact," Newell repeated as if that was the first he'd heard of it. "Right. What have you got there?"

"Another submarine, Captain. It must be. It's farther away and it appears to be on almost a steady bearing, probably heading toward that boomer, too."

"Probably a bird dog . . . a trailer waiting for someone like us. But we'll take care of him. We'll knock him off right after we finish off that boomer."

"That's a perfect *Florida.*" The words came hesitantly in a soft voice, almost a whimper.

"What was that?" Newell snapped.

It was the sonarman, Dixon. "That's a perfect *Florida,*" he repeated. "No way it could be anything else but. You can't fool a computer." His voice was unsteady, as if he were about to cry. "Slight variation in her machine noises."

"Steve," Newell said evenly. "You have about thirty seconds to straighten him out, or you're going to be short one sonarman. If you don't believe me, look what happened to Lott. We can get along without Dixon as easy as we're getting by without the others." He stalked out of the room growling over his shoulder, "Thirty seconds."

"Lost contact," Dixon croaked, tearing off his head-phones. "She's gone silent . . . like she was dead in the water. But it *was Florida,*" he added, his head cradled in his arms across the face of his scope.

Florida was silent—"like fog creeping in on cat's feet," Buck Nelson whispered to himself—making maneuvering speed. He'd given the order to reduce speed to the bare minimum, just maintain steerageway and support the hy-drophone array they were towing astern. The sounds each man generally associated with normal shipboard existence were gradually reduced to a barely audible hum. Even conversation and movement, sounds that would not pass into the water, were unconsciously restricted until men looked at each other with a strange half smile while they conversed in a combination of whispered phrases and sign language.

Buck Nelson and Jimmy Cross were both in sonar, squeezed side by side against the narrow hatch that led into the adjacent computer room. Chief Delaney paced back and forth behind his sonarmen, each of whom were monitoring a specific hydrophone array. With *Florida*'s own noise reduced to an absolute minimum, and listening conditions apparently excellent, they were in a perfect position to analyze any sound that came to them.

Delaney functioned like a concertmaster. His was more a physical job initially as he monitored his sonarmen. He moved from one position to the next, sometimes bending over a man's shoulder and lifting an earpiece to whisper something, occasionally listening over a set of proffered headphones, twisting dials, flipping switches, orchestrating sounds that neither the captain nor the XO could hear.

"Shiiit, Chief, when are you going to share some of that stuff with us?" Cross finally asked in exasperation.

Delaney winked, put his finger to his lips, and continued his performance without a word.

"I'm glad women don't treat me that way," Cross murmured to the captain. "I'd be a mighty sorry son of a bitch ashore."

Nelson was showing signs of increasing irritation. The first indication was an obvious one to his crew because he began smoothing his mostly invisible mustache. But his irritation wasn't caused as much by Chief Delaney's cavalier approach as by the fact that two solid contacts had appeared in *Florida*'s sector. Such occurrences simply didn't happen to a boomer on patrol. If Las Vegas were giving odds, the present situation would definitely be a long shot. When a boomer attracted an audience, it was either a freak happening or a serious problem.

"You may be just as sorry a son of a bitch if we can't figure out who our guests are out there." Nelson shook his head irritably. "I have a nasty feeling about this . . . very nasty."

"Captain, if I might make a suggestion at this point—although I'm sure you've already thought about it . . ." Cross paused. It never hurt to allow the captain to prepare himself. The XO had a habit, one that appealed to a powerful ego like Nelson's, of making an idea appear as if the person he was talking to had originated it. "A Marine would say something like 'lock and load,' or something to that effect, which meant he figured his men better be prepared to fire. That also means better safe than sorry, and it also seems to me that a fire-control solution for our weapons system would be a superb idea at this point." The words came out almost apologetically, as if Cross were relating the words already formed in Nelson's mind.

"You have a way with words, XO. Why don't you step outside and see if you can't set that up for us. And I'll wait here in the dark and watch Delaney play his games."

Less than a minute after Cross moved out into the control room, Delaney suddenly stood erect and folded his arms. It was his signal. His part of the symphony seemed to be completed. Then he stroked his chin thoughtfully for a moment. "It doesn't make sense, Captain."

Nelson leaned forward in anticipation. "Talk to me, Chief."

"We got a contact off our port quarter that keeps increasing speed, or at least that's the way it sounds to us, and I'll put money down that it's one of ours."

Nelson gave no indication of surprise. "Which one?"

"688."

"What's she doing out here?"

Delaney glanced at Nelson curiously. It wasn't the response he'd anticipated. "Beats me, Captain. All we do is try to figure out who's out there, not why."

"You said she's increasing speed. That would mean she's closing us." Nelson had said that more for himself than Delaney. "They're supposed to avoid . . ." His voice drifted off with his thoughts.

"Can't be so sure yet about that one dead astern, sir, but I'd say the same thing—one of ours. Can't get the computer to tell me it's a someone to worry about yet."

"Who? Which?" Nelson hadn't moved from his original position. His voice was soft and distant, as if he were more in touch with an inner self than with Delaney. The only reaction that might have expressed his real concern was a renewed effort to train his mustache. He was stroking it very precisely now.

"Dead astern, Captain. Conditions are good, but that's asking a lot in that situation. If we turned and exposed the entire array, we might just give him a title."

Nelson nodded thoughtfully. Funny how everyone was anticipating his thoughts. "I'd been planning on helping you out anyway, Chief. I thought we'd just ease around to do that at the same time we're exposing our tubes to these guests of ours. Sort of a long, slow turn so they can't figure out what we're doing, and they shouldn't be able to hear much anyway . . . and then . . ."

But they were interrupted by one of the sonarmen. "Chief, if that's a 688 on our port quarter, she's just put on the brakes. I got a definite change in her signal here. Almost drifting in and out."

"That means," Nelson commented slowly, "that either they don't know who we are, or they do and they don't want to run up our ass." He remembered SUBPAC had increased their alert condition, but that had been done before. "So that could be a 688 doing strange things, or someone . . ." He tilted his head to one side and pursed his thin lips. "Someone could have a surprise for us. I can't imagine SUBPAC sending someone out here to play games with us without some kind of warning, at least more than they have. It never makes sense to trust anyone in this life, you know."

"No, sir," Delaney agreed.

"But it's a hell of a lot more fun than we've had in days, isn't it?"

"Yes, sir." The chief was absolutely convinced now that he sure didn't understand what made the captain tick.

"I don't think I can avoid both of them. So we'll let them come nearer. Chief, I'm going to be in control from now on, I think. You let me know about the slightest change in either one of those contacts." He eased by the chief on his way out and added, "You ever have a feeling like I've got now?"

"Yes, sir." Delaney wasn't sure what Nelson was driving at, but he was glad the man was his captain. You survived with men like him.

"Good. I think between us we can handle everything." With that, he was gone.

When the Navy demands information—especially when the Chief of Naval Operations directs that he requires that information instantly—it can be done. The tomorrow-is-good-enough slogan can be tossed out the window. Secure fax lines hum.

Ray Larsen waved the glossy sheets of fax paper in Mark Bennett's direction. "So you've only read these once. You also got those stars because once is all the reading you need. The Navy can't afford to have you take any more time than that. Do you agree with what that says?" It was a copy of Wayne Newell's background investigation for a security clearance. "Is that Wayne Newell they're talking about?"

"Essentially." Bennett appeared startled by the CNO's attitude. "I mean the Newell I knew aboard *Stonewall Jackson* was an outstanding junior officer in every regard, but I didn't waste my time looking into his background. What do you expect after a guy has done sub school, nuclear power, and tours on a boomer and an attack boat before he shows up?" He spread his hands in question. "You assume that the security clearances in his jacket are exactly what they say. So you don't ask him about his family," he concluded defensively.

"I always did," Larsen responded instantly, pointing his finger at Bennett's chest. "I knew everything about my wardroom on every command I ever had."

"You never commanded a boomer, Ray . . . and stop pointing that goddamn thing at me," he said angrily. "I thought you got that out of your system."

"Sorry. How about you, Neil? Didn't you ever snoop?"

Arrow appeared troubled. "Not to that extent. Not like you, I guess. I have to go along with Mark. If someone passes a complete background investigation, there's a right to privacy. What is there in that wad of paper that says there's anything wrong with Wayne?"

"Naval Intelligence says the investigators they sent can't find any family records back in his hometown, nothing to establish his background, for Christ sake."

"I remember Myra Newell telling me that he was an only child and that his parents died right after he came to Berkeley, even before she'd met him. Everything he got, she said, he got on his own. I always respected that. Wouldn't you?" he asked defensively.

"That's beside the point."

"What the real point is here," Robbie Newman said, "is that we're chasing rainbows with that report. Four hours ago it didn't exist in our minds. Ray asks every agency that ever snooped into someone's life to come up with a report super quick and that's what we get. Wayne Newell had all the necessary clearances. His nose is squeaky clean. Fitness reports are all close to 4.0, including the ones from the man who is Mr. Undersea Warfare and sits at this table with us. All it says is that the man has no past before he showed up on the Berkeley campus, according to old records—or no old records, if you want to look at it that way." He leaned forward with his elbows on the table. They were in Neil Arrow's office. "Have any of you ever been in a town clerk's office in a small town and seen how records are handled?"

There was no response. Larsen fidgeted but thought better of speaking.

"I have. I did a little looking after my own roots once. It's entirely possible that the files on his family were pulled when his parents died, to finish everything off just right, and then the phone rang and the clerk never got back to completing the job and the files went out with the trash months later. End of the Newell family. It happens."

Ray Larsen plucked nervously with a fingernail at an imaginary something between his front teeth. Neil Arrow nodded without commenting. Mark Bennett had nothing more to say and shuffled through the sheaf of papers until he acted like he'd come to a page he was looking for.

"I'm not saying that's what happened," Newman said defensively. "I'm just saying that we can't run off and convict a man for lack of information."

"Does anyone else have any other ideas?" the CNO finally asked. "If you can't offer anything solid, then I go back to my original idea that we could have a maverick out there who has the ability to sneak up on one of our boomers and fire torpedos before they know what's going on." It sounded absurd when he thought about it, and not much better now. But there was nothing else to go on.

"How do you explain the other hundred thirty men on *Pasadena?* Do you figure they're sitting on their asses eating bonbons?" Arrow inquired.

"I don't." Larsen's response was more a shout of anger at himself than the others around the table. "I don't even know how he could get to *Alaska* or *Nevada* from where he was either. I couldn't come up with a reason if you were squeezing my nuts. I have no answers. All I know is that *Pasadena* has not responded to our emergency signal. Either she's a goner, too, or she's involved in something I don't understand." He licked his lips and looked around the table at each of his friends. "With a report on a man like this one—regardless of how fast it's been prepared—we wouldn't send him out in command of one of our 688's today. If whatever I'm reading into this is correct, the only way it could have happened is to have the Newell family records doctored when a background investigation was conducted, and then to have them disappear once the Navy was satisfied." His glance was threatening. "I'm building sand castles. Tell me I'm wrong," he growled.

Robbie Newman was about to respond when there was a sharp knock at the door.

"Come," Arrow called out.

His flag lieutenant slipped quietly into the room to hand him a clipboard containing a single message which Arrow read while the young officer muttered something softly in his ear. Arrow removed the message and waved the officer out the door politely.

"Perhaps the Russians do have us grabbing our nuts," Arrow said. "If you remember that intelligence ship of theirs, the one way up north, it's got itself in bad trouble in a storm. It seems it sent out a Mayday and the Russians are apparently throwing everything but the kitchen sink into the rescue effort—almost like the General Secretary was aboard. That's not like them, is it?"

"I'll just bet that goddamn ship has a lot to do with our problems," Mark Bennett said.

"I'll bet that has something to do with *Pasadena* and that fellow Newell," the CNO growled. He'd already taken a dislike to Wayne Newell, though he wouldn't have recognized the man if he'd walked into the room. "You don't sink boomers from an intelligence ship more than a thousand miles away. But that Russian ship did have some damn sophisticated satellite-communications equipment on it." He was picking at the same tooth with the same fingernail. "We're closer to that ship than they are. Why don't we just throw everything we've got into trying to rescue it, too. And we'll tell them exactly what we're going to do to see how excited they get. They might just want to see it at the bottom rather than have us get our hands on it. Go on, Neil." Larsen pointed at the telephone in front of Arrow. "Let's show them how we go about rescue operations. And while we're at it, let's play a little mind game," he added thoughtfully. "Let's tell them *Pasadena* seems to be missing and we're going after her with everything we've got. That ought to get a rise out of them if I'm anywhere close to right."

CHAPTER FOURTEEN

The head of the KGB stared rigidly at the phone on his desk. It was almost as if it had just talked to him . . . by itself. It was an unhappy moment. But it wasn't the phone that had spoken. It had been the voice of Captain Mersanka in the outer office. Her crisp, no-nonsense voice had come over the desk communicator—a shock, since his mind had been a million miles away—to report that the commandant of Lubyanka Prison, his own prison, *the KGB's dreaded Lubyanka,* wished to speak with him on the phone. He'd automatically reached for the instrument before realizing that he'd left strict orders that no calls be forwarded to him, at least none from those junior to him. There was enough to be concerned over without being bothered by incidentals.

He depressed the button to open the line to her desk. "I said no calls, Captain." He kept his voice low and the words were spoken as if he were talking to a child.

"Yes, sir." There was no change in her voice. There never was, nor would there be if she could help it. Captain Mersanka had been chosen for this job for her lack of emotion and her ability to put off some of the most important people in the Soviet Union. "I said you were not taking calls, sir, but he interrupted me to explain how vital this was." She paused to make it clear that she had made a decision for him. "It is vital, sir." Still no emotion to convey the real reason that she'd violated his orders.

"Very well," he answered wearily. He placed extreme trust in Mersanka and would continue to do so. Her judgment was faultless. It had been a lousy day so far, and a call from his own Lubyanka made the remaining hours seem even more ominous. He lifted the phone. "Yes." This time his voice carried the irritation of someone being interrupted at something very important by a junior.

"My apologies, General." The commandant rushed along without the niceties he normally began such a conversation with. "I have some unexpected visitors who have been placed in my custody . . . General Malik, for one . . ."

The commander of the Strategic Rocket Forces!

". . . who is in the isolation section after what appears to be a drug overdose of some kind. Also General Surkov . . ."

The assistant to the Minister of Defense!

The commandant paused to catch his breath. "I understand from a contact within the General Secretary's office that there will be more . . ."

What was the General Secretary doing! How could this be done without the head of the KGB? And his own prison! There were a few other names the commandant provided before he finally paused to catch his breath, though none as important as Malik or Surkov. And right under his nose, without his knowledge. But it was obvious that the older, more conservative ones were the victims of . . . of what? Why was this taking place when the nation was in a position of extremis? Why . . . ?

"On whose orders?" the KGB chief growled. "Where are the orders coming from?" But he already knew the answer if the commandant had a contact in the General Secretary's office.

"An accusation of treason," the commandant responded with gravity, "from the General Secretary is all that is needed in a situation like this."

The man couldn't have known about the loss of the American submarines, or the discussions that had been taking place among that very select gathering in the General Secretary's office. None of that group had been selected for imprisonment, *but some of those who supported them had been.* The commandant would, of course, be accepting of any order that came from the General Secretary. The next step would be to call around until he found out why this purge was taking place. *And his own prison . . . without his knowledge . . .*

The KGB head hung up the phone without another word. He wasn't about to provide any comment that the commandant could use, and the man was obviously fishing. Let him find out from someone else. But what the hell was the General Secretary doing? Was he sending a message to the Americans? No, not in this manner. It would take too long for the U.S. underground apparatus to learn of this. He had to be solidifying his position to . . . to what?

He wondered who the commandant would call next. Today was probably the greatest day in the man's career, or at least the most prestigious haul even for a prison of that stature. The man was persistent, and he would keep up his calling and questioning until he was satisfied. Something of this magnitude was a forecast of even greater things to come.

Then another thought struck the head of the KGB. How many more were going to end up in Lubyanka? And, if he hadn't been allowed to be part of this plan, not even notified that a major change in policy was taking place under his nose, would he be selected in a future roundup, maybe today, maybe tomorrow?

He pressed the button and told Captain Mersanka, "Have my car brought around to the front. I will be ready in five minutes." But he was careful not to tell the captain where he intended to go. She was too honest. Once he was in the car, he could use the telephone there to make his calls and find out exactly what was going on. It was much wiser to remain on the move at a time like this.

Simultaneously in another part of Moscow, the General Secretary was enjoying himself immensely for the first time in the past few days. He had done exactly what his wife had recommended—the conservative element within the Kremlin was under close control for the present. He had just given himself the gift of more time to work things out. He still had no idea what the end result would be, but he knew that the Soviet Union would not be prepared to launch a first strike in the next twelve hours. That was probably the maximum amount of time he could buy, unless the Americans allowed him the luxury of more for some unknown reason.

His military was on full alert, but they were also firmly under his control at this moment. This was one of the most important decisions he'd ever made—and it had originated with his wife! Now that he considered the situation more closely, she never had found the commander of the Strategic Rocket Forces appealing. "Too aggressive," she said. And now he had a general much closer to him assuming command of that element of the military. If a launch became necessary, it would be under his own terms.

"Dear, I'm going to take a nap." His wife rose to her feet a bit unsteadily. She'd drunk more of that pertsovka than he'd imagined she could. "I don't think I could keep my eyes open another minute."

When she left the room, he noted the level of the liquid in the bottle. It was two-thirds empty. He couldn't believe they'd drunk that much. Luckily, there was more in the freezer in the small apartment attached to his office. And food—that's what he really needed right now—there was food there and he was feeling very hungry. His stomach always acted up these days whenever he drank like that. A bit of food would make him feel much better, and he was sure it would help his wife when she awoke.

He couldn't imagine he'd be getting much sleep. And he knew he'd have to call the others soon. The Lubyanka situation would soon be common knowledge around the other offices in the building. They would have to understand there had been a shift in the power structure.

There was one other aspect of the situation he'd been making a specific effort to avoid—the American boomer

Florida. She was the final critical target in the Pacific, and her coordinates had been transmitted to that killer submarine before he'd had the opportunity to plan his next moves. Right this moment she could be in the sights of the hunter, unaware that another American submarine was about to send her to the bottom. He wished there was a way she could be warned, but that would be an admission of guilt and more than likely presage a first launch by the United States.

There had to be a way out of this puzzle, somehow, but he had no idea how . . . except to put away the vodka that offered so much solace. . . .

"Mom!" The curl of cigarette smoke rising above Connie Steel's blond hair had been sure to elicit a cry of exasperation from her daughter, Alycia. "You're smoking a cigarette." Her voice carried the high-pitched whine of the TV teenager to a new level of perfection. It was a practiced art form.

"I'm old enough." Connie made no effort to turn and look over her shoulder, for it would only encourage another obnoxious outburst. She'd been staring down the hill to the harbor at a tall-necked crane lifting crates from a railroad car on the naval-base siding. The Steels' home was situated in the hills, an older single-story building reminiscent of the Hawaii of mid-century. It was in a location people would have killed for, yet it remained unostentatious, providing a spectacular view of the harbor below and the Pacific beyond. It had been built many years before by someone who intended to keep that view well above the tree line without the necessity of clearing below.

"I never saw you smoke before." Alycia came around in front of the outdoor chaise and stared grimly at the cigarette before looking down at her mother.

Connie glanced up and smiled unconvincingly. This wasn't going to be the start of another family argument if she could help it. "I smoked years ago, and I did occasionally when you were little girls." She looked out of the corner of her eye at the cigarette. They sure as hell didn't make them like they used to. This one was half filter and tasted like she imagined a cereal box might. "I'm not going to start smoking like a chimney, if that's what you're worried about. They don't taste anywhere near as good as they used to."

Alycia appeared unconvinced. "They give you cancer. They'll kill you. It even happens to people who live around smokers without ever picking one up. I can't stand the thought of that," she added with another self-serving whine.

"I said this wasn't going to be a habit."

"Why'd you start again?" Alycia persisted, flopping down on a beach chair and dropping her school books beside her.

"I had lunch with Myra Newell yesterday. She smokes—"

"And she offered you one. That's an absolutely awful thing to do to a friend."

"Don't interrupt. It's rude. No, she didn't offer me one. I asked, she refused, I insisted, and finally she broke down and gave me one." Connie sighed wistfully and took a tentative puff. "It tasted better yesterday after a good lunch than it does today."

"She shouldn't have done it. I'm going to tell Kathy so tomorrow at school." Alycia and Kathy Newell were in the same class.

"You'll do nothing of the kind, young lady." She jammed the cigarette down, where it lay smoldering in the grass. "Her mother had nothing to do with my buying these cigarettes, and you won't embarrass either of us by doing that."

Alycia pouted. "She's a bad influence."

"Maybe you have some growing up to do," Connie said in retaliation, regretting it instantly. That was only inviting the teenage mind to react. She sensed hints of that family argument starting, the one she'd intended to avoid at all costs. It was time to retreat a bit. "You don't like her, do you? I think sometimes you judge adults a little too critically."

"She's not so bad . . ." Alycia began hesitantly. "It's him I don't like." She'd been looking down at her hands. Now her eyes settled on her mother's face. "He doesn't like kids, particularly girls." It was hard to explain something like that to your mother. "Commander Newell is so . . . so macho," she decided. "He likes to talk about things that men like, but he doesn't understand girls. Kathy can't even talk to him. Half the time he puts her off, or sometimes he just walks away. Besides, he doesn't even like Kathy. . . ."

"That's ridiculous. Kathy's his daughter. Of course he loves her." Connie absentmindedly shook out another cigarette and paused to light it. "Where do you get ideas like that?" Irritation once again crept into her voice. "Don't you have better things to do?"

Greta Steel wandered into the backyard and collapsed into another chair while a large exaggerated yawn was allowed to escape. Then she sat upright and pointed at the cigarette. "Why are you doing that . . . smoking, I mean?" Her tone was much like her sister's.

"Because your older sister is driving me to it," Connie answered sarcastically. Regardless of how good or bad it tasted, she wasn't about to be harassed into putting it out now. That would be a sign of defeat, and she wasn't about to let them get the upper hand.

"I wish Daddy was here now. He'd make you put it out," Greta said, and slumped back into the chair.

"I wish he were here, too, because he'd tell you both to either say something nice or leave me alone." She took a deep drag and blew it out in a long stream. "Why don't the two of you go off and do something worthwhile until the three of us can talk pleasantly to each other."

"I just—" Greta began.

"Now. Please. I'm being nice. Please leave me to myself for a while." She displayed a practiced expression the girls always understood. It was worth saving that one until she really meant it.

They left, hesitantly, pouting, mad at their mother because she wouldn't respond the way they expected, mad at themselves because they could tell she wanted to be in another world for a while. They'd attempted to bring her back to their own much smaller one too soon.

If Ben were here, the three of them wouldn't be picking at each other like this. She wouldn't have bought a pack of cigarettes either. Somehow there was a different atmosphere whenever he was home. Was he a peacemaker? No, not really. There was no need to make peace when he was in port. They never bickered with each other.

Ben Steel certainly wasn't a Disneyland dad either. There was discipline when he was there, but it was never hard, never overbearing. It was simply that everyone was expected to do their own job, "their own thing," as the girls said, without questioning why they did it. It was done in a spirit of family cooperation and they all enjoyed it. That was why they had so much time for those treasured family trips each weekend. No, he wasn't a Disneyland dad by any means. He was a family man pure and simple.

So many of the other men—she'd heard the stories from other wives too many times—came back and had trouble if their homes didn't run like the submarines they'd just left. Everything needed a place, a purpose, a reason, and an explanation if there wasn't. It was so much easier for them if their homes were organized just like their submarines, so they didn't have to shift personalities when they came ashore. Wayne Newell was like that; Myra had reaffirmed that yesterday.

But Ben Steel came home to get away from the Navy. He couldn't get out of his uniform and into his old, rumpled shorts any faster each afternoon. Homework with the girls was a high point of his evening during the week. Dinner was a time for all of them to plan the day trips around the island, especially to Makaha. Alycia and Greta always waited for him to complain about their bikinis, and they'd bring it up if he forgot. Yet he never once criticized them—they'd never done anything on those trips that required a lecture. He used to tease Connie afterward, when they were home in bed on a Sunday night, that the girls acted just like the ones in the old "beach party" movies, all show and no action. They never gave him reason to believe otherwise.

The other thing he liked was their solitary walks, just the

two of them. Sometimes it was on a deserted beach while the girls went "trolling for boys," as Ben called it. Other times, it was just a stroll down the hill from their home at night. He said it was good for the mind and the body, but that his aging body was more demanding recently.

The nights on their hill were perfect, especially if there had been showers that afternoon. The dampness heightened the aroma of the flowers, especially the exotic ones, creating billowy, deep perfumes that filled the darkness with images of their daytime colors. The discordant evening sounds became special also.

The longer they lived on the hill, the more both of them learned about the insects and animals that lived there with them. Connie remembered how amazed she was by Ben's knowledge of the night creatures. He could explain which ones survived by eating the undergrowth and which ones lived off each other—"the food chain is alive and well" was how he put it. Those walks just by themselves, as if the rest of the world were a million miles away, created wonderful memories. Sometimes, when they got back to the house and the girls were asleep, they made love in the front yard with the night sounds and aromas enveloping them. There must have been magic in that old house!

Privacy was something that Ben decided he'd probably always treasured, but he'd failed to realize it until they were married. In high school, in the Academy, even the first few years in submarines, he was always part of a group that did everything as a unit and succeeded because of that fact. It was Connie who taught him that the smallest unit, and the most meaningful one by far, could be made up of two people. Children became a part of that unit, but both of them understood that eventually those children would leave to develop a family of their own. Then, it would be just Ben and Connie Steel again—and that was the most vital relationship either of them would ever experience. They both vowed, silently more often than verbally, that they each would do everything possible to make their life together special for each other.

When Ben was ashore, he socialized with Navy people only as a necessity of the job. He consistently made a special effort to coordinate everything else around the two of them in their early years of marriage, dreaming of the day they would have their own home. As they transferred from one assignment to the next, it became an obsession.

That house on the hill provided the final element of their relationship—privacy. Because a career in submarines meant living close to the people you worked with on a twenty-four-hour basis, you got to know every possible thing about them. For Ben Steel there was nothing like escaping to that house to unwind from the tremendous responsibilities he carried as *Manchester*'s commanding officer. Most of all, it was where Connie waited for him.

He never talked submarines when he was home, and he avoided it when they were with other people, unless he was dragged into a conversation. Ben Steel could separate business and pleasure like no man she'd ever met.

Connie squinted at the late-afternoon sun, lit another cigarette, took a hesitant puff, coughed, and tossed it in the grass. Then she wiped away a tear that had begun to course down her cheek after a long struggle to hold it back. It was hard to think such thoughts when she was alone like this.

God, how she missed that man! The house was so empty without him.

Ben Steel remembered very few times in his career when he had found himself in such a quandary. He stood silently on the starboard side of the control room. While his eyes seemed fixed on one of the fire-control displays, he saw nothing. His arms were folded across his chest, his mind oblivious to the sounds around him.

Peter Simonds had left him alone, determining intuitively that it was better to kibitz with the OOD. Eventually the captain would come to some type of decision on their next move. That was a given, he knew, after working so long with Steel.

There was nothing hidden or implied in the orders

Lieutenant Commander Burch had delivered when *Manchester* fished him out of the Pacific. COMSUBPAC had made their mission as clear as possible. Two Tridents were missing. To send a warning to all boomers could tip off the Russians if they were involved, possibly even cause other subs to be sunk before a solution could be found. *Florida* was considered the next likely target by the admirals in Pearl Harbor. But she was in peril from an unknown source and would know no more than they did. Steel had been ordered to her sector to screen the boomer from harm and engage any enemy submarine that appeared to be challenging her.

He had yet to establish sonar contact with *Florida*. That was troubling in itself. It might even mean they were too late. But they now had passive contact with another submarine. It was a natural assumption that such a contact would be enemy because certainly no American submarine was expected to be anywhere near that sector. *Manchester* was the *only* U.S. submarine ordered into that area. Yet that contact had finally been designated as a 688-class. And soon after, David Hall thought it could be *Pasadena,* a sister ship, Wayne Newell's ship. *It didn't make sense—such a coincidence couldn't occur in a situation like this!*

Wayne Newell . . . Wayne Newell. Was it a coincidence? They had ended up at nuclear power school together, then forgotten each other until they bunked together on *Stonewall Jackson.* Their wives had become such good friends in those days, and it was only the letters between the women that had kept them in contact until they both arrived in Pearl to take command of sister ships at the same time. It seemed that every time he turned around at a critical time, there was Wayne. Coincidence?

And now, were they in contact once again in a sector in the Pacific neither of them would ever have any reason to have been, except for . . . coincidence? Steel considered the quiet, introspective Newell, equally as talented as any other C.O. in the boats, maybe more than most, but never outgoing or competitive, as others would expect. Of course, the element of competition was there, but it never came to the surface with Newell. He always appeared bland, neutral even, yet there was never any doubt that he meant to be better than anyone else. He just was going about it in his own way. That could be frustrating to aggressive officers who assumed the way to succeed was to face the competition at the line of scrimmage and then charge into the fray like a fullback. Weren't those the rules of the game?

No, they were never the rules Wayne Newell played by. He preferred to do his job very quietly, and in the end seemed to have done it better than almost any of his peers. That was why he was the captain of a superbly performing submarine. You always had to look over your shoulder to find Wayne. Except . . . except here he was in the exact same sector . . .

"Captain." David Hall was standing in the entrance to sonar. "We have another contact—an intermittent one—directly on the bow," he added tentatively.

Steel raised his head slightly, his lower lip between his teeth, and glanced toward Hall. His arms remained folded. "And?"

Hall shrugged. His captain was usually more animated. "The chief doesn't want to say yet. It's faint."

"Could be our boomer."

"I don't know yet, sir." He looked quickly over his shoulder as he was stepping back into sonar. "As soon as I . . ." Then he shrugged again, since both he and Steel knew that the captain would be the first to know any new information.

"Captain, I could add a couple of knots," Peter Simonds suggested. "It might give us a better picture sooner."

Steel nodded his assent. "Go ahead." It was logical. He should have thought of that himself. Unless the laws of physics were playing strange games with sonar conditions, *Manchester* wasn't sneaking up on anyone. It was more like a pack of dogs circling and sniffing before one of them started a fight. It was a simple matter of who was who—who was the good guy and who was the bad guy?

"Contact to port appears to have slowed," came the report from sonar. *Pasadena* was never mentioned. The name had yet to be entered in the log. Their target-motion analysis was constant at this point. The contact's speed couldn't be calculated exactly, but a change of speed could be assumed by checking their relative position. At best, it was a rough estimate.

"She's probably got us . . . if we got her," Simonds commented.

"We should be at battle stations . . ." Steel said. It seemed more a comment than an order.

The OOD looked curiously in his direction. For the past few hours the crew had considered themselves as close to battle stations as could be. That was what the XO had ordered—stand easy at battle stations.

". . . because we don't know what we have," Steel concluded, muttering in a voice so low he could barely be heard. "Where's Burch?"

"Torpedo room."

Of course he was.

"Tell him to come up here, super quick."

The SEAL was standing beside Steel in less than forty seconds.

"I need to know your exact conversation with Admiral Arrow." The voice that normally boomed in a confident, John Wayne manner had been soft and tentative for some time now. "Did he expect any other submarines to be in *Florida*'s sector, any at all?" His lips were a thin line across clenched teeth.

"Negative. He said no one else gets near *Florida*. That was why you were supposed to have a special code to alert her over active sonar, the one I gave you when I came aboard."

"And that's what keeps them from shooting at us?"

"He said that normally they'd pick us up before we found them. They should be able to figure out who we are, but there're no guarantees around a boat that's not supposed to be located by anyone. Boomers are quieter, I guess."

"Supposed to be," Steel agreed. "And if we didn't send that signal?"

"Like I said, their orders are to take nothing for granted.

Anything that gets near their position without a definite positive ID is fair game."

"What would happen if one of our own submarines wandered into a boomer's sector unawares?" He'd known the answer since his days on *Stonewall Jackson,* but this was the Steel method of clearing the mind for a decision. He was unhappy with himself and what he'd decided moments before.

"Admiral Arrow explained that they don't. No one has permission to transit a boomer's assigned sector in peacetime. The only time it might happen was during DEFCON ONE, and then every boat would hopefully be issued the appropriate sonar code to transmit if they ran into a boomer by chance."

"No other submarine—and that means absolutely none —should be in this sector, then," Steel concluded cautiously to himself. His expression showed that it was still a question that required confirmation. But his tone of voice indicated that he'd confirmed what he'd concluded earlier.

Burch wrinkled his forehead, thinking he'd made that clear already. "Absolutely, Captain."

Steel walked, almost tiptoed, the short distance to sonar and stuck his head inside. "Has there been any use of active sonar whatsoever from your contact to port?" Once again his lower lip was tightly clenched between his teeth.

"Nothing, Captain. That's something we would have picked up right away. They're playing kitty cat." Creeping . . . slowly . . . silently . . . through the grass . . . more a shadow than an entity . . .

Steel turned back to Burch. "You said other SEALs in your unit were headed on similar missions. Where?"

"I wasn't told that. But it was other parts of the Pacific. I have no idea where," he responded irritably, "but I know damn well that this was the only boat assigned to *Florida's* sector."

"Well, Commander, my chief sonarman is willing to put his nuts on the line that our sister ship *Pasadena* is off our port bow right now . . . right here in this sector, acting just like they belong here. How does that fit?"

Burch folded his arms stubbornly. His reaction wouldn't have been any different if he were facing the President. "You asked for Admiral Arrow's specific conversation. I told you everything I know."

Peter Simonds had sidled over until he was a third party in the discussion. "It seems to me that maybe we should try to close *Pasadena* and ask her what she's doing here.

Steel rubbed his chin thoughtfully before shaking his head. "Not a peep. Our orders say to make contact with *Florida* and protect her." He glanced warily toward sonar. "I have no absolute guarantee that's *Pasadena* out there. It only sounds like her. We have our orders to carry out. If that's Wayne Newell, he can make the first move."

There was no pecking order at sea at a time like this. Nowhere was it stated that the senior officers of two submarines—neither of which knew why the other was in a restricted area—were required to ascertain the intentions of the other. You operated independently until you were otherwise ordered, and you didn't stick your nose in the other guy's business. You especially kept your own counsel when the hairs on the back of your neck seemed to operate by themselves. *And you followed your instincts.*

Simonds pushed his glasses back on his nose. Steel had a habit of explaining himself to his XO. This time Simonds had no idea what was going through the captain's mind. "Yes, sir."

"We are at battle stations?" Steel asked, rubbing his eyes tiredly.

"Yes, sir." The XO was about to explain that since entering *Florida's* sector they had been about as close to battle stations as they could be. He'd made an exception—a percentage of the men could sleep near their stations until they had a solid contact. No one was sleeping now.

"Turn away a little from that contact to port, the one Moroney thinks is *Pasadena.* I want to try to keep our distance. Let's close the other if we can. That should be *Florida.*" He turned to Burch. "When you get back down below, you tell the chief he may just be using one of his torpedos shortly. It better be a record when he reloads."

"You don't think that's *Pasadena* out there, Captain?" Simonds asked curiously. He needed assurance that he still understood Steel.

For the first time since he'd considered the situation, Steel realized he hadn't been sharing his thoughts with his executive officer. He smiled broadly. "XO," he said, as if he'd just seen Simonds for the first time. "I haven't the vaguest idea what's going on. For the time being, I don't believe anything. And when you don't believe anything, you better try to do everything you can to protect your ass. So that's what we're doing until we understand things a little better. We'll proceed with the idea we may fire on either contact as soon as they're in range . . . as quiet as they are," he concluded softly. "And you better bet they already wonder what we're doing out here. I think everybody's creeping." He raised his eyebrows. "We're all a lot closer to each other than it seems. I want to be ready to shoot . . . perhaps a snapshot if I'm not careful," he mused.

Jack Tar raised his head when Myra Newell walked into the room. He continued to wag his tail even after she walked past him to stare out the window. She tapped the glass with a long fingernail, then turned and looked down at him. Hoping for attention was the hallmark of a good family dog. The tail moved faster.

"You'd much rather have him around than me, wouldn't you?"

The dog rose to its feet and came over to nuzzle her hand.

"But you'll take any affection you can get," she said, scratching behind his ears.

Once the fingers slowed down, the animal plunked itself on the floor and scratched. Myra moved across the room to the sofa and sat down, running a finger across the surface of the coffee table. No dust. Then she remembered that she'd run a cloth across everything just that morning. Jack Tar noticed she was seated and trotted over to rest his head in her lap, liquid brown eyes looking up at her, his ears forward to indicate pleasure.

"Any port in a storm," she murmured, smoothing the fur on top of his head, then scratching his ears with both hands. "Do you miss him?"

The dog continued to look up, ears cocked. Each time she spoke to Jack Tar, he acted as if he understood every word. He was a friend, those deep brown eyes always sympathetic to this understanding voice.

Was it unhappiness at times like this, or was it just insecurity, that forced Myra to dwell on past situations? Her thoughts, as always when she was alone, returned to the last time Wayne was with them. It was becoming an obsession, and she was intelligent enough to be irritated by this control over her mind. *Damn.* She was growing less enchanted with this game, this habitual process, wishing something else— anything, anything at all—would occupy her mind. But her life was too often divided into two distinct worlds, the lonely one when he was at sea and the tense one when he was home.

Pasadena had been alongside the tender for an extended availability the last time, so it had been a longer stay. The first three weeks hadn't really been so bad. Wayne had been fairly easy to get along with. He was still as tense, of course, still bringing the boat's problems home with him each day. But he'd appeared as relaxed as he'd ever been. Charlie probably had more of his time because they could throw a football together, and twice Wayne took him fishing.

His daughter, as always, wasn't as lucky. Kathy had the misfortune to be a female child growing up. She was also becoming quite attractive. At the age of fourteen she had naturally wavy hair, a clear complexion, and her figure was blossoming. Wayne Newell was more conscious each day of her rapid maturing. As much as he loved her, as much as he tried to accept this natural process, he grew increasingly uncomfortable. Each time *Pasadena* returned to port, Kathy was a different girl, a little more the independent teenager, hair a little longer, perhaps another touch of makeup—no longer *his little girl*.

While Charlie could go just about anywhere on his own, Kathy had to account for every minute outside the house. When a date came to their door to pick her up, Wayne treated the boy like one of his sailors, quizzing the youngster about every moment of their evening until Kathy left in tears one night.

The second three weeks at home, Wayne's conversations with Kathy grew more limited. When he spoke to her, it was to complain or correct—her manners, her grades, her attitude, her clothes, her lipstick, her boyfriends. It became a litany that gnawed at the household itself, until all of them were on edge.

When Myra confronted him with the damage he was causing, it was the first time he'd ever lashed out at her so vehemently. He shouted and cursed and gave every indication that he might actually strike her, though it never happened. He apologized sincerely the next morning, ashamed enough of himself to ask her forgiveness.

It was one of many personality quirks she observed that year. None of them were new, none of them even enough to drag out in the open. Each by itself was minor, but taken together they troubled her greatly. She loved Wayne Newell, but she saw his work—though she later determined that perhaps it was more him than the Navy—changing him into another individual.

It was all so subtle at first that she was sure it had to be his work—the rigors of Navy life—that was gradually taking him away from them. It couldn't be another woman. He had no time to cultivate another relationship. But others had seen it, too.

Dick Makin mentioned it casually at a party one night. It was an XO's responsibility to understand everything about his captain, and he was doing what he had to do, asking if his captain's wife had also noticed the man wholly responsible for a nuclear submarine was changing. She said little, answering only that she thought Wayne seemed to be working too hard. But she knew Dick saw the answer in her eyes, and she understood when he hugged her that night at the door and said—"I'll take care of him out there for you."

Myra could feel the tears coming to her eyes, and she struggled to hold them back, ashamed to admit that she could actually think herself into such an emotional state. *She had to be stronger than this if she was to hold their marriage together.* Dick Makin couldn't do that for her. And with that thought, she lost her composure completely.

No communications with SUBPAC!

The *word*—any word . . . whatever word might be hot at the time—was sure to spread through a Navy ship like wildfire. In a submarine, where men were more confined and quickly learned to depend on each other, the word moved even faster. The fact that Wally Snyder had reported to the captain that communications with the outside world had ceased, that there were no messages, *nothing,* when they last rose to periscope depth, troubled each man in a different way. They had no idea that their communications with the outside world had been totally under the control of SSV-516. When the link connecting her with the satellite was destroyed, *Pasadena* was completely cut off because the other circuits were being jammed. Moscow had failed to consider such an accident. They also had never considered how it would affect submariners who thought the world above them was at war.

How many days had they been under this stress? When did the conflict actually start? And where? They were unaware of any actual declaration of war. Was the Soviet Union the only enemy? Did it all begin in Europe, as the experts had anticipated? Did the Warsaw Pact nations pour hundreds of thousands of troops through the Fulda Gap to deluge the NATO countries? Or had it come down to threats between the two superpowers which eventually escalated to a missile exchange?

They knew only what they had been told. The captain of a

submarine not only holds each man's life in his hands, he also controls the minds of his crew. Their information comes at his sole discretion. Wayne Newell was both their leader and *Pasadena*'s propaganda minister. Whatever he chose to tell them had to be accepted, of necessity, as gospel.

He had told them that America was in danger. He had told them that *Pasadena* had been selected for a vital mission that just might save their country and their loved ones. One hundred thirty of them had functioned as one for him, sinking two Soviet boomers—*even though they gave every indication of being American*—because *he* had released classified information to them about a horrifying masking device the Russians had invented to confuse them. And *he* had accepted the lonely responsibilities that came with his position when challenged by members of the crew—Newell placed those who questioned his absolute authority as captain under ship's arrest and confined them before they could contaminate the rest of the crew with their mutinous ideas.

With each fearsome dollop of knowledge that came to them, they continued to hold together as one, accepting the fact that "they must face a lonely challenge with bravery, as so many of their seagoing forebears had done through the centuries." Those words had been a bit much for some of them, especially the older ones, but they were willing to be led. Their captain had successfully inspired his crew with that tradition, and they were proud of themselves in facing such adversity. Their minds were controlled by one man, and they had to place their trust in him. They had no other choices, no options.

Until this moment, they had been the hunter in a chaotic world. But now the situation had changed radically. They were closing another contact, ordered to sink one more boomer that sounded just like one of their own. But a second submarine—a "bird dog," their captain had called it—was out there, and its job was to protect the boomer, to sink them before they could hit their target. It could be nothing other than a fast, highly maneuverable submarine like their own, a lethal threat that could not be overlooked.

Now they were facing an unseen enemy—if it was truly an enemy . . . for fear spawned doubt—with the knowledge that there no longer was any contact with their country. Had there been a nuclear attack on the U.S.? Were they now fighting for what had been, rather than what once existed? Had their families perished in a nuclear holocaust?

Was there anything worth fighting for at this point? Whatever the answer might be, their training dictated that they see their mission through to the end, whether the ultimate result was protection of their country or revenge for its destruction.

Newell discerned this attitudinal change, subtle at first in its implications, almost instantly. Makin sensed it, too, as did the department heads and chiefs and leading petty officers. It could be seen in the eyes of each man. *And smell*—the nose revealed a great deal about men in conflict. Even today's nuclear submarines with their complex atmosphere control systems could not erase that unique aroma arising from tension and fear. This was uniquely different from the hard-earned sweat of a working man. It was musky, oily, and its source could be discerned simply by looking into a crewman's eyes. They told what a man was thinking even if he kept it to himself, and they explained why the scrubbers could never cleanse the air completely.

A kill was essential. Every single man understood that equally as well as Newell. Without a successful attack, and one executed very soon, *Pasadena* would be on the defensive. He knew the boomer must know he was out there. She'd gone strangely silent, or at least slowed enough so that sonar no longer had a contact. That meant any fire-control solution at this stage would be based on what the computer had developed up to the boomer's last known position. The advantage had been lost!

The mouse was now tracking the cat—the boomer must have its sonar array streamed aft—developing its own target analysis. That would be accurate, much more so than his own. Would they be suspicious enough to fire first? Although Wayne Newell was now convinced in his own mind that he was facing an enemy submarine, he remained able to discern the fact that his crew might be confused by his approach.

It all depended on who got the first shot.

How much time had passed since he was last in sonar? Newell wondered. He'd given Steve Thompson thirty seconds to straighten out that sonarman, Dixon. *That shit about the boomer's signature had better be taken care of.* He glanced about control quickly for his executive officer. *Where the hell was Makin?* Then he remembered he'd told him to make sure Wally Snyder was secured in his quarters. *Don't let stress twist your mind from your mission, Newell.* There was so much going on . . .

For a moment, eyes closed, he was back at the Charm School outside Moscow. The KGB instructors had stayed close to his group for just a few weeks before turning them completely over to the Americans. For a few days he'd been suspicious of the Americans attempting to gain control of him. But it never happened. It was months later that it came out in a discussion with his comrades that the Americans had been so brainwashed that they'd given up completely. They were no longer even capable of the desire to convert the Russian students, nor did they seem interested in escaping. Many of them had acquired Russian wives and were raising families within the bounds of the Charm School. The will to resist had been torn from their minds. And, he now wondered, had Wayne Newell been so brainwashed that he was incapable of going over to the Americans? Was that why, after all those years, after the family he'd sired, that he still remained loyal to a country he left over twenty years ago?

His eyes were suddenly wide open. Had anyone noticed? No—not a soul.

In the background he heard the diving officer cautioning the stern planesman about his bubble. A rumble of voices came from sonar, then an angry shout, then silence. They were tight. Every single one of them was tight to the breaking point.

How long could he control them?

How much time?

Once again Newell became aware of the eyes. The *word* moved quickly. *Pasadena* had turned north and increased her speed to close her target. They were attacking. But what the hell was going on? There were no communications with the outside world . . . *if one still existed!* The XO was absent from the control room, placing an officer in hack. There were angry voices in sonar arguing about the contact . . . the target that had gone silent. *The word . . . the word . . .* said that target sounded like *Florida!*

Newell had heard that name uttered outside of sonar already. *How the hell does the word get out so fast?* The eyes . . . no, not the eyes—it was the smell that bothered him the most. It hadn't been present in their first attack at all. This crew had total faith at that time. They were going to save the world. But during the second one, now that he thought back on it, it was recognizable. Now it was pervasive. *Why the hell couldn't the scrubbers cleanse it from the air, for Christ sake!*

Dick Makin reappeared in control. "Captain, I—"

"Later, XO. No time now." *Don't let this thing get any worse . . . don't lose control of the situation!* Newell fully comprehended the need to maintain full control. "Our target is still dead in the water. I want you to coordinate the attack while I talk to the crew." He was speaking rapidly now. No time to allow anyone to interfere. "Don't worry about the second target. Just figure that the Russian boomer is probably tracking us. I want to fire on his estimated position, then take evasive action. Once he hears something in the water, he's not going to sit still any longer. Then we go in for the kill . . . maybe even go active sonar for a perfect position on him."

Before Makin could respond, Newell was on the 1MC. "We are proceeding now to attack a Soviet ballistic-missile submarine off our bow. I would caution each of you not to jump to conclusions relating to our just-completed communications period. Any rumors now are dangerous. I consider such silence from shore is most likely equipment problems. So . . . no worries there." As the last words were spoken, he knew they were uncharacteristic of him. When he looked toward his XO, Makin's face confirmed that.

"Since our responsibilities," he continued, "are to destroy Russian SSBN's before they can fire, I believe we hold the key to our country's future in our grasp . . ." Even the split-second hesitation was unlike him. It was frustrating! "This target has not, repeat, has not fired a single missile, or we would have heard it. You better believe that." *Why had he said that?* "I know you are afraid only for your families, not for yourselves. If you perform as I am now asking you, you will be doing your families and your country a great service." *Thank God, a good comeback.*

There was a moment of silence, though Newell's deep breathing could be heard in the background. "If there is one thing that I deem absolutely critical to exclude if we are to complete our mission, it is rumor . . . unfounded rumor. These rumors that I have been hearing come from men who have not been able to stand up under the tremendous pressure each of you has successfully overcome. Now we are facing an enemy who knows we are on the attack, and I ask each one of you to forget these rumors, all of them unfounded, until we have successfully sunk him." *There, that should do it.*

Dick Makin studied many of the faces in the control room as Newell spoke. Everyone had listened. There was no doubt about that. He could see some faces relaxing, but there were also others that exhibited no change. It was the first time Wayne Newell had failed to convince everyone.

Pasadena was closing to attack a target that was totally aware of them and that would fight back at the first indication of trouble . . . and there was an obvious loss of confidence.

It was at that time that a voice from sonar reported—"Second contact has increased speed considerably . . . closing the area . . ."

The other submarine was racing toward them, sensing the situation—the hunter had now become the hunted for a second time.

CHAPTER FIFTEEN

Buck Nelson was on the slightly raised platform between the periscopes in *Florida's* control room, rocking slowly, heel to toe, heel to toe. His hands were folded behind his back. He would have been pacing if there'd been room. But with no more than a few feet to spare in either direction in these tight confines, heel to toe, heel to toe was the next best solution.

Jimmy Cross, whose attitudes were closely aligned to his captain's, preferred a more relaxed Nelson. Jimmy sometimes played a silent, private game that would ease his tension. He would compare this rather tall, professorial-looking Nelson with rimless glasses to the gaunt, one-armed Nelson—the heroic British admiral astride *Victory's* quarterdeck as she sailed boldly into range of the enemy's broadside at Trafalgar. After all, he would reason, the military similarities between the two men were many—boredom with trivia, tactical brilliance, introspection, even the egos. Cross preferred the control room, though, to the splinters of the quarterdeck.

Then a voice from sonar shattered the almost mystic aura building around this imaginary Nelson. "Closest contact has increased speed . . . appears to be on a direct intercept course with us."

Nelson stopped his rocking and wheeled about to stare at his executive officer as though Cross had called out the report. "What do you say, Jimmy? Who's fooling who?"

"Shiiit." This time his favorite expression was purely cover. Nelson never approached him that way, not in front of the crew. "I don't know what to think, Captain. Chief Delaney seems to be awfully damn sure that's a 688 out there."

"Have we heard a signal from her?" Nelson inquired softly, aware that nothing had been heard. It hadn't occurred to any of them that the two contacts were so close in bearing that it would have been close to impossible to determine which one sent the signal. "Anything that might confirm that suspicion?"

"Not a damn thing," the XO responded just as quietly. Quite frankly, with Nelson acting the way he was, Jimmy was just as happy any decision would be the captain's. What the hell was he asking his XO for? This was the type of problem Nelson loved!

"Then what do you say, Jimmy?" Nelson snapped. "What the hell do you think is happening? You know as well as I do that in a situation like this one of our submarines is supposed to identify itself with a coded sonar signal if it can't avoid transiting a patrol area." There it was —the first admission that he was as confused as everyone else. Nothing happening fell into an acceptable sequence, at least not according to the doctrine they'd been fed since they were junior officers. It felt good to get it off his chest.

Cross was unsure of what to say. His C.O. was generally even-tempered, never prone to reacting rashly. It was the first time since getting under way that Nelson had shown a flash of temper. "There's nothing that makes sense, Captain. Maybe he has a sonar casualty." But that was unlikely, the way the other boat had been maneuvering. It knew *Florida* was out here, and it gave every indication of closing them for a specific purpose. Nothing was covert about her approach, and there was no such thing as a submarine that appreciated company. "Outside of breaking silence and signaling him, we've got to protect ourselves."

"That second contact's increasing speed . . . radically." Dan Mundy's voice from sonar was more urgent, an octave higher. "She's not shy about any of us out here either . . . all of a sudden it's balls to the wall."

"I want all tubes flooded," Nelson ordered calmly, "pressure equalized. I also want a decoy ready." His eyes fell on Cross momentarily. "I will sink anything that comes within our envelope of safety, and that first contact is doing just that, regardless of who they are. We'll prepare tubes one and two now." There, he'd put into words the decision he'd made fifteen minutes before. There shouldn't be any doubt in any man's mind about how it had been made. The contact was neither acting like an American submarine nor following any established precepts. *It was just that it sounded exactly like a 688. How the hell are you supposed to react in this situation?*

The torpedomen were acting on Nelson's orders before he'd finished explaining his intentions to his XO. As each step was completed, the report flashed back to the control room.

Nelson's eyes swept around to the weapons-control coordinator, Lieutenant Sargeant, who had been strangely silent. "You have a good track. Are your presets entered?"

Dave Sargeant licked his lips. It was all entered—speed, gyro angle, enabling run, optimum depth. "Yes, sir. Recommend base course one eight zero, speed ten."

"Very well." Nelson looked to his right to Jimmy Cross. The XO was the fire-control coordinator. "Firing-point procedures, tubes one and two." He had yet to open the muzzle doors. That would be the last step, the one that would tip the scales. . . .

Florida settled on the recommended course and speed. "The ship is ready," the OOD said.

"The weapons are ready." This from Sargeant.

Nelson could sense every eye in control fixed on him.

"Very well. Stand by noisemakers and decoys. Pass the

word to all hands the ship may maneuver radically at any time."

Florida had been quiet as a mouse . . . quiet as a boomer gone dead silent, Nelson mused. Ten knots was still goddamn quiet. If the nearest submarine had a firing solution, he had to be a little nervous now because his target was closing. Maybe preparing to fire? Imagine that—a boomer squaring off against an attack boat! "Range?"

"We haven't maneuvered ourselves enough to provide the best target motion on him. Maybe twelve thousand yards, give or take . . ."

"Captain!" It was Dan Mundy. "Chief Delaney says . . ." Muffled voices in the background interrupted the sonar officer momentarily. "No . . . he's not positive. But Burns says he's worked excercises with *Pasadena* before and there's something about her signature at this range that just hit him—can't say what it is, just that it suddenly came to him. Delaney says Billy's never been wrong before about something like that . . ." His voice drifted off as he comprehended exactly what he'd said . . . and his captain was preparing to shoot . . .

Nelson smoothed his mustache unconsciously. "He could have fired at us by now if he was comfortable with his solution. What do you think now, XO?" he asked Cross thoughtfully. *Who, he wondered, is going to be the first to tell me to hold my fire?*

"Captain . . ." The expression on the XO's face was one of pure astonishment. *My God, we're ready to fire!* Every procedure had been carried out. "That's *Pasadena* out there. Dan Mundy just said so." The southern accent was almost nonexistent. The idea of protecting oneself was completely different from being the first one to shoot—especially on one of your own. "We can't fire on her without . . ." He was at a loss for words.

"Without what, XO? They just think that's *Pasadena*."

"Some sort of warning . . . or inquiry . . . or . . . hell, I don't know, Captain. But she's one of ours and—"

Nelson's voice cracked like a whip through the control

room. "The computer's only as good as its operators, Mr. Cross." No familiar "XO" this time. He wanted each man to understand. His words were for everyone. "Maybe there's a mistake. *Pasadena* has no business here. We don't have a clue why an enemy submarine could sound like her. That's the chance we have to take now. Only one man is positive, and I mean absolutely positive, that's *Pasadena*. The odds are just as good that could be a Soviet sub with warm torpedos and someone's finger on the button ready to fire a couple right now, whether or not they have a perfect solution." His hands gradually had fallen to his sides as he spoke. Now he folded his arms again and glared about the control room. "We are a capital ship carrying American strategy back aft. We could make the difference between home or no home at all. Anyone else have a bright idea about this contact? Don't you think one of our own would have identified by now?"

He was met with a stunned silence.

"Sonar, any change on our nearest contact?"

"Negative. Still closing."

"And the other?"

"Coming on like a freight train, Captain."

"You must have ID on that one if she's making all that noise."

"It's a 688, Captain," Mundy answered. "That's all I hear out here, 688's everywhere."

Nelson's right hand moved from his mustache to his forehead, where his fingers beat a drum roll. "Two targets," he murmured to himself, "both friendly . . . both acting aggressive . . ." He plumbed his memory for anything like this from war games. They could develop fire-control solutions on both. "Do you have a solution on the second one?"

"Not yet, sir. You didn't—"

"Then goddamn it, do it." *No friendly submarines would act in this manner.* "Danny," Nelson called through the entrance to sonar, "I need help here. There must be something different about these boats coming at us. . . ."

"No change, Captain," the sonar officer answered. "They're ours."

"But no signal?" Let everybody hear it.

"Nothing, Captain."

"I didn't hear you, Danny."

"Nothing, Captain. No signal."

Nelson turned back to Jimmy Cross, to the OOD, the weapons-control coordinator, to each of the men in the control room. Every man who stared back at him was relieved beyond belief he wasn't in the captain's shoes. Those who didn't catch his eye were ashamed they had nothing to contribute.

"Open the muzzle doors on tubes one and two." The closest contact would certainly hear that. Then they would have to respond.

"The doors are open, Captain."

"The solution is ready," Jimmy Cross stated flatly.

"Very well." Nelson waited tentatively for an identifying signal . . . anything that would keep him from shooting.

Nothing.

For a man whose red-rimmed eyes were now set off by deep, dark half-moons underneath, an exhausted Ray Larsen was still overjoyed. Once again he'd proven himself right—or at least that was the way he preferred to look at the matter from his own perspective. Clarifying information had begun to come back to SUBPAC to substantiate what had been ideas, most of them farfetched. Admiral Larsen might even have taken credit for each of those theories if he'd been working alone.

Bart Bockman had called from Bangor, Washington, half an hour before. He explained that his intelligence people had detained one of the Spetznaz operatives outside the Trident base. Neither civilian authorities nor the White House were aware of it, nor would they be for the time being. Chemicals were much more effective, he related, than past interrogation methods—they expected to know much more about Spetznaz activities shortly. But there was no doubt that the Soviets were deeply involved in the loss of the boomers.

The Kremlin reaction to the American rescue offer of SSV-516 had been quick and to the point. Any approach to the ship by any foreign power would be considered a provocative act and would be answered with force. *Stay away from SSV-516.*

In addition, scientists at the Smithsonian had confirmed that a few days before, an experimental Soviet laser-communications satellite had been maneuvered above the Pacific to a position that appeared to coincide with SSV-516's position. Nothing could be substantiated. There were no absolutes, just suspicions. But as far as Ray Larsen was concerned, that tied in perfectly with the loss of *Nevada* and *Alaska,* though he didn't bother to explain why.

Now he had just hung up the phone after a direct call with the White House. "I can read him, Mark," Larsen said confidently. "When he's hedging, I know. He's got SecDef there with him, and our Secretary, Bob Kerner. That means they're going along with us. He said he thinks the strategy of the phone conversation with the Kremlin went well, very well. Apparently, the National Security Agency insisted some satellite appeared to violate some sort of treaty, and the President didn't get an argument about it. When he indicated to the General Secretary that we're calling *Pasadena* to the surface, there was dead silence on the other end. Now the President knows it's *Pasadena.*"

"Did he say that, Ray?" Bennett asked. "After all, we don't know if something's happened for sure aboard *Pasadena.* She could just as easily be at the bottom."

Larsen shrugged off the second comment. His mind was made up. "Not exactly. That's what I mean about him hedging." The CNO held up a thumb and forefinger about half an inch apart. "But he was this close to saying I was right about *Pasadena.* When he asked the General Secretary about any problems with submarines in the Pacific, he got a runaround. Said he couldn't comment without running it past his people. Sounds like confirmation to me."

"Sounds like the same old game to me," Neil Arrow muttered. "Each word has a thousand meanings."

Larsen pursed his lips. "You've been away from Washington too long. You don't know how to interpret." He was close to shaking his finger in Arrow's direction to make his point, but thought better of it and placed both hands in his lap. "No one ever comes right out and says 'we think you did such and such.' And the other guy never just casually admits that he's done something that pissed you off. The President didn't say he thought *Pasadena* was a problem—just that we were asking her to surface—and the other guy didn't acknowledge that he knew she was a problem, but he didn't dispute it either. They're talking. That means someone over there isn't feeling too aggressive today."

"That's an interesting interpretation." Robbie Newman saw things as any engineer who was Director of Naval Nuclear Propulsion would—everything was black and white, and Larsen hadn't said a thing that wasn't distinctly gray. "If I could add five cents to this, I think it's time for a threat. If *Florida* ever gets out of this, I say use her. The only thing the Russians are going to understand is power." There was an expression on Newman's face that none of the others had ever seen. He'd always been a calm individual, an engineer who'd brought the Ohio class through early construction trauma—Electric Boat labor pains, he called it. He looked at the others around the table and blinked. "They've sunk my ships . . . killed my men. She's got to put a missile in the air . . . got to scare the shit out of whoever in the Kremlin is hesitating. Decisions are the result of pressure," he said with finality.

Admiral Larsen blinked. *Of course, that was right.* "I wish I'd thought of that myself."

"You can tell him you did if you want," Newman responded softly.

"Oh, come on. You know I wouldn't do that," Larsen

answered. No one really knew what had happened beneath the Pacific waters, but it was something tragic and something that was bringing them closer to the brink by the hour. If nuclear war could be avoided, perhaps there might be an honorable way out of it all—if honor had anything to do with the situation.

"What I really mean," Newman continued thoughtfully, "is that we have to have a method of getting even, an eye-for-an-eye sort of thing. The Russians have to understand that. I think the rest of the world also has to understand that they were willing to accept it. Whatever, the world is going to have a field day with both of us, if we avoid turning each other into glass. Imagine how many people are going to howl about this—you know, bringing the world to the brink of nuclear extinction with all our highfalutin weapons, that sort of thing."

"That's a lot of crap," Larsen retorted, "a bunch of liberals beating their chests."

Robbie Newman could be very patient, especially when he had a point to make. "There are more people who think what I just explained is absolutely logical, Ray." He leaned forward slightly. "You do remember that most civilized people don't like nuclear weapons? The only reason they're accepted at all is that they're a deterrent."

Larsen only nodded.

"You might also consider the relatives of the men on *Alaska* and *Nevada,* or any others, for that matter, who are lost. How do we balance that? If we somehow are able to stop any more submarines from being sunk, how do we gain vengeance, or at least some sort of reparation for a plot gone bad?" Robbie Newman ran his hand through his thick shock of gray hair and glanced at each of the others. "I for one want to get back to the deterrent aspect of this business, if it's at all possible. That means the President, if somehow there is a resolution to this, has to get back to the Kremlin with some suggestions for the General Secretary about how he can start grabbing his ankles if the Russians are indeed behind this whole thing."

Neil Arrow was troubled. Of course, Robbie was right, but . . . His expression betrayed his emotions. "There's no way you can make up for the loss of those men. The Russians aren't simply going to say, 'Here're a few hundred of ours for you to do away with as you see fit.'"

"That's not what I mean." Admiral Newman's reputation as a placid individual who never lost his composure remained firm. This moment was a perfect example. He looked over to Bennett. "Mark, you know where almost every Soviet submarine is right now that's at sea."

"Within reason."

"You're trailing a lot of them, right?"

"As many as we can. They're getting better at slipping a tail."

"Ray," Newman said quietly, "my suggestion would be to take out a few Russian submarines. The President has to explain it. But we would expect no retaliation for what they lose."

The Chief of Naval Operations had no idea how to respond. The idea was preposterous when he considered how he'd take the suggestion if it came from the other side—to sacrifice men and ships for . . . for avoiding a full-scale conflict? "I wouldn't know how to propose—"

"May I do it for you?" Newman was quick to offer a solution.

"I guess . . . I guess there's no harm . . ."

"No," Newman answered, "there's no harm. All the man can do is tell me to stuff it. We may never even get to that point, but conflicts are resolved by having an alternative solution before there's no way out. Would you be kind enough to call and introduce me? He's never met me before and probably has no idea who I am."

Larsen glanced at the others. He was still hesitant. But each of them nodded his agreement.

Then Neil Arrow spoke up. "I think we all agree it's a better way to reach a solution than obliterating each other. But *Florida* has to launch at least one missile. Then the Kremlin gets the message that our Trident system may be damaged but enough of it's intact to make any first strike a mistake. And it shows the Soviets they've lost their ace in the hole—if she ever does surface," he added glumly. "And, if we select a military target rather than a civilian one, that means we're willing to call it even." They were speculating. There was no assurance this plan would ever take place.

"You're right, of course," Larsen responded. "I'll tell him that."

It was difficult for the General Secretary to determine whether the sensation he was experiencing was physical or emotional. It was too complicated to put into words, but he somehow knew he was content. For the first time since this whole hideous situation had surfaced, too late for him to stop it, he felt that he had regained more control over future events—not firm control, not absolute, but he knew he was no longer grasping blindly at straws.

The "aggressive" ones had been detained. He was unsure how he would answer for that decision if Mother Russia survived the day, but much of his contentment was that he was surrounding himself with men he would not worry as much about. Even the head of the KGB was ambitious enough to accept what would have been called "a purge" in Stalin's day. *Old Joe must have felt good after one of those—surrounded by loyal, terrified comrades!*

"The Americans appear close to figuring out what may have happened to their submarines," he began tentatively. He wasn't really sure how much the Americans did know, but they were on to something. The earlier concerns he'd discussed with his wife had grown more real as a result of that call. "I've just concluded a conversation with their President. He called me. They're grasping at straws, no doubt about that, but he brought up the name *Pasadena* too often for me to believe anything else."

"They can't possibly have any clue about *Pasadena*—" the KGB head began.

"Quiet!" The General Secretary's voice was a thunderclap. He intended to maintain control. "I invited you here to discuss the situation, not to argue with me. Understood?"

The others nodded unhappily. In the past their leader had normally preferred to listen to the others first. Then he would make his decisions based on their recommendations. The KGB head was wholly unprepared for such an absolute deviation from the man.

"They will leave SSV-516 to us *if* for some reason that satellite of ours falls . . . out . . . of . . . orbit." His final phrase was uttered one word at a time to clarify the fact there were no alternatives.

"I don't understand." The Chief of the Main Political Directorate rarely spoke unless he was extremely concerned. "Perhaps being new here has something to do with my confusion." He chose his words carefully. "The objective of this strategy was to bring the United States to their knees. It sounds to me that you have second thoughts." He'd been polite and rational and now he waited patiently.

"Obviously, I've had second thoughts." The General Secretary glanced around the table aware that what he'd just said was an admission that he'd experienced those "second thoughts" well beforehand. "I think you all have had second thoughts—or if you haven't, you should be questioning your common sense," he growled, suddenly pleased with himself. "This plan was originated by people who did not anticipate today's Soviet Union, nor did they believe that the Americans would detect—" No, that wasn't quite right. "I must admit I am at a loss as to how they did detect the loss of their submarines. If not, we might not be here now."

The Minister of Defense's elbows were on the table and his chin rested on his folded hands. He'd never liked the General Secretary. He found him even less appealing now. But the man's little purge had certainly made an impression on him. There was no clue what direction might be taken. "Why did the President contact you?"

"You know as much about that as I do."

"No effort had been made on our part to contact Washington before this?"

"I can assure you none was made by me."

"We might bring them to their knees if we can take out some more of their missile submarines," the defense minister said. "Their other delivery vehicles can be neutralized within acceptable limits." His head was still down. He didn't want to look into the General Secretary's eyes, or anyone else's for that matter. "That would need some further investigation, but—"

"Your acceptable limits do not coincide with mine. A first strike is not on top of my mind right now, although I wouldn't be surprised if the Americans weren't considering one." He had no sense of the defense minister, no idea of what motivated the man. They had never fought before, nor had they ever really worked together. Now he wondered why he hadn't sent him off to Lubyanka. "Unless I am forced into a corner, unless there is absolutely no alternative, I will not launch first. Do you concur?" he finished defiantly.

"Yes, I do," the defense minister conceded. "I would follow orders to launch if they were given, but I don't believe we're in the position to initiate anything now either." He raised his head slightly and his eyes searched out the others around the table without moving his chin from his hands. Then he looked back to the General Secretary. "I doubt anyone here is ready to dispute you right now. I think we have to wait to see what happens—even if we rattle our sabers by appearing to prepare for a launch."

"Agreed!" The General Secretary couldn't believe it. Perhaps . . .

"Send the identification signal, Chief," Steel called to sonar. "We're letting it all hang out now anyway." *Manchester* was careering ahead through black water toward an uncertain resolution. He turned to Peter Simonds with a wry smile. "At least *Florida* will know who the cavalry is."

"Christ, everyone knows who we are now," the XO snorted hoarsely. "Weapons-control coordinator reports torpedos warm, presets entered, Captain."

"Very well." Steel was beaming. The tubes had been

flooded, the pressure equalized—*the weapons were ready*. All they needed was a target confirmation.

What the hell was supposed to happen now? They'd sent the identification signal provided by Commander Burch over active sonar. In unique situations it was intended to provide access to the boomer's sector, or at least security—each man hoped. It was *Manchester's* ID, her authorization that she was supposed to be there.

They waited. It was akin to waiting for someone to answer the phone.

There was no response.

"You know," Moroney remarked from sonar, "you know there is no such thing as a reply to that signal . . . don't you?"

"Right, Chief," Simonds answered. "Just sort of a letdown, I guess . . . not to get an answer, I mean," he added to Steel.

"That other boat had to hear that," the captain said.

"You mean *Pasadena?*" Simonds glanced out of the corner of his eye then quickly looked back toward the control board.

"That other boat." Steel's words were uttered carefully and deliberately. They also meant that the captain didn't want to hear *Pasadena's* name again. Steel rubbed his cheek thoughtfully, as though he might need a shave. "What would you do on that other attack boat if you heard our coded signal? Shit," he answered himself disparagingly, "you'd be trying to get your own signal out super fast so *Florida* doesn't know which end is up. Keep her wondering until it's too late. And if you weren't aware of it, and with the way we're all approaching each other like someone's going to shoot any second, you'd jump up and down and wave your arms and say, 'Hey, it's me—don't shoot.' Right?"

The XO nodded, although he found he was incapable of responding. Simonds could think of nothing to say, nothing intelligent or forceful enough that would express just how he felt. He pushed his glasses back on his nose and turned away from Steel to stare once again at the depth gauges.

"Targets, David?" Steel called out to his sonar officer.

"Both sound like they're increasing speed. Starboard bow, the one that was heading north, that's the boomer. Moroney concurs, and the other . . ." His voice dropped off.

"Talk to me, David."

"Pasadena, Captain. It's got to be . . . like . . . looking in a mirror," he choked.

"That's my target," Steel said with an exaggerated firmness. "Firing-point procedures, tubes one and two." *This had to be a trick of some kind . . . or perhaps a test of* Manchester. *Some sick son of a bitch of a staff officer with nothing better to do had dreamed up this whole scenario. No boomers had ever been sunk. It was all a ruse, even picking that SEAL out of the ocean. Commander Burch just made it more realistic. They were just testing* Manchester *. . . or more so, him, Ben Steel . . .*

"One and two . . ." was the whispered response.

"Open the muzzle doors. I want them to hear that. Maybe . . ." But Steel's voice drifted off as he was interrupted.

"I heard muzzle doors out there," Moroney shouted from sonar.

Someone else was preparing to fire! *Which one?*

"Captain, we've altered course slightly for the target," said the OOD. "The ship is ready," he concluded ominously.

"Captain . . ." Peter Simonds's voice was an octave higher than normal. "Ben . . ." he implored. No one in control had ever heard the XO use the captain's first name. His face reflected a hurt that he couldn't express.

"The weapon is ready," the weapons-control officer whispered, his lower lip held tightly between his teeth.

Both captain and executive officer turned to each other. Steel stared back at his executive officer with an expression of inner pain. The XO nodded slightly two or three times, as if searching for the correct words before saying tentatively, "The solution is ready." His eyes were tightly shut before he uttered the final word.

Manchester was ready to shoot.

"David," Steel called toward sonar, "my target," emphasizing the *my* as he spoke.

"Heavy machinery noise. Picking up speed."

Steel glanced over at Peter Simonds. Yes, he'd heard. Nothing needed to be said. The solution was still good.

The XO answered with another slight nod. Yes, that increase in speed had definitely been covered. The weapon knew about the target also. That was an automatic.

"Wind her up," Steel called out to the OOD. "Let's make the best target they've ever heard."

If they wouldn't shoot, he would!

Newell had heard the familiar words in the background as he delivered his final pep talk over the 1MC to the crew—*warm the torpedos . . . flood the tubes . . . equalize pressure* —and Dick Makin's responses as each evolution was completed and reported to him.

The presets had been entered. The torpedos were ready to respond.

"Firing-point procedures, tubes one and two . . ." Makin's voice was steady even if his face radiated an inner turmoil. He was balanced on the needle point of an enigma. His faith in the Navy—in his captain—had been challenged as never before over the past few days. It was too easy to overlook the reality of a war on the surface when the real battle, the one that he could see and smell and touch, was taking place in front of him. It had been so easy to accept everything that naval intelligence provided, especially when *Pasadena*'s captain had been briefed by SUBPAC himself. But the Wayne Newell he'd known was evaporating before his eyes . . . *had he already disappeared?* The man had been gradually consumed by the war, the devastating necessity of destroying submarines and human beings that gave every indication of being their brothers. It was forcing Dick Makin to question everything he'd ever accepted.

Wayne Newell had interrupted himself on the 1MC to call over his shoulder, "Designate the boomer target number one. And his bird dog number two." And then he'd continued his announcement to the crew in a frantic effort to keep his now fragile team from breaking apart.

"Captain, Mr. McKown reports the ship is ready." Makin relayed the fact with an unusual solemnity as the 1MC clicked off. The snap of the switch was magnified through control.

"Good, Dick, great . . . terrific." His eyes darted about the control room, never once settling on anyone. "What about the other? Must be an Alfa designated to protect the boomer, I'd say."

The executive officer stared blankly at Newell. The corners of his mouth were turned sharply down and the lines at the corners of his eyes had expanded as he prepared to speak. *This was the time he had to say it.* "Captain . . ."

"The weapons are ready." The weapons-control coordinator barked out his report in an exaggerated voice.

"Very well." Makin, momentarily sidetracked by the report, continued, "Captain, that's no Alfa out there . . ."

"Must be," an irritated Newell interrupted. "That's what I'd use if I was a Russian. Stick one of those high-speed, hard-shelled suckers out there and—"

"The solution is ready." The OOD was acting as fire-control coordinator for Makin.

"I'll take it now," Newell said loudly, his voice excessively high-pitched. He winked at his XO. "With all the problems some of these guys have with their wild imaginations about these targets being something other than Russian—"

"Captain," Steve Thompson's shout from sonar interrupted, "the other contact—the one we said sounded like one of our 688's—it just went active, some sort of signal on her sonar. It was definitely some type of code."

"Mr. Thompson, that is a method of baiting us." Newell looked quickly around the control room, then back at Makin. There was a frantic look in the XO's eyes, no different from any of the others'. "The Russians are trying to draw us away from their boomer. They are our enemy. They're deceptive. That's no 688 out there. They know that if we get this next boomer, it's all over for them. They'll do anything to stop us, and right this minute they're fooling all of you."

"But it could have been an ID for one of our own. You remember, entering a boomer's sector?" Makin's voice echoed an increasing sense of urgency. "They do that, you know. You were on one, Captain."

"That's for something entirely different," Newell retorted. "They're trying to fool us, but we're not going to be fooled . . . no, sir."

"Target number two is accelerating, *fast.*"

"Watch your depth!" The diving officer's howl of rage lashed through the control room to draw everyone's attention. "Watch it, damn it," he snarled. His face was contorted in rage as he grabbed the back of the bow planesman's neck and shook him. "You're going to lose it."

Makin's eyes moved quickly from one man to the next, his gaze darting back to the officers. He'd never seen a submarine officer treat a man like that. They were on the edge. *They were losing it.*

The OOD reacted at the same time. "Get the bow up. Get it up or I'm going to have to re—"

Newell grabbed the OOD by the shoulder and spun him around. "Get that man off the bow planes. *Now!*" He whirled in the direction of the planesman. The sailor was rigid in his chair, his arms straight, hands pushing forward on the wheel. "Look at him," Newell howled.

"Stirling," the diving officer shouted frantically, now more frightened than angry. He reached forward to shake the man again. "For Christ sake, bring her up." He grabbed the sailor by the shoulders as if pulling back on the man would bring the planes back up.

"Why isn't he off that control? Who's his relief?" Newell shouted. In the next breath he said, "I don't care who takes it."

A sailor appeared beside Stirling, to help the diving officer. They had to pry the planesman's hands from the wheel.

Dick Makin's voice was sharp. "I'm getting a problem with the solution, Captain. We have to steady up." He was trapped between two worlds. Whether it was instinct or training, he was struggling to keep an accurate solution in the torpedo. Yet he didn't want to shoot!

Newell was beside Stirling's relief, pushing him bodily into place. "Get that bow up . . . get us level if you ever want to . . ." But Newell had already turned away to shout to Dick Makin. "You call down to the torpedo room and tell them that they're going to set a record in reloading or I swear no one down there will ever see land again." He licked his lips. "We are going to hold the wires as long as possible before we turn on that Alfa and blow that son of a bitch out of the water. After that we'll finish off the boomer, if we don't get him the first time." He waved a hand at the executive officer. "You tell Chief Sanford that," he added.

Stirling, the planesman who had been pulled from his chair, lay on the deck rolling his head from side to side. Then, as if he had been stung, he opened his eyes and leveled a finger at Newell. He tried to speak. His lips moved and his tongue worked but the words he was trying to speak ran together until his hand dropped, then his head, and finally his voice.

There was dead silence in the control room for almost five seconds before Newell glared at Makin. "Well?"

"I have a solution again," he answered, expelling a deep breath.

Newell clapped his hands together. "Tube number one, shoot on generated bearings." The air-operated ram ejected the water slug and the first torpedo. The sensation could be felt throughout the ship.

"Unit's running correctly, sir."

"Tube number two, shoot . . ." Newell's voice cracked perceptibly but the order was understood.

The second torpedo leaped from its tube.

The only sound that could be heard in the control room was the low moaning of the planesman, Stirling, still lying on the deck.

The silence was not broken by the standard after-firing reports on the second torpedo.

"Well?" Newell inquired angrily.

"Doesn't sound right."

"Wire continuity on number one still good."

"Number two?" Newell shouted. "Number two?"

"Something's wrong."

"Number one still good."

Steve Thompson's voice shattered the coordination of the control room. "I heard muzzle doors. Target number two must be preparing to shoot."

"See," Newell said to Makin, as calm now as he'd been loud a moment previously. "See, that's no friendly. He intends to shoot at us. They all do. We're at war." There was a light tremor in his voice. "This is what it's really like," he said for the control room's benefit. "Now you know why they couldn't fool us," he concluded with a dramatic sweep of his hand.

"Torpedo in the water on the boomer's bearing. They've fired on us."

"Cut the wires," Newell shouted. "Come right for target number two. Noisemakers in the water. We're going to take out this Alfa before we evade. Firing-point procedures, tubes three and four."

"The ship is ready," Andy McKown, the OOD, reported mechanically. Then he wondered why he'd spoken. They hadn't settled on their new course yet. At the same time, he realized that his voice was hollow, and he wasn't sure why. The idea of a torpedo racing at *Pasadena* had no effect on him, and that was equally puzzling.

It was strange to realize that what really concerned him was this preparation to fire on the next target. McKown had been following the entire sequence of events—*and I know this is a 688, not a Soviet Alfa!* Yet he couldn't understand why he'd brought the ship onto a new course. But he had—*I don't have the guts to counter Captain Newell's orders! None of us do . . . not even the XO!*

"Weapons are ready."

"Do you have a solution?" Newell demanded.

"No . . . we need a . . ." Makin never had a chance to finish.

Newell understood instantly. "Steve, go active. I need an accurate range."

In a split second the giant bow sonar emitted a powerful sound wave to mark the second sub. The silence in control was eerie until the sonar officer reported, "Ten thousand five hundred."

"You got that?" Newell asked irritably.

There was another pause, until Makin replied, "Solution is ready."

"Tube number three, shoot on generated bearings."

No sooner was the first torpedo on its way than Newell fired the second. There was no concern about the wires this time. They had a perfect range on the target. The boomer already had fired on them. "Go deep," he shouted to the OOD. "Right full rudder. More noisemakers."

Pasadena lurched sharply as she responded to the rudder and the planes biting into the water. The men in control grabbed for support as the deck fell away and she heeled to starboard. The clatter of loose gear broke the silence that had descended through the space after the final torpedo was fired. Now *Pasadena* was running for her life.

"Those bastards in the torpedo room better be on top of it." Newell's voice was shrill. "We're going to get both of them."

"Torpedos on target two's bearing."

No one noticed Dick Makin slip into the sonar room.

CHAPTER SIXTEEN

The telephone rang once . . . twice . . . three times.

"Screw it," Myra Newell sobbed to herself. "Screw it . . . I don't want to talk to anyone." She stroked Jack Tar's ears. They were damp from her tears. "How about you? Do you want to talk?" The big dog raised his head and licked under her chin.

Four rings . . . five . . . six.

"We'll take care of each other, won't we?"

Jack Tar tired of licking Myra. He sat down and swiped a paw at his muzzle as if he were swatting mosquitoes.

Seven . . . eight . . . nine . . . ten. Ten—that was the magic number for the caller. The phone stopped ringing. The Newell house was once again deathly quiet. Jack Tar cocked an ear to the sudden silence, realized the only sound now was his mistress's sniffling, and climbed into her lap with that strange sense of comforting that dogs have for humans. She made no effort to push him down.

Who could it have been? Who was so insistent that they'd let it ring that long? Perhaps it had been SUBPAC calling. Something about *Pasadena?* An emergency? Perhaps someone had been hurt and they needed her to visit his wife? That had been before. It was something the captain's wife should do. It came with the territory. Oh, hell, maybe she should call Neil Arrow's office. No. If it were that important, if it were worth ten rings, they'd call back.

Myra knew this wasn't just unhappiness she was experiencing. She was lonely, lonely as hell. Another voice would help, a kind one, an understanding one. Maybe Connie Steel. They'd known each other for so long, even before the kids. And their conversation the other day at lunch—that was it! Myra remembered running on about Wayne . . . and Connie really had understood. Even if Ben Steel wasn't like Wayne, Connie knew so many of the other C.O.'s. And everyone's wife talked at one time or another. It was just natural for them, what with their husbands away for so long. Connie'd understand.

Myra wiggled her hips forward to get up off the couch but the dog was a dead weight. She nudged him. "Come on. Move it."

Jack Tar looked up. He was comfortable, and immovable.

"Come on, old fellow. Time to move."

The dog dropped his head to one side and rolled on her lap until one rear leg was lifted high in the air. He wanted his tummy scratched. It was an old Jack Tar trick—never move until rewarded. That was one of the first things Wayne had taught him as a puppy.

"Nope, not this time. We're going to make a phone call. Come on, up and off to greater things." She pushed until the dog rolled onto the floor. Then he stood up, shook, and tagged along when his mistress went to the phone and dialed.

Connie picked up her phone before the second ring. "Steel residence."

"It's me. You busy?"

"Talk about extrasensory perception, Myra. I don't know what it is, but I was just about to call you. It must be ESP." Connie's voice had a strange, almost false, lilt to it, as if she wasn't as happy as she sounded. "How're you doing?"

Myra paused. *How am I doing?* "Not so hot. Rotten, to be honest. I'm not even sure why."

"ESP, ESP. It must be." Now there was more confidence

in Connie's voice. "I've just got a feeling—I don't know what it is, but it's been developing all day. And it's not female problems, believe me. I know that."

"Me, too. I've been chewing on things since we last got together—you know, that nice lunch back in the hills—and . . ." Somehow the words weren't coming, or couldn't come, as easily as she thought they would. "Aw, I don't know what to say."

"I feel the same way. Maybe if the kids were home from school we'd see things differently. There wouldn't be any time to think about ourselves. It's almost a depression, and I don't know why. I'm used to living like this. You are, too."

"If I knew, honey, I wouldn't be moaning over the phone like a sick cow." The dog had curled up beside her, and she bent over to scratch his ears. "You know, outside of you, my best friend right now has four legs and soft, furry ears—and it shouldn't be that way. My husband should be the object of my dreams. But he's off somewhere a couple hundred feet beneath the sea playing war games." Jack Tar began the routine again, rolling over and raising one back leg for the inevitable tummy scratch. "And you know something else, honey?" She could feel her voice was going to crack if she didn't keep control. "I don't think I care. Wayne's last time in port was so rough on all of us that I'm not looking forward to his coming home. Maybe that's why I had to call. Maybe . . ." She could sense that she was about to lose it again and paused, hoping Connie would pick up on it.

There was no response from the other end.

"Oh, I don't know," Myra continued cautiously. "It's a feeling I've had all day that he's not going to come back"—now the words all ran together without emotion—"and I don't care and I should because if Wayne doesn't, then none of them will and it'll all be my fault and oh, I don't know . . ."

Connie heard the telltale sniff on the other end followed by the throat clearing and knew she had to say something. She didn't feel that way about Ben, not at all, but she'd also had a strange feeling about this latest patrol. It had never happened before. "I think you ought to come over because . . ." She was searching for something that would make more sense, but there were no words to express it. ". . . because I've had the same feeling all day. Except I want Ben to come back—and I want Wayne to come back, too. Myra, I want you to come over here right now. No arguments, just get your buns in gear and get over here. I'll put on a fresh pot of—no, I won't. I'm getting out some glasses and ice cubes as soon as we hang up. There'll be more days like this before the Navy retires them, but we both deserve a drink. Leave a note for the kids. Maybe we can all have a bite to eat together later."

It had been quiet aboard *Florida* during this patrol. Buck Nelson's drills were the only break from tedium. But exercises at battle stations were too often like football practice. You stuck with it just because of Saturday afternoons. That's the way they had been educated about submarine warfare, too. Wait for the big game—but that was also the one you hoped never came.

Aboard a boomer there was none of the anticipation of an infantryman, none of those tense periods of waiting as both sides went through all the processes of preparing for battle. Those grunts had to wait, and think, until intelligence would report the movement of divisions of men and artillery and tanks—and then you saw them before the shooting actually started. Or for the pilot, there were ready-room briefings, preflight checks, the flight to meet the enemy, radar contact, perhaps visual sighting, lock on, missile firing, maybe even an old-fashioned dogfight. Even on the surface the Navy had the opportunity for preparation, because spy satellites and sophisticated electronics left few surprises.

But all was quiet beneath the surface of the ocean. Submarines tiptoed around each other on cat's feet, sometimes moving so slowly, a step at a time, that the prey had no idea they were closing, sometimes remaining dead quiet waiting for the unwary to fall into their trap. There was no long-term preparation, no logistics planning, no ammunition trains, no digging in. You came with your baggage and you either left with it or went to the bottom with it.

When battle came beneath the ocean's surface, it was all around you, instantaneous, precise, final. There was no room for error on anyone's part. Each man had to cover the next. *One mistake—everyone on the boat lost.* There were no foxholes, no flak jackets, no gas masks, no armor. It all came down to reaction timing coupled with technology and each man's specialized skills.

"Coded sonar signal from farthest contact." Chief Delaney's voice rose above all the others.

"What does it—"

"Friendly, Captain, friendly," Dan Mundy confirmed.

"Closest?" Nelson asked calmly.

"Still nothing."

"Don't drop your solution on number two just yet. Do you still have a good solution on number one?"

"Very," the XO answered.

Jimmy Cross had spent a career being calm and cool. That was why he was XO of a boomer and already recommended for command. Yet right now he was beside himself. The difference in sound signatures between each of their contacts was minute, no more than the oddities of a ship's personality built in at the shipyard. "Danny, what's the difference in sound between the two contacts?" It was important that Buck Nelson reassess the situation. A hasty decision and . . . he closed his eyes tightly and waited for the sonar officer to back him up.

"One gave the right signal, the other . . ."

"Yeah, I know. I mean their signatures," Cross insisted.

"Twins."

"Captain . . ." Cross reached out and touched Nelson's forearm as one might do in attempting to emphasize a point to a friend.

"Ready noisemakers," Nelson ordered, cutting through his XO's words.

"I heard muzzle doors opening!" the chief called out.

"Which target?"

"I don't know," Chief Delaney answered. "Maybe the friendly, maybe . . . no, I'm not sure."

"Captain," Jimmy Cross continued, "recommend we reverse course and go deep. That'll confuse a torpedo if someone makes the mistake of firing."

Nelson could see it now, see it without closing his eyes. The control room of *Florida* was as real as could be, but he could also see what was taking place as the three submarines drew closer to each other. He was in no position to run. A fifty-knot torpedo had a damn good chance of catching *Florida*. *No, don't turn away, Nelson. He's about to fire—and so are you!* "Not now. They're closing too fast."

"I have a torpedo in the water," Chief Delaney said.

It was all taking place so fast. No time to think. No time to lay out all the facts and make a decision.

"Bearing?"

"Just off our bow . . . from our target . . . I think. I swear it's one of our Mark 48's. On pre-enabling run." The noise of the screw of a Mark 48 torpedo sounds like a freight train to a sonarman.

"That's it, XO," Nelson replied calmly. "Too late to take our marbles and head for the barn."

"I have a second one . . . torpedo, I mean . . . same bearing," Chief Delaney said.

"Any change in target's actions?"

"None yet."

"Noisemakers."

"Captain, I swear those sound like our own Mark 48's." The words, from Dan Mundy, expressed shock. "Forty-eights," he repeated in wonder. "Piston engine."

"That's what a 688 carries," Nelson said quietly to Jimmy Cross, a touch of surprise in his own voice. He had no more idea than any of the others why a 688 would fire at them. But the lack of change in the target's motion meant they were maintaining the umbilical wire on that torpedo. If *Florida* took any radical evasive action, new data would be sent through the wire to the torpedo.

"Now it's our turn," Nelson stated in a loud voice. "Tube number one, shoot on generated bearings."

A split-second hesitation—then the unmistakable sound of the water slug propelling the torpedo from its tube.

"Tube number two. Shoot on generated bearings."

"Decoy, Captain?" They had been fired on. As concerned as Jimmy Cross was about the submarines' identity beforehand, his mind instantly switched to the reactions he'd been trained for. It was *Florida*'s job now to counter, then evade the torpedos.

"Negative. I'll wait until they're closer . . . until they start to snake. We've already got our noisemakers deployed."

"Problems with that second torpedo of theirs, Captain."

"Both of our units running correctly, Captain. Wire continuity good."

"Target's turning. Cut his wires. First torpedo in search."

Buck Nelson's instincts told him his target would be turning to meet the 688 that was rushing toward them. He had no explanations why this would happen, but he was also sure that turn would be to starboard. "Right full rudder. Make our depth five hundred feet." *Turn away from the target, and put some space between yourself and that torpedo.* But after that he was unsure. He was under attack—from what appeared to be one of his own—and another sub was joining the melee, or appeared to be. Running was one thing, but he had to protect *Florida*, too. He had no idea what awaited him if he tried to run. The best protection was to sink that boat that had fired on him. *No, it wasn't the best, it was the only.*

"Well, what was your sense of the conversation?" Ray Larsen inquired. He was making a reasonable attempt at nonchalance. His arms remained folded, and he made a point of looking at other objects in Neil Arrow's large office. But no matter how hard he tried, he couldn't keep his eyes from drifting back to Robbie Newman.

For his part, Newman was comfortable with himself, comfortable because he felt he'd handled himself well during his phone conversation with the President, especially because his ideas had been taken seriously by the White House. Robbie Newman also experienced pleasure in the CNO's anxiety. The man's curiosity was barely held in check. "The President was both cordial and open to my suggestions. When we discussed the probability of *Florida*'s survival, he explained that if orders must be issued to even the score, we make the target selections here. But the launch message and the orders to sink any of their SSN's will originate directly from the White House."

"But we will be able to pick the targets?" the CNO insisted.

"Correct. He would like to have our recommendations within the hour since he and the General Secretary essentially have an open wire."

Larsen's eyes fell on Mark Bennett. "I assume you have some suggestions."

"*San Francisco* picked up one of their boats off the Japanese coast and she's been trailing it for more than a week. And the *Jack*'s been on the ass of one of their Victors off Iceland for four days. She's been around long enough that she deserves a final crack at something like this."

"Prepare the messages and have them forwarded to the White House," Larsen said matter-of-factly. "The bastards deserve more than they're going to get."

"There's another part of the deal," Newman said quietly. "While the President also agreed that there's only one way we can prove to them that *Florida* is safe and functioning, there are limitations. He made it absolutely clear that we can't select any heavily populated civilian area." His gaze settled on Ray Larsen. "Can't touch major commands either."

Mark Bennett'd had little he really wanted to say in the past few hours. The strategic theories he'd believed in had failed to an extent. Yet his submarines were actually being used for a specifically designed purpose. Bennett had passionately believed missile submarines were a deterrent to be retired after their useful life without ever firing a shot—that was their sole function. Attack submarines had always been intended to keep their Soviet opposites neutralized—high-tech quality competing with Russian numbers, so that a torpedo would never be fired in anger.

Even if the President succeeded in accomplishing a meeting of the minds with the Kremlin to avoid a missile exchange, this use of offensive weapons signaled a new era. To Mark Bennett, it was also as blatant a message as possible that men like himself and Ray Larsen, perhaps even Neil and Robbie, should retire. It would take a new generation to comprehend the complexities of the decisions that had been made that day, to envision new strategies that would avoid the possibility of war. The old ones now had them at the edge.

Bennett stood up. "With your concurrence, I will select an appropriate target."

Larsen opened his mouth to speak, then thought better of it.

"Thank you, Ray. I think you understand my purpose." Bennett walked to the operations room then turned back toward the table. "I'd like it if you'd all join me in this."

Neil Arrow finally said what they all knew Larsen had been thinking. "And if *Florida* isn't available for this mission?"

"Then I suppose the President has no other choice available," he remarked softly. "That would mean that one arm of our Triad has been pretty much neutralized and he has to reevaluate everything we've considered."

The sonar wave from *Pasadena* rolled over *Manchester* with an ominous note. There was just one ping, no more. Each man knew it was all that was necessary for their enemy to establish an accurate range, feed that figure into their torpedo solution, and shoot at them.

"That's it," Steel said. "Ping them, David. Stand by for a range," he called over to Peter Simonds.

"Torpedos appear to have been exchanged with the boomer," Chief Moroney announced. "Target accelerating. He must be turning away from the boomer's shots." The reports came in a matched cadence seemingly too fast to digest. Sonar picked up the sound of two water slugs. "Launch transient again on target bearing." A pause, no more than seconds, more like minutes to those in hearing range, until, "Looks like these have our name on them."

"Range—ten thousand yards."

"Got it . . ." Another pause from the executive officer. "Solution is ready."

"Tube number one, shoot on generated bearings," Steel called out, surprised at how his voice seemed to echo back and forth through the control room.

The water slug from tube one jolted the ship.

"Boomer's winding it up. I've got noisemakers on his bearing. Our unit's running correctly."

"Evade, Captain?" Peter Simonds asked.

"Negative. Not yet. We're not running from them yet. Tube number two, shoot on generated bearings."

"Target's got it wound up," Chief Moroney reported. "Can't tell if he's evading or not. He's got a problem with torpedos coming at him from two directions. If I didn't know better, I'd say he's coming right down our throat."

"Illuminate him again," Steel answered. "No secrets out here anymore." None at all, he thought. *When you're fighting your own kind after a lifetime of training to fight the other guy, how do you suddenly change everything you've been taught in a split second?*

Pasadena had the same idea. Another sonar wave struck *Manchester*.

"Both our units running correctly, Captain."

"Eighty-five hundred yards, closing rapidly."

Peter Simonds's eyes were closed as the figures raced through his head. "That torpedo is closing at three thousand yards a minute, Captain, as long as we hold course toward them . . . about three minutes if we don't change course." *Why the hell were three American submarines shooting at each other like this? How did they . . . ?* "About four minutes and we'll be waving at each other." *Fifteen years in the Navy and I'm killing my own . . .*

"Wire continuity is good on both torpedos." There was a split-second pause before he added, "He's got noisemakers everywhere. He's got to turn away from both of us."

"You're right, Peter. And I know what you're thinking," Steel said to his XO. Then, "Take her down to six hundred feet. Left full rudder. Fire noisemakers. Put up a wall. Tell you what we're going to do, Peter. We're going to drive like a sports car and try to get around behind him for another shot. No matter what he does, remember, we were ordered to help out that boomer. That means getting between them if it's possible."

"Enabling run completed on one of the incoming torpedos. It's snaking." That meant its speed had slowed. The torpedo was now searching for its target.

Manchester's deck pitched forward as the planes dug into the water. Then, with full rudder on, she banked like a plane.

"Rudder is still full left."

Steel watched the compass heading. There was a picture in his head of the relative position of all three submarines. If Wayne Newell continued to be his precise self, *Pasadena* would want to turn to starboard to intercept *Manchester*. But that would be suicide. The two sets of torpedos fired at him from opposite directions would have him in a pincer. Newell had to turn to port, away from both of them, away from *Manchester,* and continue to evade. Therefore Steel had turned to port. More than likely they would end up close to the same depth to evade the torpedos. A torpedo's greatest weakness was adjusting to a rapidly changing target depth. So Newell would want to come around on his tail. Steel knew he couldn't hold a course for long. He looked up at the course indicator. "Amidships."

"Our first unit is in enabling run." The search!

"Target's first unit is range gating. Appears to have picked up a noisemaker. Second unit range gating also—I'm damn sure on us—at a three-second ping interval." The torpedo was homing, coming in at high speed for the kill.

Another sonar wave washed over *Manchester*. Damn, Newell hadn't turned away yet. He was taking another range to . . .

"He's getting ready to shoot again." David Hall was thinking the same thing.

"He couldn't . . . I don't think. His tubes were empty. That's too fast for reloading," Simonds said. "Less than five minutes from that first shot at the boomer. He's just refining his solution." He called down to the torpedo room. "How long to reload one and two?"

"Three minutes—maybe less if we level off sometime. Christ, this reloading isn't the easiest thing to do standing on your ear."

"You're doing a wonderful job," Simonds called back. "But if you don't do it faster, you may find yourself swimming."

"Our first unit's homing on something now. Second unit's . . . something's wrong with that second one. Both the boomer's shots are range gating, but I can't tell on what. A hell of a mess out there."

Steel closed his eyes. If he held course for too much longer, *Pasadena* would eventually come in behind him. *But that would be suicidal for Newell!* He'd used four torpedos—two for the boomer, two for him—and there was at least one range gating on *Pasadena* right now. How long before she reloaded?

With his eyes still shut, a vision of Wayne Newell materialized. No, it wasn't a single likeness, more a multiple image of different stages in Wayne's life—a serious, single-minded student at nuclear power school, the faultlessly impeccable navigator, a nondrinker because he couldn't drink and maintain his perfect vision of himself, even the perfectionist who questioned superiors about anything less than 4.0 on his fitness reports. He was a man of absolutes, and it was now quite obvious that he intended to eradicate this interruption in his pursuit of *Florida*.

Once Wayne had made up his mind, there was no turning back. He was a man who established goals and met each one before he went on to the next. *Manchester*—or rather, her destruction—had become the next goal, and Steel understood that Newell would be persistent in his attack. He would go to unusual lengths, following his own concepts of pressing the attack rather than any established doctrine. He was a club fighter and he would press in for that final shot, ignoring his opponent's punches, seeking the surprise shot that would drop the other to the canvas—or the ocean floor.

Steel thought about the loss of the other boomers and imagined the tremendous pressure that Newell must be under. *What in God's name had possessed him? How had he managed to hold his crew together?* There were no immediate answers to those questions, and Steel knew in a flash that he would never know because one or both of them would shortly be dead.

There was also another thing he understood. *Manchester* could fire as many as she was capable of, and Newell would continue to press the attack as long as he remained afloat. He was that type of individual. Steel thought about how impressed he'd always been with Wayne's determination. *He still was.*

"Two-second ping interval on the one that's after us."

What was it closing on? Was it *Manchester?* Was it a noisemaker? They had turned away from the torpedos, gone deeper to confuse them. That was increasing the range, a bit more time anyway, even if it was only seconds. *How do you change everything you've been taught?*

"Our first unit's in a two-second ping interval."

Steel had two full tubes. *Pasadena* was reloading all four. "Come right. Sonar, let's go active and get another range. Firing-point procedures on three and four."

The OOD had worked with Steel for a long time. "Settle on a course off his stern, Captain?"

"Correct."

"Fifty-six hundred yards . . ."

Steel wasn't concerned with anything else. The OOD

would settle on a course. The fire-control coordinator, Peter Simonds, would have a solution. The weapons in tubes three and four had been ready before they fired the first two.

"We're turning toward that torpedo, Captain," Simonds said under his breath. Everyone else in control understood that, but none of them would want to hear it broadcast either.

"Hell," Steel answered, "he's never bothered to turn away from us." *How do you change everything you've been taught?*

The XO had one thumb in the air. "We can do it at this range. Solution is . . ."

The thumb was enough of an answer. "Tube number three, match sonar bearings and shoot."

The water slug was physical confirmation that the torpedo was on its way.

"One-second ping interval on that torpedo, Captain. I don't know what it's on to but it sounds happy," called Chief Moroney. Even with a torpedo bearing down on him, the chief was no different than he'd been during exercises.

The hell with the wire. "Add another two hundred feet," he called to the diving officer. "Left full rudder."

"Our unit is in continuous range gate." That meant their first shot was homing on a target . . . a noisemaker . . . perhaps *Pasadena*.

"Launch transient on the target's bearing . . . another single torpedo in the water."

Somehow, Wayne Newell had reloaded and held his course long enough to fire. Now he had to turn away and go very deep.

An hour before, the General Secretary had been talking about balancing on a high wire with no net beneath them. It seemed an accurate comparison. The other members of his Defense Council—*the new Defense Council*—had been in agreement. None of those remaining had any desire to become involved in a missile exchange unless it was apparent that the odds were heavily weighted on their side.

Now they were startled to note that both the General

Secretary and the Minister of Defense were visibly shaken as they reentered the council chambers. The former appeared more exhausted than disturbed, while the latter's face had become a ghostly white, vividly contrasted by his heavy beard. There was an aura of defeat about them.

"It seems there is no doubt on the President's part that *Pasadena* is the cause," the General Secretary announced, sitting down heavily. "I have no idea what his source of information might be."

"They're bluffing," the head of the KGB commented with little vigor.

"Possibly."

"But," the Minister of Defense countered, "they also seem to have figured out the purpose behind SSV-516 and the satellite."

"More bluff?" This time the KGB leader sounded even less sure of himself.

"Possibly." The General Secretary had determined before the last phone conversation with Washington was completed that he wanted each member of the Defense Council to realize that they had talked themselves into the final decision. "There is also a possibility of both sides extricating themselves before we run out of choices." How he wished his wife could join him now, see how he was turning their heads, see how he had taken control of the situation. "That high wire I mentioned has become a razor blade."

The Chief of the Main Political Directorate was a dour individual who rarely spoke until he had a sense of how the others felt. "May I assume that each of you finds that a meeting of the minds is more advantageous than seeing this strategy through to its conclusion?" He was always formal and precise, a habit that maddened the head of the KGB, whom he now turned to. He had no intention of letting anyone respond to the first question. "May I assume that Soviet intelligence services made assumptions years ago that no longer have any bearing on this situation?"

The KGB head bristled for a moment, looked to the General Secretary for some support, found none, and finally said, "Predicting the future seems to be more difficult as each year passes."

"One generation cannot think for the other?" the chief pressed.

"It is apparent that . . . this is the case."

The Minister of Defense said, "They claim that *Pasadena* has been destroyed . . . that their missile submarines are all on alert and that *Florida* will destroy every military base west of the Urals if there is further indication of any aggression against their submarines."

"What proof is there?"

"They intend to order her to launch a missile. The President says that's all the proof required. The target will have little value. If we attempt to destroy the missile, if there is any indication from any of their satellites of launch preparation here, they will launch a massive strike. They are prepared," he concluded with finality.

"So are we."

"It's a bluff," the KGB head growled.

"Possibly," the Minister of Defense responded unconvincingly. He might have added that both sides knew that in the end it would always come down to a bluff.

"At this moment they are in contact with every major nation and they are detailing the events of the past few days," the General Secretary said quietly.

"What's to prevent them from—"

"We have already intercepted those messages to their allies explaining that the Soviet Union and the United States have reached an agreement to avoid what might have been a general exchange . . ." He droned on without expression until he was interrupted.

"What if *Florida* doesn't launch? How do we know that *Pasadena* hasn't been successful?"

"There appears to be only one method of finding out. The President is quite adamant in that regard."

Neither the General Secretary nor the Minister of Defense mentioned the second set of conditions.

* * *

". . . Range gating . . . first target's torpedo on two-second interval . . ." an anxious voice reported from *Pasadena's* sonar room. The same voice a split second later, "Second target's torpedo still range gating . . . one-second interval now."

Another voice in the background, "Oh, Christ, listen to those screws. Maybe the noisemakers didn't work—they must be on us."

The boomer had fired two torpedos at *Pasadena*. The first had been decoyed and the other one appeared to have passed the noisemakers and was gradually closing in a stern chase. But the second submarine also had one working torpedo attacking them head-on.

Pasadena's crew reacted out of instinct to their situation. They had been at war for days, their enemy seemingly known only to their captain. Wayne Newell's personality had reversed itself too, often cajoling a crew that feared an enemy they were unsure of, then shifting into depressions in the last day. This lack of continuity in crisis had thrown them into total confusion. Yet the captain's face now radiated a smile of contentment that frightened those around him. Two torpedos, each one carrying enough high explosive to rip *Pasadena* apart, were range gating on his submarine and he was actually enjoying himself.

"Number-one tube loaded. The chief says he'll have the tube and the unit ready super fast. They're working on the others now."

"XO," Newell called, looking about the control room for his executive officer, "how long—"

"He's in sonar, Captain."

"Ridiculous. He's the fire-control coordinator. He's supposed to be here—with me." Newell's face shaded. The smile vanished.

"Captain, recommend more noisemakers," the OOD said for the second time. There was an urgency in his voice magnified by fear. They'd evaded after shooting at the boomer, coming right, then left, then right again. And they had increased their depth twice. Still, two torpedos had searched for and apparently found them. The XO had gone into sonar. Now the OOD found himself left completely out of the captain's plans. He fired noisemakers on his own.

"Depth?"

"Seven hundred."

"Go deeper," Newell decided, as if it was of little concern to him, "another hundred." He took a couple of steps toward the entrance to sonar. "Dick! What the hell are you doing in there? Get your ass—"

"First torpedo is on continuous range gating." *Locked on and closing.* "Must be on a noisemaker or—"

"Ohshit . . ." was cut off as a powerful explosion rocked *Pasadena.* She seemed to jump bodily to port. Yet there was no change in her forward motion after a violent shudder coursed down her entire length. The torpedo had detonated on a nearby noisemaker.

"That final torpedo got lost in the blast." Nothing could possibly be heard on the passive sonar. The voice was frantic, unidentifiable. "Maybe . . . it had to be on continuous range gate."

"Go active on the target," Newell ordered.

Christ, the OOD thought, *there's another almost on top of us and he's paying no attention.*

"Fifty-two hundred yards."

"Firing-point procedures."

Lieutenant Holloway, the weapons-control coordinator, sat at his console, his face ashen, eyes tightly closed. "Weapon is ready," he said in a soft monotone.

"Good job, Bob, good job. Not much time left." Newell's expression was one of heightened glee now. He seemed to have forgotten his executive officer as soon as the torpedo was reported ready. "Shoot on generated bearings."

The familiar thud of the water slug was felt through the length of the ship.

Done. Beautiful. Never let anything else interfere when you're making an attack. "Left full rudder. Bring her up to three hundred feet." The diving officer found Newell beside him. "Make it as big an up angle as you can. Take her right to the edge." His hand rested easily on the man's shoulder. It would be close. If they got enough water between themselves and the blast, they might just make it. "You've got a torpedo coming up your ass and you might just save our necks. I don't want to vent main ballast." Even before he had finished, he was crossing control toward sonar, grabbing the overhead supports to brace himself against the radical maneuvering of the submarine. "Dick, what the—"

His executive officer stood framed in the door of sonar, his face a grim mask, eyes boring into Newell's. "Captain, we have been firing on American submarines. There is absolutely no doubt among anyone in sonar. It is my duty—"

Pasadena jerked wildly to starboard and seemed to leap toward the surface at the same time a deafening blast rocketed through the ship. The lights blinked out. Loose bodies and gear were hurled in every direction.

The first voice to be heard shouted, "Lost steering control."

CHAPTER SEVENTEEN

Buck Nelson had read those articles in the Navy publications in his spare time. Professional reading it was called. Speculation. That's what he called them—pure speculation. *No one, especially some young buck at a typewriter, could tell what it was really going to be like until it actually happened.* Now that it had, one of the terms that had been used kept coming back to him—*melee warfare.*

Simply stated, modern sonar and silencing techniques combined with computer technology and high-speed torpedos would create the melee. Like a catfight, nothing would happen until the contestants were almost on top of each other. Then it was a high-speed melee with the old tactics tossed out and intuition and luck the deciding factors.

And that's what Nelson anticipated now as sonar attempted to keep him abreast of the nearby action. He wondered if he would ever learn why two 688s were fighting with each other after one had actually fired on him. His concern over the 688s abated with the next report from sonar.

"Torpedo still has us—or something near us—range gating now at one-second intervals."

"Time for that decoy. Shoot . . ." Nelson ordered.

"We're only at six hundred now," Jimmy Cross said. They couldn't get too deep as far as he was concerned. He'd double that depth now without blinking an eye—after the creaking and groaning of the hull contracting under pressure, it was still a piece of cake when one considered the alternative. *Either pull the plug or vent main ballast . . .*

Florida turned away from the decoy, increasing speed and going deeper on Nelson's orders. Even though the wires had been broken when the 688 turned toward the other submarine, that torpedo was persistent. But the decoy would sound like *Florida.*

"Make it a thousand feet."

"Continuous range gating . . . doesn't seem to be any change in—" Dan Mundy's calm, even voice was cut off by an explosion off her port quarter.

Florida was still increasing her depth when the blast occurred, and it seemed to give her an added push. But it was distant enough that there was no damage. *The decoy!*

"Make her level," Nelson ordered. "Speed ten knots."

"You're going to stay around for the action," Jimmy Cross commented soberly, a slight smile forming at the corners of his mouth.

Nelson nodded. "They've forgotten us for the time being. More than likely, they heard an explosion out here but they don't know what happened. It makes sonar worthless for a while. It's just mush out there between us and them. I think if we just stay near all that busted-up water where the torpedo blew, no one's going to be the wiser. I can't take the chance of running and having the bad guy come chasing after us later. If we just shut up, sooner or later someone's going to do something dumb."

"Captain," Chief Delaney reported, "we can't tell what's happening out there. Between those explosions and their maneuvering, we can't tell who's who."

David Hall had a special way with words, a method of calling a spade a spade in visual terms. There was never any doubt about his opinion of other people or a particular situation. Ben Steel had eventually developed almost a dependency on his sonar officer's critical assessments. Although it wasn't rare for David to raise his voice, this time he was anything but loud. His tone as he stood at the entrance to sonar was solemn. "Captain, continuous range gate on that torpedo." He was pointing toward their starboard quarter as if he were able to see the torpedo beyond their hull. "No doubting we're the target. Recommend we pull the plug—"

Before he could finish the sentence, Steel had barked the order and they were plunging. The blast that followed was too close. *Manchester* reeled sideways and over as if she had fallen downstairs. Hall disappeared into sonar. Ben Steel was hurled against the OOD. Together they landed at the feet of the diving officer, who was already braced against the control panel to his left. It seemed as if *Manchester*'s bow was pointing straight down.

Peter Simonds maintained a death grip on the support above him. "Up angle, Chief. Stand by the ballast tanks. We may have to blow."

The executive officer was the only one left standing as the lights flickered out. His hoarse voice was steady, barking orders. "Emergency back full."

Then the beams of battle lanterns pierced the dusty gloom. There was an eerie silence broken only by the moans of those who had been injured. *Manchester* had righted herself and she no longer seemed to be standing on her side, but there was still a steep down angle to the deck. She hadn't leveled off.

Steel stumbled to his feet. Blood from a gash on top of his head ran down the side of his face. "Can you stop the dive, Chief?"

"We're passing nine hundred feet but it's slowing, Captain. Control surfaces seem to be okay."

"I don't want to blow main ballast if I can help it, Chief. Damage reports, XO."

"Nothing yet. We're just reestablishing communications with other spaces."

"Captain, torpedo room has a loose weapon. Two men badly hurt. One's the chief."

The voice was unfamiliar. "Who's in charge down there?" Steel inquired.

"Commander Burch," the voice boomed back from the SEAL who loved the shiny torpedos.

"Secure the unit any way you can for the time being. Wrestle it if you have to. But don't slow down loading tubes. I want a status report on time to shoot again. We're in this up to our ass." Steel remembered Wayne Newell's habits well, his persistence, his lack of fear. Only the sounds of an imploding hull would stop him. *How do you change everything you've been taught?*

"Engineering reports some flooding from internal piping. Electrical system back on line no more than two minutes. No problems with the reactor. Some vibration in the shaft. Could be the propellor. Ready to answer all engine orders."

David Hall reappeared in the entrance to sonar. His left arm, obviously broken, hung at his side. His left eye was swollen shut. "The sphere and hull arrays appear to be functioning properly. Nothing from the towed array. Probably lost it. There's nothing out there but wild water. It'll take a while to regain any contact." He was still as calm as before the blast. "I think it must have detonated prematurely, Captain, or we'd be dead meat by now." The sonar officer's voice rose to its familiar level. "I would appreciate it if we could get on the other side of this mess so I can locate that son of a bitch."

More reports came into the control room. The hull was still sound. Damage to auxiliary systems was minor. Damage control reported they were even with the flooding. Most injuries were cuts and bruises, with some broken bones. *Manchester* was level and maneuvering at ten knots. The exterior controls, rudder, and planes reacted normally.

"Commander Burch reports he'll have tube one ready in about one minute. Tube four is still loaded and the unit is ready to fire. Number two's was the one that broke loose while they were loading. Tube three's unit is in position. Give him four minutes."

"Captain," Peter Simonds reported, "we've already got it together enough to fight the ship again."

Steel nodded and peered down at the deck for a moment. *Manchester* had shot a single torpedo, her third, and turned away from *Pasadena*. There had been a counter fire and *Pasadena* probably had turned the opposite direction. Newell's ego must have figured his strategy couldn't fail him.

The boomer was to the north of them, hopefully making tracks. *Shit,* Florida *wouldn't do that if Buck Nelson thought they couldn't outrun an attack boat. He'd go silent and wait, protect himself if he had to. And Newell would know that! That last shot, if it didn't hit here, was to at least keep* Manchester *occupied·while Wayne Newell went after his major target. But he won't forget us. He'll come back to see if anything's still afloat here.*

"XO, you take it. Come right and head for *Florida's* last known position. I'm going to—"

But Steel was interrupted by Chief Moroney's voice from sonar. "I've got that last unit of theirs in a search out there. It's still too turbulent to sort everything out, but that torpedo has a bad habit of operating on its own."

Goddamn. Persistence. That son of a bitch is persistent.

"Noisemakers, XO, now. And wind it up. We'll worry about any other problems later."

There is a point in a melee when the environment is contact rich but not target rich. There are too many sounds —decoys, noisemakers, explosions. Man has turned the dark, silent ocean into a maelstrom of sound. It's up to the commanding officers to select the highest-valued contact . . . and hope.

Wayne Newell struggled to his knees. His head swiveled. The battle lanterns had switched on automatically, cutting through the dust that had shaken down from the overhead. He remembered Dick Makin's outline in the sonar entrance... about to say something.. *Pasadena* was coming around to port ... away from that other boat ... they'd fired at her again ... must have sunk her ... and the boomer!

Newell rose to his knees. He recalled something being said about steering control. Yet there had been no response. Was it just from fear while *Pasadena* was tossed about in the turbulence of the blast? In the glare of the battle lanterns he could see others looking about them, some sprawled on the deck, others still strapped into their positions. Yet no one uttered a sound. Some were obviously injured. But those last words—something about steering control ...

"Does emergency steering work?" Newell bellowed. He was surprised at the strength of his voice. Or was it the silence in the control room?

The sailor at the helm position, the one who had taken over when Stirling snapped, slowly placed his hands on the small wheel and turned it. He looked up at the dial on the control panel and turned the wheel the other way. "The indicator seems to be functioning," he said blandly.

Pasadena was at a moderate up angle. Newell noticed that the diving officer was sitting on the deck, his head cradled in his bloody hands. "The bow planes," he asked patiently, "are they working?"

The control was pushed slowly forward, then pulled back. The sailor put a hand on the shoulder of the man beside him and murmured something that Newell couldn't hear. The other sailor did the same with his own control, his eyes fixed on the panel in front of him, then nodded.

"We have control, Captain."

"Depth?"

"Three hundred ten feet."

They'd been heading up to evade. "Hold her there."

The OOD—where the hell was the OOD? Newell pulled himself to his feet. The OOD lay unconscious, his body in an awkward position at the base of the periscope. Newell saw the quartermaster pull himself to his feet beside the tiny chart table. "Get damage reports for me, Clark. All I need to know is if we can shoot and if engineering can get us back to that boomer." He turned to the sailors at the controls. "Come left to zero zero zero. We'll feel our way at ten knots for now until sonar tells us what's still out there." He was talking to them calmly, logically, as if they were having a pleasant conversation in his living room. Yet the setting was bizarre—with the beams of battle lanterns arching through the dusty haze of the control room.

His executive officer was the major concern right now. He remembered Dick Makin appearing from sonar like the grim reaper, uttering words that sounded important—yet he couldn't remember what they were.

When Newell stepped into sonar, he found Makin sitting on the deck with his legs out in front of him, his eyes half shut. One of the sonarmen was tying a handkerchief around the XO's head. *What was it Makin had said?* As he looked down at his executive officer, he remembered that look on Makin's face and the words "it's my duty," after some garbage about American submarines. "Get back to your station," the captain said evenly to the sonarman. "We are still under attack. I'll help the XO." And when the sailor failed to move quickly enough to suit him, he snapped, "Now."

Makin looked up at the captain. Even in the blue haze of sonar, Makin's narrowed eyes were beacons. Was it pain? Anger? Newell couldn't be sure. Both his OOD and his diving officer were down, and he needed the XO's help. But he also sensed that he'd have to watch him like a hawk. He wasn't sure why now, but something in the back of his mind cautioned that he'd have to watch everybody. Newell stuck out his hand. "Come on there. On your feet. I need you in control. We've got Russians to kill."

The XO looked away. Then he rolled to one side with a grunt of pain and moaned slightly until he was balanced on one knee, his back to Newell. He rose unsteadily to his feet. Without looking at Newell as he turned around, he brushed roughly by him into the control room. He saw the OOD crumpled beside the periscope. The diving officer remained in a sitting position, face and hands buried in his knees, his uniform now drenched with his own blood.

Newell stepped up behind him. "Are you ready to help me now?" Makin had yet to speak a word. Newell was hesitant, unsure of his XO's intentions. *Watch him . . . watch him!* The silence pervading the control room added to the eerie glare of the battle lanterns.

Makin whirled around. The handkerchief across his forehead was soaked a bright red. Blood was running down one side of his face. He opened his mouth to speak. His lips moved but there were no words. His eyes seemed to glaze slightly as he stared right through Wayne Newell.

"Dick?"

Makin's knees buckled and he slumped forward into Newell's arms. The captain let him slide to the deck.

I'll do better at knocking off those Russians myself, Newell thought. *Those clowns on the attack team are too scared to say anything.*

Dan Mundy stood beside Buck Nelson in *Florida*'s control room and shook his head in wonder. "I don't know how, but they're both under way. I can't imagine those torpedos blew just noisemakers. I'm picking up a slight shaft problem on one of them, vibration. But they both seem to be headed this way, Captain."

"And you don't know which is which." Nelson inclined his head slightly and glanced over the top of his rimless glasses. Mundy had already explained that twice.

Mundy shrugged. "If Delaney can't tell, no one can. With those torpedos messing up the water like they did, it's not going to be easy to sort out which is which. They're both 688s. One's a good guy, I guess, and one's a rogue. I don't understand it. What do you think, Captain?"

Buck Nelson knew the bad guy, but he waved off the question with his hand. Chief Delaney had picked out *Pasadena*'s signature. Nelson knew who; he just didn't know

317

why. *What was motivating Wayne Newell? He'd fired on them. He'd fired on the other 688. He was coming back now. Which one was he? Port? Starboard?*

Nelson turned away and took a few steps back toward the quartermaster's chart table. *What do you think, Captain?* He rested his elbow in his left hand and bent his head, massaging tired eyes with his fingers. He was outside once again, beyond *Florida*, gazing down upon two SSN's jockeying for the shot that would destroy the other. One of them wanted to sink him—the other was making a desperate effort to come to his aid. But even out there, even beyond the fray, he couldn't . . . *No, I can't,* a voice inside him cried. *Can't tell which . . .*

"Designate the one to port target number one, the other number two," Nelson indicated, turning around. "Prepare all tubes."

"The one who signaled us before will be crazy if he doesn't do it again," Jimmy Cross said. "Then we'll only have one to worry about."

Nelson shook his head. "We all heard that signal," he said patiently. "They'll both use it now. It's useless. We have two targets. If one gets through, we'll sink it."

"How will we tell which one we sank?" Cross asked defensively.

"Maybe we never will."

Manchester, seven hundred feet below the surface, was proceeding toward the boomer's last known position at twenty knots. When Chief Moroney reported that *Pasadena's* last torpedo had gone into a homing run well above and astern of them, Ben Steel held his depth until the weapon was drawn into one of their noisemakers and exploded. Then he gradually brought the ship up to four hundred feet.

As they drew farther from the turbulence caused by the encounter with *Pasadena,* the other boat was detected off their starboard beam.

"It looks like they're moving close to the same course and speed," Moroney said, "maybe closing us a little."

That meant Newell would hear them, too. He'd know that somehow they'd escaped his wild attack—but he had no idea if they'd be able to hunt *Pasadena*. Newell would be wondering whether to go after the boomer first or take the chance of finishing off *Manchester*.

"Any indication of damage?"

"Nothing we can pick up. Nothing as obvious as our shaft, anyway."

Peter Simonds appeared from the engineering spaces. "Mac says not to worry. He wouldn't want to leave port with something like that shaft and he wouldn't want a full-power run, but he thinks he can sustain twenty knots without shaking anything apart. No more than that, though. And he can get us home too, he said."

"And over twenty knots?" Steel asked.

"He thinks the vibration then will be bad enough to affect sonar. Eventually we have to slow down. We're going to screw up the calibration on the fine-tuned equipment, like the attack consoles, anyway. So we better finish this off quick. Actually, Dave Hall says we're close to the edge at twenty knots. Lots of our own ship's noise interfering with his sonar."

"Any problems with developing a fire-control solution?" Steel asked.

"Not that I can tell," Simonds said. "Commander Burch says tubes one, three, and four are ready. They've got a problem with two that they're working on."

Again Steel closed his eyes and imagined the scene. If he were in Buck Nelson's shoes, he would have gone as quietly as possible after evading *Pasadena*'s torpedos. Perhaps he was as much as ten, certainly no more than twenty, miles beyond his last position. He didn't want to be heard and he wouldn't be moving at more than ten knots. And his muzzle doors would be open and weapons ready.

Pasadena was to *Manchester*'s east, so Newell would have

to come more to the northwest to search for the boomer. He couldn't go fast enough to place himself in front of *Florida*. In a picture-perfect sequence at this speed, the two 688s should intersect close to *Florida*.

Newell would be trying to place each of them in his mind in the same manner. Once his sonar picked up the vibrations in *Manchester*'s shaft—they would have had to by now—he would know exactly what Steel was planning.

"Slight change of plans," Steel said to Simonds. "They can get to the boomer before us, as far as we can tell. I want a course to come in behind them about three thousand yards because there's no way we can get in front, especially when he hears us coming like this. We'll force him to turn before he gets to *Florida*."

The casualty reports aboard *Pasadena* might have concerned a captain in full control of himself. It certainly would have altered their tactics. Wayne Newell barely acknowledged them. The boat would remain on emergency electrical power until sections of burned-out cables could be cross-connected.

There had been more damage to the crew than to the submarine. The most frustrating aspect to Newell was the fact that many of the spaces were vague about when they might return to normal operations. They didn't seem to care, and there was no time to go into each one to talk with them.

"Sonar," Newell questioned, "what do you have on our contact now?"

"Target motion indicates it might have altered course to intercept us before we reach the boomer's projected location."

"How about that noise you picked up?"

Another voice from sonar answered, "Engineering says from my description that the target must be near max speed. Probably has shaft problems."

"Range?"

"Fifteen thousand."

"Come left another ten degrees," Newell ordered. "Torpedo room, status report."

"Tubes three and four ready. Tubes flooded, pressure equalized. Both units warmed." There was a slight pause. "Damage to the piping repaired in a few minutes, then we'll have one and two ready."

"Open the muzzle doors." There was nothing to hide at this stage.

Bob Holloway, the weapons-control coordinator, stared back blankly when the captain looked over at him. He was still functioning, but more from instinct than anything else.

Newell took a couple of steps in his direction. "Your target could be at maximum speed now. I will hold this course and speed until either he shoots or we're at ten thousand yards. Then we'll adjust our course twenty degrees to port for firing." It struck Newell that he was talking to a child. "Will the weapons be ready within two minutes?" It was not a question a captain would normally ask, but the man's expression bothered him more than the possibility *Pasadena* would be fired on.

"Sixty seconds." The voice was a monotone, but the job would be done in half the time.

"That's what I like to hear," Newell said heartily. "I want you to increase the pitch on number four—deeper target." He saw Holloway staring at him uncertainly. "Problems?"

The man shook his head but said nothing. And when Newell frowned at the lack of response, the man nodded and managed, "All set, sir."

What was wrong with these people?

Newell moved over behind the two planesmen at the control panel. They'd been strapped into their chairs and were uninjured. "You men are doing a fine job. I'm going to recommend you for medals when we get home." *That would do it. They'd respond more positively to a pep talk like this.* "It's tough without an OOD or diving officer to back you up, and I've got to coordinate the attack. But we're at war, and the enemy finally gave us a little bit of what we've been handing him. I'll point out in my report that you two assumed the watch for the officers and at the same time you continued to handle the controls." He rested a reassuring hand on each man's shoulder. "You just listen to me and we'll come through this fine. I think the world just may rest on our shoulders right now. We have to get through to that boomer, you know, before she launches, so it's going to take some pretty fair boat drivers. I'm going to call for some wild maneuvers," he added with an encouraging squeeze. "I know you'll do just fine."

Then he did exactly the same with his attack coordinators. They were a disappointment, but he needed their expertise to prepare the attack. *Why was it that the enlisted men were handling this better than some of the so-called highly trained officers?* If he could finish off that attack boat with three and four, he ought to be able to take out the boomer with one and two.

He gazed about a chaotic control room outlined by the beams of the battle lanterns and wondered for a moment why no one had bothered to clean up. The OOD remained at the base of the periscope. The diving officer had now slumped over on his side in a pool of blood. His hands had come away from his face, and Newell saw that he must have been hurled against the panel—his face no longer existed. His executive officer lay where Newell had left him. Makin was moaning softly now. Perhaps he was coming around, but blood still flowed from his head.

"Eleven thousand yards."

Newell stepped over near the control panel. "Come left twenty degrees like I told you and hold your depth until I say otherwise. You're not going to have any doubts when I say go deep. Just do it." He took a deep breath. "Firing-point procedures tubes three and four."

"Weapons are ready," came Holloway's soft response.

"You did increase the pitch in number four?"

"Yes, sir." It was barely a whisper.

"The solution is ready. And *Pasadena* is ready," Newell announced proudly to those able to hear him.

"Ten thousand," David Hall called out.

Everything was ready, the ship, the weapons, the solution.

"Launch transient on the target's bearing." *Water slug!*

Same damn idea! "Tube number one, shoot on generated bearings," Ben Steel ordered.

There was the familiar thud as the torpedo was propelled away from *Manchester*.

After a pause, "Unit's running correctly."

"David, talk to me about the incoming torpedo."

"Single torpedo. Enabling run sounds normal."

"Any change in the target?"

"Not a damn thing I can tell."

"Tube number three. Shoot on generated bearings." How long should he hold the wire on these? He had one torpedo left that could be fired right away. Number two was supposed to be ready shortly. He had to protect that boomer.

"Number-three unit's running smoothly. Wire continuity good on number one."

Wayne Newell won't hold forever. Too goddamn cagey. Why the hell hadn't he fired another yet?

"Status on the target," Newell called out.

"No change. Must be trying to hold on to the wire on both weapons."

Okay. If that's the way it is. "Increase your speed to thirty knots. Come right to course zero zero zero." *Let's let them think it's going to be a chase, and maybe they'll send some conflicting changes down that wire they're holding.* Newell was behind the sailors at the control panel in an instant. "Don't worry. I'm not changing my mind. We're just playing a game with that Russian. We're going to do exactly what I said we would shortly." He gave each man a squeeze on the shoulder again. "You men are doing one fine job, let me tell you."

"Our wire's broken," Holloway called out mechanically.

"Fine." That didn't matter now. "Stand by number four. That's going to be our baby. Okay, noisemakers now, too." He'd make a screen out of them, put enough noise between them to cause confusion. Once they were confirmed, Newell called out, "Come back to the old course and speed for me. I'm depending on you while I coordinate this attack."

A short time later, "Both incoming torpedos are in search." They were pinging.

Good. The target was making a textbook attack out of it all.

One of the planesmen sounded off when they were back on the original heading.

"Tube number four, shoot on generated bearings."

When Wayne Newell heard the report that his second torpedo was running correctly, he fired noisemakers and gave the order to dive to eight hundred feet. Then he turned back toward the boomer. He wasn't worried about the wire.

Dick Makin came to with a sharply slanting deck beneath him.

"They've fired a second torpedo."

Steel knew when it was time to break the wires. "Make your depth six hundred feet," he called out, and gave the order to come around to a course that would place him in front of *Florida*. He also put noisemakers in the water, but they would be useless shortly.

That was when David Hall reported the sound of muzzle doors on a bearing approximating *Florida*'s projected position.

"Send the identification signal."

Not a moment later the sonar officer reported that the other attack submarine had sent the same signal at almost the same time. Wayne Newell has somehow convinced one of his sonarmen that imitating that signal from the Russian submarine might just save them.

* * *

324

"They've each fired two torpedos at each other, Captain," Dan Mundy reported to Buck Nelson. "And there are noisemakers everywhere. Both have probably taken evasive action by now."

"Which one do you think is the good guy, Dan?" Nelson enjoyed puzzles. This one was fascinating.

"No idea, Captain. I'd say the one with shaft problems makes a better target right now. His speed's probably limited. So I hope the other one's the good guy."

Both the weapons-control coordinator and the fire-control coordinator had reported they were ready for both targets. Buck Nelson was also. It was a shame that there were no other choices.

"Captain, I have their first torpedo in homing run."

Ben Steel was uncomfortable. He wanted more speed. But that wasn't possible. He reversed his course and left more noisemakers in his wake.

"Three-second ping interval." It had found them!

He called for another three hundred feet to his depth.

"Second torpedo is in homing run also."

"What about our own units?"

Peter Simonds was surprised. He'd heard the reports. It was the first time aboard *Manchester* that he'd ever seen Ben Steel this concerned. "They reported both units operating normally, Captain," he said. "Both of ours were in homing runs, too."

"Sorry, Peter. My mind's jumping ahead."

"Two-second ping interval on both incoming torpedos."

More speed. That's what I really need. More speed. "Increase your depth another two hundred feet."

"One-second ping interval on that first incoming. Could be on to a noisemaker. Still distant enough."

Wonderful. That's the way it was supposed to work.

Dick Makin opened his eyes. His head was a mass of pain. He saw the spotlights of battle lanterns fixed throughout the control room. And a single figure was passing back and forth through the beams—Wayne Newell. He could hear a string of familiar reports that must be . . . *Oh, God, they must be attacking* Manchester *again!*

"One-second ping interval."

Whose torpedo? He reached for the periscope and dragged himself to his knees.

"Right full rudder."

Pasadena heeled sharply to starboard. Makin wrapped his arms around the periscope and held on as tightly as he could. His world was spinning. *Don't lose it again, Makin.* A single thought persisted in the back of his mind. That attack boat had fired Mark 48's at them . . . *Mark 48's!* Sonar had identified them clearly. Only American submarines carried 48's.

Manchester was hurled sideways by a close, violent explosion. A noisemaker had barely saved them. A near-miss!

"Second incoming on continuous range gate." *Locked on!*

"Torpedo room reports severe flooding."

"Left full rudder," Steel shouted. "Increase your angle." There was nothing from sonar to indicate the incoming torpedo was hung up on a noisemaker.

The explosion that followed was not a near-miss. The blast penetrated directly upward into the engineering spaces. To those who were not killed instantly, it seemed to be everywhere in *Manchester* at once. Each man in control was aware for an instant that there was darkness as the emergency lights went out. She was on her side. A constant roaring sound overwhelmed their screams. There was no chance for the battle lanterns to blink back on. They were plunging out of control.

They were very deep when the bulkheads crashed in on top of them.

Manchester continued on its last dive.

"Target number two is breaking up."

"Very well," Buck Nelson answered. "Target number

one . . . tubes one and two . . . firing-point procedures."
Buck Nelson's voice was steady, as if there weren't the
slightest doubt in anyone's mind about the target.

"Captain," Jimmy Cross interrupted. "How do we . . .
isn't there some way we . . . ?" *How did one explain it?*

"We don't. We have to survive."

"The ship is ready."

"The weapons are ready."

"The solution is ready."

Buck Nelson closed his eyes. As soon as he opened them,
he would be committed.

A torpedo detonated well beneath *Pasadena*. It wasn't
close enough to sink her, but it did lift her bow toward the
surface and shake her like a rabbit. That was followed by a
second explosion crashing all around them at once. Instantly her bow was driven down at an incredibly steep angle.
Both Newell and Makin could hear the frantic shouts as the
planesmen fought their controls. There must have been
water in the control surface hydraulics.

"I can't bring the bow up."

Wayne Newell's voice bellowed above the chaos, "Emergency blow the forward group. All back full." *Got to get the
bow up!* There are still weapons ready for that boomer, his
mind screamed, and your boat is running out of time. *We
can still destroy that boomer. Pasadena* was beyond saving,
but he knew that he could take that boomer to the bottom
with him.

"No response, Captain. Still diving."

The sailor on the stern planes was the first to realize there
was no chief of the watch. He ripped off his safety belt and
lunged for the chicken switches on the ballast control panel
to initiate the emergency blow.

But Dick Makin was there first. He knew the C.O. would
do everything humanly possible to sink *Florida*. He grabbed
the sailor by both shoulders, dragging him back from the
panel. Pain surged through his head, through his body—
the control room seemed to be spinning away from him.

As he turned, he saw Wayne Newell staggering against the slant of the deck in his direction, rage contorting his features. "Those are Mark 48's . . . American torpedos . . . American submarine," Makin screamed. There was no reaction from Newell as he inched closer. With his last ounce of strength, Makin heaved the sailor at Newell. Both men went down, tumbling forward into the planesmen's chairs.

The helmsman's eyes were wide with fear as he saw what was happening. He was frozen in position, pulling back desperately on the planes, when Dick Makin's fist slammed into the side of his head. He slumped sideways.

As Wayne Newell struggled against the steep angle of the deck, Makin pushed the control forward as far as he could, the entire weight of his body falling across it. The bow seemed to aim straight down. Newell slid against the forward bulkhead, unable to climb back up to the controls.

Dick Makin watched Newell's frustrated attempts to rise, heard the shouts of rage with a strange satisfaction. *Pasadena* would never fire another torpedo.

She was well past her test depth before the bulkheads imploded.

Buck Nelson was about to open his eyes and give the order to shoot when Dan Mundy called for him. Together they listened in sonar until the last of the tearing, grinding sounds disappeared.

Nelson stepped back into control. "Secure from battle stations. Prepare the communications buoy."

EPILOGUE

No one aboard *Florida* was able to speak as she rose to stream her communications buoy. Two 688-class submarines lay at the bottom of the Pacific, victims of each other. One had attacked *Florida*. The other had come to her aid. They'd fought twice at close range, apparently wounding each other initially, killing the second time. It was a shattering experience. Not a soul aboard the boomer could ever have imagined that such a battle would involve anyone other than the Russians. Each man would carry this searing event to their graves.

Buck Nelson had left the control room without a word to anyone else. He'd known *Manchester* and *Pasadena*. He'd known Ben Steel and Wayne Newell. He'd known too many of the others. *And he would have sunk the survivor—if there'd been one.*

Before they could initiate their preliminary message, the ship received a single communication, a coded message for Nelson's eyes only.

Buck Nelson did not call his executive officer instantly after reading the message. Instead, he very methodically removed all the extraneous paperwork from his desk and placed it neatly on his bunk. He lay the message exactly in the middle of his desk and smoothed it with his hands until it was perfectly flat. Then, removing his glasses and tucking them in his breast pocket, he propped the photo of Cindy and his daughters on top of the message. He stared very hard at each one of them—Cindy, Jenny, Beth—as if his concentration might bring them to life right there. *You are a very lucky man, Nelson, to have been so blessed.*

Tears formed at the corners of his eyes as he thanked someone, something, anything beyond his own powers, that had allowed him such joy. *I would gladly sell my soul to be with the three of you once more.*

Then he lifted the phone and pressed the button for control. "Will you please ask Commander Cross to join me in my stateroom."

When the executive officer appeared in the entrance, Nelson pointed at the clear end of his bunk and said, "Sit down . . . please."

Jimmy Cross stared at Nelson's reddened eyes. He'd never seen his captain look that way before. Then he noticed the family picture set in the exact middle of the message smoothed flat on the desk.

Without a word Nelson slipped the piece of paper from under the picture and handed it to his XO.

Cross read it twice, the second time word by word, until he was sure he understood it completely. Quite simply, that piece of paper said that there was much more to the events of that day than they would likely ever understand.

The executive officer rose slowly and, after studying the picture of the Nelson family for a moment, squeezed Buck Nelson's shoulder and left.

Nelson picked up the photo and, after studying each face closely, neatly placed it in one of his drawers under some shirts. Then he bent down and peered at the tiny numbers on the dial of his safe. No matter how much he squinted, they remained a blur. He removed his glasses from his breast pocket, polished them unconsciously on the front of his shirt before placing them on his face, and spun the dial back and forth until the safe opened. He removed the ominous target-assignment list without looking at it and slipped the sheaf of paper under his arm while he shut the door of the safe and spun the dial.

Then he once again lifted the phone and punched the button for the control room. "Will you kindly inform the officer of the deck to sound battle stations, missile, please." After hanging up the phone, Buck Nelson put his baseball cap on his head and proceeded the few short steps to control while the general alarm echoed through *Florida*.

The entire process was conducted on a businesslike basis, just as efficiently as it had been in so many exercises. The countdown was initiated without a hitch. Jeff Sones, the missile-control officer, reported the system cycled for launch. Every member of the crew had a part but, while they were nervous, they were never anything but professional.

The red firing key was inserted.

Target information was keyed into the computer in concert with the inertial navigation system.

Final data were entered into the missile.

The cap opened on the missile tube.

The rumble as the missile departed the tube confirmed every man's worst dream—they were no longer a deterrent.

Each one in his own way felt the silent prayer that Buck Nelson had experienced in his stateroom moments before.

The four admirals sat around the table in SUBPAC's office in Pearl Harbor, each deep in his own thoughts. When the door opened and Neil Arrow's flag lieutenant was framed in the entrance, there was no real need for him to deliver the single-line message that he carried. They knew exactly what it said.

There was a speaker phone in the middle of the table, which was opened on a direct line to the White House by pressing a single button. Ray Larsen spoke for the others. *"Florida* has successfully launched her missile, Mr. President. She is now proceeding to the surface so there can be no doubt in their minds which ship completed the launch."

* * *

The General Secretary replaced the phone on the receiver, bowing his head momentarily. It appeared to the others that he had stopped breathing. But when he raised his head and spoke, there was a determined look on his face. "The launching platform has indeed been identified as *Florida*. The President has assured me that only one warhead will detonate. The target is the airbase east of Markovo. You may be sure that no part of that installation, nor any military personnel, will survive. As soon as it takes place, I will personally dispatch aid to any of the native population who may be affected. We are fortunate that such a desolate location was selected." His eyes moved about the room, settling on each individual. "We will know which submarines were chosen when they fail to return to port." He bowed his head once more with finality. "I sincerely believe this nightmare is over."

Two hundred miles southeast of Iceland, USS *Jack* required just two torpedos to dispatch a totally unsuspecting Soviet Victor-class submarine. The sounds of the hull imploding came to them before their third weapon detonated in the already sinking wreckage.

USS *San Francisco* experienced an equally successful mission. She had been trailing an older Russian intelligence-gathering submarine that had been monitoring Japanese naval operations for more than a week. Two torpedos sank the unsuspecting vessel well off the Japanese coast.

Charlie Newell was more than happy to take the other three kids with him to pick up the pizza. He was sixteen and had just gotten his driver's license. Every trip in the car was a new adventure.

Myra Newell sipped her martini, looking at it with both pleasure and curiosity. "You know, my husband would definitely disapprove if he were here now."

"I remember when he used to drink them," Connie said thoughtfully.

"Once. Ancient history. That was before he became more perfect than he already was. . . ."

The sun was still above the horizon, but damp clouds in the distance had changed its color. The ships nestled by the distant piers below were cast in a red glow. Hawaii was an island of colors, and each evening seemed to provide a new and unique tint to that scene from the house on the hill.

They talked on about inconsequential subjects to avoid what they had both sensed earlier in the day. Neither of them realized that the car had returned safely nor did they notice when their children spread the pizza out on the kitchen table. They simply knew that there was a reason they had been drawn together that evening for mutual support.

The objective remained distant but ominous until an official Navy car pulled into the driveway. Then it was all too clear. Mark Bennett, his eyes red-rimmed, appeared on the patio in rumpled civilian clothes. He should have been in Washington. They allowed Mark to tell them that *Manchester* and *Pasadena* had been lost together in a tragic confrontation with the Soviets and that they should be extremely proud of their husbands, for they had helped to prevent war.

The real story would remain buried forever on the floor of the Pacific.

Author's Note

While I have taken the liberty of employing the names of some very good friends in these pages, there is absolutely no character in this book who bears any resemblance to any individual, living or dead, whom I have ever known. *BOOMER*'s characters are purely fictitious.

Further, I have never been aware of any commanding officer of any commissioned ship in the United States Navy who was ever suspected of disloyalty, much less any captain who actually attempted to perform a traitorous act with an American ship. On the other hand, I think it is of grave importance to note that our military and our Navy have been successfully penetrated by the intelligence forces of foreign nations at an alarming rate in the past, and there is no reason to believe that this disarming practice is not continuing.

There are still too many angry old men who remember the inhumanity and the slaughter of the mid-20th century and pattern their decisions on those memories—and there are any number of brilliant, well-meaning young men who forget that history has a way of repeating itself. I offer as an example JFK's inheritance of the Bay of Pigs plan, which he allowed to continue to its inevitable and tragic conclusion. As a result, I am concerned by the complacency and naivete that believes—"It can't happen here!" It has. It will again. And there are methods that will be employed by the intelligence arms of foreign nations to penetrate our military and government that none of our current experts have yet devised. The real world of covert operations and the ends individuals and governments will go to achieve superiority are well beyond our imaginations. If it hasn't happened yet, it will. The impossible of today will become the probable of tomorrow. Eternal vigilance is not a term to be dismissed lightly.

Let us sincerely hope that a Wayne Newell never has the opportunity to achieve a position of such critical command in our military forces. *It could happen here.*